Leo the Late Bloomer

BY ROBERT KRAUS • PICTURES BY JOSE ARUEGO

Windmill Books

New York

Leo the Late Bloomer

Text copyright © 1971 by Robert Kraus

Illustrations copyright © 1971 by José Aruego

All rights reserved. No part of this book may be used or reproduced in any manner whatsoever without written permission except in the case of brief quotations embodied in critical articles and reviews. Printed in the United States of America. For information address HarperCollins Children's Books, a division of HarperCollins Publishers, 10 East 53rd Street, New York, NY 10022. http://www.harperchildrens.com

LC Number 70-159154
ISBN 0-87807-042-7
ISBN 0-87807-043-5 (lib. bdg.)
ISBN 0-06-443348-X (pbk.)

'Windmill Books' and the colophon
accompanying it are a trademark of
Windmill Books, Inc., registered in
the United States Patent Office.
Published by Windmill Books, Inc.
Distributed by HarperCollins Publishers.

For Ken Dewey

J. A.

For Pamela, Bruce
and Billy

R. K.

Leo couldn't do anything right.

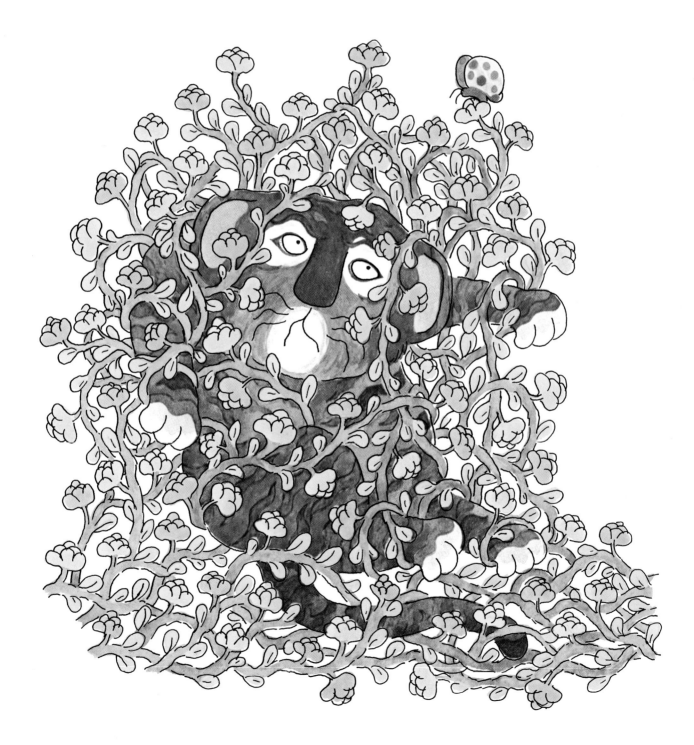

He couldn't read.

He couldn't write.

owl
Elephant
Snake
Plover
Crocodile

He couldn't draw.

He was a sloppy eater.

And, he never said a word.

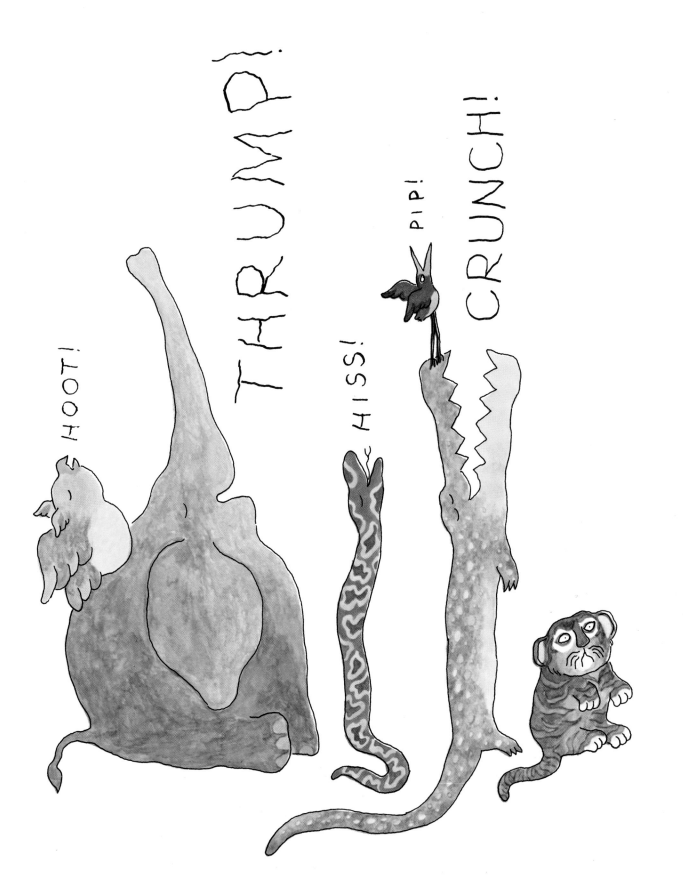

"What's the matter with Leo?"
asked Leo's father.
"Nothing," said Leo's mother.
"Leo is just a late bloomer."
"Better late than never," thought Leo's father.

Every day Leo's father watched him
for signs of blooming.

And every night Leo's father watched him
for signs of blooming.

"Are you sure Leo's a bloomer?"
asked Leo's father.
"Patience," said Leo's mother.
"A watched bloomer doesn't bloom."

So Leo's father watched television
instead of Leo.

The snows came.
Leo's father wasn't watching.
But Leo still wasn't blooming.

The trees budded.
Leo's father wasn't watching.
But Leo still wasn't blooming.

Then one day,
in his own good time,
Leo bloomed!

He could read!

He could write!

He could draw!

He ate neatly!

He also spoke.
And it wasn't just a word.
It was a whole sentence.
And that sentence was...

"I made it!"

CONTENTS

PREFACE

Salespeople who use marketing tools effectively experience greater sales. When agents have prospects in front of them, they employ their salesmanship skills. However, marketing attracts prospects to agents so they can *use* their salesmanship skills. For that reason, Part One of this text discusses real estate marketing and Part Two covers real estate sales.

There is no reason to experience only half of your sales potential. This text focuses on the processes involved in professionally marketing and selling real estate. It integrates the four elements of a marketing mix—promotion, place, product, and price—and shows how they are used within the real estate industry to create marketing strategies. These strategies help list the right properties, at the right time, at the right price, and attract prospects that are ready, willing, and able to buy.

There are many real estate salesmanship books and many business marketing books. This textbook melds the two together. Most business marketing books draw their examples from multiple industries but often have few discussions that are relevant to the real estate industry. Many how-to real estate books stress the topic of salesmanship (in marketing terms this is called personal selling), a component of the promotional mix, but often fail to discuss, in any depth, the other elements of a comprehensive marketing strategy.

When readers identify market opportunities, market segments, and target markets, their marketing strategies provide better results. When agents recognize consumer behavioral traits and learn to overcome the four reasons prospects don't buy, their sales increase. Whether the reader is a novice or a real estate agent, they grow to understand the significance and application of topics such as pricing and promotional strategies, marketing and promotional mixes, personal selling, distribution strategies, marketing research and analysis, packaging, branding, and more.

Other features of this book at a glance:

■ It is written in a straightforward, easy-to-understand format.
■ The text is divided into two parts, one on marketing and one on sales.

- Chapter learning objectives save time by suggesting a purpose to your reading.
- Concise and to-the-point chapter summaries remind you of what is important.
- Multiple choice and open-ended questions allow you to quiz yourself and apply what you have learned.
- Chapter illustrations help readers visualize the concepts presented.

You will learn how real estate agents use or create the following:

- The marketing mix, which must be balanced to create more sales
- Market research, which shows you how to find your prospects
- Data analysis and market segmentation, which helps define your target market
- Overcoming the four reasons prospects don't buy
- Pricing strategies for both listings and services
- Place strategies, which show the tools needed to get information to prospects
- Development of a promotional strategy
- A comprehensive list of interview questions (included in the text), which encourage profound, complex, and introspective answers from prospects
- A list of the most common objections heard by agents, what they mean, and how to overcome them
- A finance section that shows how the actions of the Federal Reserve affect the agent's real estate marketing practice

There are many marketing textbooks but few that explain marketing principles from a real estate agent's point of view. You will discover in this text far more than the motivational and salesmanship techniques common to many books that treat the subject of real estate marketing.

ACKNOWLEDGMENTS

This author wishes to acknowledge and thank those who contributed to or participated in the development of this textbook.

In its manuscript format, this book's chapters were used as handouts to supplement a textbook used in a real estate marketing course at Victor Valley College. Through their classroom participation, hundreds of students over the past 12 years helped refine and mold the contents of this textbook. Students encouraged the use of analogies that described everyday occurrences to help make the real estate marketing activities more understandable. This textbook is a byproduct of their influence. They encouraged it be written so that it was understandable to students of real estate and others who may have only a little experience in marketing and sales. To all of them, I wish to express my thanks.

John Kroencke, economist and retired dean of business and industry at Victor Valley College in California. His support and generosity helped start this project over 15 years ago, and his understanding and contributions helped make its completion possible. The author appreciates the motivation and patience given by Debbie and Shaun Grover during the final stages of completing this text, to Lynda Grover for her editing talents, and to Greg Grover for his almost daily encouragement to press on. The author received invaluable assistance and support from real estate educators, including Barbara Eubanks-Dietrich, retired, life member of the Texas Real Estate Teachers Association, and John N. Anderson, real estate educator, whose guidance helped organize the content and flow of this textbook.

The author enjoyed the experience of working with everyone at Dearborn. A special thanks to Elizabeth Austin, development editor, whose patient, quiet, and persuasive style helped make an enormous amount of work seem small.

FOREWORD

Almost everyone has an opinion on how to effectively market real estate brokerage services and real estate. Unfortunately, hundreds of books have been written that talk about marketing real estate but offer little or no solid suggestions on how to actually do it. Chris Grover's book is unique in that it begins by defining what marketing is and is not and then tells you how to market in a manner that will significantly increase your level of success and profitability. Throughout the book, you will find page after page filled with valuable information that will teach you how to convert solid marketing theory into practical applications to help make your business take off and soar to heights that you never imagined possible.

Sales and Marketing 101 is not a rehash of material that you have read or heard a thousand times before. The author's goal is to help you succeed by teaching you the basics of marketing, as well as how to identify your prospect's wants and needs, conduct a successful customer interview, and close the sale. Additionally, Mr. Grover teaches you how to skillfully identify buyer objections and how to overcome them.

Used as the basis for a 30-hour, Texas Real Estate Commission-approved SAE course, this book is the ideal choice for your renewal study requirement as it covers all of the required statutory topics necessary for core real estate course approval. But that is only the beginning; it also serves as a success guide for both the new associate and the seasoned real estate broker.

Mr. Grover provides a road map that gives specific driving directions to take you from being an inexperienced, unconfident real estate newbie to a wonderfully successful real estate agent earning an income that will make your colleagues green with envy. Throughout the book, he provides multiple choice and open-ended questions that will stimulate your thinking and afford you the opportunity to apply what has been learned. He also teaches you how to communicate more effectively by asking the right questions and listening for the answers that will reveal your customer's real needs and wants.

Early in the book, Mr. Grover states that "When a real estate agent no longer delivers what the consumer wants, the agent will cease to be in business." If your plan is to be in the real estate business and to prosper in that business, you must read and re-read this book.

Ralph Tamper

Ralph Tamper is the author of *Mastering Real Estate Math* and *Texas Real Estate Contracts*, as well as a series of three-hour mandatory continuing education (MCE) courses that meet the requirements to renew a Texas license. He is a senior instructor for the Graduate REALTOR® Institute (GRI) program, the Certified Buyer Representative designation course, the Accredited Buyer Representative courses, and the Real Estate Educators Association (REEA).

Mr. Tamper holds the prestigious Distinguished Real Estate Instructor (DREI) designation awarded by REEA and has been awarded the Texas Real Estate Teachers Association Certified Real Estate Instructor (CREI) designation. He also holds memberships in the national, Texas, and Houston Associations of REALTORS® and has served as a member of the Education Committee at the local, state, and national levels. In 2000, the Texas Association of REALTORS® named Mr. Tamper "Real Estate Educator of the Year" and recognized two of his courses as "Education Programs of the Year."

I

REAL ESTATE MARKETING

c h a p t e r   o n e

REAL ESTATE MARKETING

■ Learning Objectives

After the study and review of this chapter, you should be able to

■ develop an understanding of sales and how it is a part of a total marketing effort;

■ differentiate between the several levels of utility and how they affect real or perceived value and need; and

■ identify, define, and compare the four elements of the marketing mix.

■ Key Terms

effective marketing	possession utility	real estate marketing
form utility	price	services utility
place	product	time utility
place utility	promotion	

People have come to think that the real estate industry is mostly sales oriented. As we will see in this chapter and those that follow, real estate marketing involves more than sales, advertising, salesmanship techniques, telephone canvassing, and the like.

Real estate agents—in this textbook licensees and salespeople are referred to as agents[1]—are responsible for creating and applying marketing strategies that attract prospects to them so they can use their salesmanship skills. Most marketing activities do not require an agent's in-person contact with prospects. Part One of the text discusses marketing.

When agents come in personal contact with prospects, they use their salesmanship or personal selling skills. *Personal selling* is a marketing term mean-

---

1   To avoid confusion this text uses the common term *agent* to mean licensee, salesman, saleswoman, or salesperson. The owner of an agency is referred to as the broker or the broker/owner.

ing that two or more parties interact directly. These interactions are usually face to face; however, other methods are possible. Sales and salesmanship are discussed in Part Two of the text, although there will be some overlap between the two parts.

■ What Is Real Estate Marketing?

Today, **real estate marketing** balances a mix of activities that serves two functions. The first, and more common, function results in both attracting prospects to agents and creating a sale that meets the personal needs of prospects. The second function may not necessarily result in a sale, but increases the reputation of the agent or agency. Professional marketers carefully research their environment. After analyzing the research data, marketers balance the issues of property selection with service and product pricing. Marketers must consider the strategies that distribute information to the public, as well as coordinate their promotional efforts. The promotional strategy provides a mix of communication efforts that include advertising, public relations, and sales promotion, which are forms of nonpersonal selling. The best-known element in a promotional strategy is personal selling, or salesmanship. The result of a successful marketing strategy is customers sitting in front of agents who can then apply their salesmanship skills. The sale is the result of a successful marketing campaign.

Many years ago, during what was called the sales era of marketing, salespeople were trained to assume that the customer would avoid buying their goods and services. Consequently, it was their job to overcome this by using a battery of selling techniques. This was marketing in a time when personal selling and advertising were used to overcome stubborn, resistant buyers.

Perhaps because of this past, the insurance, auto, and real estate industries have had a reputation for "selling" people products or services they could not use, did not want, or could ill afford. Some agents may have heard brokers declare, "I don't care what they want. Sell them one of our listings." These industry reputations may have been well deserved. Even today, we see salespeople of this type in all three industries. Confined by education, experience, or interest, they have only one car or one insurance policy to sell. Or, as real estate agents, they take a listing without a marketing strategy to sell it. Fortunately, it is changing. After World War II, it became a buyer's market, which meant that buyers had a variety of choices, making it much easier to say no to a salesperson. Most industries moved beyond the sales era and into what's called the marketing era.

Agents in the marketing era look at the customers' needs and either match them to existing listings in the marketplace or list properties that match the customers' needs. They understand that these needs are constantly changing and modify their marketing efforts accordingly. It does the marketer little good, for example, to overprice a home best suited for a golfing enthusiast and then promote it in a newspaper read by equestrians. Not only was the price out of balance, but the distribution channel used to promote the property was inappropriate for the target market.

Effective Marketing

An effective marketing plan brings a property to market with the right mix of promotion, pricing, and distribution strategies.

Agents should note that the seller's motivation to do something differs from the buyer's. Consequently, the marketing strategy may need to be different for each. When agents work with sellers, they market only their services as competent, well-informed real estate professionals. When agents work with buyers, they market their services and a seller's property. In both situations, the agent is responsible to deliver what the customer wants.

How to Go Out of Business Fast

When the real estate agent no longer delivers what the customer wants, that agent will cease to be in business.

A purchase is less probable if the benefits from the purchase, whether imagined by the buyer or specifically expressed to the agent during the initial consultation, are not apparent in the properties; shown or the services provided. It doesn't matter what industry you are in; when you stop delivering what the employer wants, you need to find a new career. However, if an agent can market and promote the property's features in a way that solves an underlying problem thereby satisfying the customer's perceived needs, then the sale has a better chance of taking place.

Effective marketing addresses the multiple needs of the prospect. For a buyer, it provides a useful property

- in the right location;
- at the right price; and
- at the right time.

Effective marketing also addresses the seller's needs. It combines an understanding of economic utility, the marketing mix, and the total product (more on total product in Chapter 6) to create a marketing strategy that results in the sale of the property in the most efficient manner.

What's the Utility?

The word *utility* describes the usefulness of products or services. Matching the usefulness to a need requires a little practice. No matter what we say, sometimes our customers cannot see the usefulness of our product or service.

However, if a product or service satisfies the perceived needs of buyers or sellers better than a competitor's, then it has greater value for them. It is more useful to them. Nevertheless, as described below and shown in Figure 1.1, there are varying degrees of usefulness in any product.

Place utility. Marketing textbooks define place utility as making product available in convenient locations. People want property located where it suits their needs. In real estate, agents interpret this as having more to do with a property's proximity to facilities such as shopping centers, schools, religious facilities, transportation routes, and cultural centers. However, agents should not be too quick to judge how their customers interpret the place utility. Agents might rightfully assume that commuters want quick access to major highways, but market research may discover that after a long day at work and a hectic commute, the majority of commuters want peace and quiet when they get home. They may be willing to drive five more miles to get it. The marketing strategy should reflect the realities within the agent's market area.

Form utility. Form utility measures the usefulness of the product. When people buy real estate they want something that is useful to them—a home, an investment property, a bigger garage, or a fenced backyard. Others may want something less than the finished product in order to create their own environment, retain control, or gain status or prestige. This is better known as form utility. For example, which is more useful, a home that is already built or a stack of wood?

If you said the built home was more useful, you may be right. Of course, that implies that you are not interested in constructing your own home. As agents, we sometimes assume the customer is thinking the same thing we are.

Generally, it's not a good practice to make assumptions when it concerns customers. After all, customers may have a need to control things. Perhaps they want to know how the construction process works or they have an interest in building a new home. For them, the stack of wood has more value.

Time utility. Time utility calls for an adequate number of listings in inventory that are attractive to the largest market segments. Like most people, buyers want what they want when they want it, usually right now. Customers' general lack of knowledge of—or experience in—how real estate transactions work is a big problem for agents.

Some prospects assume they can move right in after signing the purchase agreement. Others believe that it may take a whole week before they can move in. Part of the agent's job is to "instruct" or "educate" the customer about time utility.

Some buyers may have a greater need for getting into a home quickly. It takes time for loan processing, appraisals, inspections, or the transfer of the title. It may make more sense for the agent to propose the tract home over a custom-built home, but then, as we said before, some people like the stack of wood.

Possession utility. From a legal standpoint, possession utility requires that

- the property be deliverable,
- the buyer be able to buy, and
- money be available and at reasonable rates.

It wouldn't speak well for the real estate company to sell a property that wasn't transferable. A preliminary title report, issued by a title company, tells the agent if the seller owns the property and if there are problems with easements, judgments, or other encumbrances.

Services utility.   Agents provide services utility when they deliver the information necessary for customers to make decisions. Agents must have a working knowledge of the inventory, financing, real estate laws, marketing, and more, and be able to convey their knowledge to customers in a format customers can understand. Customers want to know about the price, the terms, and the neighborhood. They want to know how the purchase meets their goals. When the agent lacks the perceived or anticipated services, the customer may seek an alternative agent. Every customer anticipates differently the advantage and benefit they'll get from a feature in a property. The qualifying interview helps agents discover the issues that are most important to customers, and how customers expect the benefits to affect them personally.

Figure 1.1
_____

Utilities

How useful is the product or service to the customer?

PLACE UTILITY

Is the property located where I want it?

Can I receive transfer within 30 days?

Do I have access to the main road?

Is shopping and recreation convenient?

What are the locations of the local schools?

FORM UTILITY

Are the materials available to build my home?

Is the supply of concrete and lumber affected by overseas demand?

Am I able to get the acreage I need to create my custom home development?

TIME UTILITY

Can I find the property I want within the next few days?

How quickly can I get through the permit process?

When can I break ground?

How long must I wait before I am qualified for a loan?

Can my new construction home be available within 150 days?

POSSESSION UTILITY

How do I know the seller really owns this property?

Do I qualify for a loan of this size?

What is the Fed going to do to interest rates?

SERVICES UTILITY

Can I trust this agent to give me the information I need?

Can I trust the information the agent gives me?

How experienced is this office in satisfying the needs of its customers?

Will the agent be able to help me or will the agent hurt me in the long run?

Figure 1.2

Marketing Consists of
Long-Term and Short-Term
Activities

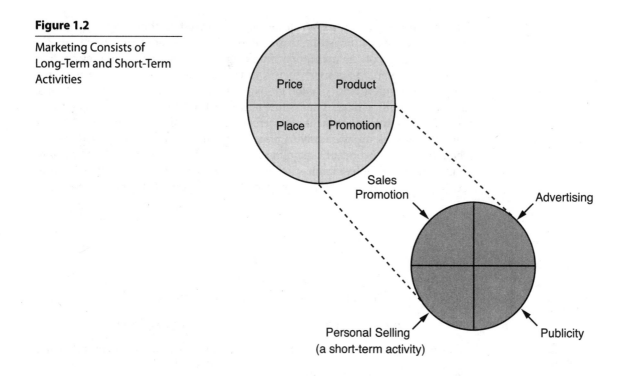

■ The Four P's and the Marketing Mix

It's difficult to succeed in the long term without marketing skills. To that extent, individual real estate salespeople must act much like corporate marketing managers by controlling the four elements of the marketing mix:

1. Product (listings/services)
2. Promotion
3. Price (for listings/services)
4. Place (distribution strategy)

Is it accurate for a property owner to say, "The property didn't sell because of my agent"? Some agents may be offended to hear such comments from sellers. After all, interest rates may have increased or the number of qualified buyers declined or perhaps a large employer closed down in the area.

Exogenous shocks, such as rising interest rates, declining numbers of qualified buyers, and an approaching inflationary market, are things outside the control of agents. Yet, real estate agents have a responsibility to use their skill and diligence in marketing their clients' properties. To overcome these seller perceptions, agents combine and adjust the four marketing activities in such a way as to produce the desired result. Products and services, from the creation of a new toy to the development of a hybrid automobile, are subject to elements manufacturers can control (product design and budget) and factors out of their control (inflation). Just as in real estate, if a new toy doesn't sell, it is partly because of how the marketer chooses to balance the marketing mix.

The four elements of the marketing mix, as shown in Figure 1.2, are product, promotion, price, and place. With a few exceptions, such as personal selling, most of the elements in the marketing mix are long-term activities to which agents must give careful consideration when developing a marketing strategy.

The Marketing Mix
1. Product
2. Promotion
3. Price
4. Place

Product

In real estate, the **product** an agent has to market is either property or service.

Property.   Agents may want to specialize in one of these specific types of real estate:

- Single-family homes
- High rises
- Commercial property
- Condominiums
- Multifamily residential units
- Mobile home parks
- Business opportunities
- Shopping centers

Market research helps agents choose the types of properties that will sell. Continuous research helps them remain flexible enough to change property types when the market changes. When interest rates start to rise, fewer people can afford to buy a home. Is this an opportunity to list for sale multifamily residential units? People must live somewhere and multifamily residential investors are usually attuned to this market environment.

Services.   Agents must decide whether to market their services to buyers, sellers, or both. They must also consider what those services will entail.

Promotion

As shown in Figure 1.2, **promotion** consists of four activities: advertising, publicity, sales promotion, and personal selling. The promotional mix uses both long-term and short-term activities to influence and encourage customers to call or visit real estate offices. Personal selling is considered a short-term activity; publicity, sales promotion, and advertising are considered long-term activities within a promotional strategy.

An agent's research will discover the factors that motivate a certain target market, such as family, comfort, status, or price; perhaps buyers just want the purchase to make them look good. Buyers may prefer investing in acreage instead of multifamily residential units. They may have sizeable down payments available or they may need to finance almost 100 percent of the purchase price. Agents use promotion to inform the market about products and pricing and often use promotion to provide the incentive needed to take action on what motivates them.

Figure 1.3

Many Factors Impact Price

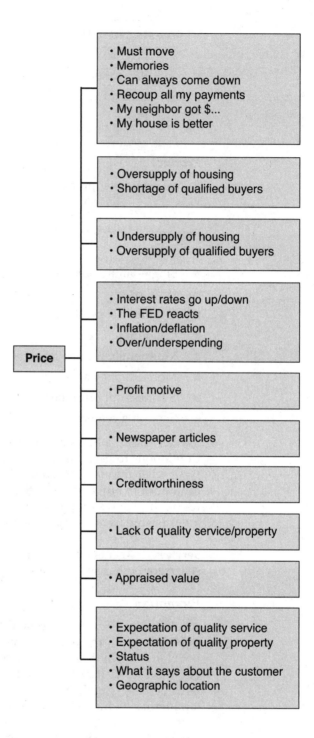

Price

Price is the value placed on the property or services rendered. As mentioned earlier, part of an agent's job is to educate prospects. Agents may discuss with the seller (and to some extent the buyer) existing market conditions, interest rates, the regional economy, buyers' demands, and how these affect the price of the property or the service provided. Figure 1.3 represents just some of the many factors that affect price and a pricing strategy. The last box suggests that geographic location affects price. This should be obvious to most. However, one of the ways a property's location affects the pricing strategy is in what it may say about the customer. In other words, a customer may be willing to pay more for a location that reflects the status and prestige that the buyer seeks. The same phenomenon can be seen in the automobile industry. Some customers are willing to pay more for an automobile because of its perceived status or prestige, even though any car can take them from one place to another. The point is that price is more easily supported when all of the elements that affect price are taken into account.

As most agents know, property prices and even the commissions charged can change quickly in a market that is rapidly expanding or contracting. As was just demonstrated, prices hold different meanings for different people. When you have a thorough knowledge of your target market, the message conveyed by your pricing strategy could be significant.

Place

Place involves the easy transfer of the property from the seller to the buyer. Earlier in the chapter, we defined place utility as having listings when and where customers want them. However, place in the context of a marketing strategy holds a slightly different meaning and centers on two main points.

First, it describes the vendors involved in taking the property from the listing stage and delivering it to the point where it transfers to the buyer. Listing and selling agencies, title insurance companies, lenders, appraisers, escrow companies, attorneys, and others are involved in delivering the property to the customer. In most states, agents are the contact point for both buyers and sellers. They are responsible for monitoring the activities of these vendors.

Second, a place strategy describes how, through channels of distribution, the potential consumer receives the promotional message. These channels of distribution (e.g., radio, television, newspapers, and others) along with the development of the promotional message provide a creative outlet for real estate agents.

Media selection should center on the most effective way to reach your target market. Media influences different target markets in different ways. With research, agents discover the one media or a combination of media needed to attract different groups within the total market. Keep in mind that place has less to do with the promotional message and more to do with how customers receive that message.

Agents must be aware of how changes in the real estate market affect their local area. Some state or local laws may outlaw some forms of delivery, such as voice recorded messages, the Internet, or For Sale signs. Each of these would affect the place strategy of the marketing mix. Agents may go out of business if they get into the rut of depending on things that worked ten years ago but are not working today.

The successful sale of a property depends on the proper mix of the four P's. The quicker product, promotion, price, and place are in balance, the quicker the potential sale.

Almost every task of a real estate marketer is included in the balanced mix of product, promotion, price, and place.

■ Summary

Real estate marketing is more than advertising, door knocking, and sales. It involves organized activities that, when balanced, help the consumer satisfy personal real estate needs. To have value, real estate must be useful to the consumer. If a property is in the wrong location or can't be delivered in a timely manner, then the property may have no value to the consumer. Agents have the responsibility to discover the utility needs of prospects and incorporate those needs into their property and service presentations.

Agents use the four marketing activities—product, promotion, price, and place—to develop marketing mix strategies. When balanced, these strategies help market property and services more effectively. Agents decide what inventory to list or services to provide given the needs of the client base. With a goal of attracting large consumer segments from the total market, agents also develop their pricing strategy, promotional mix, and strategies to distribute information to consumers.

■ Multiple Choice Questions

1. Marketing is made up of four activities that when balanced lead to a successful sale. Which of the following describes these balanced activities?
   a. The product mix
   b. The promotional mix
   c. The marketing mix
   d. The pricing strategy

2. Which of the following is *NOT* a part of a promotional strategy?
   a. Personal selling
   b. Advertising
   c. Product selection
   d. Publicity

3. In real estate, what is one of the fastest ways to go out of business?
   a. Sell only low-income housing
   b. Don't deliver what the customer wants
   c. Don't attend office agent tours
   d. Fail to submit your listing to the multiple listing service

4. To have value, something must be useful or have utility. If a married couple wants the usefulness of a fenced backyard or a productive garden, this is known as
   a. form utility.
   b. place utility.
   c. services utility.
   d. possession utility.

5. Which of the following utilities concerns itself with the availability of money at reasonable rates?
   a. Services utility
   b. Interest utility
   c. Possession utility
   d. Time utility

■ **Exercises**

Research Question 1—Real estate agencies contract for different types of listings, including commercial, residential, multifamily residential, acreage, and lots. Identify and describe the number and types of listings in a real estate office, in your real estate office or in a competitor's office. What is the rationale for having the number of listings of any given type? In what way would the inventory be affected by an increase in interest rates, a decrease in the affordability index, or an increase in population?

Research Question 2—All real estate companies offer services to their buyers and sellers yet sometimes have a difficult time articulating exactly what those services are. These services include small things, such as offering a buyer a fresh hot cup of coffee, to following the paperwork through the transfer process. What services are offered to buyers in a local real estate office, in your office, or in a competitor's office? What services are offered to sellers? Why?

Research Question 3—The direction of the economy has an effect on interest rates, wages, employment rates, and more. All of these affect national, regional, and local real estate markets. Consequently, when agents develop a marketing plan, they take into account these and other elements in the economy. Evaluate and describe existing market conditions in your area. In your opinion, what effect will the current direction of interest rates and the regional economy have on home prices and buyer demand?

Research Question 4—After taking a listing, agents must decide how the listing information reaches the public. Often, the target market that the agents are trying to reach determines the delivery method. Suppose you have just listed a property. Decide on three specific target markets. How or where will you distribute this information so that it reaches the target market? Remember, distribution does not mean advertising the information. However, distribution does include channels of distribution, such as newspapers.

THE MARKETING CONCEPT

2

■ Learning Objectives

After the study and review of this chapter, you should be able to

- explain the marketing concept and its components;
- describe the significance of goal orientation and time management for both agents and prospects;
- describe the roles prospects take when buying and the challenges of marketing property to different role players;
- identify and explain the tools used to build good customer relations;
- identify the significance of building a personal and company image and steps used to maintain that image;
- demonstrate the use of SWOT (strengths, weaknesses, opportunities, and threats) in marketing; and
- evaluate the problems in implementing the marketing concept.

■ Key Terms

buyer	goal orientation	systems orientation
customer orientation	influencer	user
decider	marketing concept	
gatekeeper	performance	

Real estate agents develop marketing strategies to help them accomplish their personal production goals and the goals of their customers. Through the use of market research and analysis, as explained in the next several chapters, the company (or the individual salesperson) has a better idea of how to describe and find its target market and how to effectively compete within its industry.

Development of a mission statement is one of the first steps major corporations take toward creating a marketing strategy. It establishes their purpose and states why they are in business. If agents used this approach, mission statements would organize and define how they approach their market, what they specialize in, and why they are practicing professionals in the industry.

Personal and professional goals, the essence of time management, are additional elements in the creation of a marketing strategy. Agents should challenge their past accomplishments while balancing them against their personal/office resources and the constraints outside the control of the operation (e.g., factory closings, inflation, or interest rates). As part of the goal-setting process, agents look at their strengths and weaknesses. They create activities and tasks that take advantage of their strengths while improving upon their weaknesses. Research helps agents discover the strengths and weaknesses of their main competitors and how they can take advantage of those weaknesses.

The information from a self-evaluation and these studies helps define the target markets (buyers, sellers, or agents) and identifies ways to find them. The marketing strategy identifies the broad-based needs of the target market and what resources might be needed to accomplish the goals of the agent. A centerpiece of today's marketing strategies is the marketing concept.

■ Marketing Concept

As we learned in Chapter 1, for many years the real estate industry was focused on convincing people to buy a product they didn't necessarily want or need. This began to change after the beginning of the 1950s, when consumers could choose from many competing products. Businesses could no longer just produce something and depend on their sales or product orientation to sell it. They slowly discovered the **marketing concept**. They learned that they had to identify consumer needs and meet those needs before developing a new product (taking a listing). There are several aspects to meeting the needs of real estate consumers. The agent's focus on customer needs is called **customer orientation**. The second element in the marketing concept, **goal orientation** and time management, is essential to long-term personal and company survival. Lastly, and often the most difficult to orchestrate for a broker, is a process whereby all agents, staff, and associate workers practice customer orientation at all times. This is done by coordinating all of their marketing activities and making sure those activities do not come into conflict with one another or with the overall activities of the company. In the textbook *Successful Small Business Management*, a similar process is called the systems approach.[2] For our purposes we will call it a **systems orientation**.

Customer Orientation

Agents who are customer oriented identify the needs of groups of buyers, sellers, or other agents. These consist of both property needs that are known to the prospects and emotional needs that may or may not be known to them. The needs of a target market should be determined before properties are listed in order to develop marketing campaigns that are attractive to large segments of the market. This doesn't mean that only one type of

---

2   Leon C. Megginson, Charles R. Scott, Jr., Lyle R. Trueblood, William L. Megginson, *Successful Small Business Management*, 5th ed. Plano: Business Publications, Inc.,1988, 449.

listing is taken in one geographic area; far from it. The listings taken should be geographically diverse but with commonalities that are attractive to the target markets.

Agents who have no idea of the composition and scope of their target market would never know when they were actually talking to a member of their target market. As mentioned above, the agent's job is to discover the needs and commonalities of multiple segments of the total market and list inventory that meet those needs. To do any less might suggest the agent is more excited about the listings than the needs of the target market.

Agents who are more excited about their listings than about their buyers' needs may have a product orientation. They are more willing to defend a property than meet the needs of their client and are likely more focused on their inventory than on customer orientation. For example, when an agent feels a particular property is suited for the customer but the customer doesn't agree, a product-oriented agent would expend more energy selling the property than reidentifying the customer's needs. Having a product orientation becomes a hindrance when the agent attempts to sell the next home on the list with the same passion. The prospect may wonder how the agent can say the same things about the second property after the agent already declared the first property was the "best" one for the customer. While it may not be the agent's intent, the customer may perceive that the agent is more interested in a commission than in serving the needs of the prospect.

When agents are customer orientated, prospects feel that the agents can effectively meet their needs. By understanding customer needs, agents can promote and later demonstrate the advantages of property features and how they satisfy those needs.

Goal Orientation and Time Management

Establishing both personal and professional goals saves time and potentially generates more sales. Many distractions in a real estate office or outside environment are not conducive to a productive workday: two or three agents enjoying the donuts and coffee in the back of the office may draw other agents into a replay of the basketball game the night before; an experienced agent may be mentoring a new licensee who has questions that must be answered now; the broker calls for a 30-minute sales meeting that stretches into an hour, and after the meeting he says he needs advertisements on two listings within five minutes. Granted, some of these events may prove productive, but they consume time that may not necessarily address the marketing concept. Time management skills and how they affect the agent and the prospect are discussed in more detail in Chapter 3. For now, think of a goal orientation as focusing on a distant point (e.g., I will earn $100,000 over the next six months) and using time management to reach that goal.

These goals may include getting a certain amount of listings or sales in a month. Perhaps you are starting to work a new geographic area in your community and your goal is to have a certain market share within that geographic area. Time management skills break down the long-term goal into manageable weekly and daily goals that must be completed. With this mindset, frivolous activities occupy less time during the workday. Setting and meeting your goals is a positive step in a total marketing strategy and further establishes your customer orientation, the essence of the marketing concept.

Systems Orientation

When agencies apply a systems orientation they successfully operate multiple tasks without conflict. This is a difficult process for most industries and particularly difficult for the real estate industry.

Suppose a real estate office has two departments, one for real estate sales and the other for property management. In a multifamily residential complex that the office manages, a tenant who has gotten behind on his rent receives an impersonal, computer-generated three-day notice to pay rent or quit. At the same time, a salesperson from another part of the company sends this tenant a solicitation to purchase a home! Do you think this lack of coordination might backfire?

The independence of agents within most real estate companies creates this difficulty. Independent contractors may have different ideas on how to provide the broker with sales and results. Agents try to bring together all the elements of the marketing concept including customer orientation and goal orientation. However, as they execute their daily goals, they bring themselves closer to their long-term goals but not necessarily the goals of the company.

The owner of the company tries to encourage the agents to abide by the marketing concept. This is difficult when working with independent contractors, but its need is apparent in many offices. In an ideal situation, the company and its agents research customer wants and discover market opportunities. Perhaps an in-house study found that consumers want more from their agents. Let's say the research revealed that many prospects wished they had a videotape of their new purchase or their old house and that none of the agency's competitors offer this service. This competitor weakness may be turned into a short-term advantage for the real estate agents within the office.

In many offices, a more realistic outcome is that agents do research for themselves but are not willing to share the information with other agents in the office. Their fear may be the potential loss of personal income.

The manager/owner may have to be responsible for all research projects, making the results of the research available to all the agents within the firm. An explanation of the marketing concept clearly defined in the company's mission statement may help encourage agents to work together, while maintaining their individuality (see Figure 2.1). This is not an easy task; whether you are a manager/owner or an individual agent, systems orientation must become a part of the total marketing concept in order to coordinate information, company policy, customer service, and agent performance.

■ Roles Customers Take

One practical application of customer orientation is understanding the roles that customers take in the buying process. Recognizing the roles that each customer plays will help the agent discover the customer's personal or emotional needs. The prospect might take on one or more of the five customer

Figure 2.1

Sample Mission
Statement

> ## *Mission Statement*
>
> ABC Realty will set the standard for professionalism in our area of operation. Our service quality will exceed the expectations of our prospects.
>
> ABC Realty is a member of the National Association of Realtors® and abides by a strict code of ethics. Our commitment to excellence and our desire to accrue more knowledge, education, and training, while maintaining a high degree of personal honesty and integrity, helps our prospects reach their goals. Our agents are dedicated to solving problems. They do not take the position of selling property to their prospects. They help prospects by suggesting solutions that meet their criteria based on a comprehensive qualifying interview. Our agents leave it up to the prospects to make the purchase decision.
>
> This firm will specialize in residential and multifamily residential properties, attempting to limit its inventory to Any Town and the adjacent city. Research and data analysis conducted by the firm each year will provide guidance for its members who use it to evaluate the seller target market and the general price range of the properties listed.

roles: user, buyer, influencer, gatekeeper, and decider. Though one person can play all of these roles, others involved in the transaction often take on separate roles.

User and Buyer

The **user** occupies the home or uses the property. The user might also be the buyer, but the buyer could just as easily be someone other than a user. Perhaps the buyer is a relative of the user or an investor who is purchasing multifamily residential units. The **buyer** is the one who has the credit necessary to buy the property.

Decider

The **decider** is the person who makes the decision to purchase. Despite the fact that the buyer makes the purchase, the buyer is sometimes not the same person who reacts to a marketing campaign or makes the decision to buy. The decider is the one who makes the buying decision, but may not be the one with the credit to make the purchase. For example, suppose your prospects are a husband and wife buying a new home. Although the husband is the sole provider of income (the buyer), his wife is the one who chose the property and made the decision to buy.

Influencer and Gatekeeper

The **influencer** is the one who responds to your promotional efforts and helps persuade the decision maker to contact the agent; the **gatekeeper** controls how and if the information is distributed to the decision maker. The influencer can play a strong role in the final purchase decision by manipulating or persuading the decider to take a certain course of action. In real estate, influencers might be the children, relatives, friends, or spouse of the decider.

For example, suppose the agent calls the prospects mentioned above and informs the wife that the property the couple saw that morning just had a small price reduction. The wife says she will talk it over with her husband; however, the agent doesn't get a call back. It's possible that the wife didn't pass along the information to the husband because she was not interested in purchasing that property. By controlling the information received from the agent, the wife plays the role of the gatekeeper.

■ Marketing to Role Players

Promotional campaigns that stress aggressive pricing strategies may be attractive to the buyer but not to the user. These properties might offer discounted pricing, which is an incentive for the buyer, but the condition of the property may not be suitable for the user. Product strategies that explore the advantages and benefits of owning a particular property, as we will discuss later, may provide the incentive needed for the user, decider, or influencer to contact the agent. Thought must be given to the promotional campaigns that agents create. It is not unusual to write promotional pieces that are attractive to the different role players. It also is not unusual to distribute them at the same time.

Let's look at a sales situation with multiple role players. Suppose an agent makes a presentation to a board that is considering purchasing a commercial property. The president of the firm attended the hour-long presentation but was more interested in getting straight to the bottom line to find a valid reason for the transaction. The president was the decider and buyer in this scenario.

During the presentation, the agent noticed that one member of the board spent a lot of time talking about how his department could really make money with the proposed property. This individual is the user and to some degree the influencer.

Another board member was very put out that no one was consulting him. As the firm's controller, it is his job to inform the president about the details of the proposal and whether the company could afford it. This individual is the gatekeeper. Unfortunately, the agent discovered that the controller didn't understand the proposal. When it was repeatedly explained to him, he asked no questions yet still failed to understand it. Worse, he did not present the information to the president. The reason for the presentation was to inform all the parties at the same time, including the president, so that a decision could be made.

In summary, if you try to sell your product to the wrong person, not only are you wasting your time but you also may be offending the buyer. It is possible also to offend the user, the influencer, the gatekeeper, and the decider. A sale takes place when the agent can balance the needs of all parties in the transaction. In every transaction, in every advertisement, and in every promotion, you have many needs to address and many needs to satisfy.

■ Building Customer Relations

Another practical application of successful customer orientation is strong customer relations. When you meet the needs of your customer by listing and/or showing the right properties and providing the right services, you remain true to the marketing concept, which improves your customer relations. Here are some specific ways in which customer orientation can help build strong customer relations.

Build a Referral Base

One of the most difficult aspects of real estate is establishing repeat customers. After all, most people live in a home for several years before ever thinking of selling it and buying another one. Nevertheless, brokers should encourage their sales force to stay in touch with past customers. One of the many ways to accomplish this is for the agents to follow up with their buyers and sellers both during and after a sale. For transactions that are less than trouble free, this may prove a challenge. Nevertheless, agents should make every effort to develop long-lasting relationships with their customers.

Build a Reputation for Performance

Performance can be defined as doing what you say you will do, and doing it in a timely manner. For example, if an agency's promotional campaign states that the office is open at 8 AM, then someone should be in the office answering the phones at 8 AM. If prospects call at 8 AM and are connected to the office answering machine, then the agency is not delivering on its promise of performance.

Or suppose after an extensive marketing campaign, prospects call the office to request information. If the agent promises to mail or e-mail the information or call the prospects back yet fails to follow through, then the agent is demonstrating poor performance, which reflects negatively on the reputation of the agency.

Meet the prospect's needs, even when there is no obligation to do so.

Stay in Touch

One agent in California built a large following by writing 20 to 25 letters every day. His letters varied in content. He wrote to past customers and customers who were waiting for property to transfer into their names. Sometimes he wrote to people who owned five or more properties in his sales region. His letters would describe a specific property that would appeal to a certain kind of prospect. Other letters described his services. This type of promotional strategy helps keep the agent's name in front of potential prospects and past customers.

The marketing concept addresses customer needs and their expectations of a certain level of service. If that service level is not delivered, they may look elsewhere for help.

The interview discovers what services individual customers demand.

Personalize Your Business

Real estate agents are in the unique position of being like a small company. They can do things for their customers that a large company may not necessarily think of doing. Agents can give the sellers a picture of their old home after they move out. Some agents loan their camera to the buyer so they can take insurance pictures of their possessions while they unpack. Your imagination can explore the possibilities, such as free use of your office fax machine, mail pickup service when prospects go on vacations (for the period you control their listing), or free home warranty insurance. Be mindful of any liability these ideas may transfer to you.

Buyer's Remorse Pill

Many agents employ the use of a "buyer's remorse pill." These "pills" are usually pieces of candy. A spice rack might be used for your "pharmacy." Fill it with the little breath mints that come in the small clear box containers. Stock a variety of different colored mints (green, orange, and white).

Each container should have a label that identifies its contents. If there is a little tension before signing the offer, give them a green breath mint (pre–buyer's remorse pill). This often helps break the tension.

After the signing, talk for a while but before they leave give them an orange breath mint (buyer's remorse pill). Tell them to keep that pill until later and take it when they wake up at 2 AM wondering if they made a mistake. Tell them that the pill will remind them of all the reasons for the purchase. (This also may avert a call to the agent in the middle of the night.)

The white breath mints are used as "forget-me-not pills," in case a prospect isn't quite ready to buy. Some agents like using the forget-me-not flower. Anything that will keep the agent's name in the prospect's mind will do.

■ Building a Company Image

Agents who practice the marketing concept orient their goals and activities toward satisfying the demands of their customers. Those customers consist of buyers, sellers, and, to some extent, other real estate agents. An evaluation of the agent and the office environment is an often-overlooked step in the marketing concept.

Self-Assessment

Agents should conduct a semiannual or annual evaluation of themselves. If you were the customer, how would you evaluate your services? When you walk into your office, what is the first thing you see on your desk? Is it a stack of unfinished paperwork or the organized desk of an executive? Observe how the support staff greets your customers because this affects how prospects perceive your professionalism. Are your listings priced within the target market's affordability range? Do you have the kinds of listings and locations that are demanded by your target market? Are you dependent on the listings of other agencies?

With regard to self-assessment in the sales process, agents must develop initial meetings that result in getting to know the prospects better. These meetings provide the agents with opportunities to help sellers understand the process of professionally marketing a property, the complexity of the paperwork involved, and the processes used to transfer a property from a seller to a buyer (e.g., lender, title insurance, and inspections).

Real estate companies that are customer oriented do not discourage their agents from taking additional college-level real estate courses beyond the minimum requirements for a salesperson's license. In fact, today, more and more agencies look for licensees who take an active interest in a college education. These companies provide additional training to help their agents comply with the laws and ethics of their industry.

Office Image

As an agent practicing customer orientation, you must measure up to the customers' expectations. How quickly does the support staff respond to incoming phone calls? Are the other agents dressed professionally for your area, or would you prefer that they not be seen by your prospects? The following is a sampling of what prospects expect of real estate professionals:

- Distinctive sign and stationery
- Informative business card
- Use of computers
- Shiny shoes and distinctive attire
- Well-organized office and desk
- Polite, courteous, well-informed staff
- Efficient use of time
- Listens to the customer
- Views property in the price range the customers say they want to pay
- Takes the time to explain how the processes work
- Follow-up

Safety and Regulations

When applying the marketing concept, customers have certain safety expectations when it comes to the purchase of a home. They expect the plumbing to work. They don't expect a fire to break out when they flip on a light switch. The buyer has the right to a home that meets minimum public health and safety standards. If a buyer asks the agent if the roof leaks and the agent says no, then the buyer fully expects the roof to be watertight during the next downpour. Any misrepresentation, as we will learn in Chapter 9, leaves agents open to lawsuits. Consequently, customers expect full disclosure of all material facts.

The marketing concept requires that agents protect the interests of their customers (another form of safety). This means that in order to avoid possible lawsuits, agents must take the time to explain the multiple components in a written listing agreement or offer. Among other things, the customer's right to safety includes such things as an explanation of lender interest rates, annual percentage rates, and other truth in lending issues, as discussed earlier. Various laws require contractors, agents, inspectors, and lenders to perform these tasks. However, the fact that the customer has a great deal of power today when it comes to a violation or even a perceived violation of their rights causes many brokers to stand up and take notice. So, as mentioned earlier, brokers are becoming more selective in their hiring practices, often preferring agents with experience, some college education, or even a degree.

Follow-Up

Follow-up is a marketing and sales process that occurs before, during, and after a sale. By staying in contact with prospects, agents demonstrate their interests in the prospects' needs. This improves the company image. After taking a listing, ask the seller when it would be the best day to call and update them on the progress of the marketing plan. Don't make this statement unless you are prepared to call even when *nothing* happened during the past week. Your calls must explain how you are adjusting your marketing plan to the changing market. Naturally, during the active weeks, you want to call them and tell them how great everything is going.

Professional agents keep buyers and sellers informed throughout the transfer process. Think of the advantages of talking with your buyer or seller at least once a week during this period. If a problem comes up, you can inform the parties and come to a reasonable solution. Some agents attempt an alternative strategy; they don't tell the parties anything until a week or so before the deed is supposed to record. By then, cumulative unresolved problems are too much to bear, and a canceled transaction seems an easy way out for everyone.

Prospect Interaction

There is no better way to apply the marketing concept in sales than to interact with prospects and help them become a part of the selling solution. When prospects become part of the sales process, helping them accomplish their goals is easier. When you interact with clients on a regular basis, the decision to renew a listing is made easier for the sellers. You have kept the sellers informed and have asked for input during the listing period. They know what you have done. They have a better sense of what it takes to sell a property and they are more willing to give you the time to do so.

■ Your Competition

Today, buyers and sellers are more aware than ever of their right to select the lenders they will use, as well as the escrow or title company, inspectors, and more. They always had this right, but now they are armed with the knowledge to use it. When you go on a listing appointment, you are probably only one of perhaps several agents the seller will meet before making a decision.

Many agents successfully secure the listings by demonstrating their uniqueness. Agents might specialize, for example, in properties within certain price

Figure 2.2

Know Your Competition

Strengths and Weaknesses

Competitor 1: XYZ Realty

Strengths:

- Aggressive, well trained sales staff
- Multiple affiliate offices
- Substantial advertising budget

Weaknesses:

- Office not highly visible from the frontage highway
- Limited sign exposure
- Not affiliated with a national franchise
- Located near an unregulated busy intersection
- Office complex has low pedestrian count

Competitor 2: 123 Realty

Strengths:

- Aggressive sales staff
- High exposure
- Good sign exposure
- Second office located on a major access road
- Office manager is active in local board

Weaknesses:

- Large sales force
- Not public service oriented
- Target market is in a higher price bracket
- Image tarnished by unethical conduct
- Located between two unregulated intersections
- Office complex has low pedestrian count

ranges, school districts, certain tracts, or properties of a specific size or use. This can also be accomplished by listing only properties that meet the needs of the target market.

Know Your Competition

One way to understand your competition is to discover their strengths and weaknesses. Suppose you were a computer manufacturer and you knew that all other computer manufacturers built computers that operated at the same speed. Each company sold its computers for $1,000. Now suppose you built a computer that operated at a substantially higher, more efficient speed and you sold it for $1,000. It seems reasonable, if all the manufacturers were similar in brand name recognition, that consumers would purchase the faster machine for the same price. This is an example of the marketing concept in that it discovers how to take advantage of a competitor that is not meeting the customer's needs. A helpful tool for assessing competitors is called

Figure 2.3

Opportunities from
Weaknesses

Opportunities from Weaknesses

- Recruit motivated, highly educated agents (look into the possibility of signing bonuses)
- Locate in newer, highly visible complex
- Target $65,000–$85,000 wage earners
- Target $250,000–$340,000 homes in the X area
- Maintain a regular, aggressive advertising campaign
- Develop distinctive signs
- Hold quarterly seminars for both buyers and sellers

a SWOT evaluation. The letters in the acronym stand for strengths, weaknesses, opportunities, and threats.

To perform a SWOT evaluation, Figure 2.2 demonstrates how you first itemize your understanding of the strengths and weaknesses of your closest competitors. When evaluating their weaknesses, evaluate what opportunities are available for you to explore. It's a given that your conclusions will be somewhat subjective based on the data gathered. As more data is gathered your conclusions may change. Don't forget to look at how your competitor can affect you. You must decide if you have the means to counteract any threats to your market share, recruitment, or sales.

Based on the weaknesses of your competitor and the opportunities they offer, Figure 2.3 shows how you might develop part of your marketing strategy. (Keep in mind that this should encompass what you found during market research. Don't speculate.)

■ Exogenous Shocks

Exogenous shocks, the environment that is outside the control of agents, may provide both opportunities and threats to agents' success. Consider the direction of bond prices (when they go up, interest rates drop), income levels, consumer confidence, new tax laws that may impact the customer's ability to borrow, regulations that require additional disclosures, decreases or increases in population density, and more. Each of these may have a positive or negative effect on an agent's market. Marketing research discovers these and the analysis of that information may reveal opportunities. For example, changes in consumer confidence coupled with a declining affordability index occurs in a particular market area may be an indication of a slowdown in single-family residential sales. This may provide an opportunity to list and market multifamily residential units as well as miniwarehouses. Depending on the expansion that may have taken place in the residential markets of a community just prior to a period of rising interest rates, a period of commercial development may follow.

■ Problems that Occur When Implementing the Marketing Concept

As smoothly as the marketing concept can and does run, there are times when its success may be in jeopardy. Fortunately, agents have time to make changes. If they observe any of the following scenarios, then it's time to become familiar with the marketing concept once again.

- There is no excuse for an agent not to get a name, address, and phone number before ending a call with a prospect. This demonstrates a pure lack of training—a system breakdown. If the agent cannot get this minimal information from prospects, then there is a major breakdown in the marketing abilities of the firm. The broker/owner is literally throwing away money on any marketing campaign he tries to implement.

  Some real estate companies and their agents do not have a comprehensive marketing plan and consequently depend heavily on advertising. If the employees or the agents who receive the calls are not trained to get the name, address, and phone number of the caller or walk-in, then the advertising dollars spent to acquire that prospect are lost.

- It really hurts when a past customer lists a property or purchases another through a different agent. However, if agents keep in close contact with their past clients, they have a better chance to get their repeat business, as well as get referrals. Agents should send past clients a note three or four times a year and follow it up with a phone call.

- When prospects don't call back even though they promised that they would, it is another indication of a problem. If the agent or employee were properly trained, then the agent wouldn't need to wait for a prospect to call back because the agent would have the caller's name, address, and phone number and could call on the prospect at a more convenient time.

  How many times have new and experienced agents heard a prospect promise to call back? When there is a problem with the marketing concept, a prospect callback is pretty rare. After all, the prospect must have a reason to do so. If the agent has already given the caller the street address, the price, and the terms of the property, why should the prospect call back? If the prospect promises to call you back, consider the call a "lost sale." Nevertheless, make every effort to get a name and phone number, if for no other reason than for the practice. After all, if the prospect doesn't call back, you have nothing. And, if you don't have the name and number, you have nothing. So, give it a shot. You have everything to gain and nothing more to lose.

- If advertising or promotions are not causing the phones to ring, something is wrong. It's easy to say that interest rates have gone up or that the economy isn't cooperating, but agents must understand the need to change the marketing mix quickly. The faster they realize that a change is needed, the faster their income will increase. In an economy similar to that of the late 1970s, 1980s, and early 1990s when home prices dropped dramatically in many areas of the country, people were losing their jobs and their homes. Though eventually interest rates started dropping along with the prices, agents couldn't seem to get people interested in buying.

  Some agents continued listing the same kinds of properties that they had in the past, but even with the low interest rates, the homes just wouldn't sell. Over a period of a year or two agents realized that the prices on existing homes were just too high for the market. They had a difficult time convincing sellers that the value of their home was less than the price they paid.

The late 1980s and early 1990s was also a period when many foreclosures hit the market at the same time, due to the cleanup of the savings and loan crisis. Some agents complained about the number of foreclosure properties that were being placed on the market. They complained that every sale caused the value of other homes to go down. In this economy, these agents continued their marketing mix of listing properties at prices that couldn't compete with the foreclosure market. They tried all the promotion ideas they used when selling was much easier and interest rates were higher, but nothing worked.

There were other agents, however, who took the time to evaluate that same market. They came to the conclusion that the market had changed and so must their marketing mix. They found, through research, that customers had changed. Customers were now often first-time buyers looking for the lowest price and interest rate possible. As these agents looked around they determined that they couldn't move interest rates one direction or the other. However, they could do something about the properties they listed. They started listing and selling foreclosure properties. For almost two years, while other agents were complaining about the difficulties they were having, these few agents were selling two and three properties a week!

Keep in mind, the phone rings for a reason. If your marketing mix is off, it won't ring. If you choose not to represent the needs of a prospect, there is no reason for the prospect to call you.

■ One of the biggest complaints among a large percentage of customers is waiting to be recognized in the office or the number of times the telephone rings before someone answers. Another complaint is the length of time a customer is kept on hold. Seventeen seconds seems to be a tolerance threshold. In an industry where the customer thinks that one agent is pretty much like the next, agents cannot afford to let customers wait. A real turnoff for many customers is to be kept waiting in the lobby for no apparent reason. We have all had the experience. We enter a store. The workers clearly see us. We wait for assistance, but we are held captive by a discussion of how the weekend rock concert went for the three co-workers. We leave in frustration because we can get batteries (or real estate) elsewhere.

■ An increase in the cancellation of listings and sales is another indication that the marketing concept may not be working. The sellers are telling agents something significant and agents must get the message quickly. The problems could stem from the pricing strategy, promotion, or follow-up practices of the company or the agent. Perhaps sellers are upset that their home has not been shown. This might have been caused by the firm's promotional strategy. Some firms establish listing contests to increase inventory. Unfortunately, contests often bring in a wide spectrum of listings that are often taken at any price so the listing agent has a better chance of winning the contest. As a result, the firm has more listings than it can effectively market. Sometimes properties are listed at prices that can't result in a sale.

Sales also cancel for a variety of reasons. A common one is that the buyer wasn't qualified. Remember, when listings or sales cancel, the prospects (buyers or sellers) perceive it to be the agent's fault. As agents, understand that buyers do not perceive it to be their fault that they didn't qualify; they may perceive that the agent should have done more to get them qualified. Also assume that it's not the fault of the lender who wouldn't qualify your buyer because they have their policies to follow; the buyer and seller may perceive that the agent should have done more to find an appropriate lender. If agents are prepared to deal with these issues before they occur, steps can be taken to keep the prospects informed of various aspects of the marketing and sales process, thus mitigating some negative perceptions. Fortunately, the anticipation of problems gets easier with experience.

■ All businesses measure their success by comparing their net income from a previous year to the current year. Agents should do the same. If you discover your net income is dropping, it could be due to an increase in your cost of living or a decrease in your sales volume. In either case, determine the cause and make adjustments accordingly.

■ Another reason the marketing concept breaks down is because agents take listings without any idea of the demographics of the target market or how to access them. Listing contests in which salespeople try to acquire the most listings may cause this situation. The marketing concept breaks down in this case because salespeople are told that if they collect a lot of listings some are bound to sell (despite the poor customer relations that are created in the interim from those homes that don't sell). A lack of knowledge of available listings that might work for the target market also hampers the marketing concept. After all, how can agents fulfill their customers' needs if they don't know what properties are available?

■ Another problem is that agents are not taking the time to determine what changes are taking place in the market. You probably know of a real estate company in your area that always seems to list properties at prices higher than market value. This is an unenviable reputation to have. Every time you look at one of its listings in the multiple listing service, you have to suspect its price is too high.

■ Brokers that hire new licensees who have little or no training can cause high-production salespeople to move to other offices. When agents can't fill out the paperwork correctly or don't understand the importance of showing up for appointments on time, they lack training. Without a formal training program, the broker may ask experienced licensees to mentor the new ones. The experienced salespeople may find their time consumed by answering the endless questions of new licensees. Frustrated with constant interruptions and declining earnings, the high-production salespeople may move to another office. Other issues that may cause experienced salespeople to leave include personnel conflicts, lack of office organization, minimal advertising budgets, and the perception that the "grass is always greener" in another office.

Marketing plans may take many forms that are dependent on their purpose and how they are used. The appendix shows a sample outline of a marketing plan that helps apply some of the material that is covered in the next several chapters.

■ Summary

A marketing strategy helps agents define and organize their approach to the market by using a tool called the marketing concept. This tool breaks the marketing strategy into three groups from which other subgroups are developed. Customer orientation requires that agents discover the needs of prospects and provide solutions for those needs. We discovered that building customer relations, improving an agent's self-image and the image of the company, and protecting the customer all center on the concept of customer orientation.

The second element in the marketing concept is goal orientation and time management. We discovered that goal orientation helps keep us focused on our short-term and long-term goals, and time management establishes the daily and weekly tasks needed to accomplish our goals. The third element of the marketing concept, called systems orientation, involves the processes of how to integrate the multiple tasks of marketing and sales without conflict. Because of the nature of many real estate offices, systems orientation could be difficult for the broker/owner to implement. However, individual agents who establish and control their marketing strategy and may find less difficulty with this element of the marketing mix.

The marketing concept may break down for several reasons. Brokers/owners should recognize the signs that indicate there are problems with the marketing concept, including the inability of agents to obtain a prospect's name and phone number, a decline in phone calls or walk-ins, an increase in listing or sales cancellations, and losing salespeople to other offices.

■ Multiple Choice Questions

1. Customer orientation
   a. identifies the features of a product and stresses those features until the product is sold.
   b. attempts to find a market's needs before listing properties.
   c. avoids conflict between the multiple tasks needed to bring the customer to the product.
   d. is another term for prospecting.

2. A prospect comes into the office after calling about an ad. You qualify them and show them a property. The prospect did not want to leave the home you showed because it met absolutely all of the prospect's needs. After several hours, and some considerable persuasion, you return to the office only to find that the house sold ten days earlier. In what area did the marketing concept break down?
   a. Customer orientation
   b. Systems orientation
   c. Goal orientation
   d. None of the above

3. Given the independence of agents in most real estate offices, which of the following is the *MOST* difficult to implement for a real estate broker/owner?
   a. Marketing strategy
   b. Customer orientation
   c. Goal orientation
   d. Systems orientation

4. What marketing strategy can agents use to encourage sellers to list properties with them?
   a. Demonstrate their knowledge of property
   b. Discount their commission
   c. Demonstrate their uniqueness
   d. Show up for the appointment on time

5. The tool most often used to discover an agency's weaknesses is identified by the acronym
   a. NASD.
   b. BARD.
   c. FWID.
   d. SWOT.

■ Exercises

Exercise 1—One of the most difficult yet profitable aspects of real estate is the repeat customer. Building strong customer relations by meeting their needs helps agents remain true to the marketing concept. What steps can agents take before, during, and after the marketing and sales process to build a database of repeat customers?

Research Question—Meeting customers' needs is the essence of the marketing concept. This is done in a variety of ways, including a comprehensive self-evaluation of both the agent and the agency. Observe for a period of several days how long the phone rings before an incoming telephone call is answered in your office. Additionally, observe how much time goes by before a walk-in is recognized in the lobby of your office. Ask fellow agents how they would describe the needs of their target market and perhaps their understanding of the size and scope of that market.

c h a p t e r   t h r e e

MARKET RESEARCH

■ Learning Objectives

After the study and review of this chapter, you should be able to

- identify the purpose of market research;
- explain how market research gathers information on market segments, product and service features important to prospects, opportunities in the marketplace, and channels of distribution;
- analyze and deduce conclusions about the significance of market research and the role it plays in time management;
- list and explain the steps taken in market research;
- define the nature of the data collected, be it primary data or secondary data; and
- describe the tools used by the Federal Reserve and analyze how they are used to control the money supply.

■ Key Terms

defining the problem	market research	secondary data
discount rate	open market operations	target market
the Federal Reserve (the Fed)	overheated economy	time management
	primary data	
gathering and organizing data	reserve requirements	

An information-gathering process helps avoid listing properties that do not meet the needs of a large potential customer base. This process is called market research. Market research provides to agents information that helps them make decisions with regard to the types of properties to list, the content of advertisements, the best channels of distribution to reach different segments of the market, and more. Without research, the marketing effort would be based on speculative guesswork. Chapter 4 will discuss how agents analyze research data and the conclusions they may draw from it.

■ The Reasons for Market Research

Market research is a data-gathering process that ultimately assists agents in making marketing decisions that reduce risk, save time, and save money. Research helps identify opportunities, customer needs, channels of distribution, and the strengths and weaknesses of the company and its competition. It also identifies pricing strategies and their impact on the market, as well as providing information needed by agents to make decisions affecting their business.

Market research is only half the equation. Data analysis and conclusions, discussed in Chapter 4, complete much of the preliminary work that needs to be done before developing the four marketing strategies that result in a sale. Before developing the reasons for conducting market research and how to perform that task, let's get a better picture of how the process unfolds.

The purpose of the research.   An agent may read in the newspaper that interest rates are about to increase. Can a marketing strategy be developed to counteract it? The agent follows up on this and gets more information to determine how it might affect their business and what the rate increase means to the marketplace.

Data gathering.   The data from multiple sources is gathered without judgment and loosely organized to help provide solutions to the purpose of the project.

Figure 3.1

The Purpose of a Marketing Research Project

The purpose of a marketing research project may be to determine the answers to some or all of the following questions:

■ What is the market's direction (interest rates, the economy, sales, etc.)?

■ What are the missed opportunities in the current marketplace?

■ What are the strengths and weaknesses of the company or the agent?

■ What are the strengths and weaknesses of the competition?

■ How do I take advantage of my competitors' weaknesses?

■ What are the external threats facing me or the agency?

■ What is the most effective advertising and promotional campaign given my current goals, budgetary constraints, and market conditions?

■ What is the size of my specific target market?

■ What is the accessibility of the target market?

■ Within the stated target market, what motivates the prospects to act?

■ What are the geographic locations and prices for listings best suited to the target market?

■ What services are demanded by the target market?

■ What are the demographics and psychographics of the marketplace?

■ How do I best promote my services?

■ What are the meaningful differences in the services offered (when compared to the competition) and the listings acquired?

■ What will be our pricing strategy and how will it be promoted?

■ What will be the appearance of my promotion and distribution strategy?

Figure 3.2

Features and Their
Changing Benefits

	Fireplace	Phone Jacks	Television Jacks
100 years ago	warmth, health	high technology and status	not applicable
50 years ago	comfort, nostalgia	2nd jack for convenience, to save time	one jack in the living room for family use
Today	nostalgia, resale value	jack in every room, Internet access, privacy	jack in every room, Internet access, privacy

Analysis. The analysis reorganizes the data so that conclusions may be drawn. Continuing with our example, the analysis confirms that interest rates are increasing and have done so on a regular basis for the past 18 months. For every 0.5 percent increase in the interest rate the affordability index drops by 8 percent. This means that fewer people can afford the higher interest rate or the higher price of homes on the market. As the number of people who cannot afford a single-family residence increases, the opportunities that appear suggest an increased need for multifamily residential units or other rental housing. The potential for foreclosures increases as adjustable rate mortgages become less manageable for some borrowers.

Conclusions. Conclusions state a course of action. The analysis above leads to the conclusion that the agent should continue watching the direction of interest rates. If rates continue to rise, multifamily residential units will see rent rates increases and vacancy rates diminish. Some existing homeowners may have to move to more affordable homes as adjustable rate mortgages increase. Start listing multifamily residential complexes and storage facilities for investors, as well as lower priced freestanding homes for end users.

Figure 3.1 suggests that real estate market research projects are created for many reasons. They may include a wide spectrum of topics from discovering a large and accessible target market to learning why it takes longer to sell a home in a particular price range. Agents who conduct research no longer limit marketing strategies to guesswork, speculation, or what the sellers think is the best way to sell their property. Creating a marketing plan assists agents in cultivating their strengths, improving their weaknesses, and embracing opportunities as they materialize.

Product Benefits

Although the general features included in a real estate product/service do not change significantly over time, agents are aware that the benefits sought by customers do change. This may mean that customers are not necessarily looking for a new feature but perhaps a demonstration of how existing features meet their changing needs. Research discovers the features in a home that are most important to different segments in a market.

Figure 3.2 provides an example of what research may uncover. It lists three common features and the benefits expected from them today, 50 years ago, and 100 years ago.

Market research gives insight into the product selection process and how agents choose to demonstrate certain aspects of a property. Today, phone jacks are common fixtures in almost every room of a home, but for years buyers thought nothing of them. When showing a home today, given the increased use of computers and the need for Internet access, phone jacks and cable TV access are features that are demanded by many in the marketplace according to research. As a result, agents may take more time pointing out these features.

Research helps agents segment the market. By grouping the total population into multiple segments, organized by demographics and other commonalities, agents can identify the types of properties those segments will most likely buy, even before listing them. As suggested before, research is not used to move segments of the market into specific neighborhoods. Instead, it helps agents list homes in diverse areas as well as discover ways to market existing and new listings to multiple segments of the market. Market research is a more formal way of identifying **target markets**—large segments of the market with similar commonalities—and the properties they are likely to buy. Imagine the results from listing only properties that most buyers want.

Let's suppose a developer is building homes in a retirement community. His regular construction methods call for a standard three-foot-wide hallway and two-foot-eight-inch-wide doors. The market research shows that many of the current residents are in wheelchairs and walkers. Based on this information, he decides to modify how the home is built and market his home not just to retirees but to retirees in wheelchairs and walkers as well. He develops homes with four-foot-wide hallways and three-foot-wide doorways. He drops the center island by an inch or two and lowers the cabinets throughout the house. He installs the lower 5.0 windows—five-foot-high windows, which reach lower to the floor—and lowers the peepholes in the front doors.

After the developer made these adjustments, he listed the properties with a real estate agent who advertised them. The agent mentioned the features above in the ad. Why did the agent do that? First, the agent operates in a retirement community. Through market research, the contractor already discovered that this was the target market. This discovery makes it easier for the agent to focus the promotional campaign to a segment of the market that should be most interested in the property. Second, the contractor identified features that are important to this community of buyers. Finding the target market did not require any effort in this case because the developer made clear to the agent the target market for which the homes were built. When agents take the time to discover target markets, it becomes easier to list properties that are attractive to those markets. It also becomes easier to focus on and locate the target markets. This saves time, creates better efficiencies, and increases the agent's productivity.

Time Management

Agents who use **time management** effectively prioritize tasks and employ their skills, experience, and education to complete those tasks. Prioritizing the most important issues of the year. month, week, or day involves the establishment of long-term and short-term personal and professional goals, as we will discuss in Chapter 10.

Market research is another time management activity when it's combined with an analysis of the data gathered and draws conclusions from that data.

Figure 3.3

Customer Analysis

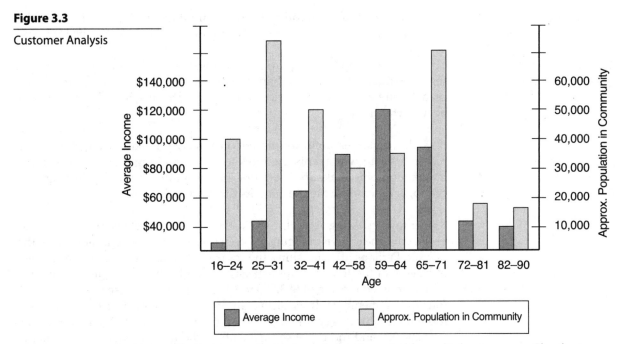

In this hypothetical case, a double barred chart is created for multiple age ranges. The chart shows an income range of between $40,000 and $140,000. The bottom of the chart shows the age ranges. It indicates that the majority of the people within a specific age range are making the average income suggested. For instance, the majority of those in the 42–58 age range are making $90,000 per year. (Note that this is not broken down by gender, which would be another interesting demographic study.)

The second bar indicates the community's population within those age groups. For instance, there are 50,000 people within the 32–41 age range within this community. (Note, once again, that this is not broken down by gender, marital status, family size, etc.)

Given the limitations of this chart, one might conclude that the largest target market(s) from which the agent could make a reasonable living would include the 59–64 age range and the 65–71 age range.

Analysis generally is not done during the data-gathering phase of marketing research, although it's difficult not to get excited by what is discovered. Data should simply be gathered and organized. The analysis and interpretation of the information is the last thing done by the agent

Prospects are the beneficiaries of research projects that help agents define the inventory and service solutions demanded by target markets.

Agents who employ market research activities use their time more productively by listing properties buyers want. Discovering the services most demanded in the marketplace, pricing properties so that they are attractive to the largest segments of the market, and demonstrating features that have meaning to prospects are results of market research and effective time management skills.

What would happen if national homebuilders didn't conduct market research studies before developing an area? What if they built homes that no one wanted? What if they built homes that didn't meet the needs of those in the community or those migrating to the community? If they built homes that very few wanted, the result would be lost time and money for the builders.

The costs for agents to acquire new listings could be equally as high with regard to time, effort, and perhaps money, especially if the agent's marketing plan doesn't work. Therefore, a careful study of the needs of the market must be undertaken first.

It is the customer analysis (based on data gathered during the market research) that gives agents the tools to attract the target market, determine its demographic makeup, list properties appropriate for the demographic group, and demonstrate the benefits the market desires.

Rather than guessing about the real estate market, simple demographic studies like the one shown in Figure 3.3 help discover the makeup of parts of that market. Perhaps after finishing the research, agents found that one segment of buyers in the total market consists of families with two income earners with combined income of $83,000 to $90,000 per year. These families include four to five members. It would be an improper use of time to list two bedroom homes for this segment. It would not make sense to list homes selling for $800,000 and more. Yet some agents without the advantage of a market study may unknowingly list properties that are priced too high for the segment of the market that has the largest number of potential buyers. The agent may not recognize that additional time blocks of their workday are necessary to sell a properly priced property to a limited number of buyers in the prospect pool.

Developing a "product," which is to say acquiring listings or providing services that are attractive to the larger segments of the total market, increases the effectiveness of a promotional campaign. The number of sales and the speed in which properties sell increases, thus increasing the number of productive workdays. This does not mitigate the obligations and responsibilities agents have to all prospective buyers. In this phase of marketing, we only are discussing how to increase the chances of attracting prospects to the real estate office.

Identify Opportunities

Through market research, agents gain a better understanding of the profit potential of the market by concentrating their efforts on one or multiple target markets. Given the high costs of marketing, it doesn't make sense to list a property and spend promotional dollars if most potential buyers in the market don't want it. Let's emphasize this point once more. You should understand that market research helps identify opportunities that appeal to the largest segments in the marketplace. The promotional efforts in a marketing campaign expose those opportunities or properties to these segments of the market. Why do agents select the largest segments from their research? The answer is simple; these segments are the easiest to find and attract. Does this mean that agents should not serve those prospects that do not fall into their definition of the target market? Absolutely not! All prospects must be served equally. The information that is gathered should *never* be used for discriminatory purposes.

Opportunities often overlooked are discovered with research. For example, through passive and active research, Steve, an agent with XYZ Realty, discovers that Ms. Henningsen of ABC Realty has been the number one salesperson in their town for five years. Without this research, Steve may not have discovered that she consistently sells 2,000- to 2,200-square-foot homes in a certain geographic area of town. He might not have discovered at which price she sells them. Without these discoveries, he would not have been given the opportunity to list properties that are needed by her target market. Ms. Henningsen can become one of Steve's channels of distribution. He supplies her with listings that her target market needs. He helps the cooperative agent, he makes a commission, and, most important, he successfully markets the seller's property, which results in a sale.

Channels of Distribution

You may recall that channels of distribution describe how the message is distributed to the public. How you communicate with your target market is best determined through research. Let's say your research shows that a large market population is retired, over age 61, and earning $45,000 to $62,000 a year. Inquiries to newspapers, magazines, radio and television stations, and other sources may result in demographic information that includes elements such as a breakdown of age, gender, and the income ranges of their customer base.

However, suppose your research discovered that the target market dines out three times a week and enjoys golf, bowling, and gardening. Different channels of distribution may come to mind during the analysis phase—channels that are more effective in letting your target market know about your listings. At this stage, however, agents should just gather the data.

Strengths, Weaknesses, Opportunities, and Threats

Chapter 2 suggested that understanding your competition is important to the survival of any business. It may be helpful to know that a competitor had one listing last month in the geographic area in which you are concentrating. This month it has six listings in your area. Agents who take the time to apply a research effort to their operational tasks are in a better position to discover how their competition might affect their career. In addition to uncovering an agent's weaknesses, research helps uncover the weaknesses of a competitor. Further study may reveal how to take advantage of a competitor's weaknesses within the agent's budget limitations. For some, a SWOT evaluation is a great tool for deciding where to operate their business. Through careful interviews with the brokers, new licensees can make a more informed decision on where they want to work.

■ Individual Agents versus Large Companies

Large real estate firms have an advantage over individual agents in that they can hire outside research companies to collect data. The research firm works with the real estate company's marketing department. The marketing department analyzes the data, including attitudes, demographics, and lifestyle changes. Together they develop a marketing campaign based on the results of the research.

An individual real estate salesperson or broker operates as a small business. Although these agents may not be able to afford an outside research company, they already are close to their market. Agents may notice a change in attitudes about a certain type of home or a geographic area within their community. They can respond by listing properties that meet those changing attitudes and avoid those that do not.

Some agents lose sight of this advantage. Some geographic regions of the country have towns that have a reputation for lower-quality homes. Job prospects in those towns may have the lowest median income in the area and/or there may be little infrastructure support from the town. Local agents may choose not to list properties in these areas, seeing them as places where their customers just wouldn't be interested in living.[3] Unfortunately, as the area changes, some agents with this bias may not see the change. Agents should try to avoid a bias from their past that can neutralize the advantage they have of being an independent real estate agent.

■ Performing Market Research

Market research has a reputation for being very expensive. However, inexpensive forms of research are accessible to agents. To help remove the myth that research has to be expensive, some of the research activities that new licensees can perform include:

- Becoming familiar with the office inventory
- Participating in the tours that view office listings
- Attending open houses
- Learning about specific geographic areas

Research identifies groups of people by the things they have in common, such as interests, income, age, needs, socioeconomic status, and lifestyle. Unfortunately, just when agents think they have finished their research, the real estate market changes. Consider this: Would your marketing mix change if several nationally recognized employers were about to enter your community? Of course it would! Just as this may affect the supply of listings, so will consumers' changing likes and dislikes affect the kinds of properties you list for sale.

Market research can be frustrating because agents often find that as soon as they have the market figured out, a change occurs—more homes are sold, there's a report of an additional 10,000 people who have just moved to the area, additional commercial facilities are under construction—and the research starts again. However, by going through the research process, agents may remain several steps ahead of their closest competitor.

Although market research is quite involved, it entails three basic steps:

1. Defining the problem
2. Gathering and organizing data
3. Analyzing data and drawing conclusions (covered in Chapter 4)

---

3   Agents may choose not to acquire listings in an area, but they should not refuse to show properties in that area. Agents may be accused of steering if they refuse to show prospects property in a specific area or attempt to channel prospects to one community over another.

Defining the Problem

Defining the problem is the first step of market research, and is similar to the first step of appraising a property or any decision-making process. Figure 3.1 demonstrated that agents may define the purpose of their research project in many different ways. The following are a few additional examples of research projects:

- How will my competitor's new housing tract affect my business?
- How do I find a buyer for my listings?
- Why are my sales down?
- Why didn't the listing contest work?
- Where do I find my next listing?
- How do I take advantage of my competitor's weaknesses?
- What are the strengths of my company and how do I take advantage of them?

A research project must start with a clear definition of what you are trying to accomplish so that the steps needed to get to the stated goal can be established.

Defining the problem correctly is half the battle. Agents know that more sales are generated by solving the right problems. Some agents provide their prospects with the right property (the right answer or the right listing) without ever discovering the prospects' underlying problem. In this environment, the agents might expect prospects to see for themselves how the property satisfies their needs. This slows the sales process. It is the problem that creates a need. Solve the problem and you satisfy the need. When agents understand the problem, they are in a better position to show the prospects how the property solves the problem and satisfies the prospects' needs. Doing anything less is like saying that the correct answer to a math problem is four without knowing if the problem was two plus two or 20 divided by five. Rather than guessing, the more time agents take to establish the correct problem, in either their market research projects or their personal selling activities, the easier it is to come up with a solution that satisfies the prospects' needs.

Gathering and Organizing Data

Research information comes from both primary and secondary sources. The second step in a research project is **gathering and organizing data**. Agents must always attempt to collect data that is relevant to solving the research problem. Let's say that before you start listing properties, you want to find out the size and demographic composition of the largest groups of potential buyers in your marketplace. Your research should determine that market's size, income range, and accessibility, among other things.

Researchers may gather the data in a variety of ways, and they don't necessarily use all of the methods indicated here. If a simple yes-or-no poll was being taken from an unscientific sampling of 1,000 people, it may prove to be more cost effective to send out 1,000 e-mails instead of 1,000 postcards or telephone calls.

Research methods used to gather data often include:

- Mail surveys
- E-mail surveys
- Telephone surveys
- Observational studies
- Experiments
- Samplings

Secondary data collection.   Market research is not easy work and involves weeks of activities including surveys, samplings, question writing, observations, and more. However, real estate agents often do not have the time for such complexity.

Secondary data sources are the result of research studies done by the government or private enterprise. There are several secondary sources of information available. Some examples include: a city's study that determined the feasibility of a gambling casino in the community; a radio station's demographic breakdown of its audience; or a large state bank's research findings that were released to its depositors. The source of the information doesn't really matter; secondary data is available to the public in one form or another and is generally free.

The list of secondary data sources is somewhat limitless, bounded only by the agent's knowledge of the sources and access to the information. Sources of secondary data that are easily accessible to the real estate agent include:

- Utility companies
- Statistical abstracts of the United States
- Almanacs
- Trade association reports, magazines, and journals
- Title companies
- Chamber of commerce studies
- Voter registration
- University/college research publications
- Religious organizations
- Newspapers/magazines
- Marketing journals

Suppose a city conducts a research study that helps determine growth trends in population, sales revenues, income of the residents, population, and directional movement in city growth and infrastructure needs. The evaluation process for a city can be intense, but from its data you can discover many things about your area. The city's data collection may have included the following elements, which agents can later analyze for their own purposes:

- Family size
- Median income
- Career fields and income applicable to the area
- Best school district scores

- Crime areas
- Labor mix and education of labor force
- The commuter population

Secondary data collection has its disadvantages because it is compiled by a second party. The information wasn't gathered to answer your specific problem. You may not be able to acquire all of the data you need, and some of the data you receive may be irrelevant to your research situation. Nevertheless, it is less costly than primary data collection, which requires that you or someone you hire collect the information that is not readily available to you.

Primary data collection.   Whether you are a real estate agent or a market research professional, the process of primary data collection is time consuming and can be expensive. Unlike its counterpart, primary data is collected by the agent and used for a specific purpose.

Primary Data Collection vs. Secondary Data Collection

Suppose you want to determine if it is worthwhile to work with the commuter market. You may want to know the traffic count on your crosstown freeway. You can hire a firm to run a cable across the freeway that counts cars. After about a month, the data will show the heaviest traffic days and times of day.

You might find, however, that your chamber of commerce or other governmental agencies have already done this primary data collection and developed conclusions about the data. The study and the information may be free and available to you as secondary data.

Individual agents need a less expensive approach to primary data collection. A reliable form of inexpensive primary data gathering is a more sophisticated approach to what used to be called "farming" a neighborhood. In this approach, agents use surveys or direct questions to gather data. In many areas of the country, it is still relatively safe to knock on doors in a neighborhood, introduce yourself, and conduct these forms of data gathering. In other parts of the country, telephone solicitations may be used but be aware of any Do Not Call lists that may be in effect in your area. Direct mail and e-mail are other forms of contact that may be used. The type of research data agents collect is unlimited, but may include the following:

- Reasons people bought property in the neighborhood
- Residents' likes and dislikes about their neighborhood
- Demographics of the people moving into the neighborhood
- Activities enjoyed by residents in the neighborhood
- Median age and family size of the residents in the neighborhood
- Marital status of the residents in the neighborhood
- General income level of the residents in the neighborhood
- Career choices of the residents in the neighborhood

These points will have more significance as agents acquire listings. After all, the commonalities of buyers who move into a neighborhood are often similar to those already living there. This creates what economists call a homogeneous neighborhood—a neighborhood with people of similar interests, incomes, and perhaps lifestyles and backgrounds.

Open houses offer agents opportunities to gather data by conducting informal surveys with those viewing the property. Perhaps an open house is used to gather data on what buyers expect of an agent; maybe agents are surveying those interested in selling their current home; or perhaps they are gathering information on first-time buyers.

Real estate agencies provide a wealth of opportunities for primary data collection. Agencies often collect the names and addresses of callers or people who walk into the office or an open house. This primary data collection continues when agents list the prices and addresses of the properties that interested the prospects. When the material is organized, the geographic location of the prospects' current address can be cross-referenced with the geographic location of the listings on which they called.

Depending on the conclusions drawn from this information, it may improve the effectiveness of an advertising campaign while disclosing the economic makeup of specific geographic areas. Agents may get 15 calls from the same community 25 miles from the listing. Perhaps they get one or two additional calls from other areas. Agents may conclude that it would be profitable to list similar properties in the same geographic area and concentrate their marketing efforts in the community that is 25 miles away. There is no "shotgun" approach here. You cannot waste valuable marketing time or dollars trying to "sell" to the entire region.

Instead of advertising in the wrong papers, sending brochures to property owners surrounding the listing, and running countless ads in the local paper, agents can concentrate their marketing efforts in the area where the buyers live and in the newspapers that service that area. As a reminder, during the research phase, agents should not jump to conclusions until the data is analyzed and conclusions are drawn from that analysis. These phases will be discussed in Chapter 4.

Closed transactions.   Closed transactions provide another form of primary data collection. If necessary, get permission from your broker to access them. Explain to the broker that you are not interested specifically in who the buyers and sellers were, you just want to review the transactions to gather general information. Cross-check every buyer's former address to the geographic location of the properties purchased. Often, agents find that people from one geographic area tend to purchase homes in the new community that have similar features. Buyers with similar interests in common may use the features to fulfill similar needs, and the prices they are willing to pay are often within the same range. If your target market of buyers comes from that geographic area, this research should help you determine which properties to list and which to let expire!

Remember, though, that secondary data collection is less costly and more time efficient for real estate agents. If you want to know the median income for a specific area, you might call the community newspaper or radio station to see if it might share some of the demographic information it has gathered. In order to market their advertising space more effectively, media publications (newspapers and radio/television stations) have a very good idea of what their market is, its size, and where it is located.

Referral power.   Another form of primary data collection that can lead to a more efficient inventory selection comes from the referred lead. Imagine a successful agent in the western part of the United States who consistently has great years. Whether the economy is strong or not, this agent consistently outproduces her peers. This salesperson knows how to work her referral market. She quickly discovered that referred leads often buy homes similar to those that her original customers bought. Her activities are evenly split between listing homes her previous customers had purchased, and selling homes to her referred leads.

Satisfied customers often send referrals. Most of these referrals make similar incomes, have similar interests, enjoy similar activities, go to the same grocery stores, and enjoy the same social activities. Although occasionally the referrals express needs that are markedly different from the group, over time this agent discovered so much about her buyer group that she has a better idea of the style of homes to list, as well as the price, terms, and locations. She outsells everyone, even during recessions, because she learned about her buyer group *before* she learned about her product.

Parts of a house.   Your data research may show that buyers regard certain parts of a property as having more value than other parts. For instance, which is more important, the fence that surrounds the property or the landscaping on the lot?

You can find out by conducting some primary research. Ask past buyers and current prospects. Go to home shows and observe which boutiques are receiving the greatest degree of interest. In what do buyers show the most interest—front doors, carpets, windows, cabinets, window coverings, insulation, roofing? Observe where the crowds gather. Data analysis and conclusions will suggest ways to market property by using specific areas of interest as points that can be highlighted in the advertising or property presentations.

Other examples of inexpensive primary data collection include:

- Using a city map to become familiar with the streets in your area
- Developing a list of for-sale-by-owner properties
- Identifying multiple geographic areas in which to specialize
- Developing a comprehensive list of questions to ask buyers or sellers
- Identifying locations of schools, shopping areas, cultural activities, malls, and parks
- Attending office and association agent tours
- Reading financial and local newspapers
- Monitoring the effectiveness of letters sent to geographic areas of interest
- Monitoring the effectiveness of newspaper advertising

■ Focus on Segments

Research helps agents answer questions that allow them to provide a better service, generate more profits, and develop advertising and promotional campaigns best suited for their target market.

A good way to get started is to break down the very large market into smaller market segments, making the large market more manageable. Market segmentation and target marketing are discussed in detail in Chapter 5. Analyzing the answers to questions agents develop about their market gives them insight into how to segment the market.

Figure 3.4

Research Questions

The following research questions represent just a few of the topics you should address when determining the viability (size) of a target market.

- What is the total number of families in your area?
- What is the total number of married couples?
- What is the total number of single people? What is their gender?
- What is the total number of single parent families? How many single parents are men? Women?
- What is the total number of unmarried couples?
- What is the average number of children per household?
- What is the ethnic background of families in your area? How is each segmented by the questions already discussed?
- Are there more 20–44 year olds or more 45–64 year olds in your area? What age range offers the largest population segment?
- What is the percentage of males to females?
- What "family size" (married with children) captures the largest percentage of all families in your area?
- What is the total population (size) of the market?
- What is the largest buyer group within the total market?
- What is the average age of the selected buyer group in your area?
- What is the average income earned by your buyer group?
- What does your buyer group want to buy?
- What percent of income is needed for a purchase?
- What dollar amount of income can be used for a purchase?
- What is the family size of this buyer group?
- What radio stations does this buyer group listen to? Why?
- What newspapers does this buyer group read? Why?
- What are the leisure activities/hobbies enjoyed by this buyer group?
- What is the religious affiliation of this buyer group?
- What is the political persuasion of this buyer group?

Develop ten more questions that will assist you in determining the makeup of a significant target market in your area.

Let's suppose you want to work with retirees. Agents should find out if this is a large enough segment from which to make a living. Agents need to know the segment well. Figure 3.4 contains just a few questions that when answered and analyzed may help agents communicate more effectively with their target market. As you go through these questions, think of others you would like answered. Although you should not analyze the answers while doing the research, give some thought to how the answers could be used when making your listing selections or marketing your existing listings.

The questions you ask are limited only by how you feel the potential answers will affect your decision making and the types of properties you choose to list or the target market you choose to attract. After a full analysis of the information, you might find yourself listing and marketing property that attracts more people to your office, rather than listing property that you will have to "sell" to a buyer. Remember what marketers tell us. There's nothing easier than selling something people want.

■ Finance and Marketing

Real estate marketing and the ability to fund loans depend on the finance markets. Through market research, agents gain an appreciation of how the finance markets affect the sale and marketability of real estate. From a marketing standpoint, one of the most important aspects of finance is the actions of the Federal Reserve. The Fed controls the supply of money in the marketplace and influences the direction of interest rates. By watching what it does, agents can better predict how thrift institutions will react with regard to credit requirements and loan rates.

■ The Fed

Almost every country has a central banking authority. The **Federal Reserve (the Fed)** regulates the banking system within the United States. However, its real power comes from regulating the growth of credit, thereby the economic growth of the country. Through its market intervention operations, the Fed can alter the value of the dollar in other countries and affect the direction of inflation, employment, and interest rates domestically.

When Fed actions cause an excessive supply of currency in the world markets, our currency appears to be inexpensive to foreigners and this creates an opportunity in our real estate markets. When the dollar declines in value, it is more appealing for foreigners to invest here because their currency will go further. Today, Europeans are investing heavily in our domestic corporations and real estate. Many foreign investors have a strong interest in the listings controlled by domestic real estate agents. Some real estate franchises also have offices in Europe and Asia. Creating relationships with foreign agencies opens an additional channel of distribution when selling domestic properties. These relationships can be developed whether the agents belong to a franchise or not.

By applying consistent research methods, agents can monitor the direction of the currency market and how the U.S. currency matches up to foreign currencies, thereby cultivating additional target markets or channels of distribution. This means that to understand how money affects marketing decisions in real estate, agents should have a fundamental understanding of the Fed and the money markets it controls.

The Fed manages the growth of the nation's money supply through the Federal Open Market Committee (FOMC). Agents should monitor the actions of this committee when trying to anticipate the direction of interest rates. The FOMC uses four monetary tools to influence the nation's money supply, interest rates, employment, and availability of credit. As a direct result, the tools affect the growth of real estate markets. These tools consist of open market operations, reserve requirements, and the discount rate. A fourth tool controls the margin requirements for the securities industry. Although fluctuations in the margin requirement affect the supply of dollars that enter the stock market and the economy in general, it is not changed that often. Our discussions will remain limited to the other three tools:

1. Open market operations
2. Reserve requirements
3. Discount rate

Open Market Operations

Open market operations provide a generally successful way of controlling the money supply through the purchase or sale of government securities. Most agents recall this definition from their prelicense courses. Agents have heard the expressions "money is tight" or "money is loose, now is the time to buy." When money is tight, interest rates have already gone up or they are rising. What causes this? What does the Fed do to cause interest rates to go down and how is it done? What should agents do if these events occur? Agents who monitor the activities of the FOMC are in a better position to predict the direction of interest rates and, therefore, the effect on their market. This gives them more freedom to anticipate changing events and inventory needs.

Interest rates have a tendency to rise when the economy overheats. An **overheated economy** occurs when the supply of goods (e.g., houses, commercial buildings, usable land, components of construction) and services cannot keep up with the demand. In real estate, agents and consumers may see an early sign of shortages when lotteries dictate who can purchase the next available home in a housing tract. Access to cash or access to affordable cash (loans) drives the demand—up or down—for goods and services.

Financial newspapers keep agents apprised of these issues as well as the successes of international economies. As agents research world economies, they may discover an increased use of limited resources within those economies. This research allows agents to anticipate an increase in the costs of the components of a house (e.g., lumber, cement, drywall). The rise in costs may be due to increased domestic and international demand and, as a result, the cost of the finished product goes up. As a result, prices rise in order to slow demand. This recovers some costs for developers and gives them time to produce more. However, increased prices that are due to shortages and increased demand often lead to inflation. To slow demand, the Fed may take steps to tighten the money supply.

When the news channels report that the Fed has increased or decreased the money supply, they are often talking about the results of the open market operation. To decrease the money supply, the Fed offers investors a rate of return, often higher than alternative cash returns, if they loan money to the federal government. By doing so, domestic investors may take money out of their local thrifts. This decreases the supply of money in the thrift, which increases the cost of money to the public. What does that mean? It can mean that home sales will decline, home prices may decline, or that multifamily residential housing will be needed soon. What can agents do? Consider listing acreage zoned for multifamily residential housing or list smaller homes that are more affordable to a larger segment of the market. Agents should reevaluate their research information to determine the makeup of what may become a new target market.

To add to the money supply, the Fed reverses the process. It does this by repurchasing its debt. Investors trade their Treasury securities (i.e., the debt obligation given to them when they loaned money to the government) for cash. When the cash is deposited into a thrift, the money supply expands. Thrifts are now in a position to lower rates.

Reserve Requirements

One of the most fascinating ways the Fed expands or contracts the money supply is through **reserve requirements**. The concept is simple enough. For every dollar that enters the banking system, a certain percentage is unavailable for transactions. In other words, that percentage of funds can't be used for either loans or withdrawals. By increasing or decreasing this percentage, the Fed has some control over the amount of money that is invested or consumed in the marketplace. Figure 3.5 shows how money is created by the banking system through a process known as fractional reserves.

Suppose the reserve requirement was 14 percent. If you deposited $1,000 into your bank, the reserve requirement causes the bank to withhold $140. In other words, it can only loan $860 of your deposit. When an individual borrows money from a thrift they are issued a check for the amount borrowed. The individual who receives the $860 check deposits it into his or her bank. That bank, in turn, may only loan 86 percent of that deposit, withholding the 14 percent reserve, or about $120. As Figure 3.5 shows, deposits made into successive banks become smaller as this process continues through the bank-

Figure 3.5

Expanding the Money Supply

	Bank 1	Bank 2	Bank 3	Bank 4	Bank 5	Other Banks
Deposit	$1,000	$860	$740	$636	$547	$3,360
Less Reserves	140	120	104	89	77	470
Loan	860	740	636	547	470	2,890

Bank 1 receives a deposit for $1,000. After 14% reserves are withheld, it loans out $860, which is deposited in Bank 2 (or the same bank, it doesn't matter) and the process starts again. After you add all of the new loans you discover that the initial $1,000 deposit created over $6,143 of new money in the economy, and $7,143 if you add in the original deposit.

ing system. Eventually, the deposits in all remaining banks equals $3,360, of which $470 is held in bank reserves. The result is a money supply that has expanded by approximately $6,143, not counting the original deposit. If the Fed raised the reserve requirement to 18 percent, the amount the banking system could create would drop to only $4,555, not counting the original deposit. The amount of potential money expansion can also be calculated by dividing the reserve requirement—14 percent—into the original deposit—$1,000. The result is $7,143 total—less the original deposit it would be $6,143.

The reserve requirement doesn't change that often; however, the availability of funds in thrifts depends on the amount of money people save. The result of a little research into how much Americans save out of every dollar may be alarming when compared to the amount people in other countries are saving. In the early 2000s, interest rates were relatively low because foreign investors financed much of the government's debt (funded through open market operations). This means that the government didn't need to tap into the deposits of domestic thrifts. Agents should monitor this issue. If foreign investors decide to stop purchasing our debt instruments, interest rates may move up dramatically given the current savings habits. Once again, this creates an opportunity for agents and investors who realize that multifamily residential units tend to appreciate in value when interest rates are high and single-family homes are not selling.

Discount Rate

The **discount rate** is the interest rate charged to member banks when they borrow money directly from the Federal Reserve. Banks must meet their reserve requirements daily. If they loaned too much during the day, they may need a loan to balance their books. Member banks do not borrow from the Fed that often and, in fact, are informally discouraged from doing so because the Fed prefers that thrifts borrow from one another. When thrifts borrow from one another it is at the federal funds rate, which is not a significant tool in the Fed's arsenal but provides a similar signal to thrifts and agents of the Fed's intentions. Nevertheless, the Fed effectively uses the discount rate as a way to signal member banks of any policy shifts. When agents read that the Fed has lowered the discount rate it means that it would like to see increased lending activity. This signals member banks to increase their loan output. Of course, the opposite is also true. If the Fed wanted to slow the expansion of the money supply, it may increase the discount rate, thus offering an opposite signal.

By monitoring the fluctuations in the discount rate, agents can anticipate declining interest rates and perhaps easing credit requirements.

So, no matter what the Fed decides to do, consumers must be willing to increase or curtail their spending (borrowing) for any of the Federal Reserve tools to work. Economics is not called a social science for nothing.

■ Summary

This chapter has defined market research as a tool used to help agents make decisions with regard to the kinds of properties to list, the content of advertising created, and how best to find segments of the market through the effective use of multiple channels of distribution. There are many reasons to conduct market research. Research helps identify opportunities, customer needs, and pricing strategies, among others.

Market research starts by defining the problem and then gathering and organizing data that provides the information needed to draw conclusions about the marketplace or the stated purpose of the research project. Data can be gathered from inexpensive secondary sources; however, the data often doesn't exactly fit the needs of the project. Larger real estate companies may hire marketing firms to conduct primary research so that the results meet their specific needs. Although primary research can prove to be very expensive, there are things that agents can do that are inexpensive or free. Agents can evaluate closed transactions, conduct surveys within their geographic area of interest, monitor the effectiveness of prospecting letters, or conduct comprehensive fact-finding meetings with their prospects.

In addition to researching the market, agents must be informed about the activities of the Federal Reserve. The ability to fund loans is directly affected by the actions of the Federal Reserve. Research helps agents gain an appreciation of how the finance markets affect the marketability and sale of real property.

The research that agents conduct is never ending because real estate markets are always changing. The kinds of research questions are limited only by how the potential answers will affect the agent's final decision making.

◼ Multiple Choice Questions

1. Which of the following *BEST* describes the reason for market research?
    a. To identify multiple farm areas
    b. To help the agent make decisions
    c. To discover channels of distribution
    d. To develop comprehensive primary data collection techniques

2. When is the *BEST* time to discover the demographic makeup of the market?
    a. Before a listing is taken
    b. After a listing is taken
    c. At the time of the sale of the property
    d. As soon as the agent becomes a broker

3. Which of the following is *NOT* market research?
    a. Learning the inventory by participating in office property tours
    b. Prospecting
    c. Conducting interviews and surveys
    d. Identifying commonalities in the market

4. Sometimes agents fail to look beyond the symptoms to a problem. More sales are created by solving the right problems and providing the right solutions. Agents may fail to establish the right problem because
    a. they fail to maintain a high degree of professionalism.
    b. they fail to ask the right questions.
    c. the symptoms don't match up to the solutions they can offer.
    d. None of the above

5. By cross-checking every buyer's former address to the geographic location of the properties purchased, a correlation between the two may find that buyers from one area tend to purchase homes of a similar price range and in a similar neighborhood in another area. This is called
    a. transitory research data collection.
    b. secondary data collection.
    c. primary data collection.
    d. base study analysis.

6. Which of the following are responsibilities of the Fed? (Choose all that apply.)

   a. Controlling the spending of the federal government

   b. Managing the growth of the money supply

   c. Increasing interest rates to control inflation

   d. Increasing taxes to control spending and inflation

7. If the reserve requirement was set at 10 percent, then $1,000 deposited into a thrift could potentially add how much money supply to the economy? Including the original deposit, the money supply would increase by

   a. $5,000.

   b. $6,000.

   c. $8,000.

   d. $10,000.

■ Exercises

Exercise 1—Working a specialized area used to be called working a "farm" area. Agents decided that it was beneficial to learn all there was to know about the properties and owners within specific areas. The areas could have included homes, multifamily residential units, acreage, or certain types of commercial or industrial facilities. Suppose your research suggests that interest rates are declining and employment rates are increasing. The housing market may be ready to take off. Your research may suggest that utility companies have expanded infrastructure in specific outlying areas within your community. Perhaps roads are about to be extended, or new housing or commercial developments are taking place in outlying areas. If growth activities such as these are taking place in your community, and even if they are not, select a geographic area to "farm." With the help of a title company, select an area of one or two square miles of acreage. The title company information will often include maps, ownership names, addresses, and phone numbers. You should make observations as to multiple ownerships or recent purchases, specifically multiple purchases by entities that share the same mailing address. Determine the average price per acre for 2.5-, 5-, 10-, 20-, and 40-acre parcels. Have the title company include all demographic data it may have for the area.

Exercise 2—Actions of the Federal Reserve affect the real estate markets. The Fed has several tools it can use to manipulate the supply of money and consequently the direction of interest rates. Evaluate the current discount rate established by the Federal Reserve by determining what the rate has done over the past 24 months, how the rate changes affected the real estate markets, and how it might affect your real estate marketing efforts today.

Research Question 1—Check with your local utility companies, title companies, chambers of commerce, newspapers, etc., and accumulate demographic information for your community. Visit or call radio stations. Ask them about the demographics for their market.

Research Question 2—How prospects perceive events or situations may determine their expectations and your success in a marketing campaign or sale. Conduct a survey among agents and ask what they feel their prospects expect of them. Conduct surveys among consumers or prospects and determine what they (buyers/sellers) expect of real estate agents. What are the perceptions among consumers of the daily and weekly activities of a real estate licensee?

Research Question 3—Research the following: federal funds rate, discount rate, results of open market operations, unemployment rate, affordability index, listing inventory levels and types of properties listed, number of housing starts, and national and local sales trends for new and used homes. Given the information discovered, discuss the type(s) of property that you should list in the current market. Describe the kind of prospect best suited for the economic environment you discovered.

chapter four

DATA ANALYSIS, DRAWING CONCLUSIONS, AND MOTIVATION

■ Learning Objectives

After the study and review of this chapter, you should be able to

- ■ describe the significance of collected data;

- ■ compare and contrast the multiple stages of motivation; and

- ■ evaluate and explain the different stages of Maslow's hierarchy of needs and what motivates people within each stage.

■ Key Terms

data analysis	motivation	summary of findings
incentives	physiological needs	

Some marketers spend time gathering data from multiple sources, only to have it stored in a folder without a plan to use it. Other marketers view the collected data and see trends, but prematurely draw conclusions without taking into account the effect other data may have on those conclusions. Professional marketing research firms look at the purpose for the research project (e.g., Why are sales dropping?) and organize the data in preparation for solving the problem. Once organized, the analysis step begins by looking at how some of the data may interrelate with other data. Suppose information from the chamber of commerce estimates that 21,000 prospective homebuyers (apartment dwellers) currently live in a small community. However, when another piece of data is interrelated with the first we may find that only 1,400 apartment dwellers can afford the average-priced home in the community. After the data is analyzed, the last step draws conclusions from the information. Initially, this chapter reviews some of the elements of market research and acts as a logical link to the analysis of data and the drawing of conclusions from it.

Figure 4.1

Research Problems

- How do I increase my market share?
- What are buyers and sellers looking for in the marketplace?
- What are the strengths and weaknesses of my competition?
- Will sales increase if I change the marketing mix?
- What motivates my target market to action?
- What are the needs of the largest target market?
- What is the direction of population growth in the community?
- Given the total adult population, what is the need for multifamily housing in the community?
- Which market segment has the greatest market potential?

■ Steps in Analyzing Data

Chapter 3 showed that agents limited by budget constraints could perform their own primary research without the cost of professional research firms. Figure 4.1 lists questions that represent the types of market research problems discussed in Chapter 3.

For demonstration purposes, let's use the last problem as our example in this chapter: Which market segment has the greatest market potential?

Figure 4.2

Collected Research Data

Research Problem: Which market segment has the greatest market potential?

Data Collected:

- Family households represent 77.9% of the population.
- There are 3.32 people per household.
- 46.54% of the population is self-employed.
- The number of households in the area is 20,480.
- 22.1% of the total population is comprised of nonfamily households.
- 36.52% of households earn $50,000 to $74,999 per year.
- Single females comprise 26.4% of the total population.
- The working population uses approximately 29% of its income on housing and 16% on recreation.
- The total population is 68,000.
- Approximately 74% of family households read the local newspaper.
- Approximately 67% of people ages 45 to 69 listen to the local country/western radio station.
- Approximately 65% of the married working segment with children is actively involved in sports activities: 83% in soccer, 10% in T-ball, and baseball, 2% in water sports.
- 79% of households making $50,000 to $75,000 read *Golf Digest*.

Note: Keep in mind that data is often collected in no particular order. Some of the data may not necessarily be useful. While collecting it, do not judge the information. Do not attempt to organize it. Just collect it. (Due to space limitations, this data represents only a part of the information used later for the data analysis in Figure 4.3.)

Unlike a professional marketing research firm that has a battery of people to help organize the data, agents are responsible for assembling the information and putting it to use. This is not an easy task. In the end, the information gathered during the data-gathering phase may or may not have relevance to the defined problem during the analysis phase. Until the data is reorganized into meaningful groups, it is just bits and pieces of data. Figure 4.2 represents data that might have been collected and organized as part of the market research phase for our example problem. We'll use this material to explain data analysis.

Figure 4.3

Data Analysis

Research Problem: Which market segment has the greatest market potential?

Categorized research information:

- Population: 68,000
- Number of persons per household: 3.32
- Number of households: 20,480
    - Household population growth: Last decade 20.3%; last two years 2.1%; next five years 4.3%
- Household breakdown
    - Nonfamily households: 22.1%
    - Family households: 77.9%
- Number of households by income
    - $24.999 or less: 30%
    - $25,000–$34,999: 13.2%
    - $35,000–$49,999: 8.35%
    - $50,000–$74,999: 36.52%
    - $75,000–$99,999: 4.3%
    - $100,000–$124,999: 2.45%
    - $125,000 and above: 5.18%
- Population by marital status
    - Single male: 17.87%
    - Single female: 32.40%
    - Married: 43.65%
    - Previously married or widowed: 6.08%
- Population by working class
    - Local government workers: 4.3%
    - Federal government workers: 2.4%
    - Self-employed workers: 46.54%
    - Minimum wage workers: 23.46%
    - Salaried workers: 23.30%
- *Golf Digest* subscribers: 5,908 households

Note: Due to space limitations, the categorized data represents only a part of the research data listed in Figure 4.2.

Figure 4.4

Hypothetical Population
Breakdown

Population Breakdown (of our research area)

Total population: 68,000

Age	White	Black	Hispanic	Others
30–34	14,256	2,184	1,368	969
35–39	10,192	2,541	1,072	833
40–44	11,731	2,030	1,350	772
45–49	10,608	1,365	1,153	696
Etc…				

Households, families, and married couples

HOUSEHOLDS		FAMILIES		MARRIED COUPLES
Number	Average Population/ Household	Number	Average Population/ Family	Number
20,480	3.32	15,954	3.16	24,412

Persons living alone

Gender and Age	Number	Percent of Total
Both Genders		
15–24	1,186	4.29
25–44	12,021	43.54
45–64	6,081	22.03
65 and over	8,320	30.14
Total	**27,608**	**100.00**
Male		
15–24	665	6.89
25–44	6,254	64.77
45–64	1,994	20.65
65 and over	743	7.69
Total	**9,656**	**100.00**
Female		
15–24	1,531	8.53
25–44	10,764	59.96
45–64	3,296	18.36
65 and over	2,361	13.15
Total	**17,952**	**100.00**

Note: This analysis is a suggestion of how to organize this information. The research
data shown in Figures 4.2 and 4.3 is not complete.

As you can see, the information gathered is a mix of data. The information makes sense, but it doesn't really tell us which market segment has the best potential; determining that would require an analysis of the information. Agents' analysis and interpretation of the material may be influenced by personal experiences and how their internal and external environment affects them. The judgments and opinions drawn from the analysis are subject to reinterpretation because new data may result in different interpretations.

■ Data Analysis

Data analysis takes raw, seemingly unrelated data from the market research phase, and reorganizes it into meaningful groups of data from which conclusions may be drawn. To do this, begin by grouping the information and developing some form of usable classifications. Figure 4.3 shows how the scattered information from Figure 4.2 might be organized.

Figure 4.4 organizes the information in another way. It provides answers based on two or more variables. The data tells us that 40.6 percent of the population or 27,608 people are single. Figure 4.4 takes additional information from the data collection and adds a variable showing the population for each age range. As agents group the data, they may choose to learn more about this segment of the market. Before ending the research phase, agents should check their data one last time to see if they have all the information that they need to reach a reasonable conclusion.

If this was all the data you collected, would it be helpful to know how many of the single women ages 25 to 44 work and what the income range was within that group? In this example database, this group of single women appears to be a large segment of people under the age of 65. You might want to know the income range for that group. What are the occupations of single women of that age group and income range? At this point, data analysis may stop until additional data is collected.

■ Drawing Conclusions

The findings of a research project should be summarized into a one- or two-page report. This report is for the agent's benefit and is generally seen by no one else. It should identify trends or opportunities in the market, but more specifically it should address the research problem. It should spell out what was discovered and what actions will be taken to address the question in the research project. It is the basis on which a marketing campaign may be launched.

The **summary of findings** in Figure 4.5 is another step toward developing a comprehensive marketing plan. Depending on the purpose of the research project, the summary breaks down into a few sentences or paragraphs the limits of an agent's resources, time, and money, and how best to take advantage of the opportunities available. Through this process, agents may segment the total market into more manageable groups (discussed in Chapter 5), learn what they do for a living, how they fill their leisure time, how much they earn, how much they can spend on housing, how best to communicate with them, what motivates them, and how they respond to marketing stimuli. A summary of findings may identify what agents are currently doing and

Figure 4.5
_____

Conclusions (Sample Report)

Conclusions

Research Problem: Which market segment has the greatest potential?

Conclusions drawn from the organized data: (Due to space limitations, this represents a small portion of a one- or two-page summary of the findings. The findings discussed may not have appeared in the previous figures.)

The primary market segments for residential housing, without reference to gender, are the 30–34 age group and the 40–44 age group. However, segmenting the market by marital status shows that those who live alone comprise a little over 56 percent of the market when compared to married couples that hold about 44 percent of the market.

Single men make up 35 percent of persons living alone and women represent 65 percent of persons living alone. Single people form the largest segment of the total market, and single women make up the largest segment of the singles market. Within that segment, the largest group of single women is between the ages of 25 and 44.

A little over 65 percent of single women in the 25–44 year old age group earn between $50,000 and $65,000 per year.

(Note: The analysis continues along these lines until the agent has defined the market segment with the greatest potential. An enhancement to the original problem might take the research data and develop a picture of that segment. Let's assume that the segment ends up being single women between the ages of 25 and 44 who make between $50,000 and $65,000 per year. The data may have disclosed some of the following information.)

The majority of the target segment read the daily newspaper at least four times per week; the highest percentage reading the Sunday paper with the greatest interest in the Home and Garden section and the Sports section. The radio stations this segment listens to are a mix of pop, rock, and easy listening music, as well as talk radio. This segment has little time for television, and spends some time on the Internet, preferring e-mail to traditional mail delivery. This segment is concerned with safety, comfort, and time management. This segment demands homes that are eight years old or newer that have security systems, fences or walls, modern kitchens, garage door openers, almost-maintenance-free landscaping, a fireplace, a spa, and trash compactors.

(Note: This form of evaluation comes from the data collected during the research phase. When it is completed, agents have a clear picture of the largest segment in the market, how to find that segment, and what type of property attracts that segment.)

compare those results to the needs of each group. A summary identifies how agents satisfy each target market's service needs and compares that to competitors. A summary also analyzes the weaknesses of competitors and finds ways to take advantage of them. Using their analysis, agents draw conclusions and form opinions about their markets. Data analysis offers agents the opportunity to list the properties that meet the needs of their target market, the agent's personality, and the constraints of their economic environment.

The interpretation of the data helps reduce the uncertainty in the market. It identifies the problems faced by the target market and the most acceptable solutions, such as the best forms of financing, the property benefits desired, and the property and service pricing models for the groups the agent is trying to attract. Agents confirm the interpretation of the data when the qualifying discussions are conducted with interested prospects.

What Motivates Prospects?

Target marketing is the topic of Chapter 5. It extends the discussion of data analysis by giving more detail on how the data breaks down the market into manageable groups. However, this process isn't quite complete until agents develop some theories about what motivates the market segments. The opinions drawn from the analysis are logical conclusions based on facts. However, as with any business decision, the conclusions drawn may not be correct. They can easily be regarded as subjective until the conclusion is proven true or false.

Our example concluded that single women between the ages of 25 and 44 years old who earned between $50,000 and $65,000 per year formed the largest market segment. What suppositions can we come to with regard to what motivates this group? We will assume that the income is substantial for the community in which the agent works. With that premise in mind, we conclude that this market segment works very hard for what they have. Our research showed that members of this segment were college educated and therefore may respond (i.e., be motivated to act) in a more positive way to a college-educated agent. This segment has no time to waste on inefficiency and ineffectiveness. Its members are motivated to work with agents who can save them time and energy. Our conclusions suggest that these women lead busy lives and would want an agent who can make a property purchase an easy transaction for them. Having worked hard for their position in the community, they are motivated to purchase quality over quantity, but they want to feel that they received a good value for their money. They may also be motivated by elements in a home that help them save time and money, such as smoke detectors, warranty plans, or a well-maintained property.

Agents discover what motivates individuals within target markets when they conduct their fact-finding meetings with prospects. The purchase decision always involves a reason to do something (a motive). Discovering the motivations of your prospects is a crucial part of the process of drawing conclusions from research data and the interview. At the same time, it's what helps agents develop a properly balanced marketing mix that is attractive to the target market.

Motivation

What motivates people to get up in the morning? Is it the scent of fresh-brewed coffee, as the television commercials tell us? Perhaps it's the big closing appointment at 10 AM, or your college final exams for which you are running late.

Motivation is that "something" that causes us to act. Motivation gives us the reason to accomplish our goals. Motivation is that hot button in a prospect that, once discovered, gives the agent the information needed to help the prospect take action.

Figure 4.6

What's My Motivation?

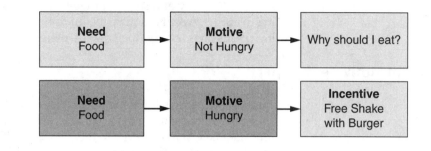

People have a need to brush their teeth. However, this need doesn't impel you to brush them every minute of the day. Having a need to brush our teeth is not a *motive* for action. However, after eating a meal, people may be motivated to brush their teeth to restore a clean, fresh feeling. Likewise, everyone has a need for housing, but that need doesn't cause us to act until a motive, such as a pouring rain that soaks us to the bone, gives us a reason to do so.

Part of a salesperson's job is to draw conclusions about what activates the reasons for buyers or sellers to take the steps that satisfy their needs. Prospects discover their needs when a state of discomfort occurs, such as a home that is too small for a growing family. Consumers are looking for ways to reduce the discomfort of unsatisfied needs. However, the course of action they take must not only satisfy the need (a larger home) but also the reason for taking the action (teenage children seeking privacy). Sometimes incentives are needed to follow a certain course of action.

Incentives are used in promotional campaigns to create a preference for one action over another. What incentives might you need to visit one fast-food restaurant over another? In this example, food is the need and hunger is the motive. Because you are hungry, you have a reason to do something. However, a two-for-one coupon acts as an incentive to go to one restaurant over another. Either fast-food restaurant would have satisfied your need for food, but the one with the coupon gives you the added incentive of also saving money (or getting more food for your money). See Figure 4.6.

When agents understand what motivates people to act, they execute their marketing plans and promotional campaigns with greater success. For example, if our target market was young families with children, our promotional campaign might emphasize security or safety features in a property. If our target market was families with children in their midteens and older, our promotional campaign for the same property might emphasize features that satisfy social and belongingness needs, such as a backyard swimming pool or a full-size billiard table in the family room.

Needs

Abraham Maslow's hierarchy of needs helps agents draw conclusions about the general needs of the market. Although the following is not an exhaustive study of Maslow's theory, it provides a basis on which agents can develop an understanding of needs and how they might be incorporated into their marketing and selling efforts.

Figure 4.7

Maslow's Hierarchy of Needs

Hierarchy	Stage	Definition	Marketing Strategy
Self-actualization	Stage 5	Self-fulfillment; a feeling that you are doing what you were meant to do, using your talents to their fullest	Enjoys sports, education, cultural events, cooking, and other hobbies. Property selections should inspire these activities.
Self-esteem needs	Stage 4	Prestige, sense of self-worth, success, accomplishment	Wants to help others as well as impress others; very status oriented. Properties should reflect these goals; must look good.
Social/belongingness needs	Stage 3	Acceptance by family and friends; belongs to groups and clubs and conforms to the standards of others	Point out places of worship, entertainment areas, golf courses and country clubs, and schools in the community.
Safety needs	Stage 2	Security, guarantees, warranties, return policies, order and stability, insurance	Demonstrate smoke detectors, warranty plans, security systems, deadbolts, owning their own home, and well-maintained property.
Physiological needs	Stage 1	Food, water, air, clothing, shelter	Promote open space, fresh air, and watertight roof.

It's a given that the main benefit of housing is shelter—a basic physiological need. However, agents can't market this benefit because it is not enough to draw a response—all forms of housing provide shelter. Nevertheless, there are many other benefits that can be promoted in an agent's marketing and promotional campaigns to satisfy the needs of consumers. Figure 4.7 outlines Maslow's hierarchy of needs.

Stage 1: Physiological needs.   Physiological needs center on the basic human needs for good health, food, medicines, exercise, fresh air, safe drinking water, clothing, and shelter. For many individuals in the United States, these needs are met in one fashion or another, which brings up another issue. What happens after certain basic needs are satisfied?

Maslow's theory suggests that someone who has just replaced the roof on his home will not be motivated to act when a salesperson at a home show tries to convince him to install a new watertight roof. There is no longer a need so the prospect isn't motivated to do anything. This is part of the difficulty of marketing the idea of home ownership to renters. The need for shelter is not a strong motivator because they already live somewhere. When they become homebuyers, it is something other than a need for shelter that motivates them.

Suppose you just listed a property. As Figure 4.7 suggests, the listed property's corner lot location (open space), its productive backyard garden, and the fresh air inside the home provided by its filtering system are features that correspond to the needs of some segments of the market. However, some buyers who are at a different stage in the hierarchy may expect to find these features in this kind of home and instead are looking for the benefits offered by other features, or different benefits of the existing features in the same home. The needs and motives for purchasing property are deduced from the analysis of data during the marketing phase, but are confirmed during the fact-finding meeting with a prospect during the selling phase.

Stage 2: Safety needs. Prospects want their children to feel safe in school; they want to live in safe neighborhoods with friendly neighbors. Although safety issues may not provide enough motivation for the customers to make a purchase decision, they are still used in marketing real estate.

Safety and a sense of order are strong motivators when they are missing. If the safety features are not pointed out, some customers may feel there is something wrong with the property. Other customers expect certain safety features to be present, but they do not bother to look for them. This puts the burden on the agents to make sure they understand the needs of their customers. During the sales process, agents use the safety motivators when explaining or demonstrating the benefits of a homeowner warranty, smoke detectors, breaker switches in the bathroom or electric panel, security systems, and other features that help make the house feel like a safe, secure home. Promotional campaigns are effective in educating the public about the advantages of home warranty plans and security systems.

Safety Issues

Some buyers see a cluttered, poorly organized home and jump to the conclusion that it's not safe. This is something to consider when listing a home or deciding how to demonstrate the property.

In the mid-1980s, hundreds of publicly registered real estate limited partnerships went bankrupt due to the rising concerns over asbestos. It was devastating to one segment of the industry; however, real estate agents can gain some control over a potentially negative environment through their advertising and promotional efforts. Suppose your local paper featured several articles about crime in the city. Your promotional efforts might include an article you write for the paper on monitored security systems. That weekend, advertise an open house that features a monitored security system with representatives from the security firm available to answer questions. Other safety issues that might be addressed using this concept include flood insurance, mud slide control, rising interest rates, proximity to fire stations, safe schools, block walls, and earthquake insurance.

Stage 3: Social/belongingness needs. The social/belongingness stage of Maslow's hierarchy corresponds to those who are concerned about fitting in, making decisions that please others, or feeling like a part of a group. Advertisements and promotions offering a home in a community that surrounds a golf course that includes a one-year paid membership to the country club may be attractive to individuals motivated by this level. Some people become motivated to buy certain clothing if they feel the purchase will result in acceptance from their friends or family. Surprisingly, the same can be said about real estate purchases. Many times the choice of one property over another is based primarily on what others might think of the decision.

Professional real estate agents point out the places of worship, entertainment areas, schools, and clubs in a community. They do this because it addresses the basic needs of many people, and the higher needs of others. Once the need is addressed it becomes a nonissue. If agents do not point out the benefits and amenities of the community or the property, then the customer may feel some anxiety or discomfort caused by an unfilled need.

Stage 4: Self-esteem needs.   When the lower order needs are satisfied, consumers often have a need for their real estate purchases to make a statement. Agents who are attuned to this, market features in ways that meet those higher needs. These people are driven by their need to succeed, get things done, stand out, and be noticed. They may respond to advertising that supports these needs. Copy in an advertisement that might appeal to stage 4 prospects could read: This home was built to get you noticed.

Stage 5: Self-actualization.   Everyone strives to have a full and rich life. Self-actualization is a way of describing one's need to be everything the individual can be. The properties purchased by individuals at this stage should inspire and encourage the prospects to enjoy life. Cultural activities and proximity to golf courses, country clubs, or tennis courts suggests to prospects a way of utilizing all their talents.

These consumers want to know more about the educational facilities, museums, and playhouses in a community. They are inspired by vacation properties or destinations, and they want to use their spare time to pursue their hobbies. Features in a home or community that support these aspirations should be included in promotional campaigns to attract this group.

A comprehensive fact-finding session helps expose what stage(s) the prospects have gone through and which are most important now. Until then, the marketing campaign can only make logical deductions (as we did in the example earlier in this chapter) based on the data gathered. After the salesperson engages clients in conversation, the agent will have a better idea of how to help the clients recognize their needs and compel them to act. When the need is exposed and a reason to solve it is provided, all that is needed is the motivation to take action. The prospect's need for finding the right house for the right reasons is the job of a professional real estate salesperson.

Conclusion

Marketers study consumer behavior. Courses in psychology, sociology, and human behavior may prove beneficial to new agents. Maslow's theory helps suggest why people buy. The initial qualifying conference helps both the agent and the prospect discover the stage(s) of prospect needs that must be fulfilled.

When developing a marketing program for your listing or service, remember the observation about fulfilled needs. This doesn't mean that homes cannot be marketed differently by appealing to different motives and need levels on the Maslow chart. In fact, consumers often are motivated by different levels of the chart at the same time. For example, they might enjoy an outstanding meal at a fine restaurant while entertaining good friends, thus filling their need for food, companionship, and self-esteem.

■ Summary

Before gathering data, professional marketing research firms look at the purpose for the research project, and then they gather data and evaluate it with an eye toward solving the problem. The volume of data makes it difficult to organize. Unlike the resources of most real estate agents, research firms have trained staffs to do this work. Nevertheless, agents can conduct scaled-down research projects and, based on their education and experience, draw conclusions from the data.

Because of this process, agents are better able to segment the total market into more manageable groups. An evaluation of the data helps determine what those segments do for a living, how they fill their leisure time, and what type of marketing stimuli may motivate them to take action. The study of consumer behavior, psychology, and sociology helps agents understand why people take the actions they do, what motivates them to buy certain products or services, and what stage the prospect is in with regard to their property and emotional needs.

■ Multiple Choice Questions

1. What is the *BIGGEST* constraint in conducting a marketing research project?
   a. A general lack of data
   b. A lack of financial resources
   c. Inability to tie the information together
   d. Identifying trends in the marketplace

2. Collected data should have relevance to the
   a. number of people in the total marketplace.
   b. total volume of sales this year compared to last year.
   c. solution of the research problem.
   d. demographics conducted by a local radio station.

3. Which of the following is a physiological need?
   a. Self-actualization
   b. Realizing one's fullest potential
   c. Exercise
   d. Being accepted by one's peers

4. Agents often suggest to sellers ways of organizing their home to create a better environment for showing the property. Some people even have started companies to help sellers prepare their homes for a showing. What need does this address on Maslow's hierarchy?
   a. Physiological needs
   b. Self-esteem needs
   c. Safety needs
   d. Social needs

5. Many times the choice of one home over another is based primarily on what others might think about the purchase decision. Which need in Maslow's hierarchy is the buyer trying to fulfill?
   a. Safety needs
   b. Social needs
   c. Self-esteem needs
   d. Self-actualization

■ **Exercises**

Exercise 1—Take the demographic data compiled in the exercises in Chapter 3 and reorganize it into categories that will help determine the largest market segments, how much members of these segments earn, and the types of jobs or careers members of these segments have within the community.

Exercise 2—After drawing conclusions on two or three prominent groups in Exercise 1, describe their commonalities. Given the makeup of these groups, make a judgment about the incentives that might be used to create a preference for your services or listings. If you are in a classroom setting, discuss these with the class to gain feedback.

TARGET MARKETING

5

■ Learning Objectives

After the study and review of this chapter, you should be able to

- ■ describe the significance of target marketing and how it accomplishes the goals of the marketing concept;
- ■ describe, evaluate, and analyze three ways to segment the market, specifically demographic, geographic, and psychographic product segmentation;
- ■ apply the principles of extrapolation to your local community;
- ■ compare and contrast the difference between externalists and internalists;
- ■ identify and explain the steps to segmenting the market;
- ■ identify why listing procedures are dependent on market segmentation and real estate marketing; and
- ■ describe how agents approach the market after a target market is identified.

■ Key Terms

demographic segmentation	family life cycles	marketing mix
differentiated market	geographic segmentation	psychographic segmentation
externalists	internalists	

Segmenting the total market organizes it into manageable groups that are accessible to agents. A **differentiated market** is one that is made up of different recognizable segments that can be attracted by creating multiple marketing mixes. Attempting to attract a group with multiple commonalities is called target marketing.

Target markets are groups within the total marketplace that have similar charcteristics in common and may react in similar ways to promotional stimuli. Agents who closely evaluate their chosen target market(s) draw conclusions about their prospects' similar interests, needs, and motivations. To attract prospects, agents develop product, price, place, and promotional strategies, which are covered in the next several chapters. Target marketing is essential to the marketing process. For the marketing mix to be developed, agents must know who they are trying to attract. It is inefficient and expensive to blanket the entire market with multiple promotional strategies directed at no one in particular. Segmenting the market into manageable groups saves time and creates efficiencies when applying the marketing mix.

■ Why Bother with Segmentation?

During the segmentation process, agents group people by the characteristics they have in common, such as age, income, lifestyle, and their motivations to purchase. Marketers in all industries use the commonalities of group segmentation or target marketing to create marketing mixes that influence purchase decisions. Agents who tap into this reservoir of information find that they can adjust the marketing mix on a single listing to make it attractive to multiple target markets. The result is higher productivity from their marketing mix strategies.

Think about this: movies often appeal to different groups of people that may not share other common interests. Though different, groups of people will respond to the same stimuli in similar ways. In the beginning of a marketing program, agents depend on this anomaly to market property. Evaluation of the data helps them find the stimulus that may be common to the group or subgroup.

Attracting a Market Segment

Suppose our research discovers a number of sports enthusiasts in the area. You have several listings that have features that might be of interest to this group, including tennis courts, basketball hoops, or large lawn areas for outdoor games.

Now suppose, as part of your marketing campaign, you give away a free sports video to qualified buyers who view property with you on the weekend. A free sports video will not attract everyone in the market; however, it may be the incentive needed to attract the part of the market segment that enjoys sports.

Differentiated Market

Real estate agents and offices carry a variety of listings at different prices and in different locations. Differentiated marketing recognizes this by creating multiple marketing mixes that are attractive to different segments of the market. Some have suggested that real estate buyers cannot be segmented into manageable groups and therefore promotional campaigns should address everyone in mass. The implication is that there are no commonalities between buyers. However, by following this logic, if each buyer's interests and needs were unique to the individual and the property that individual purchased, then for every home available there should be only one person interested in purchasing it. If each buyer were a separate market segment, there would

Figure 5.1

Market Segmentation

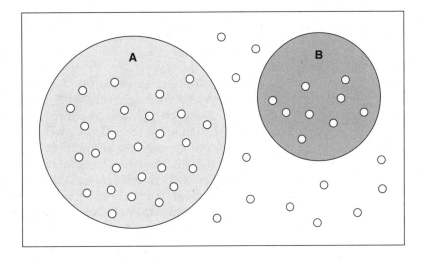

never be multiple offers on a single property; every buyer would insist on a unique floor plan suited to his or her individual needs.

Suggesting that there are no differences between groups assumes that first-time homebuyers are no different than older couples who are purchasing a vacation home, or that a woman's purchase decisions are influenced in the same way as a man's. If there were no differences between groups, we would approach the needs of someone who invests in five properties a year the same way as someone who buys one or two homes in a lifetime. In other words, we would not differentiate our market.

The box in Figure 5.1 represents the entire market. For simplicity, the box is divided into two large groups, A and B. The rest of the market is very fragmented and further segmentation is not beneficial.

Each group represents individuals with many things in common, such as age, gender, marital status, income, and the activities they enjoy. It is very difficult to know with certainty, but by evaluating the makeup of the group, agents can speculate about what motivates them and what might draw them to their listings.

Target Marketing Works

Real estate agents count on groups of people to react in similar ways to specific stimuli.

An analysis of this market tells the agent that if both groups were looking at the features of the same home, the buyers in Group A would be motivated differently by those features than the buyers in Group B. Suppose Group A is segmented to include young families with children. We might speculate about this segment's additional need for safety and security. Group B is segmented to include only single men. The young families in Group A would probably respond to the advantages and benefits of a block wall and security system differently than the single men in Group B. Now, suppose Group B is made up of single women. In this case, a safety and security feature may be of importance to them but in a way that is different from that of families with children. Each group has a different emotional connection to the feature and therefore a different motivation when responding to a promotional campaign.

The promotional strategies within the marketing mix should stress the buying motives of the largest group(s). If the phone doesn't ring, it may be because agents are marketing features that are of little interest to the larger groups. Like finding a needle in a haystack, if the distribution and promotional efforts appeal only to the fragmented groups, that is to say a small group of individuals within the total market, it may take longer for the information to reach them. Readers should remember that market segmentation is an organizational process and should not be confused with steering. Agents should *never* refuse to show homes in any area because of a prospect's race, sex, national origin, marital status, religion, or disability.

Features Don't Change

Features in a property typically don't change in the short life of a listing. What is significant is how agents prepare marketing strategies that help the target market link the *benefits* offered by the features in a property to what motivates their buying decisions.

■ Categories that Segment the Total Market

The total market is segmented by different categories. You should have a clear understanding by now that a segmentation process organizes the total market into groups that have similar characteristics. The result of the process doesn't mean that prospects in these groups will buy homes in the same neighborhood or on the same street; far from it. The process helps agents speculate about what motivates each group's real estate purchase decisions. When discovered, agents develop marketing strategies that involve price and product selections as well as promotional campaigns to attract members of the group. For our purposes, we'll organize the market into three categories:

1. Demographic segmentation
   - ■ Age
   - ■ Income
   - ■ Gender
   - ■ Family life cycle
   - ■ Marital status
   - ■ Career fields
2. Geographic segmentation
   - ■ Population locations
   - ■ Residence locations
   - ■ Climate
   - ■ Regional preferences

3. Psychographic segmentation
   - Lifestyles
   - Needs
   - Motives
   - Attitudes and perceptions

Demographic Segmentation

Demographic segmentation organizes the total market by gender, income, age, family life cycle, occupation, education, and household size. The following tools help break down a few of these in order to arrive at some general conclusions.

Gender.   Segmentation by occupation, income, or education must all consider gender. Agents who want to specialize in working with single men may need to know the age and income ranges for single men, single men with children, and those who are widowed to make sure the group is large enough with which to work. Other agents may want to help working women, and need to know how many are married, married with children, or single. Consideration for the income they earn (the next segmentation tool), the size of the market, and their accessibility must be determined. What is the income range for 25 to 43 years old (presumably the largest age segment), and within that group how many are men and how many are women? Agents might discover that within that range there are 15,140 single working men in their community of 100,000 people. This is a sizeable market with which to work. Gender is an important consideration within many of the segmentation approaches.

Income.   Most agents use income as the primary way of segmenting the market. Harper Boyd suggests that income segmentation is more useful when other factors are taken into account, such as marital status, gender, age, and other demographic data.[4] The *Information Please Almanac* is useful in finding the average income earned among various segments in the market. The following offers some interesting statistical facts that relate income growth to the growth in home prices. In 1985, approximately 26 percent of household income was used for the mortgage payment. By 1990, this number dropped to an average of 22.8 percent.[5] We have to use averages because each age range uses more or less of their income to afford housing. By Census 2000, according to information found on the U.S. Census Bureau Web site (*http://www.census.gov/prod/2003pubs/c2kbr-27.pdf*), the average percentage of income dropped to 21.7 percent, and it covered household spending, which included the mortgage payment.[6]

This suggests that up until 2000, financing became more flexible or income grew faster than the increased price of housing. Only ongoing research will tell us if that is still true today. Agents group the total market by compar-

---

4   Harper W. Boyd, Jr, *Marketing Management* (Chicago: Irwin, 1990), 202.

5   "Housing Affordability for the United States, 1990–1993," *1995 Information Please Almanac* (1995): 426.

6   Household spending is defined as the mortgage payment, property taxes, and insurance as well as selected monthly owner costs, including electricity, gas, water/sewer, oil, coal, kerosene, wood, etc., and condominium fees when appropriate.

Figure 5.2

Family Life Cycles

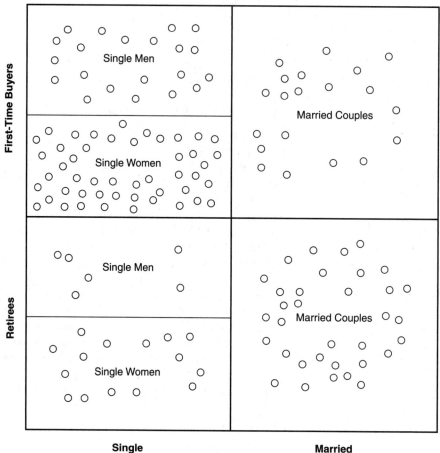

ing income information or a range of income earned to the monthly property payments the income range can support. From this information, agents determine the approximate house prices that can be supported by that group. Income statistics are also measured by the number of people who make a range of income. In other words, it's not enough to say that people who make $60,000 a year can afford X loan. What is important is a combination of information that suggests that out of a population of 100,000 working individuals, 39,000 make between $58,000 and $65,000 per year. This is a sizeable group about which to learn more. Check the *Information Please Almanac* (*www.infoplease.com/almanacs.html*) or the Census Bureau Web site mentioned previously for more information. What income range has the highest population of wage earners? The answer might surprise you. Check your local chamber of commerce or local title companies to see if they have conducted similar studies for your area.

The income levels of the target market(s), combined with other factors, should help determine the properties agents list. As mentioned earlier, most real estate agents look at income and assume that the middle-income wage earner[7] offers the largest collection of buyers. This is fine, but does the research confirm that assumption? Suppose an agent specializes in four-bedroom, two-story homes priced for the middle-income wage earner.

Agents are encouraged by the large population of the middle-income wage earners in their area; however, they also should look at the age range of the middle-income wage earner. Suppose the agents discovered that the largest middle-income segment in their area was comprised of people ages 55 to 63. This is a group that marketers call empty nesters. It consists of families whose kids have moved out of the house. This group is probably downsizing to take advantage of newly found leisure time, although this should be verified through research. Consequently, it is probably not a group that is in need of the four bedroom homes the agent is currently listing.

Family life cycles. Segmentation by family life cycles observes the different stages people go through in life. These stages include single, married, married with children, divorced, or widowed. For example, Figure 5.2 divides residential home purchasers into two groups—those who are first-time buyers (the top half of the graph) and those who are buying their retirement home. The figure could just as easily evaluate first-time homebuyers with two kids or older couples whose kids just left home.

With an eye toward finding additional commonalities, our research might divide these two groups even further, such as groups of single individuals and married couples. We can divide them further into single working men and women. This will make the whole group easier to work with and perhaps easier to find. Agents can decide which target market is the most attractive and which will give them the best opportunity to make a living.

When agents segment the entire market into manageable groups, they find target markets large enough from which to make a living and possibly in which to specialize. On first inspection, it appears that there are more first-time buyers in the market than retirees. The largest group within the first-time buyer market is comprised of single working women. If agents specialized in this area, their promotional strategy would address the buying motives of single working women. The product strategy might include listing smaller two- and three-bedroom homes with low-maintenance walled yards and a security system. Using the same graph, it is apparent that if agents wanted to work the retiree market, they would concentrate their marketing efforts on married couples. The product strategy might be the same; however, the way the information is distributed to the target markets may be different. These types of strategies are discussed in the next few chapters.

Extrapolation of demographic data. Without expensive primary research, it is hard to be precise in truly knowing the demographic makeup of household formations in a given community. However, there is ample secondary data that agents can use to get an idea of the size of their potential target market. It's not unusual to extrapolate the information from the national statistics and apply it to a local community, if local information is not available.

---

7   When people talk about a middle-income wager earner, they are usually referencing a national average. However, many communities tabulate this data as well.

If there were 250,000,000 people in the United States of which 65,000,000 were single working men, how many single men can we guess are in a community of 250,000?

A ratio can be developed from the national information and applied locally. In this case, divide 250,000,000 into 65,000,000 and you come up with 26 percent.

If you lived in a community of 250,000 people, approximately 26 percent of them would be single working men, or 65,000. If the community size were 100,000, then approximately 26,000 would be single working men, with the balance being children, single women, and married men and women.

There are obvious drawbacks to this technique that common sense resolves. Suppose your research in the almanac showed that 3 percent of the national population are chemical engineers and make $190,000 a year. If the agent lives in a remote area with a population of 250,000, an average income of $32,000, and no major local manufacturers, the probabilities are low that a significant number of chemical engineers live in the area.

Geographic Segmentation

Geographic segmentation divides the markets by the actual location of the property, population density and migration, and the political makeup within those communities. An agent's buyer target market may be more interested in the 3,000-square-foot floor plans in the Victor Knolls Tract than they are in the 2,200-square-foot floor plans in the Mesa Verde Tract. Agents often specialize in property within specific political boundaries, such as a city, or within the confines of major streets and expressways or freeways. This is very effective when the listing agent's target market is salespeople from competing companies. This is discussed in more detail later in this chapter.

A neighborhood or community that votes down or passes school bond issues gives agents a good idea of the direction the community wants to take. The analysis helps agents save time. Suppose agents are interested in listing residential acreage or lots, with small developers as the buyer target market. Does it make sense to target developers looking to build homes for young families if the community does not support school bond issues?

Prospects may address the need for a basement when looking at homes in areas of the Midwest. Prospects shopping for homes in Palm Springs may require a swimming pool or access to a golf course. Consumers develop preferences based on climate and geographic location. Later we'll discuss some of the promotional tools used to attract a market segment that has interests such as pools, horses, hiking, motorcycling, clean air, trees, swimming, or golf.

Psychographic Segmentation

Probably one of the most important areas in marketing and sales is **psychographic segmentation**. It demonstrates how different values and different needs motivate people. It is the reason agents ask if their prospects like sports, have hobbies, or are involved in weekend or after-work sports activities with their kids. Understanding what influences action or the perceptions and attitudes of the group and the individuals within the group is a valuable component in real estate marketing (to the group) and sales (to the individual).

Groups may be similar in their response to a stimulus (running out of a burning building); however, the reasons for responding are their own. People that are hungry eat food. However, the reasons for the kind of food they eat, when they eat, and where they eat are based on how they perceive the meal will satisfy their needs. People of a particular political party may have a view of the world that is different from members of another political party. People are unique individuals, but many people share the same lifestyle, the same opinions on political leaders, or the same interest in sports, and to this extent they can be organized into more manageable groups that can be attracted through the agent's marketing mix.

Although not a complete list, psychographic segmentation includes the prospect's opinions and attitudes on topics such as:

- Politics and religion
- Lifestyle
- Sports
- Hobbies
- Where they eat
- After-work activities
- Weekend activities

Lifestyle is the most telling with regard to your customer's behavior patterns. This type of psychographic data can be very expensive to acquire because it requires the use of questionnaires, surveys, or interviews. So, with the exception of prospect interviews and personal selling, which are discussed in Part Two of this book, agents may have to depend on secondary data for their marketing efforts.

In the late 1970s, Stanford Research Institute developed the Value and Lifestyle program, called VALS—later updated to VALS 2. The study helped explain consumer purchases based on the relationship between a person's self-orientation and the resources with which they have to work.

The study broke self-orientation down into multiple groups. For our purposes, we will divide them into two main groups, the externalists and the internalists.

Externalists.   Externalists try to conform to or impress the outside environment. Subconsciously, they may buy real estate to demonstrate to others the success they have achieved. Often status-oriented, they know what they want and appreciate tradition. They follow the rules and do what others expect of them. If you are listing a home on a corner lot, on a hill, or in a country club setting that has a flagpole out in front of the house, and given no other segmentation, this is the group you are trying to attract. It is the outside environment that influences the actions taken by externalists.

Internalists.   Unlike externalists, internalists do things based on experience. They are not necessarily motivated by the opinions of others. They often articulate their ideas clearly. This market segment is more likely to be respectful of the environment. They separate their trash and recycle newspapers and tin cans; they plant trees and are often leaders. Their actions and words are designed to make sure others know who they are and what they want.

These prospects respond to homes having energy efficiency, double- or triple-pane windows, Low-E (low-emittance) glass, high R-Factor (thermal resistance factor) insulation, drought-resistant landscaping, and room for a second trash compactor. In Part Two of this book, primary research, conducted during the initial meeting, will confirm to which of these two groups your prospect belongs.

Steps to Selection of a Target Market

Agents often specialize in more than one large target market. Consequently, the marketing mix for a single listing may change so it's attractive to each target market. To attract multiple target markets, agents may list other properties and, in addition to their promotional strategy, use multiple product and pricing strategies. The target markets that agents specialize in should be approachable, easily found in the marketplace, and not too costly for agents to attract. The last thing to consider is that the more things the target market has in common, the easier it may be for agents to discover a motivation for making real estate purchases. The result is a marketing mix and promotional strategy designed to successfully attract different target markets.

Steps Used to Identify a Target Market
- Identify and describe the subgroup
- Estimate the size of the subgroup
- Evaluate the accessibility to the subgroup

Identify the Market Segment and Its Size

Agents identify market segments by evaluating the differences between the groups. Agents can use an almanac to find how many people in the United States make $55,000 to $75,000 per year. Agents can identify the number of people in a specific geographic area they may want to specialize in, or how many families live in a community. Market research helps identify measurable segments of the market. Data analysis helps develop strategies for how and where to find them.

Accessibility

Can agents find their target market? Suppose you wish to specialize in prospects who are country-western enthusiasts. How do you find them? Your research will provide many of the answers, but for now, think about where they dine out, the stores they frequent, and the recreational activities they pursue. Local country-western radio stations may prove helpful with income and other demographic information, and the list goes on. Let's demonstrate how you would use the information you discover. Suppose you discover the restaurant that is most frequented by country-western consumers. Talk with the manager about paying for a portion of the cost of printing menus if an

Figure 5.3

Two Ads

Come See

Three bedrooms, 1 3/4 baths, formal dining room, large master bedroom, indoor
laundry. Approximately 1340 square feet.
Asking $X.

Agent Name   Phone Number

HOME ON THE RANGE

1900 square feet, four bedrooms, two
baths; sits on one acre. The barn and
stalls are ready for your horses. The
home is in "tip top" condition and yards
are landscaped. It is a buy, so call now.

Agency, Phone Number

institutional advertisement about you or your firm can be printed on the
menus. Develop a placemat that features your name or agency, a map of the
community, and perhaps other advertisers.

Listing Procedures and the Target Market

The next step after researching a target market is developing a marketing
campaign aimed at that market. Take a look at the two ads in Figure 5.3 and
decide which is emphasizing a product description and which is inviting a
target market to call.

The first ad is not written to attract a segment of the overall market. The cre-
ator of the ad may be hoping the potential customer can figure out what the
advantages and benefits are of having a large master bedroom or an indoor
laundry. In fact, the first ad does not make an effort to target any particular
market. These "shotgun" ads rarely "talk" to a target market.

Now look at the second ad. It talks to people who enjoy the outdoors. That
agent appears to have identified the target market as a group that enjoys
yard work. Perhaps the agent's research discovered a large population of
families with children. The agent creates a promotional campaign (which
includes this ad) that might be attractive to families that enjoy horses. Written promotional pieces should be created after the agents have identified and
described a target market.

Let's look at two more advertisements. In each, determine what incentives, if
any, are presented that give the customers a reason to do something.

The second ad in Figure 5.4 is stressing a home that is well suited for two
segments of the market: first-time buyers and the commuters.

The fact that the second ad says it is a home for a first-time buyer or commuter is the incentive that helps convert the reader's motivation to action.
An incentive helps readers believe their reason for doing something will be

Figure 5.4

Incentives in Ads

ANY CITY AFFORDABLE—Three bedrooms, two baths, 1845 square feet;
fenced and partially landscaped, circular
driveway. Only $X.

Agency, Phone Number

ANY CITY VALUE—Excellent home for
first-time buyer or commuter. Three
bedrooms, two baths, brick fireplace in
living room, breakfast nook, fenced and
landscaped. All financing available. $X

Agent, Phone Number

satisfied. Can you hear it now? "Hey Stacy, here's the house for us. It's probably closer to the freeway because it says here, 'for commuters.' I bet I can cut 20 minutes off my travel time to work."

What helps motivate the reader to action in the first ad? On first reading, it seems to describe the property with the hope that readers will figure out why they should be motivated to call. This is not an atypical ad. If we were to read into it we might note that the property is fenced and partially landscaped. The fenced yard might attract an individual looking for safety. The partial landscaping may address certain social needs in that people want to have control over their own property and at the same time fit into their neighborhood. For other buyers, this might imply that the landscaping isn't finished and it would require more work. The added work would take away from their enjoyment of other activities. If the latter proves to be the largest segment in the market, expect few calls from the ad.

Overall, however, despite the fact that the ads describe the same property, the second ad seems to be the more powerful of the two. Your promotional efforts should state the benefits of features that are meaningful to your target market. This means that you may have to write different ads to accommodate the needs of the two or three target markets you are trying to attract.

An Overlooked Target Market

Two frequently overlooked target markets are the co-operative agents and companies who need the kind of properties you list. Your primary research tasks may have included approaching co-operating agents. Many of these agents are not hesitant to tell you what kinds of properties they sell. In so doing, they are indirectly telling you something about the target market they attract.

There is nothing stopping you from supplying these agents with the inventory they need. Listing property for the target market of other agents works well for those more interested in marketing and less interested in selling. Listing procedures require you do what is necessary to get the property sold. When you research your market, you'll discover who the top agents are in your area. By doing so, you also discover the types of properties they sell, the frequency of their sales, the price range of the sales, and geographic areas where they are located. Work with those co-operating agents by supplying them inventory that you have listed, inventory that meets the needs of their target market.

Summary of the Target Market and the Marketing Mix

People in the Midwest are more likely to look for homes with a basement than people in Oregon. Homes with swimming pools might sell with more frequency in states such as Florida and California. This demonstrates that people from different parts of the United States have different needs, buying habits, and purchasing patterns.

Real estate agents in the farming states must meet the needs of that segment of the market. Real estate agents in California and New York work with people from literally all over the world. In both cases, the way agents satisfy customer needs and deploy their marketing mix affects their number of sales.

In Chapter 4, Maslow's hierarchy of needs showed that as products fill a need the motivation to fill that need is lessened. In other words, if members of the target market already have a place to live, then the marketing mix must tap into undiscovered needs and motivations of those in the group. Think about this: lots of homes have many features that are similar to other homes—three bedrooms, two baths, two-car garage, carpeting—but that is only half the story! If the only thing that mattered in the decision were having three bedrooms, then the buyer would buy any three-bedroom home that came along. This doesn't usually happen, so something more must be needed. Consequently, some products are not marketed to satisfy a basic need, but rather a higher need. For instance, clothing designers don't market their lines as garments that keep us warm. They market them as items that help us appear younger, look slimmer, or be with the in crowd. Yet, through all of this, the product never changes. Real estate is marketed the same way. It is difficult to change a property's features, but agents can change the marketing and promotional mix, thus attracting different segments of the market.

■ Alternative Strategies

The markets that an agent works with are sometimes difficult to segment into workable groups. Other times, agents find similarity in the needs of a group. For this reason there are several alternative strategies used to help market your listings and your services effectively.

Mass Marketing

Mass marketers often have only one product to sell or take a narrowed approach to marketing the properties they list. Consequently, their marketing mix is unimaginative and not directed to any particular segment in the total market. As we saw in the advertisement examples in Figures 5.3 and 5.4, some agents write ads without a specific target market in mind. This is mass marketing. Agents produce a more effective marketing mix when they segment their market and differentiate their marketing efforts toward the larger segments of the total market.

Differentiated Marketing

As explained earlier, a differentiated market assumes that properties can satisfy multiple needs. Differentiated marketing develops different marketing mixes to attract different segments of the market.

Why is this important? Minimally, it gives agents who use it a competitive edge. In the classified section of a newspaper on any given day, there are often real estate advertisements that offer few differences from the advertisements of multiple competitors. The properties are unique, but there seems to be something missing that helps differentiate one ad from another; something that helps the advertisement appeal to a particular target market. The following are strong motivators for some real estate prospects and may help differentiate your listing from other advertised listings:

■ The desire to make new friends in a new neighborhood

■ Precision and craftsmanship

■ The recognition for one's success and accomplishments

■ The ability to control the final look of the home

■ A house design that saves time

> **DIFFERENTIATED MARKET**
>
> Sample ad: Home for sale. Four bedrooms, three baths, detached guest house with bath, one acre, block wall, security system, fully landscaped, three-car garage (30x46), four-foot-wide hallways, three-foot-wide doors, gas-start fireplace, tile roof, circular drive. Kitchen, den, family room, and dining room all have a view. Dual-pane windows with vertical blinds. Six-inch exterior walls.
>
> What are some specific features of this home? Who would have an incentive to purchase this home based on those features? One feature is listed below. Try adding at least five more features to the chart below and list the benefits of each feature and what type of customer would be interested in it.
>
> | Feature Benefits | Who would buy |
> |---|---|
> | 1. Block wall security | Families with kids, retired couples, single women |

As you completed the exercise in the example above, you probably noticed that it is not so much the feature but rather the advantages and benefits that the buyers are seeking. Your market research helps identify the preferences, needs, desires, and aspirations of the target market. In other words, it helps agents formulate logical conclusions regarding the benefit the target market expects from the block wall and other features.

This exercise goes a long way in helping agents associate the features in a home with the benefits and incentives needed by target markets.

Niche Marketing

A concentrated marketing plan literally concentrates the agent's efforts toward one end. This is called niche marketing.

Suppose a new agent is very young but has just experienced purchasing a first home. This agent can relate to the first-time buyer and share experiences on what to expect throughout the buying process. The agent decides to aggressively work that segment. After developing a marketing mix for this group (product, price, promotion, and place), the agent directs *all* marketing effort toward the buyers in the group. This can prove to be a profitable marketing tool as long as the research showed a market segment large enough from which to make a living.

"What everyone knows is valueless."   Market segments should be large, so that the segment has the potential of being profitable. However, beware of the larger, more obvious market segments.

These segments include doctors, lawyers, accountants, and others. A stock market executive once said, "What everybody knows is valueless." Segments that receive intense concentration become rather unsympathetic to the volume of salespeople who approach them. After all, it doesn't take a lot of work to figure out what everyone knows.

■ One Last Point: Markets Constantly Change

Gathering and evaluating the data needed to choose a target market is an interesting process. However, agents should keep in mind that just as interest rates change or house prices increase, target markets change. Agents may find that there are fewer people in a targeted group who can afford the $550,000 homes they are listing. Additional research may show changes in the age range, income levels, and marital status of a targeted group. A complete evaluation of this new material results in a new marketing mix. A **marketing mix** is the combination of the right product at the right price given the right promotion through the best channels of distribution that produces a buyer who is ready, willing, and able to buy your product or service. This can only occur if you stay current with your market.

■ Summary

Agents want to know how to increase productivity, attract buyers, list properties that sell, and design promotional and pricing strategies that are effective. The more agents know about their prospects and the real estate environment they work in, the more efficient their sales. Market segmentation is one of the by-products of data gathering and analysis.

Segmenting the total market into manageable groups helps agents understand that a group of people receiving the right stimuli will respond in similar ways. Agents should evaluate the segments in their marketplace and draw conclusions about their similar interests, needs, and motives. Attempting to attract a group with multiple commonalities is called target marketing.

A shotgun approach to marketing or trying to appeal to all individuals within the total market is a very expensive approach and often counterproductive for real estate agents on a limited budget. By evaluating the market and segmenting it into smaller, similar, and more manageable subgroups, agents can match the similar interests (commonalities) of segmented groups to the amenities/benefits in homes they list.

The market may be grouped through demographic, geographic, psychographic, and product segmentation. Several large segments may be discovered after grouping the total market. The reality is that agents may select more than one large segment with which to work. Consequently, this involves more than one product, pricing, or promotional strategy. The segments worked by agents should be approachable. In other words, they can be found easily in the marketplace. If they can't be found easily, then it would be costly to attract them, and following the precepts of time management, the agent's time should be spent elsewhere. The last thing to consider when selecting a segment is the meaningful differences between groups. The more similar the members are within the groups and the more they have in common, the more likely they will have similar needs to address.

When following the listing procedures of a state, agents are reminded of their responsibility to do what is necessary to get the property sold. An often-overlooked segment of the market is the top co-operative agents in an area. Co-op agents who have identified their target market of buyers are often very busy selling to that market and too busy to list additional inventory. Agents who research the activities of co-op agents discover the types of properties they sell, the frequency of their sales, the price range of the sales, and geographic areas where they are located. Having an understanding of the co-op agents' target market gives agents the opportunity to supply the co-op inventory that meets the needs of the target market.

When applying market segmentation, agents discover that a single product is sold in different ways to different segments in the market. The marketer must use different incentives to motivate different segments of the market to action. Over time, a target market may change. Agents need to keep on top of any changes in the demographics because this creates changes in the way they should approach their market. As agents begin to appreciate their shifting target market, they begin to develop an understanding of how to find that market.

■ **Multiple Choice Questions**

1. Through data analysis, agents can discover large segments of the market that share similar characteristics in common. These potential target markets must meet certain criteria to be viable groups on which to work. Which of the following is *NOT* one of those criteria?

    a. They must want to buy a home.

    b. The must have an ability to buy.

    c. They must have the authority to buy.

    d. They must be accessible.

2. Creating a promotional campaign designed to appeal to all prospects within the total market is expensive and often counterproductive. This is called the

    a. segmentation approach.

    b. nonsegmentation approach.

    c. shotgun approach.

    d. direct approach.

3. There are multiple ways to segment the market. Which of the following represents demographic segmentation?

    a. A prospect's preference for colder weather

    b. More and more women are working in the marketplace

    c. Values and needs motivate people differently

    d. Some people choose to separate their trash and others don't

4. Suppose you find that families with children ages 1 to 9 represent a large segment of the market. Further research shows that they participate in weekend sports activities and frequent fast-food restaurants three to six times per week. Which of the following represent the segmentation activities described above?

    a. Product and psychographic segmentation

    b. Psychographic and geographic segmentation

    c. Geographic and product segmentation

    d. Demographic and psychographic segmentation

5. Groups of people may respond to an advertisement, but the reason for their response may be different. One group may buy a brand of toothpaste because it whitens their teeth. Another group may buy the same toothpaste because it freshens their breath. This says that people are motivated to do things for their own reasons. Which of the following describes this kind of segmentation?

    a. Geographic segmentation

    b. Product segmentation

    c. Psychographic segmentation

    d. Demographic segmentation

■ Exercises

Research Question 1—Competing real estate agents provide listing sales-people with an opportunity when they treat their competitors as their target market. Competing agents may have channels of distribution that are different from the listing salesperson. By discovering what successful competitors sell, salespeople can list properties that fill their competitors' needs. With the help of the multiple listing service, evaluate the volume of sales and list the agents or agencies that created the sales. Correlate the volume of sales, pricing, square footage, and geographic locations with the agents or agencies creating the sales.

Research Question 2—Sometimes local information is just not available. In these instances, agents do not want to consume a lot of time and expense trying to understand the demographics of their market. With an almanac or online census Web site, calculate the total population of the United States. Break that population down by gender, income, age groups, marital status, and career fields. Extrapolate those numbers to your community.

PRODUCT AND PRICING STRATEGY

6

■ Learning Objectives

After the study and review of this chapter, you should be able to

■ analyze and explain the difference between selling a product and selling the total product;

■ explain how value is defined and how prospects may perceive a difference between price and value;

■ evaluate the significance that inflation has on price and value and its effect on home values and sales;

■ define the purpose of the property price in the overall pricing strategy; and

■ discuss the concept of enhancing value.

■ Key Terms

enhancing the property's value	packaging	total product
	price niche	value
inflation		

Two elements of the marketing mix include the product and the price. In this chapter and the next we define value, the purpose of price, how real estate is affected by inflation, and how agents react in different ways to inflation. Pricing strategies for property and services can enhance their perceived values, which helps the prospects feel they are getting more value for their money.

The services provided by agents are considered products, but there are multiple products to consider. Agents may choose to market multifamily residential units, industrial buildings, commercial structures, acreage, lots, or single-family homes. Real estate agents can also provide what is known as total product.

■ Product Strategy

Although customers ask about a property's features, they really want to know the ways the property can benefit them. They want to know how the product (property/services) can solve their problem and satisfy their needs. This means that agents must demonstrate more than the property's features; they must also demonstrate how those features solve the prospect's situation. **Total product** is a way of describing a quality product or service that exceeds the customer's perceived expectations.

Total Product

We can no longer say that agents only market homes or property. Sellers want more from agents who sell their property. In most states, agents generally earn their commission at the time they present an offer from a ready, willing, and able buyer that meets the conditions of sale. However, given the concept of what William Zikmund calls a "total product,"[8] sellers expect agents to handle all of the paperwork and problems that may arise prior to the transfer of the property to the buyer. For this reason, commissions are often paid at the end of the transaction, rather than at the beginning. Buyers want agents to return phone calls in a timely manner, show up for appointments on time, and explain the features of a property in terms that help them understand how the solution solves their problem and satisfies their needs.

The Total Product

Product
A three-bedroom home

Total Product
A home
- that offers years of enjoyment;
- built for a growing family;
- that is fun to live in;
- that makes the buyer look prosperous;
- that adds to personal prestige;
- with quality touches…

When agents embrace the total product idea, they develop another competitive advantage over their peers. To be cost effective, listings should meet the needs of the larger market segments in the area, so that promotional campaigns have a better chance of attracting interested prospects. The presentation of any elements in the total product should coincide with what agents learn about the market segments or the individual prospect.

---

8 William Zikmund and Michael D'Amico, *Marketing*, 2nd ed. (New York: John Wiley & Sons, 1986), 11.

Intentional Presentation

A real estate agent's product strategy includes such things as identifying features within the home; through intentional, repetitious, or conspicuous presentations agents help the prospects remember that feature. Conspicuous presentations of a feature implant it into the prospect's mind in such a way that it makes it difficult to forget. For example, when showing a property that has a fireplace as its main feature, what better way to demonstrate the fireplace than to have the owner start a low burning fire before the prospect views it? The room remains comfortable and the fireplace is memorable and conspicuous.

Packaging

Many consumer product companies use the concept of packaging to get their products noticed. It has application in real estate too.

Successful **packaging** of a property or service (the product) makes the prospects want to experience more. Packaging draws attention to the product; it creates curiosity and encourages comparisons. Often, as part of the product strategy, agents make sure the house is in showcase condition. Clutter, disrepair, and soiled carpets or walls demonstrate a potential lack of quality, or generate a feeling on the part of prospects that the property is unsafe. Agents know what prospective buyers are looking for. Consequently, agents can suggest to sellers ways of making their home more appealing without offending them. This can be done with a computer and a publishing software program. Initially, agents prepare a one-size-fits-all, boilerplate list of common elements within most homes that are usually in need of attention. To keep the list inoffensive, it should look like it was prepared in mass and given to all sellers. The form should list general suggestions, such as mowing the lawn once a week, whether or not they apply to the specific seller. The list could suggest that sellers clean the windows once a month, paint the trim if needed, and wash down the walls before the first open house (even if the home is immaculate). However, because you control the form, you can also add items that are of concern for a particular problem, such as the overwhelming scent of animals when entering the home. You might suggest spray or powder products that help neutralize the smell. The form might also ask that sellers help prepare (package) the home for a showing by turning on the lights in all the rooms, preparing the air-conditioning or fireplace, or putting a drop of vanilla extract in a warm oven just before agents demonstrate the property. Agents want the outside of the home—the curb appeal—to be such that the buyers want to enter, and feel comfortable enough to stay while asking questions about the property.

Packaging

Here's another example of how packaging encourages prospects to want to learn more. Suppose you are a consumer in a grocery store without a grocery list. You walk the aisles, and somehow you know what you want when you find it.

As you walk down one aisle, you remember that you need cereal. If all of the cereal boxes had no recognizable packaging, you really wouldn't know what kind of cereal was inside. Yet, when you see a cereal box that is orange with a sports figure on the front, you know it is Wheaties.

The lesson here is that even if the contents of each cereal box were the same, different buyers can be attracted with different packaging. If a box were yellow with no other markings, many might think it is Cheerios. We still don't know its real contents, but we may be more interested in opening the box.

Initially, it doesn't matter what the box contains, as long as the prospect can identify with the "packaging." In real estate, prospects may choose to have their agent skip a property if the home has poor curb appeal. Packaging holds other meanings for prospects. Agents are closer to a sale when prospects feel agents have a thorough understanding of their needs and they can satisfy those needs through the presentation and packaging of a total product.

Properties could be virtually the same, but different packaging will attract different buyers. This means that the home does not have to change for every prospect. However, by packaging specific real estate features we attract different groups from the total market. We do this because we know that the amenities of specific features benefit prospects in different ways. Therefore, those features must be packaged in different ways, even though the house never changes. Once these features are packaged, they are put into the promotional mix.

Services

The services agents offer tie in nicely with the total product concept. For example, the buyer and seller may demand more in the way of follow-up during the listing period or the processing period before the property transfers to the buyer. Agents must be prepared to adjust their schedule to meet the needs of their clients. Some prospects may want to save time and are looking for someone who can listen to their needs and respond accordingly and quickly. Others may prefer to look at 15 to 20 homes before making a decision to write an offer. Chapter 7 addresses agents' services and their value to the buyer and seller.

For now, as agents develop a marketing strategy, thought should be given to the elements discussed in this chapter especially with an eye toward integrating the marketing mix, which includes the four P's of product, price, promotion, and place.

■ Pricing Strategy

Price provides a way of measuring the value of real estate or comparing one product with another. If we said we could get a car for $50,000, we would probably perceive the car to be a quality vehicle. What would you think if we said we could get a house in southern California or south Florida for $50,000? Prospects (buyers or sellers) may perceive value in many ways. What someone will pay for a property or service is often based on the utility value of the item purchased. You will recall the utility values discussed in Chapter 1. As an example, time utility suggests that someone who was late to joining a real estate market rally might assign more value to a home purchase today in the fear of having the price go up even more over the next several months.

Defining Value

There are several ways to define and exchange things of **value**. Value is indicated by price. Value is also a perception that buyers and sellers may hold of the products and services they buy. One prospect may look at a home with a beautifully landscaped front yard and see a loss of time and money to maintain its look. For them, the property has less value than for someone who perceives the yard to be something that may help get him noticed.

Let's Barter

Books on economics talk about the system of barter. Barter was used for centuries before a money system was established, or when money was not available. Like today, people bartered for things that were useful to them. Think of two baseball card enthusiasts who work an exchange of two cards of one player for one card of another. These exchanges are possible because each of these items has a perceived value; a value that the other party wants.

Value and Price

We are conditioned to think that price indicates value or quality in some way. However, for our purposes, value does not necessarily mean only price. This is important to remember, and it will be repeated later. When agents discover the demands or needs of their target market, and list properties accordingly, their listings have more *value* to the target market. Value is integrated into the total product. In other words, if you supply a quality property that meets the needs of the target market the buyer may feel they are getting more value from their purchase decision.

Real estate prices rise and fall over the short term, but have experienced a general upward trend over the long term. Therefore, when agents interview with sellers, they must educate them on how the four P's are interrelated. If any element, such as the price, is out of balance with the others, a sale is less likely to take place quickly. Suppose an agent placed a long-term advertisement into a magazine suggesting that inflation has been crushed, interest rates are declining, and now is a good time to buy. However, by the time a prospect reads this advertisement, inflation could be running rampant and prices may be rising rapidly. It is easy to change the price on the listing, but more difficult to change the magazine advertisement. This is a marketing mix that is out of balance. If inflation starts rising rapidly during the listing period, the seller may want to raise their listed price accordingly. Conversely, if prices start declining, it's the responsibility of agents to inform their prospects of changes in the marketplace. Once again, a price adjustment may be necessary.

How We Name Price

In the real estate industry, some agents do not like to use the word *commission*, preferring instead to say that they are compensated by a fee. Some agents have been trained to say "monthly investment" when they talk to prospects about their monthly payments. It is not uncommon for real estate agents to run advertisements without the price of the property. Agents have said that they do this because they feel the price might stop some prospects from calling; others explain their actions with the overused phrase "the quality of the home cannot be represented by the price." Because there are many ways of saying price in real estate, we will limit our discussions to commissions and the price of a property.

Another Purpose for Price

Price may be used to reflect the quality of a property or the services provided by agents. From a supply and demand standpoint, if customers have a specific need and the supply is limited, then prices will go up. In this sense, the best definition for the purpose price plays in a capitalistic society is the effi-

Figure 6.1

Demand Curve

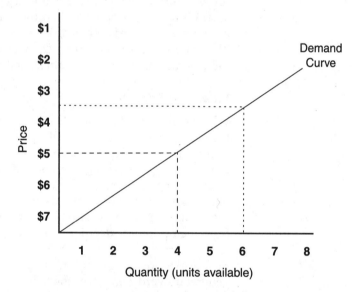

The demand curve shows that the quality demanded in the marketplace is six units and that the consumer is willing to pay $3.25/unit. (This is like saying you can sell 2,000 square foot homes for $3.25 all day long.) However, as inflation increases the price of the product goes up, which causes the demand for the product to go down to four units. (This means that it becomes more difficult to find enough buyers willing to pay $5.00 for a 2,000 square foot house, which may have cost only $3.25 just a few weeks earlier.)

This chart also demonstrates that, given the demand curve, as the supply of an item declines the price for that item increases. Conversely, if the price of an item increases (higher property prices, higher interest rates, higher costs of qualifying or acquiring a loan, etc.) the demand for the item declines.

cient allocation of goods and services to those who need them and can afford them. Five-bedroom homes are scarce and their higher prices reflect that scarcity. Consequently, those who need the utility of a five-bedroom home may pay more for it, even though the square footage may be the same as a four-bedroom alternative.

■ Price and Inflation

Inflation is the result of many factors that cause prices to rise. Rising demand for a product that is in declining or stable supply is one of the more common reasons prices rise in the real estate market. At some point, inventory cannot keep up with demand. Increasing prices eventually hit a level that is too high for the market to accept, thereby choking off demand. As demand decreases, prices decline.

The economic term *price elasticity* suggests that it is not unusual for some sellers and agents to be slow in accepting market price declines. This creates a general slowdown in the volume of real estate sales. However, this opens up an opportunity for the professional real estate agent.

Figure 6.1 suggests that as prices increase consumers demand fewer properties within certain price ranges, which may translate into an increase in unsold listings, at least in the short term. When sellers trust you and accept your information about the direction of prices, it results in listings priced closer to market value and probably below those of your competitors.

The Effect on Housing Demand

The Federal Reserve is well aware that shortages and the rising cost of the components used to build a home cause home price fluctuations. Price fluctuations are caused by:

- Changes in the cost of lumber and plywood
- Increased costs of permits and environmental paperwork
- Increased costs of appliances, concrete, or lumber
- Increased costs of labor
- Increased energy and transportation costs

To slow the growth of inflation, the Federal Reserve must take steps to reduce demand. Through the open market operations and other tools at its disposal, it takes steps to encourage thrifts to increase interest rates. Higher interest rates make it more difficult for people to afford a home. Sellers who must sell should reduce their prices to compete with the higher price of money (interest rates).

Inflation changes the value of the dollars a buyer uses to buy a home. Suppose a buyer has $450,000 cash to buy the $450,000 home he needs. However, because of inflation, that home now costs $464,000. The buyer is $14,000 short because the dollars do not have enough value to exchange for the new inflated price of the home.

As prices rise, some prospects remain qualified, but they quickly realize that without higher down payments they can't buy as much as they could six months or a year earlier. If they must pay more, they will demand more in the way of services and the total product. Consequently, agents must take more time enhancing the value of the properties they list by promoting features that provide the benefits needed by the prospects.

Although priced at market value, when agents satisfy more of the prospect's property and emotional needs, the property may appear undervalued to the prospect.

■ Agents React to Inflation in Different Ways

No Reaction

Professional agents are aware of what is going on in the financial marketplace. They can connect rising interest rates, rising home prices, rising rent rates, and a declining affordability index with slowing sales. They evaluate the facts and avoid talking about how this market is different, how everyone they talk to wants to purchase real estate, or how upbeat the lenders, title companies, and escrow representatives seem to be. That optimism is fine, but professional agents temper their optimism with what is taking place in the market.

Take Lower-Priced Listings

During periods of rising prices and slowing sales, some agents approach the market differently. Rather than continuing to list properties that do not sell, agents may list bare bones tract homes with minimum FHA carpets, no fireplace, unfinished garages, and hollow core doors. Although the prices for these cheaper homes are also inflated, agents can promote the lower monthly payments to attract a new level of buyers. Agents must familiarize themselves with Regulation Z and the Truth-in-Lending laws before promoting monthly payments in their advertising.

Finding the Value

Some agents list properties at higher prices, but they do so only after taking the time to find the value for which their buyers will pay. No matter which approach agents take during periods of high prices, they must consider how they will market the price.

Agents can increase the value of their listings without changing the price, but in doing so they should not sell things that are not inherent in the property. Recall our discussion of the total product. When prospects buy real estate, they often look at many homes. This can be a long, drawn-out process. Frustrated after not finding a home that satisfies their needs, they may go to a second agency, only to end up putting in an offer on a home the first agency already showed them. Prospects may do this because of the perceived higher value that resulted from the personal selling of the second agent, or the fact that the agent listened to the prospects' needs and delivered. Real estate agents increase the perceived value of their listings and service by creating promotional campaigns. These campaigns include personal selling messages, advertising, or promotional messages that stress greater value and benefits (fulfillment of property and emotional needs) from the purchase decision when compared to alternative promotional messages from their competitors.

■ The Purpose of the Property Price

How Sellers Price Their Property

Sellers usually have a preconceived idea of what the price of their property should be, even before calling for the agent's professional opinion. Therefore, the agent is responsible for finding out the motives behind the seller's demand for a certain price. For example, consider this actual case: a seller required $72,000 for his acreage, with a $10,000 down payment. The market interest rate at the time was 11 percent, but the seller was willing to go 7 percent and take payments for 30 years (a good incentive). Unfortunately, the price was about $20,000 more than buyers were willing to pay.

After an extensive interview, the agent discovered that the seller wanted payments of $412 per month. He pulled out an amortization book and said, "At $72,000, with $10,000 down at 7 percent for 30 years, the monthly payment is $412." The seller and his wife wanted exactly $412 per month to supplement their retirement income. Once the agent knew this, he restructured the listing to $53,200 with $10,000 down. The balance of $43,200 (with prepayment penalties) was payable at $412 per month including 11 percent interest until paid (about 29.7 years).

During qualifying interviews with the sellers, take the time to find out what motivates their pricing decisions. Doing so establishes a more realistic price and helps keep the marketing mix in balance. If agents took listings at prices above market value, then channels of distribution may close down (e.g., some agents may be unwilling to show an overpriced property), and advertising costs increase because it may take more time to market the property.

Discover the Result the Seller Wants

Sellers have different motivations for pricing their property the way they do. There is always some kind of reasoning behind what they are demanding, though it may not seem so at first.

In the early stages of the listing appointment, agents may not bring up pricing objectives. Instead, they should find out what results sellers were seeking when they established their price. Remember that selling a property for a certain price is not necessarily the "result" sellers want. In the example above, the result the sellers wanted was not a particular price; it was $412 in income per month. Once you and the seller settle on a result, look for alternative routes to get there, especially if the seller is initially demanding too much for the property.

Real Estate Values Never Go Down

Sellers have been *educated* to expect a profit from the real estate they own. Unfortunately, the resulting price they demand may or may not have any relevance to current market value. Sellers may have paid too much for the property or they may have overimproved it. However, in addition to a profit, some sellers expect to recover all their principal and interest payments, property taxes, and property insurance.

The reality is that it has only been over the last 35 to 45 years that real estate values have seen significant increases. This is probably due to the baby boom

Figure 6.2

Why Sellers Sell

Two sellers each want to sell their home for $400,000.

Seller A: Why?	Seller B: Why?
Carry paper for retirement income	Needs cash
Sell quickly for medical operation	Earn highest profit possible
Move closer to the kids	Get away from the kids
Job transfer out of state—must sell	Job transfer across town—can commute until sold
Need an extra room for an office	Cannot maintain this large house

explosion after World War II. For many decades prior to that, homeowners purchased their home with the intention that when the home was sold they could get most of their money back. Home prices just didn't go up significantly in short periods of time prior to the early 1960s. If sellers overprice their property, several things may occur in the short term:

- They may get lucky and sell the property.
- The sellers may realize continued disruption to their daily lives as buyers walk through their home yet make no offers.
- They may reduce their profit expectations and lower their asking price.
- They may end up taking the property off the market until they can get what they want.

Meeting the Sellers' Price

Comparable sales prices help establish the listing price for the agent. It's interesting to note that although each property sells for a price consistent with other sales in the area, each sale met a seller's unique pricing objective.

This means that if a home sells for $400,000, a comparable home should also sell for about $400,000, but for different reasons. The key to a successful listing is to determine the objective or result the seller wants. Figure 6.2 details the different reasons two sellers have for selling.

Although both homes in Figure 6.2 have the same value on the same street, each seller's motive or the reason to sell is not the same. If an agent can discover the unique reason the seller wants to sell, it makes the presentation and acceptance of an offer much easier.

■ Enhancing a Property's Value

After taking a listing, agents must look for ways to increase the perceived value of the property before they attempt to market it. **Enhancing or intensifying the property's value** is quite a challenge, but it is part of the total product obligation. Obviously, you cannot change the features of a home, nor can you say things that are untrue. However, in both the marketing and sales process you can determine the buyers' motives for purchasing a property and explain the benefits of owning the selected listing so that the buyer perceives, understands, or recognizes a value that is at least equal to or higher than the listed price.

Figure 6.3

A Unique Headline

$435,000

~~$432,000~~

If you have always wanted a home that provides the complete range of family comfort for informal living…

Suppose a contractor builds two homes on adjoining lots. The homes are identical in almost every way. However, they are built for two speculators who intend to sell them immediately for a profit. Different agencies list each property. They are both priced at $328,500. One property sells for $328,500, the other sells for only $324,500. Shouldn't they have sold for the same price? What happened?

One of several things may have occurred to create this situation:

■ The seller accepted the $324,500 and the buyer outsold him, or the seller got what he wanted in the first place.

■ The buyer outsold the seller's agent. In other words, in the second home, the agent's sales techniques did not increase the perceived value of the property enough to warrant the $328,500 price.

■ The agent for the first home may have reinforced the prospect's perceived needs to the extent that the buyer felt she was getting a $330,000 value for only $328,500. An agent's marketing and sales efforts should create a perceived value that is higher than the price demanded.

Agents who are having a difficult time marketing a home that is priced just under market value may try this pricing strategy: Suppose the home is listed for $432,000. After getting contract approval from the seller to change the listing, emphasize the property's new price in the headline. In the new headline, cross out the original price of $432,000 and put $435,000 above it, as demonstrated in Figure 6.3.

Although the price was increased, this actual case produced so many calls that the agent sold this listing in three days, and two other properties besides. The consumer who purchased may have been motivated by the price increase, perhaps fearing that prices would rise even further.

Getting More for Their Money

The more features you convert to benefits and solutions, the easier it is for the buyers to accept the price and make the purchase. You also make it easier for the buyers to "look good" in the eyes of their friends. The buyers can brag about the great "deal" they got. When they brag about the low price they paid for the property, they almost always tell their friends about the agent who helped them discover such a find.

Agents who produce real estate infomercials for their local community stations can help enhance property and service values. They can explain the benefits of high R-Factor insulation, sturdy construction, wide overhangs, or a hip roof compared to a gable. Perhaps the buyers purchased the home because it met their size requirement. They may have purchased because it was in the neighborhood in which they wanted to live. Maybe the house had insulated windows and wide overhangs, which as the agent explained, would lower utility bills and perhaps allow the buyer to have more money for recreational interests. Perhaps this aspect of the total value or total product was not explained by another agent the buyers worked with when showing another home in the same tract. Some agencies have explored the benefits of increasing their service value by having all-in-one offices—escrow, lawyer, lender, and real estate company. All of these examples share a common theme. Prospects expect more.

■ Factors Influencing Property Pricing

In addition to comparative market data, other factors, such as the ones below, influence how you price the properties you list, or whether you take the listing at all.

■ You arrive at the property for a listing appointment only to find five other homes on the street with For Sale signs in their lawns. If you were a buyer, what would you think of the street? Many prospects might look at the number of signs and wonder why so many people want to move out of the neighborhood. Efforts should be made to work together with competitors so that perceptions such as this do not develop.

■ Your competition includes other agencies that are trying to beat you to that for-sale-by-owner (FSBO) property down the street. However, the competitive circle may be much broader than this. The biggest competitors facing you are sellers of their own property. After all, how many open houses and advertisements could a seller run for the amount of commission they might pay an agent? It's something to think about.

■ In some markets, another form of competition is the low cost of renting a house or an apartment. The low rent means that there may be a surplus of available housing on the market. This has a direct effect on the price of properties in the community.

■ Sellers are sometimes surprised at the total fees and commissions necessary to market a property. These costs include the underlying mortgage payoffs, the transfer costs, and potential capital gains taxes. Although there are significant tax exemptions on capital gains for personal residences, not all real estate sold is a personal residence. Some sellers may refuse to sell for any reason until their tax status or the capital gains taxes come down.

■ Successful agents know the price range and the style of homes to list. They list property based on what their research tells them about the size of the potential buyer pool. After all, what is the value of taking listings that are priced at $600,000 if there are very few in the marketplace who can afford them? In this case the pricing and the product strategy is affected by the demand for the products that are put into inventory.

■ Your Competition and Property Prices

Prices are known to fluctuate in a broad range because of economic expansions, recessions, increasing or decreasing interest rates, strict or easy credit requirements, increased foreclosures in a given area, and seller carry-back financing. All of these elements have an effect on the ultimate price of services and property.

Price Niche

Agents who specialize in properties within a certain price range employ a **price niche** strategy. Suppose you list property priced between $480,000 and $500,000. Perhaps you develop an advertising and promotional campaign around this niche. You generate a number of sales. What if an agency discovered an increased number of retirees moving to their area? It modifies its marketing efforts to list properties at prices that are affordable to this market segment. Its promotional campaigns attract retirees. Sales increase. Other agencies see what this agency is doing and start copying its actions. This form of competition could cause the agency's source of buyers or listings to diminish. However, additional market studies will help find another niche market that bases its decisions on price.

Overpriced Property

If a property is overpriced, advertising and promotional efforts may only yield more overpriced listings. Normally, an overpriced listing does not produce a quick sale. One can only imagine the long-term impact on the reputation of agents who consistently list overpriced properties.

■ Pricing, Product, and Your Target Market

Selecting a specific target market helps draw agents to particular types of homes, school districts, neighborhoods, price ranges, and more. When agents define their buyer segment, it helps establish the price range for the properties they list, as well as what features may motivate the prospects to take action.

As agents target their market, they may develop concerns that their competition will see their success and copy their actions. Other agents may start listing the same type of property. Oddly enough, to compete, you will not have to list properties at lower prices just to attract your target market.

Buyers negotiate several things of value. What the agent sells them is not so much a house and shelter, but a solution to their problem at a price they can justify. Their problem is not necessarily lack of a den. A den solves a property need. The problem may be the desire for the *recognition* they gain from acquiring a room big enough to show off their 100-year-old billiard table. Perhaps the need is a *hope* for the future or the *pride* they show by providing the best home they can for their family. Some people want to expend *less effort* or have *more power* and *control.* The purchase of one property over another may give buyers more *choices.* As discussed earlier, it is the *total product* that will ultimately justify the prices you charge for your services and products.

■ Summary

It seems like every buyer wants to negotiate the price. Often, they do this so they can brag about the great "deal" they made for the property. By selling the total product, agents enhance the value of the property without reducing the price. By increasing the value in the buyers' eyes, the buyers feel they were able to "pay less" for the property than it was really worth to them. Most agents don't bother selling the price; they sell the benefits. This increases the perceived value of the property or service, gets the sellers their price, makes a commission, gets referrals, and gives the buyers the opportunity to talk about the great "deal" they got through an agent who really understood them.

■ Multiple Choice Questions

1. Marketing the _____ is when you supply a property that meets the property and emotional needs of the target market so well that it appears underpriced to the buyer.
   a. property
   b. price
   c. total product
   d. agent's services

2. Which of the following causes real estate prices to go up?
   a. A declining supply of housing with a faster decline in demand
   b. A declining demand for housing with rising supply
   c. A rising demand for housing and a declining supply of housing
   d. Rising interest rates

3. Given all that buyers consider when making a purchase, which of the following *BEST* completes this statement: When buyers consider making an offer, they negotiate
   a. the price.
   b. things of value.
   c. improvements.
   d. the transfer date.

4. Why do most five-bedroom homes in a community hold a higher price than their four-bedroom counterparts?
   a. A slowing demand for five-bedroom homes causes the price to rise.
   b. Lenders take a greater risk financing loans on homes that are out of the norm.
   c. The supply of five-bedroom homes is often small.
   d. The increased supply of four-bedroom homes causes five-bedroom homes to rise.

5. If the Federal Reserve sees prices rising for the components of a house it may conclude that shortages will cause inflation, assuming demand stays constant or increases. What can the Fed do to slow this eventuality?
   a. Decrease interest rates now so that more people can buy before the prices rise further
   b. Decrease taxes so buyers have more money to work with
   c. Increase taxes to slow spending
   d. Influence thrifts to increase their interest rates to slow spending

■ Exercises

Exercise 1—Packaging a property for marketing and sale is a process familiar to many agents. A packaging event includes agents who ask sellers to keep the lawn mowed or turn on the lights just before a showing. Develop a list of items that will help sellers package their property for marketing and sale. The list should concern items both inside and outside the home, and it should be applicable to all sellers. In other words, it should be a one-size-fits-all, boilerplate form. When used in the field, agents would replace one or two items for items specific to the listed property.

Exercise 2—Develop an argument for the kinds of listings you would take given the following economic scenario: House prices have increased steadily for the past five years. The component costs of construction are rising. The availability of acreage for continued development is declining. Interest rates have steadily increased for the past six quarters. The affordability index is declining.

Exercise 3—When agents take a listing, they must look for ways to increase the perceived value of the property before they attempt to market it. Enhancing the value of a property is a challenge; however, by doing so prospects may perceive a value greater than the price paid for the property. Agents must not misrepresent the facts nor suggest things that are untrue. Instead they point out the amenities or features and how they benefit the prospects. Define a target market and what motivates them. Enhance the value of one of your recent listings or your existing home.

chapter seven

PRICING YOUR SERVICES

■ Learning Objectives

After the study and review of this chapter, you should be able to

- explain how to justify your service fees by enhancing their value;
- identify and describe some of the elements that are used to justify an agent's commission;
- anticipate questions from your prospects so that you can be paid what you are worth; and
- identify and describe some of the elements that are used to justify service pricing objectives for the real estate firm.

■ Key Terms

enhanced value	quality service	turnover
profit	standardized output	

Agents work for a fee or commission for services rendered. Commissions are usually a percentage of the selling price, but like fees, are always subject to negotiation. Federal law reinforces the act of negotiating the commission. In Chapter 9, we will find that under deceptive trade practices it is always illegal for agents to conspire together to fix brokerage fees or commissions. The rates and fee structures acceptable to any given state are beyond the scope of this text. Because laws are subject to change, you are encouraged to fully understand the federal laws and the laws of your state with regard to implementing any of the services pricing strategies within this chapter.

During periods of deflation, home sales decline, prices tumble, sellers' equity dries up, and few buyers are in sight. When sellers must sell, they want to negotiate the lowest commission possible. Agents want to negotiate a commission equal to their worth. However, until agents demonstrate otherwise, sellers presume that most agents employ similar marketing plans: they put property into the multiple listing service and have an agent tour, place a sign on the property, place a lock box on the property, have an open house, and advertise it.

As we have discussed in various parts of the text, sellers know that they can do all of these things without an agent. Multiple listing associations cannot prevent sellers from becoming members, and even if they did, they can still distribute the information on their property to all agencies in their area. Sellers can invite multiple agents to attend in-home brunches, they can put a sign on the property, and they are always home so a lock box is not needed. They can have an open house every day, and use thousands of dollars (what they would have spent on the agent's commission) to advertise the home. Therefore, agents must address how their services are different from those of their competition (including for sale by owners), and how to avoid the competitive spiral of negotiating a lower compensation for services rendered.

■ Personal Pricing Decisions

Some might say that pricing agent services depends on the price of the property or the economy. Although negotiated real estate commissions vary from office to office, most agents offer similar services. Without significant differentiation between agents or agencies, sellers' perceptions of the quality of services do not fluctuate very much. The pricing decisions for agent services are a reflection of the increased value prospects look for, such as quality, expertise, and the ability to perform. Additionally, issues such as the cost of the service and profits are recognized as company objectives and are considered when pricing agents' services. Other company objectives include the time and expense involved in the promotional strategies, and the desire to increase turnover and market share. Company objectives are discussed later in this chapter.

What Influences Personal Pricing Decisions?

Commission pricing decisions are influenced by many factors. The main factors, discussed below, are:

- Enhanced value
- Quality
- Expertise and professionalism
- Profit
- Performance
- What the market will bear

Enhanced Value

Enhanced value helps prospects perceive and understand that they are receiving more than what they are paying for. The added benefit involves two elements. The first is the mechanical aspects of the service, such as marketing/selling the property, returning phone calls, follow-up, and processing the paperwork. The second is the emotional aspects of the service. The emotional issues concern things such as how prospects feel when they hire what they perceive to be the best agency in the area and what that might say about them. Agents want to negotiate a fee equal to what they are worth. At the same time, they want to differentiate their services from their competitors. Increasing the value of agent services helps prospects perceive them to be of greater value than those represented by a competitor's fee. When the perceived value is increased, prospects are more likely to pay the agent's stated fee, even though a competitor's fee might be lower or the same. Nevertheless, with a higher fee and the perception of enhanced services comes a higher expectation of performance.

From a pricing strategy standpoint, higher commissions and bonuses yield faster sales. Properly priced listings with higher commission structures or bonuses offered at the beginning of the promotional campaign help assure that a listing will be on the show list of cooperating agents. Exposure to the marketplace sells real estate. This pricing strategy assures additional exposure in a shorter period of time. This often causes a quicker sale, and that is what the seller wants. If this is not the seller's goal, then agents should find out why.

The list below shows a few of the expanded services agents provide sellers that help substantiate the negotiated fee and/or the motivations behind a seller selecting a specific agent to market their property.

■ The prospect's use of an agent's special knowledge of a specific aspect of real estate (some prospects will only work with the best in their area)

■ Weekly updates on the status of a listing (often sellers are left in the dark after they sign the listing agreement or experience their first open house)

■ An attitude that the agent is helping the prospects purchase a service or listing, rather than selling it to the prospects (people do not like being sold things)

■ A quality of service that's measured by the reliability of the agent and responsiveness of the agent to the needs of the prospects (a well-prepared interview helps agents understand the prospects' needs and discover what is important to them, so the agent can perform accordingly)

■ A reputation for performance (positive word of mouth advertising is always a strong enhanced value)

■ A firm with a successful, long-standing history in the community (the reputation of the office is just as important as the reputation of the salesperson)

■ A commitment to follow up with the prospect before, during, and after the sale (prospects often feel they are ignored until there is a problem)

■ An empathic ability to listen to and understand the prospects' property and emotional needs (tie the emotional need to the property and help prospects recognize a higher perceived value that cannot easily or quickly be duplicated by the competitor)

Quality

The definition of quality is different for everyone. The intangible nature of a quality service is like water running through your fingers; it's difficult to get hold of. There are tangible attributes of quality, such as office appointments, professional attire, attitude of the personnel, and responsiveness to the prospects, but are these enough? Referrals to agents also suggest quality service. However, the prospects may wonder if the agent can perform as well for them too.

A quality service can't be evaluated as you would evaluate the quality of a laptop computer. If the quality of the laptop is not what was perceived, it can be returned for a refund. However, if the quality of the service is not as perceived, the prospects lose time and perhaps money. But how can the prospects evaluate an agent's services without potentially suffering the loss of time and money? Do they know enough about real estate or the duties of licensees to be able to judge a quality service over one that is not?

Although difficult, if agents prepare prospects during the qualifying meeting, quality services can be measured. This can be accomplished through **standardized output**. When you go into your favorite fast-food store anywhere in the country you know in advance the quality of the product you'll receive and the approximate price. One weakness of the real estate industry is its lack of a consistent or standardized output. Technology may standardize services over time. However, today this weakness in the industry provides some agents with an opportunity when pricing their quality services.

In many service industries, there is no standardized output or expectation that the quality services received from the one vendor will be repeated by the next. The unfortunate perception and perhaps the expectation among many is that poor services are the standard in the real estate industry. Fortunately, the qualifying meeting with the prospects gives agents the opportunity to understand how the customers define a quality product and a quality service. By listening to the prospects and quietly educating them during this meeting, agents prepare them for what to expect during the buying/selling process. When the unknown can be somewhat eliminated and an expectation of quality can be created, there is the development of a standardized product and a way to measure if quality services were provided. If prospects perceive that quality services were provided, then the agent's reputation is reinforced by word-of-mouth advertising. For some, the value of the services may have exceeded the price paid.

To help your prospects grasp the issue of standardized output, explain how one agent can sell a tract home and close the transaction in 45 days, yet a different agent, selling in the same tract with all of the same service companies, closes it in 90 days. Many things can cause this, such as changing interest rates, difficulty finding comparable sales, or qualifying the buyer at a higher rate. Ask the prospects how they feel about these issues. When prospects recognize what may transpire, it lessens their anxiety. A **quality service** is measured by letting prospects know what to expect, telling them what you will do, and then doing it.

Saving quality services. Prospects cannot "save" your services, so you could become less than a memory after the sale unless you have a marketing strategy to stay in touch. Keeping in touch and following up with your clients makes your quality service "tangible," something that your clients can retain. They will continue to appreciate your good service each time you follow up with them, just as they would appreciate their purchase of a laptop each time they used it. Tangible, quality service generates referrals—the most productive way to increase sales.

Expertise and Professionalism

The degree of expertise agents have in an area not only provides an example of enhanced value, but it also suggests a level of compensation. Agents may have an expertise in marketing commercial buildings or businesses. Because there are fewer agents with this kind of expertise, they should demand and receive a higher commission than those selling homes, for which the supply of agents tends to be much higher. If agents have a reputation for selling homes within a week, then they should be compensated accordingly.

When it comes to fees and commissions, agents must comply with the federal and state laws and the policies and procedures of the brokerage firm for which they work. Generally, agents have control over the price of their services because they can

- discount the price of their services,
- charge a higher price for their services, or
- charge what the market will bear.

If agents lower the price of their services, they may end up with more listings than they can properly handle. If they can't sell the high volume of properties they are listing, it may negatively affect their reputation and that of their company. Sellers may be attracted to low-priced salespeople or agencies because they perceive few, if any, differences between them. If this is the case, then prospects do not see the connection between higher brokerage fees and the agent's professionalism and expertise. It is the agent's job to change this perception.

Profit

Profit is the amount remaining after all expenses have been paid. We modify that in the personal services area to suggest that it is the commission paid for the services rendered. An agent's profit is affected by the pricing strategies he or she selects. Suppose you charged a low commission. Low commissions may directly affect profit margins. Certain channels of distribution close because of the lower fee. Co-op real estate agents may look at alternative properties before moving your listing closer to the top of their show list. If your agency developed a reputation for low commissions, co-op agents would have little incentive to get information on your listings. On the other hand, if you offered a bonus on every new listing if it sells within two weeks, the incentive to sell your listings would increase. This is a form of branding and positioning that is discussed later.

Unfortunately, the cost of the agent's services is of little concern to buyers, and they are probably right in feeling that your commission doesn't affect them. After all, if the seller didn't use the services of an agent, the savings most likely would not be passed on to the buyer. Therefore, reducing your commission is not necessarily an attraction to the buyer.

Agents can look to how the retail industry operates to develop a strategy for pricing a listing. Retail stores purchase their inventory wholesale and mark it up to account for operating costs and profit. During difficult retail cycles, they have the flexibility of decreasing their prices, thereby increasing the number of units sold and possibly increasing their bottom line.

Let's make this last point very clear. If the retailers' products don't sell, they have recourse. They reduce their expectations of profit and reduce the retail price. In other words, they originally bought the product for their shelves at a price too high for their current market.

Suppose agents were like retailers. When they take a listing, they are in essence "buying" a home wholesale. The wholesale price includes the sellers' profit. The resale price includes your commission, that is to say, your profit.

If the property doesn't sell, what happens? A retailer can't go back to the wholesaler and ask for a reduction in the wholesale price. If an agent acted like a retailer, the agent would have to take price reductions solely from the commission. (Sellers often request that agents reduce their commission to put the transaction together.)

One difference between a retailer and an agent is that the agent must always get the seller's authorization to make any changes. Can you imagine going back to the property owner and demanding that the seller allow you to reduce your commission? The seller would be very pleased. Instead, the offsetting effect is a reduction in the price of the property, which the seller must approve. This reduction pleases prospective buyers and may create a sale without reducing the seller's profit.

In this example, the agent was forced to reduce profits for one of two reasons. Either the agent did not properly "wholesale" the property (list it at the proper price) or other elements of the marketing mix were out of balance.

We can all understand how a decrease in prices may increase the demand for a listing in the short term. After all, this opens up another level of consumers who could not purchase the property prior to the price reduction. However, as we have seen in previous chapters, agents can increase demand and profits by increasing the perceived value of their listings or services.

One last point about profits: market values can change quickly. In down markets, it costs more for agents to sell a property. Property prices may have to be adjusted lower. Commissions often suffer in these markets. At the very time when costs are increasing for the agency, the sellers want to negotiate lower fees. Remind the sellers of what was discussed earlier. A smaller commission is not attractive to co-operative agents, so a major distribution channel closes to the agent and the seller.

Performance

We discussed the negative effect of discounting your commission too much, resulting in an increase in inventory. This affects your reputation with regard to performance. If you cannot sell the properties you list, word may get out that you can't perform. Therefore, at least one part of the continued demand for your services has nothing to do with their cost. It is more accurate to say that it is positive performance that results in continued demand.

During the interview, agents should take the time to learn what value sellers place on the commission earned by the agent. Agents should take the time to learn if the sellers have some preconceived ideas of what agents do to earn their commission. When you ask, the prospects will tell you how they expect you to earn your commission.

When sellers interview agents, they want to know what the agents will do to market or sell the property. Let's say the negotiated commission for a sale is $33,000. The sellers expect to hear a marketing plan that consists of more than putting a sign in the yard, securing a lock box on the property, putting the property in the multiple listing service, having an open house, and advertising it. Those are probably the same services that the last agent promised to perform for the seller. If you provide the same services, how are you different from your competitors? What motivates the sellers to list their property with you? Sellers want to know that the agent can do more for them than they can do for themselves. It is during the interview that the prospects and the agent discover the services needed, and therefore the value of those services.

The price of your service is directly related to the benefit received by the seller of the property. When you provide or offer a greater benefit (more than sellers expect), you have the right to ask for and receive a higher fee, or the right to be designated the exclusive listing agent.

The bottom line is that the price of your service is not really a factor in getting more listings. The thing that creates the demand for your service is your reputation for the ability to perform. Your ability to perform and your reputation are examples of enhanced value.

Ask for what you are worth.   If you wish to try for a higher commission and the sellers are a bit apprehensive, it's partly because they may have a lower threshold for disappointment. Even though they don't pay a commission unless the agent produces results, they don't want to lose the time it takes to show that the agent can't perform. The sellers must be assured that the services meet or exceed their expectations. To help overcome any apprehension, demonstrate confidence in your ability to perform by suggesting a sliding commission schedule. (Make sure you get the permission of your broker before trying this.) The conversation may sound something like this:

Seller: "I see that your commission is negotiable."

Agent: "Yes, that's correct. For homes, I charge anywhere from 7 to 9 percent. Which would you prefer?"

Agents must know their market environment, increase their service performance, and explain to the sellers the advantages of this form of pricing strategy. Higher commissions on real estate aren't needed for every property. However, some sellers need all the equity they can get out of their property. Increasing the brokerage fee is sometimes a better way to retain equity and speed the sale than decreasing the overall price of the property.

The following is what you may say:

> "If you would like, my fee could be 9 percent for the first 30 days, 8 percent for the next 30 days, 7 percent for the following 30 days, and then 5 percent until the expiration of the listing. Would that work for you?"

If you are confident in yourself, your marketing plan, and your ability to perform, the chances of receiving a rewarding compensation are quite high. As mentioned earlier, when high commissions are integrated into the marketing mix, additional distribution channels usually open up. As more agents show the property, the likelihood for a sale increases. Agents' marketing efforts can get very creative when they consistently get 1, 2, or 3 percent more than their competition, even in markets where the fees are generally declining. Real estate commissions are always negotiable; however, you must be aware of your market, state laws, or office procedures before attempting this kind of strategy.

When you perform, by consistently executing effective marketing plans that create sales, you have earned the right to charge a higher price for your services. To compete, your competition must match your services, develop a unique niche, or reduce their commission structure.

For some, higher prices suggest better services or a better ability to get the job done. Although some prospects only want to work with the best in the industry, and a higher price often reflects that quality, agents should not charge excessive fees. The prospects should not be put in a position to say that the services were fine, but the fee was too high.

Preparation avoids having to lower the price of your services or even the price of the property. So, list properties that meet the needs of your target market at the price they will pay, and provide a service where the value exceeds the commission charged.

What the Market Will Bear

Real estate commissions are negotiable. In addition to compensating agents for their experience, performance, and quality services, another element must be considered: commissions are negotiated by what the market will bear. Sellers may negotiate a lower fee when there are more qualified buyers in the market than agents know what to do with; however, when buyers are rare, commissions can and should be negotiated higher.

Usually at the peak or near the end of a strong real estate cycle, some agencies find it difficult to obtain listings because sellers are being approached directly by buyers. In this case, neither the sellers nor buyers recognize the need for an agent. Because listings are hard to get in these markets, some real estate franchises attempt to avoid competition by offering a low fee for their services in an attempt to capture as much of the limited market share as possible. Unfortunately, as we have said, many channels of distribution close and the seller may have to rely on the listing agency alone to sell the property.

Unless constrained by state or local laws, agents can negotiate whatever commission they wish with their customers. If a property owner needed to sell quickly, the owner might consider paying a higher commission to an agent that could perform. The agency and its agents must be careful with this strategy if they do not or cannot perform.

Many offices that operate on 100 percent commission give their agents more latitude. The owners of these offices require that the agents produce a certain amount of commission for the office before receiving their 100 percent commission for the balance of the year. They can also be charged a monthly fee in exchange for receiving 100 percent of the commission (less splits to other agents or offices). Subject to state laws, agents working in an office that pays a 100 percent commission may have the authority from their broker to negotiate whatever commission or fee they like. For example, the seller and the agent may negotiate a flat fee for full services, or a fee to follow the sales through the transfer process. Agents could reduce the negotiated commission if the seller supplies the buyer to the agent. They could charge as little as a 1 percent commission up to a percentage as high as can be negotiated with the seller.

Why pay more when I can get the same service for less?

Take the time to differentiate your services.

◼ Real Estate Companies: Service-Pricing Objectives

Real estate companies, independent of other agencies, may establish policies on how they price their services and the price range of properties they list. Their profit targets may require that they specialize in upper-end homes or acreage sales. Other offices may look for increased turnover to reach their profit targets, or have specific market share goals.

◼ What Influences a Company's Pricing Decisions?

The major factors that influence the decisions companies make about the price of their services are:

- ◼ Time and expenses
- ◼ Turnover
- ◼ Market share

Time and Expenses

Agents should determine what amount of time and cost are involved in selling a property. If they can't get an appropriate price for their services and the property, then in theory they should refuse the listing. Agents generally do not build a property for their inventory, but they can select the types of listings they accept. More costs are incurred the longer it takes to market a property. Every real estate company establishes its own pricing objectives. The policy and procedures manual, sales meetings, and the business culture within the agency pass these objectives along to the agent. Some offices list properties for a flat fee, others for a small commission plus expenses. It is a violation of federal law for brokers to conspire with competing agencies to set commissions or fees. However, based on the elements discussed in this chapter, they may establish commission targets within their privately owned office. These targets may never be met, however, because the commission is *always* negotiable with the prospects.

A Progressive Pricing Strategy

Imagine you are a new licensee. You read all about marketing and now you are ready to apply some of your newfound techniques. After discussing a comprehensive property and service pricing strategy with the seller, you get very excited about your first house listing at 8 percent! It is a well-priced property, in a slightly down market. The seller understood the advantages of a high commission, and needed to sell the home quickly. That night you set about organizing the marketing campaign you would start in the morning. You wondered what your broker would think. Perhaps he'd parade you out into the middle of the office and tell everyone about the listing and the high commission you were able to get.

The next day you took the listing in for the broker to review. When the broker got to the commission he looked up at you, and then down at the commission, and then up again at you. "What is this?" the broker asked. "I negotiated an 8 percent commission on a home!" The broker said, "We don't do that here."

The broker made you go back to the seller and rewrite the listing agreement for a lower commission. This isn't unusual; in fact this is a true story. You shouldn't expect this kind of reaction from all brokers, but it does make sense to understand an agency's pricing strategies before you accept a job with the company.

The more progressive offices allow their agents to price their services while in the field. Whatever method an agent uses, the commission negotiated will be dependent on the pricing strategies set by the office or the individual agent.

Turnover

Turnover measures how long it takes to sell homes in a particular price range in a given year. For example, if it takes six months to sell a home in a particular price range, then the turnover ratio for that price range is 2 (12 months divided by 6 months equals a turnover ratio of 2). Property turnover within the firm is another pricing approach some agencies monitor. The faster the turnover, that is to say how long it takes to sell the average home, the more commissions generated. If listed properties are not selling and all the other elements of the marketing mix seem to be working, the conclusion must be that the property prices do not represent the needs of the buying public or the pricing for the services is not generating enough activity. This doesn't necessarily mean that the agents' listings are overpriced. It may just mean that the inventory and/or prices are not what the buyers or cooperative agents want.

Knowing the needs of one or more target markets helps agents avoid listings that are of little value to them. Listing properties that are demanded by the market increases turnover, sales, and profitability.

Suppose you can put one of two types of properties into your inventory. Each is listed in a different price range. Assume you know your target market well. If $400,000 homes have a turnover ratio of 6 and $500,000 homes have a turnover ratio of 3, the marketing opportunity and pricing decision is made easier. What this means is that to sell a $400,000 home, it takes an average of two months (12 months divided by 6 turnovers). That equates to $2,400,000 in sales for the year ($400,000 multiplied by 6 turnovers). The $500,000 homes take an average of four months to sell (12 months divided by 3 turnovers). That equates to $1,500,000 in annual sales ($500,000 multiplied by 3 turnovers). When the turnover ratio is high, then the profit potential for the firm and its agents increases. However, as shown below in the discussion on market share, this may not always be the case.

Market Share

Having a good market share means that an agency or its agents are responsible for most of the sales in a geographic area (neighborhood, city, county, or state). The strategy used to price property or services can increase or maintain sales growth and market share. Agents can increase sales when they consistently price their listings in a way that is attractive to their target market. During recessions, agents have the flexibility to consider flat rate fees or fees for seller/buyer counseling to maintain market share.

Market share is used to evaluate the effectiveness of pricing. To do so, agencies measure the size of their total market. The total market may be as large as the geographic area of a particular state or city or as small as a 500-home tract. The agency's market share measures what percentage of the total sales it controls. Setting a base point, brokers watch the changes in sales to determine an increase or decrease in market share. The number of total sales in a given region is easily available through a title company. In addition to the other elements of the marketing mix, when measuring market share, consideration should also be given to the price of services.

Many agencies have discovered that profits do not necessarily go up when the number of sales increase. Suppose two companies are competing for total market share. One company lists and sells a $100,000 property for a $10,000 commission. The other company lists and sells three $30,000 properties, for a commission of $3,000 each, or $9,000. The second company produced three of the four sales that took place in the area. It has a 75 percent market share, but it did not make as much profit as the first company, which had only a 25 percent market share.

Agents should attempt to know everything there is to know about what's going on in their market. Though it is somewhat difficult to get the information on what other companies are doing, it can be done. For example, by researching past sales through the multiple listing service, you can generate records of the sales made by your competitors. This will not necessarily tell you everything they are selling, or the exact brokerage fees charged, but it should give you a good idea.

For points of comparison, you want to know where your competition is selling property, the sale prices of the properties they are selling, and what commissions they are charging. If you get the reputation of being a firm that lists overpriced properties that don't sell and you want a high commission on top of that, your market share will suffer.

It's a Property Sale!

Most retailers understand that price cuts are meant to be temporary. A unique idea in real estate is for an agency to select three or four properties for a special "sale."

Get the seller's written authorization to temporarily reduce their price (perhaps offset by your reduced commission) for a three- or four-day sale. Promote your weekend sales prices just as the retailers do. At the end of the "sale" period, raise the prices back to the original amount, or even higher. Make sure you advertise the changed price after the sale is over.

■ Summary

This chapter has explored how to enhance the value of agent services so that the commission charged appears inexpensive to the prospect. Decisions that affect service pricing include the quality of the service, the ability to perform, the expertise of the agent, and the profit goals of the salesperson and the broker. Commissions are negotiable and are ultimately the result of what the prospect is willing to pay.

In addition to a profit incentive, the real estate company's pricing objectives include the time and expense it takes to market the property. The brokerage fee must be enough to cover these expenses. The faster the agency can turn over its inventory through a balanced marketing mix and a service pricing strategy that encourages agents to show the property, the faster the commissions are generated. Ultimately, brokers would like to control a larger market share each year. The service pricing strategies used by their agents help increase turnover, increase profits, and secure a reputation for performance. This translates into high market share over the long term.

■ Multiple Choice Questions

1. Which of the following offers the *BEST* reason for enhancing your services?

    a. Enhanced services increase turnover, consequently decreasing profits.

    b. Providing enhanced services helps differentiate the agent from competitors.

    c. Higher commissions put more money into the agent's pocket.

    d. Enhanced services cost the broker less and therefore the turnover ratio is lower.

2. Which of the following represents the *BIGGEST* disadvantage of charging a low commission?

    a. Overall company profits decline.

    b. Prospects can't "save" the services.

    c. Channels of distribution close down.

    d. The turnover ratio increases.

3. Which of the following is not considered when a real estate company establishes its service pricing objectives?

    a. Turnover

    b. Performance

    c. Market share

    d. Time

4. What does a property turnover ratio of 3 mean?

    a. It means that the real estate office is selling three properties each month.

    b. It means that the real estate office is selling three properties a year in a particular price range.

    c. It means that properties in a particular price range take an average of three months to sell.

    d. It means that properties in a particular price range take an average of four months to sell.

5. Suppose a real estate company had 75 sales out of 100 in a tract of homes last year. This year they had 120 sales out of 130. This is an example of increasing the company's

    a. profits.

    b. turnover.

    c. market share.

    d. expense.

■ Exercises

Exercise 1—Agents want to get paid what they are worth. Minimally, they want to represent the seller over all other competitors. To do this they must offer what sellers perceive to be a better service. Until you are face to face with prospects, you will not know what perceptions they hold with regard to the service they need. So, during the marketing campaign agents must demonstrate how they are different and how those differences relate to their perceptions of the target market. List ten ways you would differentiate or enhance the value of your services and why they would be important to your target market.

Exercise 2—Professionalism is a determinant for getting paid what you are worth, but what is professionalism? Is it something that is seen or felt? How can it be measured? Is it possible to provide a quality service for one customer and be considered a professional and to provide the same service for another customer and be considered something less than professional? Prepare a report on how prospects may define and measure professionalism.

chapter eight

PLACE AND PROMOTION STRATEGY

8

■ Learning Objectives

After the study and review of this chapter, you should be able to

- define the concept of place and the elements it involves;
- describe the importance of speed, convenience, and condition to prospects;
- explain channels of distribution and recognize the difference between promotion and distribution;
- list and describe the three functions of real estate promotion;
- list and describe the four elements of the promotional mix;
- evaluate the steps prospects must take before making a purchase; and
- describe how promotional campaigns integrate the four elements of the promotional mix to provide a consistent message regarding a property or service.

■ Key Terms

branding	positioning	publicity
functions of promotion	promotional campaigns	sales promotions
noise	promotional mix	

Chapter 1 identified all of the elements of a marketing mix, better known as the four P's—product, price, promotion, and place. Chapter 7 discussed product and pricing strategies. This chapter examines place and promotion, the last two elements of the market mix. The chapters that follow—Part Two of this book—begin our discussions of real estate sales, and provide more detail to that aspect of the promotional strategy. Nevertheless, you should be aware that sales are a part of promotion and are discussed throughout this chapter.

Marketing professionals expand the use of the term *place* to include not just the location of the property but also how fast the property can be transferred to the prospects, and how the prospects learn about the availability of property listings.

It is one thing to make the information available through place strategies; it is quite another to develop the promotional message. These strategies have one thing in common. They all attempt to successfully communicate with prospects, persuade them to take action, and through repetition, remind them of who the agents are or what services they provide.

■ Place

From a marketing standpoint, place is defined as the agent's ability to deliver the property or service demanded by the marketplace. This requires that agents organize the activities needed to speed the delivery. Place also explains how the marketplace learns about the property or service. Place ties in well with promotional strategies because it provides the vehicle, or the channels of distribution, needed for the promotional strategy to be heard.

The four elements of the place strategy are:

1. Speed
2. Convenience
3. Condition
4. Channels of distribution

Speed, Convenience, and Condition

Speed. Multiple issues relevant to prospect needs and agent activities are addressed when using the word speed in a place strategy. Prospects want to know how long the real estate transfer may take, what to expect during loan processing, and how agents can save them time when looking for a home. From the agent's point of view, speed describes how quickly information can be disseminated to the public.

Convenience. The place strategy calls for the convenient and easy transfer of property to prospects. The prospects may want a newly constructed home but do not want to take the time to search for a lot and build. The convenience of a well-designed floor plan may motivate their interests in a new tract home development. If prospects know that there are five or six homes almost immediately available just behind the model, they may be willing to wait a short period for their completion.

Real estate offices must be convenient to the markets they serve. It may not be necessary to open additional offices, but the use of kiosks in malls or having an occasional presence at trade shows, swap meets, or career nights act as additional channels for the public to gain access to promotional information. The properties listed must meet the perceived location needs of the target market. Agents must coordinate the activities of the other professionals that contribute to the sale of a property. These include lenders, lawyers, title companies, escrow companies, and appraisers. Each of these carries part of the responsibility for delivering the title of a property to the prospects. Agents are responsible for making sure the process runs smoothly.

Condition.   The condition of the property and title are both part of the place strategy. The features within the home must be in good working order and the title must be verified as deliverable before an agent considers listing a property.

Channels of Distribution

Information about agent services or listings must be delivered in an efficient manner. Channels of distribution, which have been mentioned a few times in the text, now will be discussed in some detail. These channels describe the processes used by agents to deliver the promotional message to the public. Unlike the aspect of promotion that involves the message, the place strategy addresses how the message reaches the public via television, newspapers, radio, and others sources. However, in real estate, there seems to be some crossover between promotion and place. It is worthwhile to distinguish between the two and how information passes through various channels of distribution.

Not discounting other factors, sellers hire agents for their channels of distribution. This topic should be included in an agent's discussions with sellers of promotional campaigns without giving away what those channels are. Agents should spend some time explaining how buyers are going to become aware that the seller's property is available for sale. Sellers could hire any agent from any office. You want them to hire you, so show them how you are different from your competitors.

After agents take a listing, the sellers want the public made aware of the property as quickly as possible. Agents have some choices to make. They can personally take the information door to door, paint the billboard signs, create a newspaper and devote its use entirely to running real estate ads, or they can hire others who are more efficient at spreading the word. This suggests that agents could specialize in listings and distribution, and let another agent sell their listings. Assuming that listing property is one of the agent's strengths, then specializing in that area improves efficiency.

Figure 8.1

Examples of Channels
of Distribution

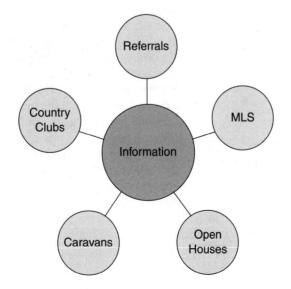

The importance of the message (promotional strategy) is matched only by the methods used to get that message out (place strategy). Think about a multiple listing service (MLS). Is the MLS service considered promotion or a channel of distribution? For the most part the MLS gets property information out into one channel. The agents who subscribe to the MLS have access to property information that is in that very important channel of distribution. Therefore, it serves a dual purpose.

Agents use a variety of channels in the hopes of finding a buyer as shown in Figure 8.1. This gives them a lot to think about when they consider that their competition has access to the same channels. However, their channels become decidedly more effective after a careful evaluation of their target market.

Types of channels. Real estate agents use a variety of channels of distribution. The following is an incomplete list of the more common channels. Can you add any?

- Multiple listing service
- Media selection
- Other real estate companies
- Client base
- Religious groups
- Referrals
- Open houses
- Previous customers
- Agent tours, sometimes called caravans
- Newspapers
- Magazines
- Television
- Radio
- Trade associations (e.g., medical, education, legal, apartment, mobile home)

When agents take a listing on a property, the sellers want to know how they are going to sell it. Keep in mind they want to hear something unique—different from what the other five agents they just interviewed said. Agents should explain that they could be the agent who sells the property; however, they intend to *market* the property by employing multiple channels of distribution, which include all agents or agencies in the community. This will enhance the exposure for the seller's property and open the possibility that other agents may sell the property, creating an opportunity for an even faster sale. The marketing channels used should not be limited to those mentioned above. Prior to 1990, few people had heard of or were using e-mail, the Internet, or cell phones. Today, they serve many real estate agents as additional channels of distribution. The point is to keep your eyes and ears open for opportunities to develop new ways of getting information to prospective buyers.

> ### Be Your Own Channel of Distribution
>
> A CPA entered a community with absolutely no clients. When asked how he was going to establish his client base, he explained that he was his channel of distribution.
>
> When asked what he was going to do, he explained that he'd created fliers and was going to distribute them at the local discount store every Saturday for six weeks. He did this and within a year he had 350 clients and sold his practice. Later, he was doing the same thing in northern California. This place strategy offers an underused method of distributing information. Have you ever seen a real estate agent passing out fliers at the local discount store? Try it. It works. (Be sure to get permission from the store manager. And don't leave the fliers on cars—hand them to individuals.)

■ Promotion

Promotion plays an instrumental role in successfully marketing real estate. It is probably the best-known strategy in real estate marketing. When we think of the word *promotion*, the first things that may come to mind are those pens with the agency name and address on the side. Thankfully, promotion involves more than free giveaways. The four elements of a promotional strategy are personal selling, advertising, sales promotion, and publicity. Personal selling is the best-known aspect of the promotional mix and is treated in more detail in the next section. When properly balanced, these four elements become a powerful marketing tool.

■ Functions of Real Estate Promotion

Promotional strategies develop a message that informs prospects about the availability of a property or service. Once prospects are attracted, the agent's message attempts to persuade prospects to overlook the distractions created by the competition and to use the agent's services. Reminding the prospects why they used the agent's services in the past and encouraging prospects to remember them in the future is an often-overlooked role of promotion and advertising. Louis Boone, and other marketing textbook authors, suggests that the **functions of promotion** are to inform, persuade, and remind prospects about listings and services.[9]

The Three Functions of Real Estate Promotion

- ■ Inform
- ■ Persuade
- ■ Remind

Inform

Communicating information is the foundation of a promotional strategy. The method of communication is broken down into two parts: direct and indirect communication.

---

9   Louis E. Boone and David L. Kurtz, *Contemporary Marketing Plus*, 8th ed. (Fort Worth: Harcourt Brace & Company, 1995), 601.

Direct (two-way) communication involves a marketing concept known as personal selling. There is an interaction between two or more parties. These interactions are usually face to face, however, telephone and Internet discussions may sometimes work.

Indirect (one-way) communication features one party providing information and the other receiving information, but the agent and the buyer are not necessarily interacting with one another. It's possible that a face-to-face meeting occurs, but if the prospects do not interact with the agent, then it is a one-way communication where the agent does all the talking. One-way communications most often involve advertising in newspapers, magazines, billboards, radio, and television. Indirect communications also include publicity and sales promotions. Many agents have successfully used the telephone to inform and sell multifamily residential properties and land. Some investors are familiar with the units in a given area, and don't need to see them, except as a condition of the closing. They are more interested in the numbers. Many land investors and developers are well aware of the geographic features of the land in which they are interested. These well-informed investors may respond to telephone and mail promotions. An offer and deposit is possible if they trust the numbers. However, most homebuyers would not buy a home without seeing it.

Finally, always keep in mind who you are informing. Don't lose site of your target market(s). This will ensure that you are getting the best use of your promotional dollars.

Communicate a solution.   The promotion process should describe how buyers benefit from owning a property. The development of a promotional strategy depends on the market segment agents are trying to attract. Suppose you have discovered several groups in the marketplace in which you would like to specialize. One group demands the very best, and seeks precision and accuracy. Another group wants to be recognized as having an elevated position in the community or high status, or perhaps just wants to be noticed. Still another group wants to appear prosperous, but save effort in doing so. How do you communicate a solution to these emotional or personal needs? Suppose you are listing on a 20-acre parcel with a large ranch house, corrals, and barns. The property is situated on a gentle rise, and very visible from the main road a quarter-mile away. From that distance, the passerby sees thousands of feet of shiny, white, double-rail fencing. The fencing is made of a durable plastic that never needs paint, and appears straight and even throughout.

Figure 8.2	PROSPECT	FEATURE(S) TO PROMOTE
Communicating a Solution	Precision and accuracy	Thousands of feet of shiny, white, double-rail fencing, that appears straight and even throughout
	Someone who wants to be noticed	House on a gentle rise that is visible from the main road; thousands of feet of shiny, white, double-rail fencing
	Someone who wants to be part of the elite in their community, but save effort in doing so	Large ranch house, visible from the road; shiny, white, double-rail fencing that never needs painting

Through your promotional efforts, communicate and inform the target market of solutions to their personal/emotional needs as shown in Figure 8.2.

Send a consistent message. Your personal selling tasks should be consistent with the rest of the promotional strategy. This means that advertising, sales promotion, publicity, and personal selling should not contradict one another. Suppose a prospect walked into your office and presented you with a coupon for a free appraisal. It wouldn't be appropriate to say, "We don't do those anymore." The promotional message to past and present customers should remain consistent among all publicity, advertisements, and sales promotions. In other words, if a sales promotion says one thing, then the other elements of the promotional mix should communicate the same thing.

Daily promotions. Communications with the marketplace should never stop. Daily promotions inform and remind the public that agents are still in business. Certain things are promoted on a daily basis. In other words, from day to day, there should be consistency in your communication efforts. This is not a complete list, but consideration should be given to the following:

- A real estate sign provides a daily reminder of the firm's existence.
- An office that maintains regular office hours suggests stability.
- A real person available to answer phone calls during the workday suggests reliability. If prospects call a real estate office and calls are connected to voice mail or not answered at all, they might wonder, "How will they have any time for me?"
- Promoting the benefits of in-office specialists, such as a lawyer, escrow company, property management, or lender, if these are available, adds value to your services.
- Returning telephone calls quickly or following up with brochures, in person or by e-mail, provides the level of attention propects may be seeking.

In each case, consistent communication helps inform the public of the benefits of your product or service.

Persuade

The second function of real estate promotion is to persuade the prospective buyer or seller to use that agent's services or buy their listings. The process of persuasion is something that can take a considerable amount of time. After all, can you imagine meeting someone for the first time and within ten minutes selling him or her a $650,000 property? The general size of a real estate transaction often prevents such a spontaneous purchase.

Persuasive Idea

Develop press releases about a property that coincide with your open house advertising. This promotional mix is even more persuasive when written to a targeted market.

Overcoming noise. Although messages seem clear when they are first written and conveyed, misinterpretation often distorts the meaning. As the message is forwarded through the channel, consumers can get distracted by other messages that affect the persuasiveness of the original message. This is called noise. Today, when comparing properties, lenders, interest rates, and real estate agents, your prospects face many choices. When you are trying to market your services or your listings, you don't want the prospect distracted by other messages, nor do you want them confused by your words or actions. Unfortunately, this does happen. It takes persuasive communications for the prospect to see through the noise.

Educated prospect pool.   Today, buyers and sellers are educating themselves about the market and the competencies of agents. To avoid the noise and other distractions of competing agents, your written and verbal communications must be persuasive and compelling. There must be a reason for the prospect to hire or call you over anyone else. Today, most families consist of two wage earners. These people are tired at the end of the day. Some have a need for a better home, but don't want to waste their free time with an inefficient, ineffective agent.

Agents must persuade buyers to choose to work with them over all others. After all, the buyers can buy a home listed in the multiple listing service from virtually any agent in town. They don't need any particular agent. Your promotional mix must differentiate your services and inventory from your competitors. It must demonstrate that you have a solid understanding of the buyers' needs *and* that you can provide them with solutions.

Remind

Promotional efforts not only communicate information and persuade people to action, but through repetition they remind customers of who you are and why they took the actions they did to work with you. Repetition is the key to this and any promotional effort. Staying in touch with past customers should yield referrals. At the same time, continued promotional efforts that remind the public who you are help secure new customers.

Professional real estate marketers are also aware of the distractions to which past customers and current prospects are subjected. Most buyers wait three to seven years before they are ready to sell their home. That is a lot of time for the buyer to forget the agent's name. When they decide to buy or sell again, they often use a different agent. Part of your promotional campaign should be to stay in touch with past customers, through direct mail, e-mail, the occasional phone call, or newspaper advertising. When the buyers are ready to sell the home you sold to them, you want to be in a position to help.

Reminders are useful during the presale and the postsale. In fact, agents have several opportunities to remind prospects that they are working for them.

Examples of tools agents use to remind prospects include:

- Advertising a name and slogan. This simple idea promotes the name of the firm and reminds sellers of the benefit they get from working with the agent. For example, "XYZ Realty, a HouseSold Name."
- Calling buyers/sellers once a week with an update. By calling the customer, you demonstrate your professionalism, rather than just talking about it. The call gives you the opportunity to remind the buyer/seller of the sometimes-cumbersome processes of the closing paperwork.

Sharing with the seller the multiple marketing steps agents use to create a sale may help renew the listing if just a little more time is needed.

- Sending two or three greeting cards each year. There are companies that will do this for you for a fee. In addition to handwriting the envelope and mailing the cards from your zip code, they also send you a list of the prospects that received a card within the past week. This way you have the option of calling those propects just to say hello or ask for a referral.

- Including your prospects on a mailing list. There are times when you have a property of tremendous value. You want to tell everyone about it. The first people on your list should be your past sellers, past buyers, and current prospective sellers and buyers. Send information on all kinds of properties. However, you want to assure your current prospective buyers that you are aware of their individual needs, so send other properties under a separate cover letter.

- Sending general boilerplate letters to all past customers. Let them know you are still around and find out if they are interested in more property, or if they know someone who is.

Examples of Tools Used to Remind

- Advertising your name and slogan
- Calling buyer/seller once a week throughout the transfer period
- Sending greeting cards throughout the year
- Placing all prospects on a mailing list
- Placing all past customers on a mailing list

Repetition. One communication isn't usually enough to get through the distractions of other competitors. Distributing promotional messages repeatedly helps break through the noise that is created by the promotional efforts of other agencies.

Although you advertise each week, a part of your promotional message or the promotional look should remain consistent until it no longer works. If agents in your community have not discovered how effective a photograph is, start running ads with your picture. Do this until several other agencies start doing it, and then look for an alternative promotional technique. In other words, don't create your own noise.

Don't I Know You?

Run advertising with your picture in the ad. When you are the first to use this technique you will find people take notice. Waiters and waitresses, store clerks, and people on the street will say that they think they know you. They don't know why. You must look familiar. It's really interesting to watch their facial features as they try to remember where you met. When you tell them you are in real estate, it's like you were a long lost friend. They tell you about how they saw you in an ad—just one ad, mind you! Agents should strive to stay ahead of their competitors' promotional messages. This technique may continue to work after it's discovered by two or three other agencies. To avoid the noise of competing advertisers, decide whether it is worthwhile to continue it. If not, drop it and move on to another technique.

Repetition acts as a solid way to remind prospects of the availability of your product or service. Remain creative, however; the same message repeated over and over becomes its own noise. Just like the FDIC sticker on the outside of a bank or the Equal Housing sticker in a real estate office, most consumers don't notice overused messages anymore.

Recessions.   If you slow down or stop reminding prospects of your existence during recessions you are in effect extending your company's recession. Real estate offices that do not practice marketing techniques have a tendency to get frustrated with their advertising results during economic recessions or other slowdowns. Instead, they try to hire more bodies, offer free sales training, and hope someone will sell something, while cutting back on their expensive advertising budget. After all, the advertising isn't working anyway.

Unfortunately, people are very slow to change, so it could take several months for a real estate company to convince prospective buyers that a recession is actually over. If agents stopped promoting themselves or their company, their recession could be extended.

Through a repetitive message, project the position that you are not going to participate in the recession. As others begin to believe your repetitive message, they may stop participating in their personal recession.

■ The Promotional Mix

The **promotional mix** is a combination of personal selling, advertising, publicity, and sales promotion with the purpose of informing, persuading, and reminding prospects of your products and services. Personal selling has the advantage of direct communication with the prospects. This is advantageous because it allows agents an interaction that is not possible in advertising. Agents sometimes forget that advertising is only the message; the place strategy, discussed at the beginning of this chapter, makes decisions on the vehicles used to deliver the message. Publicity is a form of free advertising. It's used to deliver a reminder message, educate the public, or tie in to other promotional messages. Sales promotion is a helpful tool in reminding the public of your services, as well as providing an incentive to act. The four elements of the promotional mix are discussed below in more detail.

The Four Elements of the Promotional Mix

- Personal selling
- Advertising
- Publicity
- Sales promotion

Personal Selling

Personal selling is a marketing term that describes prospects and agents who meet face to face and interact with one another. It is a direct form of communication, unlike advertising, publicity, or sales promotion.

There was a time when brokers who acted as land or tract home developers hired real estate salespeople to take the orders. The broker promoted the project to get buyers in front of their salespeople. The salespeople didn't have to list and market the property; they only had to have good salesmanship skills. Perhaps real estate offices stress salesmanship skills because it was done that way in our early history. However, things have changed. Today, salespeople are responsible to the seller for marketing *and* selling the property.

Personal selling is the element of promotion most familiar to agents. Many new agents dread personal selling. This is not unusual. New agents are afraid of saying the wrong thing. When they first start out, they are taught what seem to be disjointed techniques to get the buyer or seller to say yes. The office sales training seems overwhelming until they put it to use.

Training and other costs.   Real estate training is very expensive and time consuming for the broker/owner. Some offices prefer hiring only trained licensees. However, in order to differentiate their firm from others, some of the larger franchises offer extensive sales training.

Even after extensive training, it may take time for a new salesperson to produce a positive return for the broker. Unfortunately, some companies discover that after the training, new agents sometimes leave the firm to work for another agency. This suggests an inefficient use of the brokers' time and money. Increasingly today, more brokers are attempting to minimize their out-of-pocket costs by expecting salespeople to pay for the training themselves or attend college courses in real estate marketing.

Sales training can take many forms, from learning how to fill in the paperwork to techniques used to respond to an objection. As we will see in Chapter 12 and 13, agents learn phrases they can use to get a listing or close the sale, such as this alternative-choice closing question: Would you prefer to move in on June 12 or June 18? Some agents spend laborious hours learning multiple closing techniques. Yet without a basic understanding of marketing skills, it would be difficult for an agent to use this training. Salesmanship techniques require direct communications with prospects. Marketing skills help bring prospects to agents, so they can apply their salesmanship techniques. Without marketing skills, the costs to the broker and the agent, in time and money, can be even higher.

Figure 8.3

Sample Ad

Any City	**$118,000**
2182 sf, 3 yrs young! 4 bd, 2 baths. Small down.	
ABC Agency	**555-4321**

Advertising

An advertisement is often a printed message and is one part of the promotional strategy that informs, persuades, and reminds prospects about a product or service. It's easy to associate advertising with how messages are delivered to the marketplace. However, the messages in an advertisement and how those messages reach the public are two different topics. Nevertheless, it makes sense at this point to combine both for our discussion. Earlier, we saw that radio, newspapers, and television are often used in the place strategy to deliver the advertising message.

As a reminder, advertising consists of messages that are delivered through any nonpersonal media, meaning they require no personal selling. The radio offers a convenient distribution channel for persuasive messages because listeners can be doing something else at the same time. Television is an excellent delivery medium when an audio and visual message is desired. When agents intend to have the message last more than a few seconds, they use newspapers and magazines. Prospects clip out an ad and may have it lying around the house for several days before calling an agent. The ad offers a persuasive or informative message about a property or service. Agents prefer advertisements because they can reach a much larger market than one-on-one personal selling.

Rewrites.   When the advertising message does not produce calls agents often rewrite the advertisement. It is impossible to prepare promotional messages that appeal to everyone so agents should take the time to define their target market before spending the broker's limited funds on advertising. In fact, a rewrite generally takes another step toward finding a larger buyer market. If the phones are not ringing, a rewrite may help attract a different target market or discover a new target market.

Suppose an agent you know spends five minutes and comes up with the ad in Figure 8.3.

It's a gem, but it receives no calls. Apparently, no one in the total market was able to convert the features offered in this ad to discernable benefits. Consequently, with pressure from the seller, the agent commits more time to a rewrite, shown in Figure 8.4.

Suddenly, the phones start ringing. The agent says, "It's about time." Through the rewritten ad, the agent inadvertently discovered a target market—married couples with small children. We can't estimate the income level of the callers because no price was listed in the ad. However, we can deduce that the callers are concerned about the safety and security of their family. If this agent had identified this target market and other information that comes from

Figure 8.4

Rewrite

> ### Children Are Happier...
>
> ...in a roomy home. This 2,182-square-foot, 4-bedroom, 2-bath home lets you breathe a little easier. It's across from a park, offering your children room to play within your sight.
>
> ABC Agency, 555-4321

market research, the ad may have been more on target the first time. When preparing advertisements, you need to carefully consider word usage. Figure 8.5 contains a list of acceptable words and words that cannot be used in certain contexts in real estate advertising. This list changes from time to time, with both additions and deletions. To use these words improperly within a real estate advertisement could be a violation of both state and federal fair housing laws.

To avoid rewrites or to develop a more effective ad

- define your target market;
- identify elements in your listing that meet the needs of the target market; and
- advertise those features and their benefits in your first series of ads, not your last.

Emotional connection.   An agent's job is to develop promotional strategies that connect with prospects at a deeper level.

Prospects that have developed a need for a home have a sense of what it should look like. They have a sense for the kinds of activities they want to pursue in and around the home. Photographs of various activities are an excellent way to connect to the prospect emotionally.

Yet why do the pictures of homes in local newspapers seem so sterile? Keep in mind: prospective buyers want to know if your listings can provide them the benefits they perceive. Agents should not be afraid to experiment with photographs that have real people in them (just be sure to get any necessary releases from the people photographed). Imagine a summer advertising campaign in your local paper. You know what your competitors' picture ads look like. However, you want to create that emotional attachment. Here are some things to consider:

- Create a picture ad with backyard setting. Have a small boy doing a cannonball off a diving board.
- Perhaps you can demonstrate a low-maintenance yard by showing someone resting in a hammock with a tall glass of iced tea nearby.
- In the winter, take an interior picture of someone enjoying a book next to the warmth from a glowing fireplace.

Figure 8.5

Advertising Word List

This list of words and phrases is intended as a guideline to assist you in complying with state and federal fair housing laws. It is not intended as a complete list of every word or phrase that could violate local, state, or federal statutes.

Additional notes follow the list.

BOLD = not acceptable	*ITALIC = caution*	<u>UNDERLINED = acceptable</u>

<u># of bedrooms</u>
# of children
# of persons
<u># of sleeping areas</u>
55 and older community*
able-bodied
active
adult community
adult living
adult park
adults only
African, no
agile
AIDS, no
alcoholics, no
American Indians, no
Appalachian, no
Asian
<u>assistance animal(s)</u>
<u>assistance animal(s) only</u>
bachelor
bachelor pad
blacks, no
blind, no
board approval required
Catholic
Caucasian
Chicano, no
children, no
Chinese
Christian
churches, near
<u>college students, no</u>
colored
congregation
<u>convalescent home</u>
<u>convenient to</u>
couple
couples only
<u>credit check required</u>
crippled, no
curfew
deaf, no

<u>den</u>
disabled, no
domestics, quarters
<u>drug users, no</u>
<u>drugs, no</u>
employed, must be
empty nesters
English only
<u>Equal Housing Opportunity</u>
ethnic references
exclusive
executive
<u>families welcome</u>
families, no
<u>family room</u>
<u>family, great for</u>
female roommate**
female(s) only**
<u>fixer-upper</u>
<u>gated community</u>
gays, no
gender
golden-agers only
<u>golf course, near</u>
group home(s) no
<u>guest house</u>
<u>handicap accessible</u>
handicap parking, no
handicapped, not for
healthy only
Hindu
Hispanic, no
HIV, no
housing for older persons/ seniors*
Hungarian, no
ideal for . . . (should not describe people)
impaired, no
Indian, no
integrated
Irish, no

Italian, no
Jewish
<u>kids welcome</u>
landmark reference
Latino, no
lesbians, no
male roommate**
males(s) only**
man (men) only**
mature
mature complex
mature couple
mature individuals
mature person(s)
membership approval required
<u>membership available</u>
mentally handicapped, no
mentally ill, no
Mexican, no
Mexican-American, no
migrant workers, no
Mormon Temple
Mosque
<u>mother-in-law apartment</u>
Muslim
nanny's room
nationality
near
Negro, no
<u>neighborhood name</u>
<u>newlyweds</u>
<u>nice</u>
<u>nonsmokers</u>
<u>nursery</u>
<u>nursing home</u>
Older person(s)
one child
one person
Oriental, no
parish

<u>perfect for . . . (should not describe people)</u>
<u>pets limited to assistance animals</u>
pets, no
Philippine or Philippinos, no
physically fit
play area, no
preferred community
prestigious
<u>privacy</u>
private
<u>private driveway</u>
<u>private entrance</u>
<u>private property</u>
<u>private setting</u>
<u>public transportation (near)</u>
Puerto Rican, no
<u>quality construction</u>
quality neighborhood
<u>quiet</u>
<u>quiet neighborhood</u>
<u>references required</u>
religious references
responsible
restricted
retarded, no
retirees
retirement home
<u>safe neighborhood</u>
school name or school district
<u>se habla español</u>
<u>seasonal rates</u>
<u>seasonal worker(s), no</u>
secluded
<u>section 8 accepted/ welcome</u>
section 8, no
secure
<u>security provided</u>
senior adult community*

senior citizen(s)*
senior discount
senior housing*
senior(s)*
sex or gender**
shrine
<u>single family home</u>
single person
single woman, man**
singles only
sixty-two and older community*
<u>smoker(s), no</u>
<u>smoking, no</u>
snowbirds*
<u>sober</u>
sophisticated
<u>Spanish speaking</u>
Spanish speaking, no
<u>square feet</u>
straight only
<u>student(s)</u>
students, no
Supplemental Security Income (SSI), no
synagogue, near
temple, near
tenant (description of)
<u>townhouse</u>
traditional neighborhood
<u>traditional style</u>
tranquil setting
two people
unemployed, no
<u>verifiable income</u>
walking distance of, within
wheelchairs, no
white
white(s) only
<u>winter rental rates</u>
winter/summer visitors*
woman (women) only**

* Permitted to be used only when complex or development qualifies as housing for older persons

** Permitted to be used only when describing shared living areas or dwelling units used exclusively as dormitory facilities by educational institutions.

All cautionary words are unacceptable if utilized in a context that states an unlawful preference or limitation. <u>Furthermore, all cautionary words are "red flags" to fair housing enforcement agencies. Use of these words will only serve to invite further investigation and/or testing.</u>

Source: Miami Valley Fair Housing Center, Inc., Dayton, Ohio (www.myfairhousing.com). Used with permission.

Take a moment to reflect on how a prospect might respond to these visual ads. Do you think the seller would want to become involved in the development of the advertisement? More importantly, do you think a buyer might become more emotionally attached to the benefits you are portraying through the visual media?

Advertising and other forms of promotion are often broken down into two categories: product advertising that promotes listings and institutional advertising that promotes the firm. Unless the ads give prospects a reason to call, it is difficult to measure the results of institutional advertising. As a result, many brokers use publicity to promote their office and individual salespeople, rather than the listings they market.

Publicity

Publicity is a message that is not paid for by agents but must be controlled by the agent as much as possible. Publicity can be a powerful tool when controlled by agents. Publicity educates the public about issues involving the real estate industry or the image of the agent/agency. The credibility of the message is enhanced when published by an outside vendor, such as a newspaper. There can easily be good publicity and bad publicity.

Good publicity.   To accomplish good publicity the agent has to exercise as much control as possible by helping the newspaper or other media outlet to get the right facts.

For example, suppose an agent conducted an "open lot" by posting three balloons at each corner of the lot. Near the front of the lot, the agent set up a desk, a roller board, chairs, a filing cabinet, and even a potted plant and an office telephone (not connected to anything). Somehow, the local paper heard about it (a well-placed telephone call may do the trick) and the press was invited to come to the open lot. After all, everyone else was holding open houses that weekend and where's the story in that?

This was a unique promotional idea, and worth the extra coverage. To manage the publicity, the agent provided the reporter with information on how he developed the idea. The next day, he gave the reporter additional information on how well it was received.

Bad publicity.   Publicity can also have a negative impact on your business. It doesn't always have to be about you or your agency. You may open the morning paper and find a front-page news item about the real estate industry in general. There are almost always articles about the economy. If inflationary pressures cause interest rates to rise there should be a concerted effort to counter this bad economic news by using a press release. This is a difficult task for an individual real estate company, but is something the local real estate associations should be encouraged to do.

Who writes the press releases and how?   Your real estate broker is not the only one who can write press releases. Unless the contract with your broker says something to the contrary, you can write publicity stories and press releases about your accomplishments, unusual properties, or perhaps your unusual sales methods. It is still a very good idea to pass these through your broker before publication.

Vary the size of your press releases. Each release can be on the same topic, but write one that is only two paragraphs long, make another a page long, and the last no longer than two pages. The paper will appreciate the time you take to edit your releases to various sizes. It saves reporters and editors the work of trying to come up with short articles to fill space.

Your releases should be double-spaced and typed. Try to include a photograph because it helps draw attention to the press release. Important to the continued placement of your articles is a reputation for writing well and a working relationship with your newspaper account executive.

Sales Promotion

Sales promotion includes activities that persuade, remind, or inform, but that do not involve personal selling, advertising, or publicity. Sales promotions can be more than ink pens and calendar giveaways.

Sales promotions are used as incentives for buyers, sellers, and agents to do something. The problem with certain types of sales promotions is that they have been used so much that many are not as effective as they once were (such as offering a free home appraisal). Nevertheless, sales promotion provides an enormous opportunity for agents who have learned to differentiate themselves from other agents by using thoughtful marketing techniques, including unique sales promotion ideas.

Sales promotions may help get a prospect in front of you so that they can compare your services to other agents.

Use your imagination.   Promotions are aimed at four receivers: the prospective buyer, the seller of property, and the sales forces of the listing office and competing selling offices. Effective promotions vary with the imagination of the agent and the needs of the targeted market. Although the following ideas are not unique, they may help stimulate your imagination:

■ Offer a bonus to the selling agent (through their agency) if a property is sold within three days. This is most effective when the property is first listed for sale or offered at an agent tour if it's within the first week or so of listing availability.

■ Have an annual party for all of your buyers and sellers. One agent had his usually around Christmas. He never forgot those on the other side of the closed transaction. In other words, if your office represented only the seller, don't hesitate to invite the buyer to your party. It is highly possible that they have been "orphaned" by the co-operating agency.

■ Develop a fold-over business card or a note pad with local emergency phone numbers.

■ During the summer, hold raffles for game software, sporting equipment, and bookstore gift certificates.

■ If you work a specialized geographic area, walk it on a rainy day and give away rain hats. The prospect will never forget it.

■ Offer free warranty insurance with every purchase of homes within a certain price range.

- Offer free special services to people that have active listings with you. These include use of your copier and fax, Internet access, and substantial referral fees to agents outside your area.

- Offer a limousine shuttle service to and from the office for that special buyer.

- With every closing, present the buyers with a gift certificate for plants, flowers, or shrubs for their new home.

- Pay half the title or escrow fee for the buyer, the seller, or both—it depends on which target market you are going after.

- To attract a buyer, offer a one-year subscription to the local newspaper and one other paper.

- Offer free landscape planning software if your target market includes those who enjoy the outdoors and have a need to create and control their own environment.

- Put a property "on sale." Depending on the price and the permission of the seller, offer a $5,000 discount until X date.

- Some of the more traditional promotional items include note pads, free pens, T-shirts, and watches with the company name prominently displayed. Coupons for a free appraisal are becoming more common, and therefore less effective.

(Note that each state requires that agents be in compliance with local real estate laws and regulations. This list is provided to stimulate ideas; however, a comprehensive review of state laws is beyond the scope of this text. Agents should review the regulations and laws within their state before implementing promotional strategies.)

With your imagination, you can easily expand this list. Consider electronic sales promotions, a minicatalog of your listings, a three-day price reduction on selected properties, computer disc programs to manage personal property inventory, and videocassette or DVD promotions. Keep in mind sales promotions are typically short term in nature. Long-term promotions are possible but lose their value when the competition observes your success and copies it.

In some offices, sales contests motivate salespeople to perform at a higher level. The contests could result in anything from a preferred parking spot to a one-week luxury cruise. When brokers have sales promotions for their agents they might include a percentage or dollar bonus to their selling salespeople or a higher commission split if they experience a certain level of dollar activity within specific periods of time.

■ Before the Purchase

There are several reasons prospects in need do not respond to well-prepared promotional messages that are directed at specific target markets. Almost all buyers go through a process that prepares them to purchase.

At the earliest point in this process, prospects may learn about their need for real estate from an agent's advertising, publicity releases, brochures, newsletters, or news articles. As buyers become aware of their needs, they become aware of specific agents and agencies. Additional promotional efforts, such as a postcard that shows that a neighbor down the street is selling their home, helps prospects become aware that others, perhaps friends or neighbors, are buying and selling real estate while they are not. The economy, prices, and interest rates start to affect their motivation to do something.

All buyers probably find it difficult to make a higher-priced purchase without some knowledge of the property or service. As prospects gain more knowledge about their needs and an agent's services, they move closer to making a purchase decision. The last critical steps come when prospects consider contacting an agent. They may tell others that they are thinking of buying real estate or selling their home. The reason for telling others is to confirm how their friends will respond if they decide to purchase. If the feedback they get is positive, the prospect may choose to work with one agent over another. The sale is almost made. Prospects buy after they have educated themselves, looked at the alternatives, and discovered their needs. They buy after they have an idea of what people will think of them for the purchase decision. Prospects buy when all of this is learned and understood.

Your communication efforts must be designed to attract members of specific target markets with the understanding that all prospects are at different stages in the purchasing process. This means that your promotional campaign should address those first-time buyers who have yet to start looking for a home as well as those who purchased their last property 20 years ago and are now looking for a new agent to represent them. Just as you wouldn't give a book on biology to someone who wants to read about history, you should not develop promotional campaigns that do not address the interests of the targeted market.

> ### Promotions Are Often the Best Way to Attract Targeted Customers
> Your research shows that working women head more than 25 percent of U.S. households. If your target market included women who were heads of household, how would you attract them?
>
> Here's a suggestion: Develop office parties during which you serve cheese and crackers and offer a variety of beverages. Give tours of the office. Offer door prizes such as books on investing, free home warranty insurance, and subscriptions to newspapers and magazines. During the party, display color pictures and slides of properties best suited for your target market. Make presentations on property and financial alternatives to meet their needs.

■ Promotional Campaigns

Promotional campaigns distribute information in a coordinated way. The campaigns seek to position the company or the licensee ahead of all competitors, differentiate its services and products, and characterize (brand) the reasons people identify with its listings and services. The three elements of a promotional campaign are:

1. Branding
2. Differentiating the product or service
3. Positioning

Each element of a promotional mix can act independently of one another. Agents can write ads in an attempt to sell a property. They also can promote an upcoming weekend open house, and execute sales during the week. However, promotional campaigns coordinate these efforts in an attempt to point out the differences between properties and agencies, and to position the property or the agent's services in the minds of the consumer.

For example, a company that specializes in view properties uses the following slogan: The sky is the limit. Its *publicity* during the week might talk about a unique open house on the weekend on top of a hill with an unlimited view. The *sales promotion* during the same week could mention the open house and a tethered balloon ride to get another perspective of this spectacular home. Lastly, the *advertising* could promote the open house.

Branding

In the traditional marketing sense, branding a product includes things like the product's trademark or a brand name, such as Kellogg's®, Tums®, and Campbell's® Soup. For our purposes, envision branding as searing into the mind of the consumer the usefulness of a property or the reputation of an agent or agency. **Branding** creates the reasons people identify with the product. For example, branding points out the differences between real estate franchises, such as Century 21®, Coldwell Banker®, or Keller Williams®.

Agents can also work to brand a listing. Though similar to differentiating a product like an antacid or a breakfast cereal, when branding a listing, agents attempt to find how its unique features affect the prospect personally, and demonstrate how these features are different from anything else on the market. Don't get this confused with pointing out unique brands within the home, although that can be part of it. Having Pella® windows in a home in a particular community may differentiate that listing from others in the area. However, try to go a bit deeper. A home that is in a retirement community may be branded as attractive to someone who wants to develop closer relationships with others. Conversely, a Frank Lloyd Wright home is a brand unto itself; however, it may be alternatively branded as attractive to someone who is interested more in accuracy, precision, and correctness. Promotional campaigns are used to point out these elements and what they mean to prospects.

Promotional campaigns are useful in branding agents, as well. For example, an agent could be branded as someone who offers a unique style of customer service, specializes in specific types of listings or market segments, or is known for his or her reputation in the community. Some agents use their pricing strategy to develop a brand that stands out from their competitors. Imagine having the reputation for paying agents, through their brokers, a bonus of 20 or 30 percent of your commission for selling your listings within two weeks of the listing date. This kind of branding increases sales and demonstrates to property owners your commitment to creating an environment that helps satisfy their needs.

A buyer can purchase property from any real estate agent or directly through the seller. Buyers may be persuaded to use the services of a specific agent because of a successful promotional campaign. Building positive first impressions helps agents brand their name into the minds of the public. Part of the promotional campaign should consistently remind the public of your professional image and self-image, which is demonstrated in many ways and will be discussed fully in Chapter 10. When you enter your office take a look around to see how it affects your reputation.

- Are the agents' desks so cluttered and unorganized it appears there is not enough room to write up a sales offer?
- Are the agents well mannered or are they having their lunch over a trashcan?
- Are the agents on time for appointments?
- Do they call their buyers and sellers with weekly updates?
- Are the office secretary and the agents using computers to help the client or are the computers just window dressing?
- Are any of the following present?
    - Articulate, well-educated licensees and staff
    - Distinctive signs and stationery
    - Well appointed office including wall hangings, furniture, decorations, lighting, plants
    - Efficient use of the customers' time

Information Exposes the Differences: Differentiation

Because of the public perception that all agents' services are the same, it can be extremely difficult for agents to develop a brand that is truly different from that of their competitors. How can agents go beyond branding to educate the public about the differences between them and their competition? Promotional campaigns create the message that differentiates agents' services and properties from those of their competitors. Let's address the service side first.

The services: stand out among your competitors.   Your promotional efforts help you stand out and become memorable and different. Without distribution strategies and promotional campaigns that develop information that shows how you are different from your competitor, buyers/sellers have no reason to seek you out. The key to differentiating your service from that of others is to be original. If you are not original, you are not different; you are just the same as someone else. One way to differentiate your service could be to offer to pick up clients on a motorcycle with an enclosed four-seat sidecar; now that's different.

You're Full of Hay!

One dynamic salesperson sends a small box full of hay to those special ranch properties he is trying to list. Inside the box, resting on top of the hay, is a card that reads: "Trying to find a professional agent is like trying to find a needle in a haystack." On the back of the card is his address and phone number. The card is attached to a piece of yarn. You guessed it. As the card is pulled, the yarn slithers out of the hay, and at the end of the yarn is a needle. It's impressive and is very successful.

The property.   The second kind of differentiation agents face involves the property. How can agents make their listings different without changing them? Agents must find that unique feature in a property and point out its uniqueness as it relates to the needs of the target market. The purpose of this process is to build a preference for the agent's listings.

Through personal selling and other forms of promotion, the agent helps buyers differentiate between two seemingly identical properties.

Environmental concerns and the increasing use and cost of energy have influenced what buyers look for in a home. During the 1970s, buyers were more concerned about energy efficiency and insulation. Today, energy, radon, and asbestos are the hot issues. Let's use the energy crisis to demonstrate how you might differentiate between two similar homes.

Suppose you find that the target market has a growing concern about energy supplies and the increasing costs of their utility bills. Your promotional efforts should describe features that stress energy savings. In the presentation, remind the prospects that your area of the country requires that attics have a minimum of R-39 insulation. Then inform them that for improved efficiency the attic in the home they are currently viewing has R-60 insulation.

"It helps keep the heat out in the summer, and it's like putting a warm blanket over you in the winter."

Even though the five homes you showed that day were all similar, your statement helped differentiate the last home from the others.

Find the centerpiece.   Using one component of a property as the centerpiece of the promotional campaign attracts a certain kind of buyer. A home advertised as using 30 percent less energy than other homes its size (confirmed by a utility company), shows how the property is different from the others. Then again, your promotional campaign may focus on another aspect of the same property, perhaps the view, which you use to further differentiate the property from its competitors and attract a different target market.

Use your research.   Suppose your research concluded that the largest portion of the total market wanted a large side yard or other area in which to store a boat or RV. If your listing has this feature, then the promotional campaign should feature the storage area.

Doing what is different gets you noticed.   Take the time to identify how your product compares to that of your competition. There is no point in promoting the same things as your competition. Suppose your competition's advertisement promotes three bedrooms, two baths, a large patio, and a two-car garage for $X. There's no need to promote the same features, unless you promote them with a purpose that is directed to your target market. Instead of just mentioning the large patio, say, "This summer, your neighbors will appreciate the scent of steaks sizzling on your built-in BBQ on this family-sized patio." Be different in your approach. If your competition does not or cannot offer the limousine service or a motorcycle pick-up service we discussed earlier, promote it like crazy.

If the property only consisted of four exterior walls, a concrete slab, and a roof, how would you promote it? By now, you should realize that the answer comes more from the target market of prospective buyers than it does from the property itself.

Don't get in a rut. To make a property unique relative to other seemingly similar properties, describe its benefits. Do you remember the insulation example from above? The agent mentioned the insulation and described the benefit—it would feel like a warm blanket in the middle of winter.

When evaluating the promotional campaign for a property, pretend the property is just the same as everyone else's (three bedrooms, two baths, a living room—you know how the ads look). However, instead of thinking about the property's features, concentrate your promotional campaign on the benefits that your target market will receive by owning your listing.

Ask the seller for help. When you take the listing, ask the sellers what they feel is unique about their property. Ask them why they bought the property. When you identify what attracted the seller to their home, you help identify a target market that can be attracted with your promotional campaign.

In the last several chapters, you have discovered that the properties you sell are more than a building on a lot with a view. They have more value than the walls, paint color, carpeting, new roof, and three-car garage; but what is that value? Suppose you advertise or show a home with a view. You go on and on about the view, the benefits of the view, and how much you enjoy the view. If the view doesn't mean anything to the buyer or the target market, it is of no value. When developing a promotional campaign be sure to enhance the value of a property with features that mean something to the target market. Often those features will be the same things that attracted the current owner to the property.

Positioning

When a market segment thinks of one agent or one agency, that is the result of **positioning**. Where branding concerns the uniqueness or usefulness of a property or the reputation of an agent or agency, positioning ranks the agent or agency into the minds of consumers. Consumers are more informed today about products in the marketplace than at any time in our history. Multiple forms of media, such as television, radio, the Internet, telephones, billboards, magazines, and newspapers bombard consumers with promotional messages on a daily basis. How is anyone to hear your message?

Positioning helps brush aside some of the noise that consumers see, hear, or read every day. There are a number of breakfast cereals that contain 100 calories per serving, without milk. Yet, in 2005 Kellogg's Special K® positioned itself to attract consumers who wanted to lose weight. Kellogg's promoted that you could lose six pounds in two weeks by eating a bowl of its cereal for two of your three meals per day. This may prove to be a profitable short-term positioning campaign. However, General Mills® Corn Chex® has the same amount of calories as Kellogg's Special K. If General Mills and others feel their position in the market weakened in any way, they may come out with similar claims and weaken the positioning attempted by Kellogg's.

Positioning helps attract an element of the market to your product. Untrained salespeople are attracted to agencies that have positioned themselves as providing the best training for new licensees. It could be that they are attracted to the office that has positioned itself to be a specialist in acreage or multifamily residential sales. Smaller companies often suggest that they can be more responsive to the needs of their prospects compared to their larger counterparts. This will not pose a problem unless the competition feels threatened and decides to come out with its own promotional campaign designed to reduce the threat. As an agent, you must be aware of how your competition has positioned itself and be prepared to meet this challenge if it begins to infringe on your market share.

Real estate is a competitive industry. As an agent your promotional efforts must help position you in the minds of the target market. What does this mean? Who sells the highest quality, higher-priced homes in your community? If you know the answer, you have discovered a firm that has positioned itself in the market.

Here's something to ponder. When a real estate agency claims to be number one, does anyone claim to be number two? No? Perhaps a small firm can position itself to be number two in the community because it is flexible and more responsive to the needs of its customers than the high-volume agency that is number one. Agents also position themselves among other agents. Agents who pay a bonus to any agency that sells their listings within two weeks of the listing date may have positioned themselves to be number one among their peers.

Can you be positioned as number one or number two in your area? Of course you can, but first you must take a bold step and declare it.

■ The Marketing Plan

You should now have a strong sense of the many marketing tactics that bring customers to an agent's office. The final step in deploying a complete marketing strategy is to develop a marketing plan. A marketing plan guides agent decision making for a period—a month, a quarter, or the entire year—so that marketing activities are fully planned and integrated into day-to-day operations. It is the result of market research and analysis and the integration of a balanced marketing mix (product, price, promotion, and distribution). You should keep in mind that there is no one format for a marketing plan. Its design is based on what the agent wants to accomplish. In the appendix is a sample outline of a marketing plan with explanations and examples for the topics and subtopics. You are encouraged to review this appendix and add additional topics as needed to create your own marketing plan.

■ Summary

The marketing mix consists of the four elements of product, price, place, and promotion. This chapter discussed place and promotional strategies. Place strategies include property availability, the speed of transfer, and the channels used to distribute information about an agent's listings or services.

Promotional strategies may be the most influential in the marketing mix. The promotional mix consists of four areas—personal selling, advertising, public relations, and sales promotion. Agents typically place the most emphasis on advertising and personal selling. Promotional campaigns integrate the four areas of the promotional strategy so that messages are consistent in all of them.

■ Multiple Choice Questions

1. Which of the four P's addresses activities such as explaining what to expect during loan processing or delivering a home to the prospects in a timely manner?
   a. Product
   b. Price
   c. Place
   d. Promotion

2. Which of the following is *NOT* an element of promotion?
   a. Publicity
   b. Advertising
   c. Personal selling
   d. Product development

3. The function of real estate promotion is to communicate, _____, and remind.
   a. list
   b. position
   c. persuade
   d. understand

4. Which of the following is used in a place strategy?
   a. An advertisement
   b. A listing
   c. A newspaper
   d. A price reduction

5. Offering a bonus commission to the selling agent is a form of
   a. advertising.
   b. publicity.
   c. sales promotion.
   d. good publicity.

■ Exercises

Exercise 1—Sales promotions are used as incentives to get prospects to act. The prospects include other real estate agents, as well as buyers and sellers. It's sometimes difficult to create a unique sales promotion. A free appraisal has been done so much that most prospects are not motivated by it. Develop a list of five sales promotions that may be attractive to your target market.

Exercise 2—Pull a listing from the multiple listing service, or visit an open house, and develop an advertising message. The message should stress benefits instead of property descriptions and should be applicable to your target market. Describe the place strategy you would use to reach your target market.

Exercise 3—Promotional campaigns distribute information in a coordinated way. Select a listing from the multiple listing service, or visit an open house and develop a promotional campaign that incorporates publicity, sales promotion, and advertising. The campaign should be directed toward a specific target market.

Exercise 4—Develop a comprehensive strategy to brand your name (or the agency's name) and position it within the community.

part two

REAL ESTATE SALES

ETHICS AND REAL ESTATE PROFESSIONALISM

9

■ Learning Objectives

After the study and review of this chapter, you should be able to

- list and describe the steps involved in real estate sales and marketing;
- evaluate and explain the steps in any presentation;
- identify and describe the characteristics of a successful salesperson;
- evaluate the history of ethical regulations and laws and explain the need for ethics in the real estate industry; and
- describe with examples the guidance used in avoiding deceptive trade practices.

■ Key Terms

blockbusting	misrepresentation	qualifying
Civil Rights Act of 1866	negligence	redlining
fraud	prospecting	steering
group boycott		

Salespeople in all industries successfully close transactions by persuasively overcoming objections and solving problems. Preparing for the activities of the profession and prospecting for and qualifying customers are only a few of the activities in the sales process and are discussed over the next several chapters. The act of selling is the last stage in most marketing campaigns because marketing is what gets a prospect in front of an agent. Personal selling starts when agents can talk to and interact with prospects. Although kept to a minimum in Part Two, there may be some discussion of marketing, as it relates to the sales function. Lastly, this chapter explains that in addition to following a strict ethical standard, professional real estate licensees share similar characteristics.

Figure 9.1

Agent Activities that Result
in Sales and Referrals

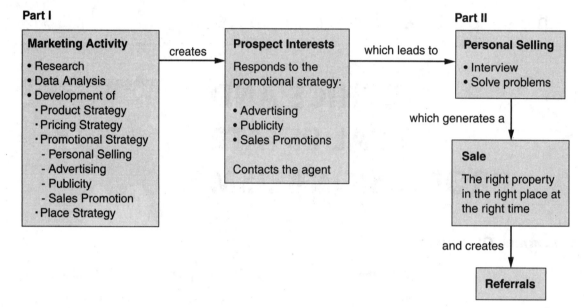

The Professional

Many real estate professionals hold up their hand and promise to abide by a code of ethics and standards of practice as set forth by the National Association of REALTORS®. All licensees, members and nonmembers of the association promise to abide by the laws of the state in which they are licensed. Professionals mold their practice to a certain ethical standard. In fact, a professional can be defined as someone who conforms "to the technical or ethical standards of a profession."[10]

When salespeople apply comprehensive marketing strategies they experience more opportunities to apply their salesmanship skills. Without some form of marketing, the chance of a face-to-face meeting with a prospective buyer or seller is compromised. It is very difficult to try out salesmanship techniques or get referrals if agents don't have a prospect in front of them. Figure 9.1 summarizes the activities from the two parts of this text that result in sales and referrals.

Personal Selling Activities

The following section describes the activities in the sales process. The activities include preparation, prospecting for buyers and sellers, qualifying both buyers and sellers, and applying appropriate sales techniques.

---

10 *Webster's Seventh New Collegiate Dictionary*, s.v. "professional."

Preparation

Preparation and knowledge build self-confidence and cut the time needed to put together transactions. Salespeople are not necessarily paid for the hours they work. They are paid for how they apply their knowledge of real estate to produce results.

When preparing to sell a property agents use the data and analysis gathered during the marketing phase to determine how it relates to the customer. Cumulative data and preparation helps agents build a degree of self-confidence that ultimately helps the customer trust the agent.

Preparation helps agents effectively compare the advantages of their services, or selected properties, to those of other products or services on the market. It could prove quite embarrassing if the customer knew more about the services of a competing firm or its listings than the agent did. Can you imagine a prospect suggesting that XYZ's services are better than yours? What would you do? How would an agent's selling skills overcome this if the agent didn't know what services the competitor provided?

Preparation for a sale (either to a buyer or a seller) includes multiple activities that for now we will break down into tasks involving research and planning. This is not meant to be an exhaustive accounting of how agents prepare, but should set the stage for further evaluation.

Research.   Research helps agents understand the property market, their competition, and specialized areas. When agents tie in the research results to their sales process, they can demonstrate with more confidence how a property's features and advantages relate to the benefits required by the target market or individual prospect and how the property (or service) provides the required solution.

Research helps agents understand their market and the strengths and weaknesses of their competitors. Salespeople use a tool from their market research called SWOT when analyzing the competition. Agents who are on a listing appointment are in a much stronger position when they are aware of and understand a competitor's strengths and weaknesses. That agent can now take advantage of opportunities that may be revealed. They can also prepare themselves for any threats posed by the competition.

Through research, agents may choose to specialize in certain geographic areas. Properties bordered by specific streets, geographic obstacles (rivers and mountains), and political boundaries make up an area of geographic specialization. These may consist of a residential neighborhood, a commercial district, or perhaps an entire town or city. Agents become familiar with the neighborhoods, street names, grocery store locations, parks, utility providers, and the market segment most attracted to the area.

Planning.   Planning helps anticipate needs or expectations and puts into place strategies to satisfy them. In preparing to contact prospective clients, agents should take the time to anticipate questions the prospect may have about their company. Some prospects don't want to work with just anyone. They may want to know about the broker's plans for growth, additional offices, or more agents, or they may like to know if the agency is well known in the area or if it's just a start-up. Planning ahead will overcome some of these issues.

Agents should become aware of the policies of their local multiple listing service, and the office procedures with regard to listings, advertising, and signs. It would be quite an embarrassment to say, "I will have our sign company put the For Sale sign up by this afternoon," only to have it posted on the property a week later.

An agent's sales goals are based on the results of earlier research. Where research may tell them the weaknesses of their competition, planning puts into motion sales strategies to take advantage of those weaknesses. Suppose your competitor hasn't reacted to rising interest rates and the declining number of qualified buyers. Your sales planning activities may consider prospecting for and listing multifamily residential units.

When properly executed, a comprehensive interview gives agents the confidence and information needed to act as a counselor[11] in the sales process. Acting as a counselor, agents don't need to give advice, but instead act as a sounding board for prospects. In other words, they provide multiple opportunities (property or services) that meet the needs of the prospects and help them work through a process of making a decision. Meetings with prospects help agents determine the property and emotional needs of the prospective buyer/seller. It helps agents understand what the prospect thinks. As we'll discover in Chapter 13, interviews don't just happen; they must be carefully planned.

Agents often develop multiple forms and fliers to explain their services, educate prospects, and prepare buyers and sellers for upcoming activities. These sales activities include buyer and seller net sheets; fliers explaining what title companies, lawyers, or escrow companies do; how to prepare the property for showing; how to prepare for an open house; how an agent determines market value; how to pick an agent; and a host of other topics.

Working through the sales process with prospects requires listening. Listening takes practice. Empathic listening (understanding the prospect's point of view) is even more difficult. Agents who do not prepare or plan to talk less than their prospects open themselves to a sale more difficult than it needs to be. Practice listening as part of a planning regimen.

Agents can't be expected to know everything on their first day at work. Planning for sales means practicing many things, such as speaking clearly, learning how to smile when they answer the phone, listening empathically, and writing offers that are clear and to the point.

---

11 The term *counselor* should not be interpreted to mean one who offers consultative services for a fee, as per Standard of Practice 11-3 of the Code of Ethics and Standards of Practice of the National Association of REALTORS®.

Figure 9.2

Steps in the Sales Effort

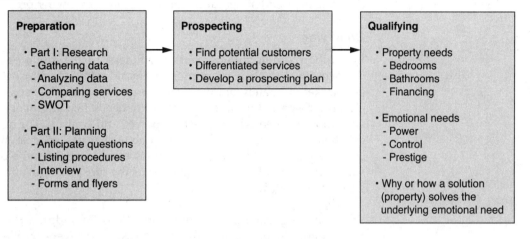

Preparation

In Part I (Marketing) agents gathered and analyzed information. They now prepare a sales strategy around that data.

In Part II (Sales) agents use the information in Part I to anticipate questions and prepare promotional materials as well as interview questions that require profound answers from prospects.

Prospecting

Prospecting generally requires in-person contact with others (although telephone contact, written letters, and e-mail may also be considered). Agents' marketing efforts determine how agents find potential customers for their in-person contacts and what they say to differentiate their services from others.

Qualifying

Qualifying involves three steps in the sales process.

The first identifies the property needs of prospects. The second two steps identify the emotional needs that must be satisfied and why or how those needs are met.

Prospecting

Prospecting is the method used to find potential customers who can benefit from your product and who are ready, willing, and able to make a buying decision. Preparation and knowledge set the stage for prospecting and the remaining steps in the sales process.

As mentioned earlier in the text, consumers don't think there are any differences between agents. One agent is just as good as another. Prospecting and the advantages of in-person contact help change that. Consumers respond to differentiated services. A new licensee usually needs to devote more time and effort to this task than established agents do. He or she must get organized quickly and concentrate heavily in this area.

Real estate sales and listing activities seldom remain constant. This means that your volume of business may slow if you do not maintain some kind of a prospecting plan. Knowing what and where to prospect comes from the results of your market research. Chapter 12 discusses some of the mundane tasks in the sales process, including sending out prospecting letters each day, meeting new people every day, making prospecting phone calls every day, checking expired listings, and working for-sale-by-owner properties.

Qualifying

In addition to determining creditworthiness, **qualifying** a prospect means discovering both their property and emotional needs. Prospecting the target market ultimately produces an interested buyer or seller. Agents should qualify prospects for both their property needs (e.g., number of bedrooms) and emotional needs (e.g., prestige, power, and control). The qualifying process helps agents understand the unique wishes of a specific customer. Successful agents quickly learn that there is more to qualifying a prospect than simply finding out what price and terms the prospects can afford, and what size home they want.

The qualifying task serves multiple functions. In addition to establishing a friendly and trusting relationship with prospects (buyers or sellers), the initial qualifying meeting gives agents an opportunity to differentiate themselves from their competitors. At these meetings, agents should demonstrate that they can provide solutions for the perceived needs and wants of prospects. Agents want to understand how their customers reach their decision without the prospects feeling that they are being judged for those decisions.

In addition to finding out whether the buyer prospect has the ability to pay, agents must discover who makes the decisions to buy, who has the authority to buy, and who will use the property or service.

■ Selling Styles

Preparing for the sale, prospecting, and qualifying the prospects make up some of the activities and methods used by professional real estate agents during the selling phase. Education, time, and experience add power to these activities and methods and those that will be discussed later in the text. Development of the marketing mix and the process mentioned above eventually mold the selling style of professional agents. There are multiple selling styles practiced in the marketing industry. Agents may adapt one or a combination of the following:

- Consultation approach (a process of asking and listening)
- Depending on the client for guidance
- Waiting for the prospects to say they are ready to buy/sell
- Pushing the prospects until they buy/sell

Some agents may go to a listing appointment, view the home with the homeowner, and then wait for the homeowner to bring up the idea of listing the property. Sometimes agents show property to buyers only to miss multiple closing opportunities. They chauffeur the prospects from one property to the next, hoping that the buyer will say they are ready to buy. Very few agents still follow the old sales era philosophy of forcing the prospects to buy something they don't want. This text follows the consultative sales approach in which the agent asks questions and listens intently to the answers to help provide the prospects with the best solutions available. A discussion of the many salesmanship techniques you might find in the marketplace is covered in Chapter 12. The remaining part of this chapter describes the common characteristics of successful salespeople, and the ethics involved in real estate sales.

■ Characteristics of a Successful Salesperson

Satisfied customers are the result of a common trait among professional salespeople. That trait is the ability to solve problems. A successful sales career employs the strategies presented in this chapter and those that follow. Agents who employ these strategies have additional qualities or commonalities that differentiate them from others. The following lists these attributes to help agents identify them and build upon them throughout their real estate career.

Characteristics of a Successful Salesperson

- Patience
- Trust and credibility
- Motivation and persistence
- Communication skills and creativity
- Knowledge

Patience

Above all, the salesperson must be patient. It takes time to build a client base. Your knowledge of real estate will increase as your career matures. However, as you gain more knowledge and insight, it will seem like year after year your clients' lack of knowledge remains the same. Be patient; this is why you are needed. Your client base might always be filled with first-time buyers, people moving into a new area, and people who have left friends behind in their old neighborhood, all of whom are experiencing a major change in their lives. It can be overwhelming for your customer and frustrating for you. Have patience. It is the part of your job that will never change.

Trust and Credibility

One issue we have already mentioned, and will talk about in some detail later, is trust. You must have enough credibility in the eyes of prospects so that they like and trust you.

Motivation and Persistence

Motivation is the reason for doing something. We all have reasons for buying certain products repeatedly, such as reliability, price, taste, value, and utility.

As an agent you will have to have a reason for getting up in the morning and possibly working another 14-hour day, addressing yet another series of inane questions, and selling a room with a hole in the carpet the same size as the hole in the last home you sold. Is it challenging enough? What do you expect from the career? An answer to the question "Why am I in this business?" should be considered.

You must have the persistence to know that your goals are well founded. After you break away from an employer who might have directed your work assignments, it can be very easy to sit back and relax. After all, you are in charge now. No one can tell you what to do. It is very easy to lose touch with the reason for getting into the business when you put in long hours sometimes never seeing any tangible results.

You may recall the story of the old gold miner, who after years of persistence gave up, only to have the next miner discover the mother lode only three inches from where he stopped digging. Know that what you are doing is what you want and that it is right. This will motivate you and give you the persistence needed to reach your goals. You don't want to sell out just short of the mother lode.

Communication Skills and Creativity

Agents are responsible for writing offers that articulate what the buyers want. Communication skills are vital to an effective salesperson. Perhaps you are familiar with a transfer process that generated one amendment after another. Why is that? Was there miscommunication in what the buyer wanted, what the seller wanted, or what the agent wrote down?

College courses or seminars in language, language composition, journalism, creative writing, speech, and similar topics help improve an agent's command of the language. Agents must also be able to produce exciting and creative promotional campaigns that speak to a specific target market. They must be able to explain unique real estate concepts and terms in ways that make sense to the prospects and that are interesting and engaging.

Knowledge

In most states, agents are required to complete a minimum number of college-level real estate courses to obtain a real estate license. Unfortunately, many stop their education at that point. To add to the college courses and seminars mentioned above, agents might consider broadening their base of knowledge with courses in psychology, sociology, business marketing, and business law. When agents just start out, knowledge and education is almost all they have. Thirty years ago some readers might have attended one of many motivational seminars by Tom Hopkins, a national sales trainer. He used to say that we all start with knowledge and enthusiasm. It's not until later that we are transformed with knowledge and experience.

Agents who review the volume and content of the real estate laws in their state need only compare them to the laws written 25 years ago to realize that there is much more to know to stay current. The last ten years have seen changes in interest rates, legal forms, Internet marketing, telephone technology, how property is financed, and even how a brokerage firm is organized. Today, most offices and agents have their own Web site. Many offices include specialized services such as property management and loan brokering. These require additional knowledge beyond the scope of listing a property and trying to find a buyer for it. The pursuit of knowledge should be never ending.

■ Real Estate Professionalism, Ethics, and Deceptive Trade Practices

Ethics are not unique to the real estate profession. Industries such as agriculture, management, communications, religion, sports, construction, finance, and health care have high ethical standards that members within their industry attempt to reach. Most industries are guided by a set of laws or an ethical code established by the federal government, state governments, or an industry association.

Many of the ethical codes established by industry associations are already a part of the laws of states or the federal government. Many law classes remind us that an ethical issue may or may not necessarily be legal or illegal. For instance, every community has minimum standards for home construction. Perhaps the city requirements call for R-36 insulation in the ceiling. The developer may have an ethical standard that is either higher or lower than the minimum standard within the community. If the standard of construction the developer uses is R-70 in the ceiling, the developer's ethical standard exceeds the legal standard, and it is an ethical standard that offers the right course of action for that developer.

Ethics and morals provide the basis on which we attempt to make the business and social environment a better place to work and live. With that in mind, the following laws give ethical guidance to those in the real estate industry.

The Civil Rights Act of 1866

Thirteenth Amendment. On April 8, 1864, the Thirteenth Amendment passed in the Senate and was moved forward to the House, where it passed on January 31, 1865. By the end of that year, on December 6, 1865, the amendment was ratified and slavery was made illegal. This meant federal law abolished any state law that made slavery legal.

The Civil Rights Act. Passed April 9, the Civil Rights Act of 1866 defined citizenship in the United States as belonging to anyone born in this country. This act provided clarity to the Thirteenth Amendment. Slavery was abolished and now former slaves were citizens with the right to hold, use, and sell property. Many thought the Civil Rights Act of 1866 to be unconstitutional and approximately two months after the Civil Rights Act passed, both the House and Senate passed the Fourteenth Amendment to the constitution in June 1866.

The Fourteenth Amendment made the Civil Rights Act very clear: "All persons born or naturalized in the United States and subject to the jurisdiction thereof, are citizens of the United States and of the State wherein they reside." It went on to say that, "No State shall make or enforce any law, which shall abridge the privileges or immunities of citizens of the United States." This amendment allowed no state the right to "…deprive any person of life, liberty, or property, without due process of law; nor deny to any person within its jurisdiction the equal protection of the laws." (Source: *www.gpoaccess.gov/ constitution/pdf2002/032.pdf*)

This was a huge step forward for civil rights. With the exception of the Civil Rights Act of 1870, which clarified that the 1866 act was still the law, and still provided remedies in court, there were few major civil rights laws enacted until 1964.

Antitrust and Fair Housing Laws

Although most states have their own antitrust laws, they are generally only effective within their state. The Sherman Antitrust Act of 1890 gave an interstate connectivity that was not there before. The act encourages the preservation of competition in the marketplace. It has seven sections, but the first two (see textbox below) help describe it, and the intention of most state laws.

The Sherman Antitrust Act (1890)

Section 1—_Trusts, etc., in restraint of trade illegal; penalty_
"Every contract, combination in the form of trust or otherwise, or conspiracy, in restraint of trade or commerce among the several States, or with foreign nations, is declared to be illegal." (The balance of this section considers the penalties for violating Section 1.)

Section 2—_Monopolizing trade a felony; penalty_
"Every person who shall monopolize, or attempt to monopolize, or combine or conspire with any other person or persons, to monopolize any part of the trade or commerce among the several States, or with foreign nations, shall be deemed guilty of a felony..."

(Source: _www.usdoj.gov/atr/foia/divisionmanual/ch2.htm#a1_)

How do these laws relate to real estate?

Price fixing. The antitrust law is dependent on a conspiracy, which means that two or more people must be involved. Competing agents may not talk about the commission rates of other offices, nor may they conspire to charge the same rate for similar services. Suggesting to their customers that they charge the same rate as everyone else is unwise, as this may suggest that competing agencies got together and fixed prices. Under the antitrust laws, these may be considered illegal acts.

Group boycotting. Agents cannot conspire to put other agencies out of business, speak badly of those agencies, or refuse to assist co-operating agencies that are asking about their listings. If two or more competitors conspired to follow any of these actions, they may be conducting a group boycott, which is illegal. Some agencies may feel a little territorial if they operate in a rural to semirural area. Although these agencies may not have gotten together to discuss the issue, many may simply make it difficult for an outside real estate company to show a property listed by a local agency. This may prove to be unethical because agents have a responsibility to do everything they can (without violating any law or ethical standard) to sell their listings.

Civil Rights Act of 1964

Several states enacted civil rights acts based on the safeguards created in Title VI of the Civil Rights Act of 1964. In part, the act said that if any person, state, or agency provided a federal financial assistance program or activity, then it was illegal to discriminate or deny benefits based on race, color, or national origin. This became the first in a series of new civil rights acts.

Civil Rights Act of 1968

Discrimination based on race, color, religion, national origin, or gender is unlawful when it relates to the offering of brokerage services or to the sale, rent, or financing of housing. Those who experienced violations of this act could go to the Secretary of Housing and Urban Development for assistance. The act also brought with it specific forms of discrimination that would no longer be tolerated.

Steering.   Agents who show properties in specific areas because they feel the buyer is best suited for that area due to a stereotype or bias based on race, color, religion, national origin, or gender may be accused of steering, a form of discrimination. For example, suppose a buyer can afford a $400,000 home. Based on a racial bias, the agent shows properties in a neighborhood occupied by residents of the same race, rather than expose the buyer to multiple areas of the market. Steering is morally wrong and therefore unethical, as well as illegal, and is not tolerated.

Blockbusting.   The illegal practice of blockbusting occurs when agents incite panic among sellers to sell before home prices decline because buyers of a different race, color, religion, or national origin are moving into the neighborhood.

Redlining.   It is illegal for lenders to practice redlining, in which they refuse to loan or limit the loans in specific neighborhoods based on the racial makeup of that neighborhood.

Advertising.   It is illegal to discriminate in any form of advertising. Agents must be aware of what constitutes discrimination and how different individuals perceive the meaning of words differently. If an ad reads seniors need not apply, this may appear to be an obvious form of discrimination. However, other wording such as just down the street from several churches may be equally offensive and may violate fair housing laws.

Seller discrimination.   If the seller asks the agent to discriminate (e.g., "I don't care who you sell the home to, just make sure they aren't X") and the agent says nothing, then the agent is violating the fair housing laws as much as the seller. This is when the agent needs to stand up and refuse to take the listing. Agents must not participate in the discriminatory actions of a client or customer.

Brokerage services.   It is a violation of fair housing laws to provide an inferior service to a customer based on race, color, religion, or national origin. Agents must be careful. Suppose an agent is in the habit of contacting all buyers and sellers once a week to update them on the status of an escrow. Now suppose they do not provide this service to those of a different race. Even if it was unintentional, they may be accused of violating the ethical standards of the National Association of REALTORS® as well as the fair housing laws. If you increase the value of the services you provide a seller (free Internet access, use of the copier and fax machines, free coffee, mail pick-up service) for the brokerage fee you charge, then you must provide the extra services to everyone charged the same fee. In other words, if you have a marketing plan that consists of A, B, C, and D for a 6 percent commission, you should not have a problem in offering A, B, and C for a 5 percent commission as long as you provide consistent services to everyone.

Fair Housing Amendments Act of 1988

The 1988 act amended and added significant changes to the Civil Rights Act of 1968. Under the 1988 amendment, HUD attorneys helped victims bring cases before judges. The penalties for discriminating under the Fair Housing Act could include fines up to $50,000. Additionally, the protected classes now included those with handicaps and families with children under the age of 18. This act also included new provisions starting in 1991, which required greater accessibility to new construction and multifamily dwellings.

Americans with Disabilities Act of 1992

This act extended the 1988 act by improving handicapped access to existing structures. Real estate agents who market commercial and industrial structures that are available for public access must be aware that accessibility must be available for everyone, including those who are blind, deaf, and have difficulty walking. So far, only personal residences, buildings that house religious organizations, and private clubs are exempt from this act.

The best advice is don't discriminate. One has to wonder why a businessperson, whose existence depends on successfully marketing and selling their product to those who need it, would want to discriminate at all.

Deceptive Trade Practices

The Federal Trade Commission Act of 1914 originally protected merchants and manufacturers from deceptive trade practices. However, in 1938 the law was amended to include consumers. The Uniform Deceptive Trade Practices Act identified activities businesspeople could no longer engage in when attracting or marketing their products to consumers. Many states have created their own laws over the years, or simply follow those in the federal act. Agents violate basic ethical standards and deceptive trade laws when they conduct or engage in any of the following.

Misrepresentation. Agents that make false statements or conceal information from buyers that may be useful in making a purchase decision are responsible for misrepresentation. Agents may say that the roof doesn't leak. If this later proves to be untrue, this is a false statement of material fact. Agents are responsible for gathering that information. Some agents make statements such as, "You can't go wrong making this purchase today." The marketing and selling industry calls this puffing. It is simply a statement of opinion. Misrepresentation of material facts crosses over to not only what agents know, but also what they should have known about the property. Although every state is different, successful court cases involving misrepresentation may lead to dollar damages, a revocation of the offer, and possible suspension or revocation of the agent's license.

Fraud is another form of misrepresentation, but it relies on deceit. For example, an agent knows that the roof of a home leaks. They are not asked about the roof; however, they do not disclose this material fact. This may be considered fraud. Consider the following fraudulent acts:

- An agent says the plumbing is fine when they know there is a persistent leak under the foundation or crawl space.

- The agent produces a certified roof inspection; however, no inspection was conducted and the agent signed a falsified certificate.

- When asked about the age of the building, the agent, knowing it was built before 1978, says it was built after 1984 to prevent any concerns about the potential of lead-based paint in the home.[12]

Negligence.   Agents are charged with the responsibility of employing reasonable care when evaluating a property for resale. For example, agents may be guilty of negligence for not finding out if a permit was pulled on a patio cover for a listing they have secured.

The Uniform Deceptive Trade Practices Act.   The following topic headings come from the Uniform Deceptive Trade Practices Act, Section 2 [Deceptive Trade Practices], and were created in an attempt to define unfair trade practices.

Pass off goods or service as that of another.   Suppose a buyer is somewhat impressed by status. He or she comments to the agent that the home they are viewing looks very much like a Frank Lloyd Wright design. The agent says it is a Wright design, even though the agent knows it is not. In this case, the agent has committed a fraud against the buyer by suggesting someone other than its true designer designed the home.

Causes the likelihood of confusion or misunderstanding as to the source, sponsorship, approval, or certification of goods or services.   This may be more difficult to assign to real estate; however, there are a few examples that again lead back to misrepresentation or fraud. Agents cannot suggest that a roof is certified for 15 years if no certification exists. In most states, the name of a real estate salesperson cannot exist in the name of the real estate company. Real estate salespeople cannot represent themselves as real estate brokers if they hold no such designation. Agents may not say they hold an associate's degree, bachelor's degree, or other degree or certification of higher learning, such as a Certified Financial Planner™ designation, if no such degree or certification exists.

Causes a likelihood of confusion or misunderstanding as to affiliation, connection, or association with, or certification by, another.   This is similar to the previous example; however, under this guidance agents may not say they are members of the National Association of REALTORS® or the American Bar Association, for example, if they are not.

Uses deceptive representations or designations of geographic origin in connection with goods or service.   Suppose in light conversation, the seller tells the agent that the walls are supported by actual two-by-fours and not the smaller-sized

---

12 Starting in 1978 with the Residential Lead-Based Paint Hazard Reduction Act, the federal government requires that agents disclose all lead-based paint hazards in homes constructed prior to 1978, and cause sellers to remedy those hazards, if any.

lumber cuts seen today. The owners are proud of the quality of construction in their 70-year-old home and they let the agent know that the lumber came from old growth forests and not a tree farm. A violation of this guidance may have the agent misrepresent the property by telling buyers that the lumber in the house came from a tree farm.

Another example of a violation of this guidance might be to suggest that a home is located in a prestigious area when in fact it is not contiguous to but just outside of the area.

Represents that goods or services have sponsorship, approval, characteristics, ingredients, uses, benefits, or quantities that they do not have or that a person has a sponsorship, approval, status, affiliation, or connection that he does not have. Violations of this guidance occur when a real estate agent sells a property and tells the buyers that it is zoned for horses, when in fact it is not. An agent may represent that the ceiling insulation is R-36, when in fact it is only R-24. Perhaps a buyer is considering a home on a golf course. A violation occurs if the agent suggests that the golf course was designed by a well-known golfer and is PGA sanctioned, when in fact it is not.

Represents that goods are original or new if they are deteriorated, altered, reconditioned, reclaimed, used, or second-hand. Agents violate the Deceptive Trade Practices Act when they suggest new paint, new carpets, or new landscaping exist, when in fact it may have been a year since they were new. Agents must be extremely careful when using the word *new* in their promotional material or verbal presentations.

Represents that the goods or services are of a particular standard, quality, or grade, or that goods are of a particular style or model, if they are of another. Suppose a couple tells an agent that they want to purchase a home that has a very quiet interior. They are looking for a home with 5/8-inch-thick drywall on all walls and the ceiling. They want all of the exterior and interior walls insulated. A violation of this guidance would occur if the agent represents the drywall to be 5/8 inches throughout and all interior walls to be insulated, when in fact they are not. It might even be suggested that a violation is present if an agency advertises a standard of quality service that doesn't exist at the agency.

Disparages the goods, services, or business of another by false or misleading representations of fact. It's a violation of this act and the ethical guidelines within the National Association of REALTORS® to misrepresent the actions of another agency or agent. When you think about it, it really doesn't speak well of the person making the remarks either. Agents may not misrepresent or degrade the listings of their competitors, or the housing tracts they represent.

Advertises goods or services with intent not to sell them as advertised. Sometimes agents write powerful advertisements that are backed by successful promotional campaigns only to have the phones ring off the hook. When the property sells, the advertisements should cease. If agents continue advertising and promoting the same property, they may be in violation of this guidance.

■ Summary

Real estate professionals abide by the laws of their state; they meet a high ethical standard, and share many commonalities such as patience, motivation, persistence, and communication skills. Often taking a different approach to the market, professional agents are profoundly familiar with the steps of preparing, prospecting, and qualifying their buyers and sellers while applying sales and marketing techniques that help the prospect accomplish their goals. Over time, with additional education and experience, agents develop their unique selling style, which helps them apply the four elements of a presentation and persuasively overcome objections before successfully closing the sale.

Virtually every profession has ethical standards by which it abides. Many of these have become a part of the laws of states or the federal government. Ethical standards and state and federal laws have provided guidance for the avoidance of unfair or deceptive trade practices.

■ Multiple Choice Questions

1. Several things occur in the initial steps of a marketing effort. Which of the following words is *NOT* a part of these steps?
   a. Referrals
   b. Preparation
   c. Qualifying
   d. Prospecting

2. Which of the following is an activity that anticipates questions about how your firm is different from other firms?
   a. Preparation
   b. Prospecting
   c. Action
   d. Qualifying

3. Real estate professionals take on several tasks when they first start the marketing and sales effort. Which of the following should new licensees spend *MOST* of their time on, at least until they are somewhat established?
   a. Preparation
   b. Prospecting
   c. Qualifying
   d. Understanding all ethical standards

4. It is illegal for lenders to refuse to loan or limit the loans in specific neighborhoods based on the racial makeup of that neighborhood. This is known as
   a. blockbusting.
   b. redlining.
   c. steering.
   d. misrepresentation.

5. Which of the following defined citizenship in the United States as being anyone born in this country?
   a. Civil Rights Act of 1872
   b. The Thirteenth Amendment
   c. Fair Housing Laws
   d. Civil Rights Act of 1866

■ Exercises

Exercise 1—You have just been told that it costs $100 for every ad call. If the phone rings, the broker wants you to do everything you can to set an appointment. Minimally, the broker wants you to get the caller's name, address, and phone number. Work with another, or, if in a classroom setting, divide into two groups. One group represents the agent and the other group the caller. After the initial greeting the caller says, "I saw your ad in the paper, could you give me the address?" What can the agent say to the caller to achieve what the broker wants? As an agent, try not to create long speeches, especially those similar to what the prospects probably heard from their last call to an agent. (e.g., "The outside just doesn't do the home justice…") Remember your purpose. Get an appointment and if you can't, get the caller's name, address, and phone number. As the caller, make it difficult for the agent.

Exercise 2—Part of any listing presentation is a discussion of price and market value. By planning ahead, agents prepare fliers for sellers on how to determine market value. Many times these fliers are mailed, faxed, or e-mailed to sellers in advance of the listing presentation. Prepare a flier that offers a straightforward explanation on how prices are determined. Keep in mind that this flier should sell the idea of pricing a home properly. Revisit Chapter 6 for ideas on how to explain the use of price in marketing and selling real estate.

Research Question 1—Agents can apply a SWOT analysis to help evaluate their personal strengths and weaknesses as they pertain to real estate marketing, and anticipate any threats or any opportunities as they materialize. With regard to the things that can be controlled, identify the strengths and weaknesses of you and/or your office. Identify the threats (things you cannot control) from the outside marketing environment (new competitor in the area, interest rates are rising) and any opportunities that may be available to you or your agency.

Research Question 2—Planning is an important part of sales. However, sales depend on cooperation from sellers. Research and develop a flier for sellers (unlike those of your competitors or your office) on how to prepare for an open house.

INSIGHTS INTO A SUCCESSFUL SALE— NO TRUST, NO NEED

■ Learning Objectives

After the study and review of this chapter, you should be able to

- list the four reasons most prospects don't buy;
- identify the steps that overcome no trust;
- explain the role of self-image and time management in overcoming no trust;
- list and explain the steps needed to overcome no need;
- develop questions for prospects to overcome no need; and
- explain the reason for solving the right problem.

■ Key Terms

competence	no need	objective
goal	no trust	relating
need		

Today many how-to salesmanship books talk about the four nos that can impede a sale. These obstacles may be overcome in one of two ways. The first method uses the old-fashioned sales era approach in which a salesperson often says whatever is necessary to close the sale. Some of the closing techniques that are explained in Chapter 13 were developed in the sales era but do have relevance today. The second method, developed by Mac Hanan and others, uses a consultative approach to sales. The emphasis is placed on building relationships by questioning the prospects and employing empathic listening skills—methods that are so common in salesmanship training today.[13]

---

13 Jeff Thull, *Motivating Sales Forces with Enhanced Learning, www.clomedia.com/content/anmviewer.asp?a=621*

Every salesperson has experienced a sale that involved what seemed to be the right property for the right prospects, yet the prospects didn't buy. Frustrated, the agent might have convinced himself that the buyer wasn't really interested anyway. That may be true, but it may not.

Reasons Financially Qualified Prospects Don't Buy

■   No trust

■   No need

■   No help

■   No hurry

What's more likely is that the agent didn't address one or more of the four reasons financially qualified prospects don't buy.

■   The prospects don't trust the agent. If they don't feel they can do business with the real estate agent, then business is not likely to happen.

■   The prospects don't have a need for the product. You can try all day long to sell a three-bedroom, two-bath home to a family of four, but if they don't feel they need the home, they won't buy.

■   The propects see your solution as providing no help to them. There are times when the prospects' need is well established; however, the prospects cannot see how the three-bedroom, two-bath homes you are showing solve their problem.

■   The prospect may not be in a hurry to do anything. The agent may have to use incentives and other techniques to motivate a prospect who is in no hurry.

The rest of this chapter will address the first two reasons prospects don't buy—no trust and no need. Chapter 11 will cover the last two—no help and no hurry.

■ No Trust

As salespeople, we have very little time to develop trust and overcome any negative perceptions prospects may have about salespeople. This is one of the most difficult tasks for any agent. It's one thing for agents to know the product well, to know the neighborhoods, and to know how to get a prospect to sign a purchase agreement; it's quite another to gain the prospects' trust. It takes time to develop trust in someone. Many things are going on in the prospects' mind. They might have talked to the agent for a few minutes on the phone before setting an appointment. Now they are driving to the agent's office to meet for the first time. Will the agent be what the prospects expect? Will the agent be able to find them the right house within a reasonable period and at the right price? Can they trust this agent to satisfy their needs?

When prospects first meet you, they don't know who you are and they are uncomfortable. The prospects may have been slow in setting an appointment because of a bad experience with an earlier agent. They may have a difficult time opening up to agents. This may be further compounded if they are annoyed by agents' constant interruptions or if agents appear hesitant in answering their questions. All of these create a lack of trust. Trust must be earned quickly if you are to help them and make a sale in a reasonable period of time. Before we explore how agents earn the trust of prospects, let's review how prospects express their lack of trust.

It's difficult to hear, but when property owners try to sell their home without an agent, it may be because they don't trust agents. They may perceive them to be unprofessional, unable to get them the price they want, or unable to answer their questions. Agents who understand that these perceptions and others exist are in a better position to deal with them. Today, when agents are on listing appointments, prospects express their lack of trust in a variety of ways, as demonstrated in the textbox below.

How Sellers Express Their Lack of Trust

To demonstrate their lack of trust in you the seller may say any of the following:

- "I can explain the features of my home better than you."
- "I can have an open house every day if I want."
- "If I don't hire you I can save the commission and advertise more."
- "If I don't have an agent, I can show my home when I want."
- "I appreciate your coming over, but I already have an agent I work with."
- "I've heard about your company. No thanks."
- "Isn't your company the one that's had the listing on the Miller property for the past year?"

Overcoming No Trust

To overcome a prospect's lack of trust agents must enjoy a strong self-image and they must relate to the prospects by getting to know them better through open communications. During this process, agents demonstrate their competence and desire to help. Prospects want agents to listen to their unique situation and do not want to be hurt by agents' actions.

First Impressions

Trust is more easily developed when agents have a strong self-image (not to be confused with egotism) that is based on a solid work ethic as well as personal and professional goals. Consumers that purchase products requiring a salesperson's involvement can sense when the salesperson is not interested in what they are doing or a salesperson that may be just passing through to another career. This does not make a good first impression. To develop trust, agents must believe in themselves and have confidence in their abilities. Prospects can tell when agents do not believe in their services, or if they do not have a strong conviction for the properties they demonstrate.

Development of a strong self-image is a step in overcoming no trust. How people feel about themselves and what they aspire to be relates to the self-concept or self-image people have. Mary Ann Oberhaus also suggests that a self-concept centers on the beliefs people hold, their values, their likes and dislikes, and how these are portrayed to the public.[14] When people make the decision to become real estate licensees, they demonstrate confidence in their abilities. Perhaps they wanted more than a nine-to-five job. Their strong self-image gave them the opportunity to dictate their work hours, and gave them control over their destiny.

Projected Self-Image

Agents' success depends partly on their projected self-image. This begs an answer to the question: Can someone who cares so little about themselves care enough about the problems of their prospect? The following actions and characteristics have an effect on the prospect and how they perceive the abilities of the agent, sometimes even before they meet them:

- Correspondence full of misspelled words
- Written correspondence with multiple syntax errors
- Unpolished verbal skills
- Lack of follow-through with customers
- Not doing what the agent says he or she will do
- Worn-out, unpressed, frayed wardrobe
- Company signs in need of repair
- Company signs on the site that are crooked or lying on the ground
- Wasting the customer's time by not working smart
- Unkempt or unclean automobile
- Unorganized desk space in the office
- Inappropriate, unprofessional attire
- Poor manners
- Sloppy, unorganized Web site

Self-image, how you see yourself, is projected to your client with that positive first impression. Prospects are trying to decide if an agent is someone with whom they want to work. Is the agent well mannered? Is the agent up to the challenge? Does the agent appear prosperous? Has the agent decided to work in a professional setting or doesn't the agent care what the office looks like? Prospects' first impressions often dictate whether they will go further with the agent. It's considered proper etiquette for agents to stand and introduce themselves when their prospects enter the room. However, some agents introduce themselves while they remain seated, protected by their desk. Some agents may be perceived by prospects as being self-important, preferring to hear what they have to say and not what the client has to say. This lack of consideration does not develop trust. Sometimes it's a matter of what prospects perceive to be a professional appearance that creates trust or loses it.

Suppose you are a buyer looking for a home in the highest price range for your area. You call and set an appointment. The next day, you arrive at the office where the agent introduces himself. You are unimpressed with his tight

---

14 Mary Ann Oberhaus, *Professional Selling: A Relationship Process*, 2nd ed. (Fort Worth: Harcourt Brace College Publishers, 1995), 112.

slacks and open collar, silk-like, long-sleeve print shirt. Around his neck are three gold necklaces. His pierced ear has hanging from it a gold bauble reading SOLD, and his gold ring is big enough to be a corporate seal.

Immediately, you feel your preconceptions about real estate agents might be true. The agent appears more interested in himself than in your problem. A feeling of discomfort is creeping up the back of your neck. You are searching for a polite way to terminate the meeting. What you see does not build trust. Is there anything wrong with the way the agent is dressed? The agent didn't think so and there may be some prospects that agree. However, most people have a general idea of how professionals dress in their community. The example above did not capture that professional image. The agent must now work harder to demonstrate that he can be trusted. So, appearance, manners, consideration, and dress all have a part in developing a successful first impression.

Goal Setting, Time Management, and Your Prospect

Many people like to be around those who are successful. Personal goal setting and your approach toward accomplishing your goals have a lot to do with prospects developing trust in you. Perhaps it's the hope that something will rub off. In real estate, prospects hope a successful agent can help them realize their goals too. They don't want to work with someone who is not capable of helping them or someone who can't focus on their needs and solve them.

Personal goals and objectives.   Agents are encouraged to set daily, monthly, quarterly, and annual goals and objectives. We will not go into detail here on setting goals, but let's define these two terms before we move on.

A **goal** is something you desire or want to achieve. A goal might be to take a week off every three months or to earn $70,000 per year.

An **objective** is the means by which you intend to accomplish the goal. For example, if your goal is to earn $70,000 in income per year, then your objectives might be: Make 65 cold calls per day (See Figure 10.1). From those calls you expect to set three appointments per week. From those appointments you expect one or two listings or sales per week that will equate to commissions of approximately $1,500. If you are successful and you make $1,500 every week, it equals $78,000 for the year. This puts you on track to reaching your goal of $70,000.

Figure 10.1	**Personal Goals**	**Objectives**
Personal Goals	Earn $70,000 this year	Make 65 calls per day
		Create 3 appointments per week
		Generate one sale per week
		Earn an average commission of $2,000 per week

You should note that each objective could also become a goal. One objective was to make 65 calls per day. You could restate this and say your goal is to make 65 cold calls per day. Great idea, now how will you do it? Your objective will define how are you going to make those calls, who you are going to call, and when you are going to call them. Another consideration is whether it is legal in your community to make cold calls.

Prospect's goals.   Prospects want their agents to provide successful results. Your personal goals are important. Prospects can tell when agents have a track record for accomplishing personal goals. There is that air of confidence that prospects can sense. The agent's attire, the office décor, and a new automobile all suggest someone who is successful, someone who knows how to meet or exceed his or her goals. Agents also need to understand the prospects' goals. They must encourage the prospects to articulate their goals so the prospects have a clear understanding of the solution when it is revealed.

Focus on your goals.   Suppose apples, hammers, and clocks are placed on a carousel that spins slowly throughout the day. Let's suggest that these represent opportunities that pass you by each day. Without a goal, you don't know which opportunity to grab. Can you imagine trying to accomplish your goals by grabbing anything that comes along? Knowing what to grab (before anyone else) is resolved by having a goal. If the goal is to satisfy your hunger, you know to grab an apple.

This example shows how easy it is to accomplish a goal when you keep the goal in mind. It is not much different than saying, "Tomorrow you will see a red VW bug." You can't help but see one. If told, "Don't think of a purple giraffe," you can't avoid the thought! In the same manner, when your goals are clearly fixed in your mind, the ways to accomplish them become apparent.

Prospect's focus.   Can you imagine the power you have when you get your prospects to focus on a goal just as clearly as you focused on the apple? Imagine getting the prospects to realize they were hungry just before you show them an apple. The same can be done just before showing them the house that will satisfy their needs.

This is a powerful tool and represents part of the discussions to follow. It is also part of what the prospects are looking for when deciding whether they will trust you. When prospects understand their goals, your selling efforts become easier. You don't want to tell them to set goals, but you don't want to waste time on someone who is wishy-washy about identifying the solutions they are seeking. Chapter 13 will cover specific interview questions that will help prospects get a clearer understanding of their problem (goal) and how to solve it (objective).

Dependability and competence.   Prospects measure dependability by how reliable agents are. Prospects may wonder if the agent is organized enough to do what they say they will do. Dependability can be demonstrated in several ways, such as returning phone calls when promised or mailing information in a timely manner.

Competence deals more with how capable the agent is and how they use the knowledge and experience they have. It's demonstrated in many ways, such as mailing letters in which all the words are spelled correctly, having a clean car, or wearing a shiny pair of shoes. Being prepared and sharing with the prospects the ways you have solved problems in the past helps demonstrate that you are capable. Agents who can develop questions that they feel the prospects will ask and develop answers to those questions show competence. Prospects need to know that the agent they have hired to solve their problems will ask the right questions and solve the right problems.

During the initial meeting, prospects want to know if you have the experience and background needed to solve their "unique" problem. Because these concerns are almost universal, take the opportunity and address them. Tell the prospects that after they called, you were thinking about the meeting, and then take a moment and tell them about the firm and yourself.

Prospects want to know what experiences agents may have had in the past. These experiences might include your education as well as actual sales transactions. Give them examples of how you helped other people. You might provide them with references that demonstrate involvement in unique transactions. Don't limit your discussions, however, to your experiences. Talk about the office operation, its position in the community, and the experiences and background of those you draw information from, such as your broker.

If you are new in the industry, you may be concerned at this point. Let's explain a technique that can be used to help demonstrate competence, even without calling upon years of experience. When sitting before the prospects, identify yourself as a problem solver. As a problem solver explain that your job is to get a clear understanding of their situation by asking questions.

With the prospects' permission, find out as much as you can about their situation. Develop questions that allow the prospect to both thoroughly define their situation and describe a solution that will already exist in your inventory. It makes for a much easier sale when the prospects tell you what they want to buy, rather than you telling the prospect what to buy.

When the prospects have answered all of your questions, tell them that you would like a few moments to process the information and perhaps share it with your broker in order to provide them with the best property selections for their situation. Make sure to ask them if that seems reasonable. It would be hard to imagine them telling you that they don't want the best selections possible.

Relating

Relating to prospects occurs when agents and prospects get to know one another and discover the things they have in common. In a previous example, we knew we didn't trust the salesperson with the gold necklaces and earring. We didn't know why we didn't trust him, but we had that feeling. Perhaps, as they say, we just couldn't relate.

Have you ever noticed how quickly people respond to others who seem to be very much like themselves? We can relax around friends who are like us. When two people have similar things in common, when they enjoy the same hobbies, when they have the same friends or the same value system, it is easier to communicate. It's easier for prospects to say that they don't like some aspect of a property to an agent who is like them. The reason they are able to do this is that they feel the agent won't like that part of the home either. Trust is more easily developed when the prospects feel they are working with someone who is like them. Answering these questions will help you better relate to your prospects:

- Do you and the prospects have similar interests, goals, beliefs, or values?

- Do you have enough in common with the prospects for them to feel comfortable opening up to you?

- Are you interested enough in what the prospects say to ask them to tell you more?

People discover things they have in common at various levels. Sometimes they have the same friends or acquaintances, go to the same church, and watch the same television programs. As they become closer, they may talk about how they *feel* about the economy, interest rates, or the prices of homes in certain areas of town. Expressing how one feels allows people to see into their psychological central core. One indication that trust has been developed is when prospects tell you how they feel about certain subjects.

The qualifying interview develops trust and credibility through the selective questioning of the prospect. The first meeting allows agents the time to develop the rapport needed to make a sale. Asking specific probative questions helps prospects share their feelings. The key is asking at the right moment. If you ask "feeling" questions too soon you will lose any credibility you may have developed up to that point. The result of a successful meeting is that the prospects feel you understand their situation and are interested in them.

Listening

Understanding your prospect's situation is accomplished by listening. Whether you are new in sales or an experienced salesperson, a competent salesperson must be interested in the prospect's unique situation. Active listening, focused listening, empathic listening should strive to clearly understand what the prospect is saying. Understanding the prospect's position is a critical research activity needed to overcome the four reasons why qualified people don't buy. Let them tell their story. Be patient. Put yourself into their shoes and listen intently. If agents are patient, the prospects will give them *all* the information necessary to lead the prospects to where they want to go. Listening is developed more thoroughly as we discuss the other methods of overcoming a no.

What Is Your Intent?

Larry Wilson says that the "greatest cause of no trust"[15] is not knowing what the caller intends to do. Some marketers of consumer products may cold-call an area for leads, but many of us hang up quickly on such callers. A better approach for cold-callers would be to quickly identify the intent of their call (see textbox).

---

15 Larry Wilson, *Counselor Selling: Relating Eden Prairie*: (Wilson Learning Corporation, 1978), 35.

The Reason for My Call...

Suppose you are making cold calls to apartment tenants. After identifying yourself, explain the reason for your call. For example:

"The reason I am calling is because you are in my service region (this is announcing your intent). I wanted to see if there is a basis on which we might do business (another way of stating intent: "I'd like to make a commission"). We have helped many tenants move into the security of a new home. I don't know if we can do the same thing for you; only you know your situation. However, I'd like to sit down with you and see if we can put our experience to work for you. How does that sound?"

This approach may yield better results, as long as the calls are not made at those inconsiderate times, such as during the evening meal or when the football is on the one-yard line. In addition, be sure to always follow the guidelines of the federal Telemarketing Sales Rule when calling prospects.[16]

Don't judge the prospect.   Agents do not want prospects to perceive that they are judging the decisions they make. You'll recall that when trust is developed, prospects often feel that your opinions may be similar to theirs. If the prospects pick one property over another, it is not the job of agents to judge that decision. Agents should supply prospects with information and alternatives and assist them in the decision-making process. If prospects feel that the agents consider their decisions to be poor ones, the agents may be setting themselves up to hear, "I'll think about it."

Suppose a husband and wife are reviewing a home with an agent. The wife asks how large the lots are in that area. The husband says they are all 1/2 acre. However, the lots are 1/3 acre in this neighborhood. Agents must be very careful in how they disclose this material fact without appearing to judge the answer given by the husband. This technique is discussed in more detail in Chapter 12.

To overcome no trust, create a positive first impression by assuming a role suitable to the professional standards for your area. Show your prospects that you are capable of handling their unique needs without judging their decision-making process. Remind them that your intent is to make property suggestions based on what was discovered during the interview. Suggest to them that the more information they give you, the better the selections you can provide from which they can make a purchase decision.

No Need

When prospects come into a real estate office it's presumed by most agents that they know they have a need. They may have said they need a three-bedroom home and they made an appointment with an agent in a real estate

---

16 In 1995, the Federal Trade Commission created the Telemarketing Sales Rule. It was amended in January 2003 to prohibit calls to people who registered their home phone or cell phone on the National Do Not Call Registry. At the present time only thrifts, telephone companies, and other common carriers, as well as nonprofit organizations, are exempt from this rule. Agents can access more information by going to *www.ftc.gov/donotcall/*.

office to solve that "need." Yet when several three-bedroom homes are shown, they don't buy. The conclusion we must draw is that there is more to their need than just three bedrooms. Prospects often have needs that may or may not be apparent to agents, and sometimes they are not apparent to the prospects. Until prospects trust the agent, they may not share with the agent the underlying motivational forces that brought them to the agent's office. When agents discover these needs, they become persuasive selling tools.

Property and Emotional Needs

A **need** is a force that when activated provides the motivational trigger to act. Property needs identify things such as the need for a larger home, a bigger garage, or more bedrooms. The more difficult part of overcoming no need is discovering the emotional or personal needs of customers. Emotional needs concern personal or psychological issues, such as being in control and the need to be right.

People who are thinking of purchasing their first home may have a fear of doing so. After all, they are comfortable in the apartment in which they live. However, their fear probably has nothing to do with the advantages of homeownership or the physical elements of the home. Prospects may fear a purchase decision that decreases the security they already have. Prospects fear losing the respect of others. After all, what would their friends think if they purchased in a declining neighborhood? These are not property no need issues, they represent emotional no need issues. Consequently, some prospects don't purchase that perfect listing because of a need that has not been addressed. Although their property needs of a three-bedroom, two-bath home are met, they put up a no need roadblock because the purchase may also affect them emotionally. Emotional needs, such as the fear of making a mistake, fear of criticism, or fear that they paid too much should be addressed during the interview and are discussed in more detail in Chapter 13.

Causes of No Need
- The need is unknown to the prospects
- Complacency or fear of losing something
- What motivates the need is not addressed in the sales presentation

---

Suppose your target market is tenants in high-rent, two-bedroom multifamily residential complexes. You have a meeting with a couple in an apartment unit. The tenants have said they were not interested in moving into a three-bedroom home, but for future reference they were willing to listen to what you had to say.

During the meeting, you discovered that he is attending college and that they operate a home business together. The young couple has a two-year-old son. During the day, she takes care of their son. The needs of their son make it difficult for her to operate the business during the day. When he gets home from school, the textbooks land on the dining room table—which is in the living room—right next to the operational books for the business. They both feel they needed more control over how they use their time. You learned that each night he would try to concentrate on his studies and later work on the business. When asked if he felt distracted by working in the dining room, he admitted that he was. He felt that it would take only two or three hours each night to complete the business paperwork and his college studies if there were no distractions. When asked how long it was currently taking, he said they were often up until one or two in the morning.

This is a close-knit family that wants to spend more time with their son. The meeting helped the tenants rediscover that the whole reason for having a home business and working as they were was to have the money and the time to spend with their son. That was not working out.

This example provides a basis for discussing the no need objection. Here's an example of a couple that had a need, but didn't realize they had it. The need is not a house with a third bedroom; the tenants made it clear they don't need that. In this case, to satisfy their underlying needs, problems had to be discovered. The tenants explained that the two-bedroom apartment worked well for them. However, what they discovered was that they needed a way to spend more quality time together and quality time on their business and college studies. A third bedroom (solution) would allow them to accomplish that. This limited example involved several steps for overcoming the no need objection: discover the problem, discover the cause of the problem, question the prospect, and listen intently to the answers. Let's review each of these and discuss them in more detail.

To Overcome No Need
- Discover the problem
- Discover the cause of the problem
- Question the prospects and listen intently
- Clarify the need
- Solve the problem

Discover the Problem

The tenants in our example had a time problem, yet they were unaware of an unfilled need. They were not interested in purchasing a three-bedroom home; however, they did purchase a solution that afforded them more time together. The problem was not the need for another bedroom, but the third bedroom satisfied the underlying need, which was to create a solution that allowed more time for family activities. When agents solve problems they satisfy needs.

Agents must take control of the information-gathering process as early as possible. They shouldn't talk about the inventory too quickly. Instead, agents should join the prospects in discovering what results they are looking for by making their real estate purchase. Agents often assume that prospects know, but if they don't then agents are throwing out solutions and just hoping the prospects buy something. The reputation of agents may suffer in a community if comments circulate that the agents showed properties that were nothing like what the customers wanted or that agents don't listen to their customers. In other words, the prospects perceived that their property and/or emotional needs were not satisfied. This ties in a little with the no help objection that we will discuss in Chapter 11. Discovering the underlying emotional need is critical to overcoming most no need objections. Take the time to learn all you can about your prospects and their property and emotional needs.

Discover the Cause of the Problem

The cause of a problem is what motivates prospects to take action or not. Remember that the cause of an action is more than the desire to have a larger home. Prospects often go to agents with what they perceive to be clear needs. "Our house is too small" is clear, but it represents a problem, not necessarily a need. Agents must question what motivated the prospects to visit them. After all, wasn't the home the same size last year? When did it become too small? The needs of the prospects are what make the small home a problem. When agents take the time to explore this kind of question, they are closer to finding the cause of the problem. No need objections may develop because the emotional needs have not been discovered or disclosed to the agent.

Prospects who use the no need objection want to gain something in the transaction. They do not want to lose anything of value. Perhaps the homes viewed offered fewer benefits than the one in which they were currently living. Is "fewer" defined as fewer bedrooms, less square footage, lower status, or less convenience or comfort? All of these add up to no need when they go undiscovered. Your job is to get down to the cause of the problem before attempting to provide a solution.

Sometimes agents miss something in the qualifying meeting that would have either put a transaction together or kept it together. Agents might have presented the right property to satisfy what they perceived the prospect's needs were, only to have it rejected. It's like participating in a qualifying event to become a member of the Olympic archery team and shooting a bull's eye, only to realize it hit the wrong target. This happens in real estate sales too. Let's revisit the prospects that have determined their "need" is a three-bedroom home. After the agent calls the lender and qualifies the prospects, he spends the entire day showing them three-bedroom homes. He finds one the prospects really like and writes it up. They are very excited because they got the home they wanted, but that night the prospects get into an argument about the new house and they cancel the transaction. Why?

In this case, both the husband and wife wanted a three-bedroom house. He wanted the third bedroom for an office. She wanted it for a sewing room. Obviously, they wanted a larger home, but the underlying needs—an office and a sewing room—were not discovered and so the three-bedroom solution the agent came up with did not satisfy those needs.

Understand the cause of the problem (the customer's motivation for buying) before showing any property.

Before showing any property, encourage your clients to share with you the reasons for their purchase decision. Agents who solve the cause of a problem are more on target than those who shoot arrows into the air, hoping that one might hit the bull's eye. Often the difficulty an agent has in closing a transaction can be traced to the interview. By using questions that require complex answers, the prospects develop a burning need to solve the cause of their problem.

Question the Prospect and Listen Intently

The best way to discover the prospects' needs is to ask questions and listen empathically. Empathic listening means that agents take the position of their customers to better understand what they need and why they need it.

Interviews should be more than a rushed formality. It is *rushed* because some agents (fortunately very few) feel they can't sell something if they can't show it, and an interview slows up that process. After all, they can ask questions while driving down the street or waiting at stop lights. It's a *formality* because most prospects expect some period of time to get to know the agents and to tell them what they want.

Needs are understood by addressing *what* the prospects expect from the physical features or property and *why* they are motivated to purchase. As we have demonstrated, it is not enough to say the prospects are motivated to purchase because they need a three-bedroom home. The three-bedroom home is a potential solution, but not the motivation for doing anything. During the course of an earlier interview, we discovered that the tenants needed an area in the home where one of them could spend time alone working the books while the other stayed with their son. Working in a small apartment was the cause of the problem. However, knowing *why* the third bedroom solves the problem makes it easier for the agent to point out the benefits of purchasing a home with a converted, detached single-car garage or a den that is separated from the family area. Once the agent solves the problem, they satisfy the underlying need for having more time with their son.

Question.   The questioning process gives agents the opportunity to discover what the prospects say they want as well as helping prospects understand why they want it. Meetings should be conducted in a quiet environment where both the prospects and the agent can relax. The room, preferably a conference room, should have no distractions. However, if the meeting takes place in the prospects' home, then make sure the radio and television are off, and that the prospects have made arrangements for someone to watch the children.

We'll save many of the questions for Chapter 13, but let's discuss the essence of how to discover both property and emotional needs. One type of question you can ask concerns issues about what the prospects expect—of the property, of a neighborhood, or of the agent's services. These address property needs or *what* the prospects want. Asking prospects how they *feel* about an issue addresses emotional needs or *why* they want it. The answers may be telling with regard to what the prospects want and why they want it. Near the beginning of an interview, you should ask this question: What do you expect from a real estate agent?

After a question like this, just sit back and let the prospects tell you everything you must do to overcome no need for your services.

Later you can ask: When working with agents in the past, what did you like the best about the experience? If you listen carefully, the prospects will tell you everything you should not do. It doesn't seem to matter what industry the salesperson is in, this question is rarely answered positively.

You can ask the prospect how close your available inventory of homes must come to their stated needs with specific exploratory questions such as:

- JoAnn, as I understand it, you need a home with a 25-by-26-foot living room. You want the kitchen facing the street, and you need a three-car garage that is attached to the home. Is that correct?

- John, how would you feel if we could find all of the features you want, but the living room was only 20 by 25? (Emotional needs are learned when agents ask prospects what they feel. This discovers why they need something.)

- JoAnn, is that about the way you feel? (Always confirm whether you must address one or more emotional needs by asking this of others involved in the buying decision.)

- If we could find a home with all the features you want, except it had a two-car garage instead of a three-car garage, how would you feel about losing that extra garage space, John?

With each question agents should slowly get closer to the prospects' psychological core. Prospects who can prioritize their property needs take away from the experience a realization that they may not get everything they want. The prospects are given the opportunity to discover how many of their "vital" property needs can be moved to a lower spot on their list. This list of nonmandatory items may be used later to pull the transaction together. In the interim, you don't want to make a full-blown presentation on the benefits and advantages of features that are not that meaningful to the prospects. If you solve the wrong problem, you won't make a sale.

Listen.   After posing a question, the next step is listening to the prospect's response. As we will discover during the interview, this requires active listening. Interviews require careful listening because you do not want to miss a key point that might be relevant to the reasons why prospects need to make a purchase. You also don't want the prospects to ramble, and listening helps keep them on track by reinforcing the things you want to hear and focusing their attention on the topic when necessary. If prospects tell you they need a three-car garage, you may respond with a nod or an "I see." If they get off track and start talking about what they had for lunch the other day, for example, you want to bring them back to the topic at hand. You might say, "You know, you said something important a moment ago." Most agents have never heard a prospect continue talking until they were told what was so important. This helps the agent regain control of the discussion once again.

This process of questioning and listening helps prospects discover underlying problems and encourages them to express a solution that might have been hidden, even to them, if you hadn't conducted your interview. More importantly, it lets them get involved with the total process and the solution. When prospects can discover their needs with you, you can encourage them to share with you the importance of satisfying those needs. If the prospects say, "We need four bedrooms," don't jump in the car and begin showing them four-bedroom homes. Question them further by simply asking, "Could you tell me a little more about that?"

Clarify the need. By listening carefully throughout the interview you encourage prospects to clarify their needs. As they tell you more about their situation, the prospects take ownership of the problem, which intensifies the need for a solution. One agent had a prospect that said he needed a third bedroom to use as an office. The agent asked if he could elaborate on that a little more. The prospect explained that he was writing a novel about the Revolutionary War. It was his first novel and he wanted to get it published. The third bedroom was where he planned to do his writing. Through the prospect's feedback, the agent understood that he wanted his novel published so that he could get the recognition he felt he deserved as a high school American history teacher. For him, he needed the recognition to validate his competency as a history teacher. The cause of his problem was a small home. The solution was a third bedroom. By solving (the third bedroom) the cause of the problem (a small house) the agent satisfied the prospect's underlying need and problem (recognition). Through your questioning, you want to encourage prospects to understand the reason for how their perceived solutions satisfy their needs.

Solve for emotional and property needs. During the initial meeting, confirm your perceptions of the prospects' needs. Remember, agents should always strive to solve the right problem the first time. When the agent above says, "As I understand it, Greg, you are very interested in a home that provides the appropriate environment so that you can complete your novel. Is that right?" the prospect is given the opportunity to confirm that this is one of his emotional needs. If it is not, he will correct you. Either way you are getting closer to discovering the problem that needs to be solved.

Let prospects talk more than you. Take notes and pay attention to everything they say. Then remind them of these discoveries when demonstrating the property. Prospects want agents to remove the no need roadblock so they can move forward. Through qualifying questions and careful listening, agents can prepare the prospect for what is about to take place. Careful listening and feedback demonstrates to the prospects that you are fully aware of their situation. Careful questions by agents encourage prospects to describe the solution they are looking for—a total solution that overcomes no need.

■ Summary

Many people have trouble trusting in others and opening up to strangers. One can almost feel the tension in a room when agents and prospects first come together. Agents start the process of overcoming no trust by closely evaluating their self-image because this affects the way they work and how people perceive them. Achieving your personal goals gives prospects the feeling that you can help them succeed with their goals. Agents must encourage prospects to articulate those goals so prospects have a clear understanding of the solution when it is revealed.

Agents continue the process of overcoming no trust by relating to the prospects, getting to know the prospects, and giving the prospects an opportunity to understand them as well. As agents demonstrate their dependability and competence, more trust is developed. When prospects like and trust agents, they are more comfortable telling them what they think and how they feel about the solutions presented to them. This can be lost if prospects feel the agent will judge them for the comments they make.

Prospects sometimes fear making a move because they don't know if the solution will actually solve their problem. This fear brings on procrastination and the feeling of no need. Questioning and listening to the prospects and carefully feeding back what they say can overcome no need. Sometimes prospects activate the no need defense because they don't have a clear understanding of their need. Agents should always attempt to solve the right problem.

■ Multiple Choice Questions

1. Agents who believe in themselves have taken the first step in overcoming
   a. no trust.
   b. no need.
   c. no interest.
   d. no help.

2. An agent who has the experience to ask the right questions of a prospect is
   a. relating to the prospect.
   b. demonstrating dependability.
   c. demonstrating competence.
   d. developing a relationship with the prospect.

3. Which of the following suggests to the prospect that you are interested in their unique situation?
   a. Asking questions
   b. Telling them about yourself
   c. Listening
   d. Not judging their comments

4. Which of the following is a tool used to help overcome no need?
   a. Relating with the prospects
   b. Questioning and listing to the prospects
   c. Arriving at an appointment on time
   d. Showing the prospects how they are similar to the agent

5. A home with a beautifully landscaped backyard is shown to prospects. They say they don't like the yard, yet the yard is an improvement over the one at their current home. To solve this issue, problem solvers find the _____ of the problem.
   a. results
   b. effect
   c. cause
   d. parts

■ Exercises

Exercise 1—Knowing who you are and where you are going in life helps develop a strong self-image. Prepare a report that is titled "Who Am I?" To have the greatest effect, try to write about 20 pages or until you have exhausted an introspective description of who you are. The more your write, the more you will discover about yourself. Describe what you have accomplished so far in life, and what problems you overcame to get to where you are. Identify how you perceive yourself and how you interact with others. Describe where you want to go, how you will get there, in what time frame, and why. By addressing these issues and more, you will gain a stronger understanding of yourself, your strengths, and your weaknesses. When it's completed, only you should have access to reading this document. Please understand how the process usually works. After you start typing, it often takes three or four pages to get through the "fluff" (how you present yourself to the world) and down to the more profound introspection. Having goals and understanding who you are and where you want to go improves your chances for success in real estate or any industry.

Exercise 2—Develop an annual goal such as increasing market share, income, or listings sold, and describe in detail the daily, weekly, monthly, and quarterly activities that will bring you closer to your goal. For example, suppose you have established a goal to earn $100,000 this year. That's $25,000 per quarter. What steps will you take to earn the $25,000 for the upcoming quarter? How will you manage your time each week and each day to accomplish your goal?

chapter eleven

INSIGHTS INTO A SUCCESSFUL SALE— NO HELP, NO HURRY

■ Learning Objectives

After the study and review of this chapter, you should be able to

- explain why it is important to understand the difference between no need and no help;
- list and explain the three steps needed to overcome no help;
- describe the signs of no hurry;
- explain the difference between your success in solving problems for others and the prospects' fear about whether your solutions will work for them now;
- evaluate the significance of fear and the roadblock it places when attempting to overcome the four reasons people don't buy; and
- explain the five steps in overcoming no hurry.

■ Key Terms

advantage	no help	no hurry
benefit	no help presentation	

When addressing the issue of no need agents gather information on the property and emotional needs of prospects and what motivates them to take action. However, the results of some interviews may leave agents with a different perception of the prospects' needs. When the agents present solutions, the prospects cannot see how these solutions address their needs. A miscommunication or a misunderstanding of the prospects' needs can result in solutions that prospects view as offering them no help. Many times prospects fear the risk of making a purchase, and are in no hurry to do so. Agents are often faced with prospects that perceive their product or service as providing no help and they are in no hurry to move forward.

■ No Help

A property is of no help when prospects do not understand *how* it satisfies their needs. Overcoming no help requires an explanation of the usefulness of the property or service, how it is advantageous to the prospect, and the benefits it provides. If the prospects perceive that the listings shown come up short of expectations, then the solutions are of no help to them. Agents should understand that while the prospects may have said they wanted a three-bedroom home with a view, if they don't understand how your listing solves their needs you won't have a sale. This description creates a strong link to the no need objection. No help is about the *communication* of your solution to the no need problem. Agents will have a difficult time explaining how a property helps a prospect if they do not understand what motivates them (emotional needs). Agents may get frustrated with prospects, but that is overcome when they demonstrate how the property helps the prospects.

Cause of No Help

No help arises when agents poorly communicate *how* the solution satisfies their prospects' needs.

Suppose an affluent individual had a need for a wristwatch. The salesperson presents the individual with a very fine quality, brand-name watch. It satisfies the product need, but the prospect wants something more. After discussing the issue with the prospect, the salesperson discovers a personal need for prestige and recognition. To make a sale, the salesperson must satisfy not just the prospect's reasons for the purchase, but demonstrate *how* the personal or emotional needs are satisfied. He opens another case and has the prospect try on a different watch while he describes the reputation, craftsmanship, and quality of the Rolex timepiece. No help is overcome and the sale is made.

By properly determining the motivations behind prospects' needs, as detailed in Chapter 10, and then demonstrating how their solution meets those needs, agents can largely solve the no help problem before leaving the office. The best way to demonstrate this solution is to repeat the emotional need back to the customer. Let's look at part of an interview that establishes the needs of the customer (as discussed in Chapter 10) and examine the types of questions and statements that overcome no help.

Prospect: "I need a home with a view." (This is a property need.)

Agent: "A view? Which direction would you like the view to face?"

Prospect: "The view must face north."

Agent: "I see. That's interesting. The view must face north. Could you tell me more about that?" (This is an important question that will elicit the cause behind the need.)

Prospect: "Yes. I enjoy painting pictures. I want a room in the front of the house that I can work in. I want indirect light."

Agent: "What kind of pictures do you paint?"

Prospect: "I paint mostly landscapes. I have them on consignment at a small gallery. Art critics come in there a lot. One of these days I will paint a picture that will put my name right up there with other famous painters." (Now we see the emotional need behind the property need—the cause of the problem. This is what the agent will repeat back to the customer to overcome no help.)

Agent: "I see. So a view with a northern exposure is *very* important."

Prospect: "Yes."

Sometimes agents hear that the buyer wants a view and then they move on to list the next feature the buyer is looking for, thus missing a critical component in how the view helps the prospect. They would have missed knowing that the view had to have a northern exposure, and they would have missed the reason why. If the agent conducted a limited interview and didn't discover the reason or the need for a northern exposure from the front of the house, the agent likely would show the prospect some homes that did not satisfy the buyer's need—leading to a no help objection.

During the interview the prospects' responses must be copied as accurately as possible. To overcome the negative effects of a no help objection, the agent must evaluate what was said during the interview. This analysis should be converted to a well-thought-out presentation of the property. The presentation should address not only the *needs* of the prospects but also how the property or service *helps* the prospects get what they want or need.

■ No Help Presentation

There are three steps used in a **no help presentation** to overcome the no help objection for a product (property, feature, or service). Those steps include identifying what the product does, demonstrating the advantages of the product, and explaining the benefits so prospects can understand how the product helps achieve their perceived needs. Some, such as Michael Bosworth in his book, *Solution Selling*, have suggested that you develop presentations that focus on the *feature*, the *advantage*, and the *benefit*. Other marketing textbooks use the words *product*, *advantage*, and *benefit*; and still others use *solution*, *advantage*, and *benefit*. They all address the issues of the advantages and benefits of the property. For our purposes, to overcome no help, focus your presentations on the property, the advantage, and the benefit.

Steps to Overcoming No Help

1. Identify the property
2. Demonstrate the advantage
3. Explain the benefit

Property

The real estate property solution presented to the buyer should match up as closely as possible with the property needs stated during the interview. After all, how does a three-bedroom home help someone that has a property need of five bedrooms? If the prospects said they wanted a five-bedroom, three-bath home with a view, then the property should match up as closely as possible to those property needs. As mentioned in Chapter 10, each component of a home provides an opportunity to satisfy both property and emotional needs. Some features in the home may be more important than others. Spend time discussing the features that mean the most to the prospects.

Let's suppose that during the interview the prospects described where they currently live. You discovered that they do not have a fireplace but want one. When you asked about their hobbies or recreational interests, they said they liked camping. Your follow-up question asked what they liked the least about camping, and they said they didn't like trying to light up green or damp firewood. These are two seemingly unrelated issues, but how can we use them in our sales presentation?

"Greg, did you and Lynda notice the corner location of the fireplace? Do you see the large, key-like wand coming out of the brick wall? That turns on the gas starter for your wood fires."

By presenting the feature in this way you have satisfied the prospects' property need.

Advantage

The **advantage** helps the prospects understand how the product is useful or how it works. Agents often turn on switches to overhead fans, fluorescent lighting, or the garage door openers to indicate their presence and show that they work, sometimes letting the prospects decide how these features might help them. However, agents should also take a moment and address each feature's usefulness in light of what is known from the interview. To overcome no help issues, agents must move to the next step and explain the advantages.

"One of the advantages of having a fireplace with a gas lighter is that it is easy to light a fire every time, without hassle. Turn the wand to low, light a match, and start your fire."

You want to help the prospects understand the advantage of this feature. The solution to a minor problem (lighting a fire) is the gas starter that does the work for you. The advantage helps the buyers start the fire. If you remind the buyers why the solution and the advantage are important to them, you are helping the buyers overcome any feelings of no help.

Advantages remind prospects of their motivation to seek a solution. The agent's next job is to reinforce for the prospects how the advantages benefit them.

Benefit

The **benefit** describes how the feature or property satisfies an emotional or product need. Without this element, the prospects may recognize the feature and understand the need, but they may not understand how the property helps satisfy the need. The agent needs to complete the presentation.

"What this means, Lynda, is that you will be able to save time and start a fire even when the logs are a little wet. And, as you know, it does get rather damp here during the winter, doesn't it?"

The interview helps you discover the prospects' problem, how they hope to solve that problem by working with you, and what motivates them to action. The benefits they seek are based on both product needs, such as the physical features in a home, and personal or emotional needs, such as saving time, maintaining control, or making friends. By spelling out the benefits, agents help prospects understand how the property satisfies their needs. By explaining the benefits of the property and overcoming no help, prospects will feel that the solution more than satisfies their needs.

■ No Hurry

No hurry stems from the prospects' perception of potential negative consequences resulting from the purchase decision. Skydiving may sound exciting, but many people are in no hurry to try it because of the perceived consequences. In real estate, prospects may be excited about the purchase but more fearful of the consequences. Often agents get prospects through the elements of no trust, no need, and no help, only to hear them say, "I'd like to think it over" or "I'd like to talk this over with my wife (or aunt, next door neighbor, etc.)." Agents must overcome no hurry objections so prospects can make a buying decision.

Signs of No Hurry

Prospects convey that they are in no hurry to make a purchase in many different ways. In a business setting, the signs of no hurry may be subtle and agents need to learn to recognize these no hurry situations.

Prospects question your competence or make excuses. Suppose you go to a listing appointment and make one of your best presentations about why the sellers should list with your firm. If the sellers feel uncomfortable with you for any reason, they will be in no hurry to hire you. If you are new to the industry, they may not want to be your first experiment. Perhaps they feel that because of your limited experience you will take too long to sell their property. In different ways, they suggest that they do not want to move forward. How can you tell there is a problem? If you tell them that your brokerage fee is 6 percent and they promptly tell you that they have never paid more than 5 percent, this may be an indication of no hurry. Or maybe they say that they don't see many of your signs around town. They may even be more direct and say, "I worked with your company once. John Doe works there. I'm in no hurry to work with your company again!" These may or may not be factual statements, but they are an indication that the sellers feel no urgency to list their property with you.

Sometimes sellers like you or your presentation. They have a need, and can see how services like yours can help them, yet they are still in no hurry to hire you. Instead, they just want you to leave their home or to hang up the phone. They may suggest, "We appreciate your time and we'll get back to you."

The prospects just want the pain to stop.   Prospects will avoid a purchase decision if they think that it's more trouble than it's worth. Suppose your prospects are thinking of buying their first home. After they found the right house, they started to experience one of the most stressful moments in their lives. They felt there was something wrong. How many agents have heard prospects say that perhaps the purchase was not meant to be? The prospects may think, "If we purchase this house, will this enormous pain continue? Perhaps we should think about it." As soon as they say to the agent, "We'd like to think about it," the stress melts away and they feel better.

Prospects may also express an interest in avoiding the purchase process altogether, saying, "I am starting to think I shouldn't move. I have lived in this apartment for 12 years. From what you are telling me, the qualifying, the processing time, and finding a home could take a long time. I just don't think it's worth it to me. I am really happy where I am."

Common concerns of a prospect in no hurry.   Prospects' excuses are based on real concerns that may not have been shared with the agent. Some of these concerns include:

- What if this is the wrong house for me?
- What will my friends think of this particular purchase?
- Do I really know what I am doing?
- Can I really trust this agent to suggest what *I* need?
- Is this a reputable company that is concerned about *me*?
- How do I know if I am paying too much?

Even if these concerns were discussed in the interview, when the prospects are closer to making a purchase decision, they want additional assurances that what they are about to do is best for *them*.

Risk of Purchase

The foregoing discussion still doesn't explain what causes people to fear something that may not exist. Understanding prospects' fears is an important part of overcoming no hurry. The fear goes beyond the property or service and is often a part of the emotional side of the solution.

Suppose the prospects have finally found the house that they really want, but suddenly you are confronted with no hurry. Without further investigation and probing you may never find out that they have a fear of being rejected. Maybe they are afraid that the seller won't accept their offer or the lender will refuse to qualify them. Or they may be concerned with what their friends will say if they offer more for the home than the appraiser says it's worth.

Risk of Selling

Suppose you are trying to get a listing on a property. It is one of many homes already listed in a neighborhood. This particular neighborhood has natural boundaries and covers over three square miles. You are making headway with the sellers. Trust and credibility are well established. The sellers have a need for a smaller home and they thoroughly understand how your marketing plan will help them sell their home. However, no hurry sets in.

All of a sudden the sellers don't want to list their home. What is the problem? By supporting the seller's thought processes, you discover that the sellers fear moving to another neighborhood where no one knows them. There are many ways of supporting the sellers through this crisis. First the agent must determine what they mean when they say that no one will know them. Do they mean they will not know their next-door neighbors or those in the overall neighborhood? Are they fearful of losing the friends they already have?

These issues and more must be addressed before asking for the listing. The following steps create the environment needed to overcome no hurry.

■ Steps to Overcoming No Hurry

Prospects want to make sure your solution is best for them. To overcome no hurry, you must overcome their doubts by supporting and reassuring them. As the time for a decision gets closer, agents will hear more objections, which can prove helpful in creating a close. Again, objections are ways for the prospects to slow down the process of accepting the agent's solution by indirectly asking for more information. If prospects get anxious or feel that headache is coming on once again, they may need time to calm down to feel better about what they are doing.

Agents overcome no hurry by taking a supporting role with their prospects throughout the decision-making process. *Supporting* means reassuring, comforting, or calming a customer by suggesting that "more positive experiences will occur"[17] as a result of the purchase. One way to get prospects to move forward is to demonstrate how they will feel after they make the purchase decision. Depending on the situation, agents must explain that with just a little inconvenience up front (e.g., a little more down payment, the packing and confusion of moving, or the time it takes to locate a property) the prospects will be able to realize positive benefits (e.g., move into the home at the end of the month, have a home that should appreciate in value over time, or make them the envy of all their friends). Agents must demonstrate how and why the benefits of a purchase outweigh the inconvenience of finding the property and moving.

Keep in mind that some prospects may perceive all kinds of risks when making real estate purchase decisions. These risks are similar to those that cause no need and no help; however, they are addressed differently when overcoming no hurry. There is the risk of paying too much for the property, the risk of losing friends, the risk of increasing the time needed to maintain the property, and the list goes on.

Why are these problems coming up again? Were they not resolved when dealing with no need and no help? Someone who is demonstrating no hurry may

---

17 Mary Ann Oberhaus, Sharon Ratliffe, and Vernon Stauble, *Professional Selling: A Relationship Process*, 2nd ed. (Fort Worth: Harcourt Brace College Publishers, 1995), 276.

feel that everything is moving too quickly. They may feel a certain amount of pressure when making a life-changing purchase decision. They will start to question your motives. Just as patients get a second opinion before undergoing major surgery, most people need reassurance before making a big decision. When prospects express no hurry, they just want some assurances that what the agent is suggesting is right for them.

Listen to Their Anxiety

Although it seems like agents should do more talking when a no hurry objection arises, the truth is they are better served by carefully listening to the prospects. Let them talk. Let them tell you what is on their mind. The more they talk, the more you will understand why they are in no hurry. Suppose the prospects say, "No, I don't think I would be interested. The yard is too large." Encourage the prospects to tell you all about why the yard is too large.

There is no need to tell them that the yard is not too large or that the interest rates are at their lowest level in years or that the price is lower than anything else on the market. Instead, discover why the prospects feel the way they do. Ask them to elaborate and then listen and let them tell you everything that is bothering them about the yard. Then find a way to overcome these objections and reassure the prospects.

Empathize with the Customer

After taking the time to listen to your customers, demonstrate your understanding of what they have told you. Many times when prospects hear their objection fed back to them it may seem ridiculous, even to them, and you might be able to move immediately to the last step. Nevertheless, by feeding back a prospect's concerns, it helps the prospect understand that you are listening to them and attempting to resolve their concerns. Remember, if the objection is legitimate, it is brought up because the prospects need more information before making a decision. Your job is to make suggestions, given your knowledge of the inventory, but this is difficult if you don't understand the problem. You encourage prospects to tell you more when you convey that you understand what they are saying.

"I understand what you mean. You are saying that a yard of this size will not allow you enough time to spend with your kids on the weekends. Is that right?"

Question the Problem

Agents should now question the objection in order to confirm its existence. Asking, "Is that right?" helps discover if this is the real reason for the lack of urgency. We'll assume that the prospects have shared all they can. By repeating it back to the prospects in the form of a question, agents can help the prospects prioritize the objections using what was learned during the interview. When questioning the problem, agents have to put the prospects in the position to say yes so the process can continue to move forward.

"As I understand it Jim, the real problem is not the home or the yard as much as it is the time to care for the yard. Do you feel the same way, Duana?"

You are allowing the prospects to be more specific about what is bothering them. You have allowed them to say that they will buy the home with the big yard, if you can figure out a solution to the real problem.

Solve the Problem

After the prospects have specified the problem, paraphrase the prospects' words, if possible, and suggest a solution.

> Agent: "As I understand it Jim, the real problem is not the home or the yard as much as it is the time to care for the yard. Do you feel the same way, Duana?"
>
> Prospect: "Yes."
>
> Agent: "How do you see the back yard, Jim? In other words, how much landscaping would you like there to be? How much would you want to maintain?"
>
> Prospect: "I would only want to maintain the area behind the garage, the grass next to the patio, and the bushes next to the house. The rest is just too much."
>
> Agent: "So, you would prefer the rest of the landscaping to not be there. If it weren't for all this landscaping, you would probably purchase this home. Is that about right?"
>
> Prospect: "Perhaps. What do you have in mind?"
>
> Agent: "Based on what you have said…"

Any number of solutions can now be presented based on the problem. Perhaps a price reduction is warranted to cover the cost of decreasing the size of the landscaped yard. Maybe the sprinkling system is such that certain areas can be shut off causing the plants to die without detracting from the value of the home. Perhaps the seller will agree to create a low-maintenance yard if he gets his price, or perhaps the seller or the agent will prepay into an escrow account money that could be used for two years of yard maintenance service. The point is to find out the reason for no hurry, and then solve the problem.

Ask for the Order

After solving the problem and getting a confirmation of its solution, the last step in this process is to ask for the order and close the sale. Additional closing techniques will be explored in Chapter 13.

The key to every step is to carefully listen to the prospects tell you how they feel about your solution. Don't discourage them from being specific in their concerns. Empathize with the customer, but question the specific problems they bring up. Let them hear what you think their problem is by paraphrasing what you heard and feeding it back to them. Often the prospects will come up with workable solutions that can be applied to the listing you are showing. Don't lose your opportunity to have the prospects help you close the sale. By this time, you should have noticed that to overcome all these objections, questioning and listening are a consistent element.

■ Summary

Many times prospects don't understand the solutions provided by their agents. Prospects may agree with the agent on the fundamental problem, but they don't understand how the agent's solution addresses it. Sometimes prospects can connect their need to the property's advantages and benefits. However, if they can't understand the advantages and benefits of an agent's solution, then agents may have a difficult time overcoming no help.

There are many signs of a prospect in no hurry to take action. Prospects may not return phone calls or perhaps will question your motives. Prospects who fear the consequences of selling their property or making a purchase decision are in no hurry to do so. To overcome no hurry, agents must take the time to listen to the prospects' anxiety and empathize with their situation. Once a concern is raised, question the problem, feed it back to the prospects so they can hear it, and then solve it. When the prospects agree that the problem is solved, ask for the order.

■ Multiple Choice Questions

1. Which of the following is a sign of no hurry?
   a. The prospects want to be noticed by their co-workers.
   b. The agent demonstrates the benefits of a feature.
   c. The prospect questions the competence of the agent.
   d. The agent demonstrates the advantages of a three-car garage.

2. Which of the following is *NOT* a step in overcoming no help?
   a. Demonstrating the advantage of a feature
   b. Reassuring or supporting the prospects' decision process
   c. Explaining the benefits
   d. Identifying a property or feature

3. Which of the following is overcome when the agent supports and reassures the prospects and their decision making?
   a. The risks of purchase
   b. No trust
   c. No help
   d. No hurry

4. What are prospects telling agents when they pose a legitimate objection?
   a. They are in no hurry to buy.
   b. They need more information.
   c. They don't trust the agent's solution.
   d. They are unwilling to act.

5. When prospects avoid a purchase decision because they feel it might be more trouble than it's worth, they
   a. are expressing a no hurry objection.
   b. are expressing a no trust objection.
   c. are expressing a no help objection.
   d. are expressing a no need objection.

■ Exercises

Exercise 1—Agents overcome no help by explaining the usefulness of a property, how it is advantageous to the prospect, and the benefits it provides. Work with another individual, or, if in a classroom setting, break into two teams. One team should describe a listing and its multiple features. The second team should summarize the product needs and emotional needs of their prospect. (Make the assumption that the prospects qualify for this home.) Working together and using the property-advantage-benefit formula, the two teams should choose any given feature from the first team's property description and describe how they would overcome no help based on the product needs and emotional needs compiled by the second team.

Exercise 2—We have all employed a variety of excuses that suggests we are in no hurry to make a purchase. Recognizing these signals puts agents in a better position to overcome no hurry. Without referring to the text, list five ways you have indicated no hurry to a salesperson in the past.

chapter twelve

PERSONAL SELLING

■ Learning Objectives

After the study and review of this chapter, you should be able to

- ■ explain the advantages and disadvantages of personal selling for both the owner and salesperson;
- ■ list, from a broker/owner's point of view, the different styles of salesmanship that salespeople bring to an office operation;
- ■ compare and contrast the differences among the three styles of salesmanship;
- ■ list and describe the multiple methods used to promote your personal selling services;
- ■ evaluate the complex role of qualifying the prospects by identifying their property and service needs and their emotional needs; and
- ■ review the property and personal or emotional reasons people buy.

■ Key Terms

action	order getters	problem solver
attention	order takers	referral
interest	personal selling	
desire	pioneers	

In virtually every marketing textbook, **personal selling** is the term used to describe the face-to-face interaction salespeople have with their prospects. Personal selling makes use of the primary and secondary data collected during the marketing phase. It is one of the oldest methods used to sell real estate. Once again, you should be aware that selling is a part of the promotional strategy, which is a part of marketing. Personal selling is the culmination of a significant amount of work that went before it, including marketing research, discovery of a target market, selection of channels of distribution, product selection, and pricing strategies. The marketing effort is used to get the prospects in front of agents. However, selling requires the use of some of that marketing information. Prospecting is a face-to-face activity, but requires marketing research to identify the best group to prospect. To that extent, this chapter may mention marketing concepts as they apply to selling.

Real estate brokers depend on their sales force to apply their personal selling skills to attract prospects and sell inventory. For the broker and salesperson alike, there are advantages and disadvantages to the personal selling side of the promotional strategy. Because the salesperson is in direct communication with the prospect, agents must be able to articulate their message in an understandable way. The salesperson is involved in various tasks including telephone techniques, qualifying a buyer or seller, presenting offers, and closing the sale.

This text divides the discussion of personal selling into two parts. This chapter discusses activities involved in prospecting and qualifying. Chapter 13 discusses the interview, its use in the qualifying process, and how it relates to the presentation and demonstration of property.

■ Personal Selling: Advantages and Disadvantages

The advantages and disadvantages of personal selling focus on several main issues (see Figure 12.1). One advantage of personal selling is that agents can make a presentation, observe the prospect's response, and adjust the message accordingly. Unlike advertising, which is a one-way communication, personal selling offers the opportunity to interact with prospects and understand more completely their needs. Personal selling is not without its disadvantages. These include the time and expense involved in sales training, whether the agent can generate a sale as a result of that training, and the fear that new agents may say something wrong or violate some obscure law. It is generally more expensive than other forms of promotion when it comes to prospect contacts. An agent may contact only one prospect during the same period of time that an advertisement may reach hundreds of prospects.

Figure 12.1

Advantages and
Disadvantages of Selling

Advantages

- Modify the message if the environment changes
- Observe the prospect's body language
- Hear the prospect's voice inflection
- Personal satisfaction
- Potential for unlimited income

Disadvantages

- Time and expense in training
- Fear of doing something wrong
- Limited number of face-to-face presentations
- Long workdays

Expense of Recruitment and Training

It is quite expensive for a broker to recruit agents and train them in proper selling techniques. However, this process is necessary because, with the exception of their own efforts, brokers are dependent on the sales force for production. There must be a fine balance between training new and experienced licensees.

Brokers need trained agents on the floor. Anything less than a well-trained agent costs the broker money. Suppose the phones are ringing because of a successful advertising campaign. If agents with ineffective personal selling skills answer the phone, it's very likely that the caller will outsell the agent, resulting in a system breakdown. The caller might get the agent to mention the price, the address, and other information about the property before the agent thinks of asking for the caller's name, address, or phone number.

The training provided by some brokers doesn't go beyond a basic understanding of the procedures to follow when processing a listing or an offer. In other offices, sales training is a consequence of linking a new licensee with an experienced agent who might provide them on-the-job training while in the field. Larger offices may have the advantage by absorbing the high costs of sales training for their licensees.

Training can include the following topics, though this is not an exhaustive list:

- Writing down the names of people you know
- Deciding how many seller contacts to make in a week
- Making a listing presentation
- Inspecting listed properties
- Cold-calling by telephone or in person
- Prospecting
- Learning how to demonstrate a property
- Overcoming objections
- Asking for the order
- Presenting an offer to which the buyer and seller will agree

In most real estate offices, salespeople are responsible for marketing their listings and personal selling. Salespeople identify target markets and develop prospecting tools to locate and attract prospects. After prospects respond to the promotional efforts and come into the office, the agents can use their personal selling techniques.

A costly by-product of sales training meetings is that productive agents sometimes sit through them out of respect for the broker, when they should be prospecting, listing, or selling property. Some brokers strongly suggest that newly licensed agents attend the sales training courses offered by their franchise, or attend costly private-vendor motivational courses. The cost of these is generally borne by the salesperson, not the broker. It's often more efficient for brokers to have an operation that lists and sells real estate than it is to have one that spends time and expense training its sales force. Some agencies have encouraged their local community colleges to create courses on real estate salesmanship and marketing. They often have input into what goes into the courses. This may provide an inexpensive alternative to training new licensees in house.

Fear of Doing Something Wrong

Some new agents fear the act of selling because they feel overwhelmed by the process. Without some form of training, they may fear that they will say the wrong thing or not know what to say. Some are apprehensive about approaching or talking with people about real estate. They don't want to appear to be "selling" something. Others are concerned that they may have sold a property that the buyer didn't actually want, and fear contacting that buyer again.

To help overcome the fear of selling, keep this in mind: If buyers can see how one of your listings will solve their problem, they will buy. If sellers can see how your services will fill their needs, they will work with you. If they can't see how your solution solves their problem, most of the time, they won't do anything. Most prospects prefer that agents not sell them anything, so don't try to sell. Take the time to find out what is troubling the prospect. Find out when this problem arose and why they haven't solved it in the past. By interacting with prospects, agents can take on the role of problem solver, rather than salesperson.

Problem Solver

Most agents like the feeling that comes with selling a property or services that satisfy the customers' needs. Gardening centers have lawn mowers to solve their customers' problems. Pharmacists have medicines they dispense that help customers overcome their problems and satisfy their needs. Real estate is the product used by agents to solve problems. Brokers hire salespeople to help prospects solve their problems through the purchase of real estate. As a **problem solver**, the agent offers facts, choices, information, and counseling to prospects to help them make decisions. As part of marketing's promotional strategy, personal selling involves reminding or informing the prospect about a product or service. Persuading prospects to buy may take time and interaction to help them discover how a property or service satisfies their needs.

Interact with the Client

The advantage personal selling has over other forms of promotion is the ability to interact with a buyer or seller. With advertising and other noninteractive promotional tools, you wait for something to happen. As part of a marketing campaign, suppose you developed, printed, and distributed over 30,000 brochures about a property. You placed the brochures in four different newspapers. Once the brochures are made, you cannot make changes to them without incurring additional costs, and you have used all your promotional dollars for the next four weeks to create the brochures.

If nothing happens, it's probably because the message wasn't the right one. But how would you know? The prospects aren't in front of you. Without the benefit of face-to-face contact, you cannot gauge their reactions. You can't see their eyebrows go up after reading a small detail in your promotional piece. With personal selling, however, you can modify the presentation as you deliver it, and changes may appear so seamless that the prospects never know the difference. This is not unusual. The needs of two different prospects—even married individuals—are rarely the same, so agents often make changes in the presentation when showing property to different people.

Let's say you show a three-bedroom home to your prospects. It has a security system, three-car garage, and a view. Some prospects may have indicated a concern for safety. Obviously, the agent should spend time demonstrating the security system. Other prospects may suggest they want a good value and the ability to stretch out and breathe fresh air. In this case, you demonstrate the beautiful view and explain that the corner lot and the home are included in the price.

Today, Web sites, e-mail, voice mail, and fax machines have created more sophisticated ways for prospects to interact with agents. This new technology suggests that being in the physical presence of the prospect is not always needed. Through technology, prospects can indeed interact with agents and some forms of advertising, publicity, and promotional strategies. Agents that have a personal Web site may stay in contact with prospects via e-mail and voice mail. Some agents have made presentations with the use of Web camera and computer. Prospects can see the agents and listen to their presentation, and agents can interact and see the prospects on their computer. For many, the interaction between salespeople and prospects offers the best way to quickly respond to prospects' questions, concerns, misunderstandings, or unaddressed needs.

Presentations to a Few at a Time

Selling a product or service is all about getting in front of prospects. An agent might spend a week visiting 20 or 30 prospects, yet that agent could put on an investment-planning seminar and see the same number of people in a three-hour period. The use of seminars, classes, and other forms of public speaking can increase the agent's exposure to the market.

■ Types of Salespeople

Brokers must make decisions about what types of salespeople are necessary for their operation, given the type of sales situations that take place in the office. You should keep in mind, as we go through the following types of salespeople, that each salesperson can have the traits of more than one type, but usually has stronger tendencies toward one type.

As we started this text, we suggested that everyone is a salesperson. It seems that no matter where you go, or what profession you are in, everyone has something to sell. Perhaps it's your next-door neighbor who is trying to borrow your lawn mower. Or maybe it is your five-year-old daughter who is trying to get you to put a quarter in her piggy bank to show you how it works. Sales are made every day by teachers in every elementary and high school, every college and university. Depending on the skills of the salesperson, the buyer will be persuaded to accept or reject the information.

Everyone has a certain style—a way of selling his or her idea, product, or service. A child's style is usually very direct. As people mature, some tend to be less direct for fear of offending others. Some agents are very direct, which can offend some prospects but be very effective with others. In most industries, there are generally three types of salespeople: pioneers, order getters, and order takers.

Pioneers

This is a rare type of salesperson in the real estate industry. **Pioneers** sell franchises or are responsible for establishing a client base or a method of selling before moving to another project. In industries other than real estate, they may be found cultivating new prospects and then turning them over to another salesperson. Developers of real estate franchises may employ real estate agents to sell their franchise opportunities. Housing developers may have an internal staff to train local agencies on how they want their housing tracts marketed and sold. Once that is done the pioneer moves on to another of the developer's tracts.

Order Getters

Order getters fall into what many marketing textbooks call creative salespeople. They have a different role in marketing. Rather than depending on the customer to find them, these agents aggressively seek out past customers and search for new ones.

Generally the order getter makes more sales and more income. Order getters are in great demand by real estate brokers.

Order Takers

Developers who are looking for agents on which their pioneers can rely may need order takers. By definition, **order takers** are employed to maintain customers and their repetitive orders. However, the term *order taker* has some application in real estate. Agents have occasionally interviewed customers who knew exactly what property they wanted to buy and how much they would pay. All the agent had to do was take the order.

Order takers are very effective in tract developments. After building its models and developing a marketing and sales campaign, developers may hire local agents whose sole job is to guide prospects into the five or six models offered, answer questions, and take orders if there is an interest. Often the developer remains responsible for getting the prospect to the tract. Some developers require that agents represent only their product, so it may be rare that the developer allows the agent to leave the tract to show properties other than what is in the development. In other words, if an agent is sitting in the model home that day and a prospect comes in but doesn't like the models, the agent usually can't close the model and show other listings. The agent is primarily there to take orders. Without a doubt, the agent may have more skills than are required by the developer, but the situation may not allow for them to be used.

■ Customized Presentations

Customized presentations are usually designed by the agent. They emphasize the use of the agent's speech patterns and personality. On the other hand, canned presentations are boilerplate, one-size-fits-all, scripted speeches that are often ineffective. Fortunately, few, if any, real estate agents use the canned approach to sales.

There are times when every salesperson gets momentarily distracted during the selling process, which may lead to missing the opportunity to close. If this happens, the salesperson can fall back on certain memorized phrases to help change the direction of the presentation and create another closing opportunity.

These transitional phrases offer ways to get back on track and may possibly lead to a successful close.

- ■ "Just to clarify my thinking…"
- ■ "As I see it…"
- ■ "Could you elaborate on that?"
- ■ "I am sure you wouldn't ask unless …"

Using these and many other customized phrases allows agents to regain their composure while restating the problems the prospects have identified in the interview. By restating the problems, agents can summarize how the features of the property solve the prospects' problem.

Brokers are responsible for improving the sales efficiency of the brokerage operation. They do so by the sales agents they ask to join their firm. Their hiring selections may be dependent on the types of projects or the niche markets the agency is known for attracting. If the broker represents developers' tracts, they may want to hire agents who are specialized order takers or train new agents to be order takers. Agents who choose to conduct phone canvassing may need training in development of customized presentations. Personal selling takes training and is not necessarily the easiest promotional tool to implement. Brokers who have a reasonable idea of the strengths and weaknesses of their salespeople can create sales training programs suited to their needs.

■ Activities of Personal Selling

Selling requires that agents and prospects interact with one another. A variety of marketing media are employed to distribute messages about agents' services. These include direct mail, newspaper ads, radio, television, billboards, and others. Some activities are regarded as marketing, such as public events, yet put agents in direct contact with prospects.

Tools to Promote Agents' Services

We'll cover several tools that agents can use to promote their services: the referral market, business cards, public speaking engagements, real estate courses, and public events.

Tools to Promote Agents' Services

- Referral market
- Business cards
- Public speaking
- Real estate courses
- Public events

Referral Market

A **referral** is the direct result of a satisfied customer telling others about an agent's services and encouraging them to contact the agent. Some offices aggressively work referrals. One example is an office that holds a dinner each year for all of the buyers and another for all of the sellers they assisted during the year. They even invite past sellers and buyers who were represented by co-operating agents, perhaps thinking the co-op agents were not going to invite them to a similar party. The guests participate in raffles for gifts; short seminars update the audience on local developments and growth trends; and the broker asks the guests to recommend the company's services to those they feel could benefit from them.

Working the referral market requires an investment of time and money into the agent's business. Activities agents can do to generate referrals include:

- Keep track of all closed sales (buyers and sellers)
  - Write past customers three or four times per year
  - Follow up with a phone call
- Send small gifts to "bird dogs" (people who refer customers to you) for no particular reason. Let them know you are thinking about them.
- Stay organized
- Return phone calls and reply to e-mail or mail quickly
- Ask for a letter of recommendation when the situation presents itself
- Professionally print wedding-like announcements showing the change of address for your buyer or seller. Contact the sellers and buyers directly and offer to mail them.
- Stop by the homes of your past customers. If they are not home, leave something so they know you were there.

Business Cards

Business cards share with others the fact that you provide a service. They are a form of introduction when first meeting a prospect. They are an excellent promotional tool. Business cards that provide useful information or a useful purpose (magnetic card) are often held longer. If business cards are held by prospects, the agent's name may sound more familiar at the next call or visit.

The prospects are more likely to keep a card if, in addition to reminding the prospects who the agent is, it provides an additional useful service. The back of a card might list emergency phone numbers for local hospitals, police, and utility companies. Getting a vendor, such as a pizza company, to pay for a small portion of the cost of business cards is not that uncommon. In return, the pizza company's delivery phone number is listed on the back of the card. Some agents have also included specially approved discounts for local restaurants or retailers. These forms of business cards can be handed to buyers when they first move into their home, or to sellers after a hard day of packing.

Public Speaking

Public speaking provides a platform for marketing your services. Because you are speaking to and interacting with a number of people, it is considered a form of personal selling. It presents you with a unique opportunity to deliver information that may not be available otherwise. Public speaking comes more naturally for some than for others, but learning how to do it is not impossible. The receiver of the information perceives the agent to be more knowledgeable than other agents. This puts that agent far above the competition. One company in California used a computer software program to create a slide presentation. The presentation described recent changes in the tax laws and how they influenced investment decision making. Well over 300 people attended the seminar. It is still conducted twice a year, or by appointment, and is updated as the tax laws change. Another agent joined with a Certified Financial Planner®/stockbroker to present the real estate portion of a monthly nine-hour financial planning seminar.

Agents might consider taking public speaking courses to polish their natural abilities. For topic ideas, think about the concepts taught in every real estate principles textbook. Many of those concepts are unknown to the general public and would make interesting subjects for a public seminar. There is nothing better in personal selling than when an agent can speak to a lot of people at one time.

Real Estate Courses

Creating real estate courses or volunteering to teach real estate classes at a local community college is a tremendous way to demonstrate your expertise and promote your services. To become involved, call the personnel department at your local community college and ask what the requirements are for teaching real estate courses. See if you can contact the department chairperson or dean about writing a new course not currently represented at the college. Teaching real estate courses is much like public speaking except that in a semester system you are doing it for about three hours every week for 16 to 18 weeks.

Initially, agents should prepare an outline of the course. Share that with the dean or department chairperson. Sell your idea and explain why it is needed in the community. Keep in mind, the subject must be marketable. That means that at least 20 or more students in a community would want to attend, which is not as easy as you might imagine. Also keep in mind that unless you take additional steps, the public's exposure to your new courses is limited by the marketing abilities of the college. You may want to consider talking with the public relations officer at the college about preparing press releases and special advertising about the course.

Courses must be prepared in a specific format that is approved by the state. Volunteers, or curriculum committees, as they are called in many colleges, review the contents for completeness. Agents can check with their local colleges for more information.

Public Events

Although it is difficult to measure their effectiveness, sponsoring public events is sometimes useful. Many of the larger franchises are heavily involved in this kind of promotion. However, agents should strive to go beyond indirect promotion and move toward creating personal contacts. If your agency sponsors public events, ask to be the agent who represents the company. Remember, it's difficult to sell without personal interaction.

■ Steps to a Sale

The activities described in promoting your personal selling services should never end. Agents want the most exposure possible in the shortest period of time. Passing out business cards, asking for referrals, and writing publicity pieces on your education and experience help the community learn more about you. In the meantime, agents should take the next step toward attracting a prospect and executing a sale.

Prospecting

Prospecting helps agents find potential customers who are ready, willing, and able to make a buying decision. Prospecting is the most well known selling activity in which agents are involved. Virtually every real estate licensee starts his or her career learning how to prospect for listings or buyers. Prospecting is like taking a calcium tablet every day to maintain strong bones—on a day to day basis, you don't really know if your efforts are working. Nevertheless, prospecting must never stop. Most agents have heard of "stuffing the pipeline." It's that imaginary pipe into which you stuff the three people you met yesterday, the five listing appointments you had today, and the 200 phone calls you made last week. As you keep stuffing that pipeline, the theory goes that something has to come out the other end. It often does, and sometimes at a furious pace, leaving little time to continue stuffing the pipeline.

As we said, prospecting must never stop or there could be dry spells between periods of great activity. Prospecting incorporates many different activities, once again, limited only by your imagination.

Closed files. A good source of personal contacts comes from the review of closed and canceled transaction files in your office. These files include buyers' phone numbers, new addresses, and the addresses of the properties from which they moved. If the buyers purchased within the same town, they often transfer their phone number to the new address. Many buyers have cell phones, whose numbers may transfer with them if they move to a new carrier.

Generally, homeowners move every five to seven years. Ask the broker if you can call the buyer for a listing appointment. If the responsible salesperson is still with the firm, ask if it would be alright to work those old files. Write the person who bought the buyers' old home (unless they were represented by someone in your firm). It's been five to seven years for them too.

Agents can call, and say, "Hello, my name is Shaun. I represent ABC Realty. We helped you purchase your current home six years ago. The reason I am calling is to see if you were thinking of making a move in the near future."

Lists. Some agents depend exclusively on lists for their prospect leads and personal contacts. These lists come from a variety of sources:

- Rosters from community service organizations
- Country club membership lists
- PTA members
- Voter registration
- Companies that sell lists
- The parents of kids who participate in youth sports teams in the area
- The blanket e-mail addresses from your favorite online Internet service provider
- Title insurance companies; they can generate lists of every homeowner in an area within a few minutes. These lists can tell you when the owners moved in and when they last financed the property, as well as providing data about the property itself.

Expired listings. Brokers sometimes suggest that new agents consider renewing the expired listings in the multiple listing service.[18] The expired listings include those of all agencies. They are not limited to the licensee's office. When just beginning a real estate career, an agent may not have had time to do any market research. The agent needs to get an income stream started. If agents can just get a listing, they will have something to advertise and something to promote to other offices. Expired listings provide a good source of sellers who were once motivated to do something. Sometimes sellers just need a new agent with a marketing plan and an ability to execute it.

Agents can call sellers and say, "Hello. This is Betty from ABC Realty. The reason I am calling is that I noticed that your home is no longer available for sale. Is this what you had intended?"

Farm area. Agents who learn as much as they can about specialized geographic areas are working their "farm" area. These areas often consist of residential homes but can include acreage of a certain size, lots, or commercial or multifamily residential units in a variety of neighborhoods. Unfortunately, when it comes to single-family homes, safety issues have limited the use of "farming" in some areas. However, some agents have discovered that few take advantage of this technique, even with safety precautions added.

This method requires quite a bit of self-discipline. A farm usually consists of about 400 to 500 homes. Your goal is to know every owner of every property. You should know the names of their kids, their ages, hobbies, where

---

18 Agents must check the policy of their local multiple listing service to see if there is a wait period between the time the property expires and the time when the original listing agency can attempt to re-list it.

they work, and as much about their property as possible. It takes dedication to visit or contact each property owner at least four times per year. Most agents take a meticulous approach to organizing a farm area. They generate maps and biography sheets on each owner; they even highlight their assessor maps showing the route they walk. They visit each property at least once (the easy part), but soon find out that persistence is needed, at which point many just give up. The lack of competition is why farming an area generates so much success for those who stick with it. The persistent approach needed may require less face-to-face contact initially, and more contact by direct mail, e-mail, or telephone.

Phone calls. Another approach is to make phone calls. With the use of the Internet, it's easy to find the name and address of almost every property owner with a listed phone number. You can find all the property owners on a street in a certain town within a specific state.

Agents active in this form of sales make between 150 to 200 dials three mornings a week. The term *dials* means they dial the number and let it ring no more than three times. After the third ring, they hang up. Phones that ring more than three times are perceived to be urgent calls. The best approach is to let it ring three times and move on to the next call.

If the owner answers, introduce yourself and your company affiliation: "Hello Ms. Prospect, this is Judy, representing ABC Realty. Do you have just a moment? (If they don't, thank them very much and move on to the next call). The reason I am calling is that your home is in the area I service. I wanted to introduce myself and see if you were thinking of making a move anytime soon."

The conversation could go in many different directions from there. Your purpose is to set an appointment to present them with more information on the listing you called about or on your services.

Prospecting taken a step further. Some real estate agents achieve extraordinary success by taking many of the extra steps discussed throughout this text. In other words, they do more. They go beyond a prospect's expectations. So, aggressively market your listings, be outrageous, and get noticed.

■ The Art of the Successful Sale

After attracting prospects, agents must be ready to make a presentation. The presentations are made to buyers, sellers, or other agents. Presentations have four underlying activities that prospects may not recognize: gaining their attention, maintaining their interest, creating a desire, and demanding action. Before closing the sale,[19] professionals use these steps to persuasively overcome objections by providing solutions to the prospects' perceived needs, wants, or desires.

---

19 *Closing the sale* means the prospect agrees to the purchase—a buyer may choose to purchase a property, a seller may choose to list their property with the agent, or a cooperative agent agrees to demonstrate a listing.

Attention

The first step in making any presentation is to gain the attention of the prospect. It is not uncommon to approach the presentation much like the approach used to develop an advertisement. First, you must gain the attention of the prospects and then hold their interest while developing their desire to take action.

An attention-grabbing sales presentation requires planning and rehearsal. Rehearsal helps develop selling skills that agents can fall back on, especially when involved with unique or stressful selling situations. As agents gain experience, the presentations can become more flexible.

To improve the chances that the prospects will listen to what agents have to say, every effort should be made to avoid distractions during the presentation. Agents cannot grab prospects' attention if they are distracted. The first 30 seconds of a presentation are critical.

Phrases That Grab Attention
- "I'm here to show you how to save $120 per month on your house payment."
- "I have a property in this area that you can own for less per month than your current rent payment."

Interest

Agents gain the interest of prospects when they demonstrate to the prospects what the product or service means to them. Knowing what benefits the prospects are looking for helps agents demonstrate property in such a way that maintains interest. Agents should encourage the prospects to tell them what they need and how they expect their solutions to satisfy those needs. Agents' skill, experience, and imagination in responding to an evolving situation helps guide them toward the best ways of gaining and maintaining the prospect's interest while demonstrating their product or service.

Suppose you are showing an owner-occupied home. The family room has a couch, chair, tables, and lamps—things that make the current owner comfortable. You can walk through the doorway and stand against the wall, as all agents are taught, to make the room look bigger. You can talk about the nice baseboards, the paint color, the view of the backyard—innocent, everyday issues that are a part of the sales process but probably don't do much to sell the home.

Conversely, rather than demonstrating the way the home is currently used, reflect on the extensive first meeting you had with the prospects (presented in more detail in Chapter 13). Keep your presentation flexible. Help the prospects interact with the home. Help them imagine a different use. Help the prospects visualize their goals and show them how your solution satisfies their needs.

Let's look at another practical application that helps generate interest in a property. Suppose the prospects have a difficult time imagining how their furniture might fit into a room. Using a laptop computer and one of the many inexpensive home design software programs, agents can draw the room's dimensions and place the doors, windows, arched openings, and fireplace exactly where they should be. The prospects can help their agent measure the room and provide measurements of their furniture. Using the computer, agents can place their furniture in the room. Once the flat image is exactly as they like it, it can be converted into a 3-D view of the room.

Now the prospects can add window coverings, wall coverings, carpet, change the color of the walls, and add furniture they have yet to purchase. After this is done, agents can use the software's 3-D tools to create a walking tour of the room. If the prospect wasn't sure if a new pool table was going to fit, this type of software program helps put their mind at ease.

Desire

Desire is the motivation or need to solve a problem with a specific product or service. The desire to solve a problem and satisfy their perceived needs motivates prospects to contact agents. If the desire for a solution is not present, then solving the problem or closing the sale is unlikely.

As we mentioned earlier, the sales presentation also involves persuasion. Desire can be influenced by a persuasive message. The influence agents have on the prospects' decision making should not be judgmental or manipulative. Pressuring prospects to take action will only serve to damage your reputation in the end. Persuade them to see the advantages of your solution. Suppose your father would like to access the information in the Library of Congress, but doesn't want to travel to Washington, D.C. Give him a computer. When he looks at you and wonders what he's supposed to do with it, explain how he can access that information on the Internet. Persuade him to use the computer by showing him how much easier it is than traveling to the Library of Congress. With some prospects, it may take a bit of persuasion to get past the learning and on to the solution. In other words, it may take time for the prospect to understand how your solution satisfies their needs.

Action

Taking action in a sales presentation means that the prospects "buy" your solution. Using a home design software program to demonstrate how a room could look and helping the prospects understand how a property fills their perceived needs are some of the steps used in the selling process to persuade prospects to take action.

Encouraging action starts as early as the first extensive qualifying discussion held with the prospects. During this step, agents should ask questions that require profound, complex answers. Agents need to spend time listening to the prospects. Agents are not as concerned with how large the living room is in a home as they are with how the space benefits the prospect, or how it provides the solution they are seeking. Questions should be created that help the prospects understand why they are motivated to take action. Examples of these kinds of questions appear in Chapter 13.

How to Ask for Action

Agent: "Would you like to play billiards in your home in 45 or 60 days?"

Customer: "The quickest we can—45 days?"

Agent: "We will do our best to get you into your home in 45 days. Would you please acknowledge this agreement right here?"

Objections from buyers and sellers are often nothing more than ways of telling agents to slow down. The prospects just need a little room to think. Objections often slow the call for action. By treating objections as if they were questions, agents can help the prospects work through their concerns by making sure they understand the solution that is being presented. Most agents do not feel threatened when prospects ask questions, so there is no need to feel threatened if the prospect brings up an objection.

Closing the Sale

Closing the sale is the last element in the sales process. Agents can close the sale only after the prospects understand the solution. A variety of closing techniques are in Chapter 13; however, all of these activities, when properly executed, should generate the most important factor for future business—a satisfied customer.

■ The Process of Qualifying

Chapter 9 introduced qualifying as one of the steps in personal selling. Although determining the creditworthiness of prospects is very important, of equal importance is discovering their property and emotional needs. Most agents are taught to ask questions such as How many bedrooms are needed? How many people are in your family? or How much do you earn per year? Consequently, those issues might only be touched on here. Agents who take the time to segment the market into manageable groups during the marketing phase learn some of the common product needs of that market segment before meeting with prospects from that segment.

Suppose your market research discovered a sizeable market of registered nurses in the area. Let's make the assumption that being a registered nurse is a high-stress job. In practice, you would use research to back this up. What features in a home might appeal to registered nurses?

Perhaps a spa, a tranquil backyard, or several quiet areas in the home would help relieve some of their stress. When you thoroughly know your market segment, you can use your selling skills to solicit listings that have a better chance of meeting the needs of that target market.

In other words, the reason you want to know your target market so well is so you list the right properties in geographically diverse areas the first time for the largest segment of your market (in this case, registered nurses). Once the prospects are in your office, you can qualify them to confirm what you learned from your research.

Figure 12.2

Qualifying the Prospect

Prospects consider the following things when being "qualified" by an agent.

PROPERTY QUALIFICATIONS	EMOTIONAL QUALIFICATIONS
The number of bedrooms needed	Is the purchase right for me?
The number of bathrooms needed	Will the purchase make me look good?
Size of the garage	Am I paying too much? Will I look like a fool if I am?
Price range they are seeking	
Financial qualifications	Will the home's features save me time and effort?
Geographic area they would consider	
School districts	Is the information detailed enough to make a decision?
Access to shopping, schools, entertainment	Who has done this before me? Were they satisfied with the result?
Quality of construction	Why should I commit to this purchase?
Landscaping	Can I trust this agent?
Etc.	What will my friends think if I work with this agent?
	What will my friends and relatives think of me if I sell? What will they think if I buy in a different area?
	How will this decision change me?
	Will I be noticed?
	If I buy, how will it save me money?
	How do I know this property will work for me over the next several years?

Without a comprehensive qualification process, agents might come across buyer prospects that say they want a three-bedroom, two-bath home with a fireplace on a half-acre in a particular neighborhood for $450,000. However, when they present their "qualified" prospects with the "solution," the prospects don't want to buy. This suggests that there is more to qualifying than getting an indication of what they can afford and a list of the desired features.

The qualifying interview establishes not only the needs of the prospect, but the things that drive those needs. Figure 12.2 helps describe some of the many emotional decisions prospects may consider before choosing to work with the agent. These and other emotional qualifications should be addressed during the qualifying process to make the decision to work with the agent and to purchase easier for the prospect.

It is almost impossible to find everything the prospects are looking for in a property or service. After agents are satisfied that the prospects have a want/need, they must determine how close they must come to the solution the prospect is seeking. Prospects may say they want a four-bedroom, three-bath home with a large yard, but given the knowledge that agents have of their inventory, agents may want to test this need by determining what is more important—a large yard or the third bathroom. In other words, if they could get the third bathroom, could they live with a smaller yard?

We have learned that qualifying prospects is more than asking them how much they earn and what they have in the way of a down payment. It is more than asking them the number of bedrooms they need, how many bathrooms they desire, how close to the freeway the home must be, what school district they prefer, how close they want to be to shopping, and so on.

The property and economic information above is a part of every sale. However, in agents' excitement to make the sale, they sometimes overlook the dynamics and purpose of getting to know more about the prospect. The interview is so important to the qualification and selling process that Chapter 13 is devoted to it.

For now, keep in mind that many different how-to real estate books tell agents that the qualification stage is the most important phase of the sale. Let's explore the reasons with a brief example. In addition to the information mentioned above, you want to find out during the qualification process what the prospects think about certain issues. What are their property and personal/emotional reasons for making a buying decision?

Wouldn't it be powerful to learn that the prospects think interest rates are about to go up? It's a valuable closing tool. You could learn this by asking, "Fritz, what do you feel about the direction of interest rates?" Or, "Increasing inflation usually means increasing interest rates and higher monthly payments." Make sure you include the other spouse. "Is this the way you feel Diane?"

In this example, getting information on how the prospects feel about interest rates helps create a sense of urgency that can be restated when agents present the "best" property to the prospects. Prospects should feel that it is better to buy now than later, when interest rates could be higher.

As explained earlier, until the prospects like and trust the agent, they don't really care what the agent thinks. As we said in Chapter 11, it does little good to tell them interest rates are going up or interest rates have never been this low or you better buy now because the market won't go any lower. Spend the time finding out what they think and what their reasons are for making the purchase.

■ The Reason to Buy

People Buy for Unique Reasons

The qualification process establishes, in the prospect's words, their reasons to buy. Recall from Chapter 11 the importance of listening to the prospects and helping them meet their needs. Interviewing the buyers long enough for them to articulate their reason for buying always makes for an easier sale.

With limited qualifying techniques, agents will leave the initial interview without having gathered the knowledge they will need for the presentation. It's a given that propects expect the plumbing to work, the cooktop to light right up, and the electrical switches to operate. However, if the features of a home were the only things talked about in the interview, this doesn't leave the agent much to talk about when they get to the property, other than the basic features.

If the agent does not know that the family wants a large double oven because they entertain frequently, then just showing them the kitchen is really not going to satisfy their need. However, if the agent discovered this need in the qualifying interview as well as the reason for the need (so that the agent can describe the advantages and benefits of that feature), then demonstrating the kitchen to the prospects may have more significance.

"As you can see, Mae, the double oven is about four inches wider than your current oven. You also might note that the lower oven casing rolls out. It's much like those refrigerators that have the freezer on the bottom, isn't it, Don? This means that it is easier for you to baste a turkey and take it out for carving when ready (advantage). That should make things more convenient for you (benefit), shouldn't it?"

Talking to a Friend

Prospects are more likely to buy from someone they trust as a friend. One of the reasons agents take time to qualify prospects is to build a measure of trust before showing properties. Friendships take time to develop, but are very necessary in life. A friend is someone in whom you can confide. You can talk about anything from your goals to your illnesses. A friend is someone you can trust. Most successful real estate agents become friends with their customers during the process.

Good agents rise above any misconceptions prospects might have of those in the industry. If prospects don't trust them enough to tell them all the symptoms of their problem, the agents would be like a doctor prescribing an aspirin for an aneurysm that was about to burst. If they don't know what their prospects want, they end up showing the wrong property, thereby losing more credibility. And the prospects will tell their friends, "He never listened to what I wanted. He showed me properties that were overpriced, not on a corner, and too far from shopping." In the eyes of the prospects, you are just like all the other agents they have heard about.

Stretch beyond the simple, quick interview, and learn the prospects' reasons for buying. Those reasons provide you the compelling rationale the buyer uses to make a purchase. Once the right property is visited, use that rationale; paraphrase the buyers' own words to help demonstrate how the property meets their needs.

As we will see in Chapter 13, the interview is a time to engage the prospects in a discussion. We have established that prospects don't expect too much of agents, so agents should surprise them. Prospects do expect agents to ask the mundane questions—How many bedrooms? What area? What's your income?—just like all the other agents, so don't disappoint them. However, to lock in those prospects and to get them to like and trust you, ask questions that require more profound thought. It will be unexpected.

Prospect Is Asking for Help

There is almost no reason for the prospects to come to your office unless they have a problem. When people go to the hospital, they are there with a problem and they expect the doctor to provide a solution. It is no different when prospects come to your office. Your job is to discover, often with the prospects, the cause of their problem. Brokers have observed their agents sometimes get frustrated with their buyers. One agent told his broker that his buyers said they wanted a four-car garage. The buyers were very demanding on this point. The agent said he showed at least 10 or 12 homes with four-car garages, and still the buyers wouldn't make an offer.

The broker asked him if he explored the reasons why they wanted a four-car garage. The agent admitted that he hadn't. He assumed the buyers knew what they wanted. This is an example of the results of a common (incomplete) interview—take down what the buyers say they want and fill the order.

After conducting a more thorough interview, the agent discovered the cause of the problem. The reason they didn't make any offers was that the garages they were shown were too small to handle their 24-foot boat and trailer (the cause of the problem). Once the agent understood the cause of the problem, it was much easier to focus his personal selling tasks on a selection of homes that would solve this problem and satisfy the need.

Well-thought-out interview questions help prospects understand their need, the cause of their problem, and the kinds of solutions that will solve it.

Know the Inventory

Professional agents stay familiar with the changing inventory in the market. When questions are skillfully prepared, agents find that they can help prospects identify a solution that is available within their existing inventory of properties. There comes a time during the interview when the prospects so completely understand the cause of the problem, they can't wait to go out and find the solution they now clearly visualize. After all, it is their solution. They own it. Again, depending on how the agent structures the questions, the prospects should have described a property that is currently on the market.

As you can tell, the interview is a significant aspect of personal selling. If you show properties that are not getting favorable responses from the prospects, you did something wrong in the interview. The importance of discovering the prospects' reason to buy can't be stressed enough. So ask questions of the prospects and listen to their answers. Most people like to hear themselves talk and they are even more impressed with you when you take notes.

■ Why Don't They Buy?

Without a careful review, it never seems to make sense why a buyer doesn't buy from the listings you present them. Agents know that it's easier to sell people something they want; that's why they conduct the qualifying interview—to find out the price they can afford or the number of bedrooms needed. The fact of the matter is, there are many reasons people buy or don't buy real estate (see Figure 12.3).

Figure 12.3

Reasons to Buy

PRODUCT REASONS FOR A PURCHASE	EMOTIONAL/PERSONAL REASONS FOR A PURCHASE
"The corner lot gives you a bigger back-yard for the kids."	Prestige, love of family, power
"This home is only one mile from the main highway to work."	Saves time, money
"You will be one of the first to purchase in this new tract."	Desire to be noticed
"You will note that this is a well-established area."	Gain the respect of others, pride of ownership

A product reason for purchasing a home might be a job transfer, a pay raise, or the fact that the current home is too small, underinsulated, or too far from the main road that takes the owner to work. Through questioning, the prospects can share a list of features they want in their new home. After an interview, some agents are excited. They select a list of properties that meet the product list almost exactly—three bedrooms, convenient location, better insulation—but the buyers make no offer.

Emotional Reasons for Buying

Agents get frustrated when prospects don't buy when presented with what they said they wanted. A comprehensive qualifying interview discovers that people don't always buy for the product reasons disclosed to agents. Purchasing real property is a complex decision and prospects are usually motivated by both product and emotional stimuli. Albert Bandura points out that emotions play a role in our purchases. Many times it isn't only the large living room with a view that prospects buy, but the sense of self-worth or self-satisfaction that plays into their decision making.[20]

Emotional reasons for our purchases concern how the purchases affect us. Suppose prospects had a choice of purchasing a home on an inside lot or purchasing the same floor plan on the same lot size that was on a corner. The prospects may choose the inside lot if they feel it improves their ability to develop new relationships without being too demonstrative. Others may select the corner location if they feel it gives them more power or prestige. Prospects rarely share their emotional reasons for a purchase. Emotional reasons for a need are deduced from the interview. These deductions give agents an overall impression about the prospects and the tools necessary to overcome no help, as we discussed in Chapter 11. Agents can develop follow-up questions that confirm their impressions of the prospects' motivations.

Some prospects may have never really assigned a conscious reason for their emotional purchases. We all developed a preference when we purchased our last car. Why were you first attracted to your particular model? Was it that

---

20 Albert Bandura, *Self-Efficacy: The Exercise of Control* (New York: W. H. Freeman and Company, 1997), 450.

the promotional campaign addressed an emotional need (e.g., the need for speed, to look good in traffic, to appear younger, to protect your family) or did you buy it because of its side-impact safety features?

Use your personal selling skills by reconfirming what you learn during the interview until you have defined what truly motivates the prospects. The fact that an agent was finally able to find a home with a garage big enough for a boat may not have been what motivated the buyer above. What might have motivated him could have been

- his desire to maintain the best-looking boat on the river,
- the need to preserve an old wooden boat to ensure the memories of him and his father fishing when he was a boy, or
- his plans to buy a boat when he retires.

Take as much time as you need during the interview to discover what motivates the prospects. In addition to the property or product needs, find the emotional reasons for the purchase.

Emotional Motivation

Suppose you were a candy salesperson. If you found that your customers craved strawberry (a motivation to eat candy), why would you offer them chocolate?

The same is true in real estate sales. Remind the prospects what motivates them to action when demonstrating features in a home. "I would imagine this location on top of the hill can be seen from several miles away. What do you think?" Obviously, this question reinforces an underlying reason to purchase. Satisfying emotional needs is often more powerful than solving for the product needs. When you know what motivates customers, why waste time telling them or showing them something that does not motivate them to buy? If you don't know what motivates customers, then the process of showing a property may be a waste of time for the prospects and frustrating for you!

■ Summary

Personal selling is one of the most challenging yet influential elements of the promotional strategy. It is challenging for brokers because of the high cost of recruitment and training. Many licensees don't want to appear to be selling something to prospects. From most prospects' point of view, that's a good position for agents to take. Prospects don't want to be sold something, but they do expect agents to solve their problems. The ability to interact face-to-face with prospects makes personal selling the most influential aspect of promotion.

Brokers should take the time to become familiar with the personal selling strengths and weaknesses of their sales staff. Those who recognize the different types of salespeople on their staff have a better opportunity to develop training programs to meet their needs and those of the office.

Agents promote their personal selling services through multiple media, including business cards, the referral market, public speaking, and public events. These promotional activities help expose the agent's education and experience to the public while they take additional steps to create a sale. These steps involve advertising for listings or buyers, prospecting, developing farm areas, telephone canvassing, or evaluating closed transactions and expired listings.

At some point, prospects approach you and you are charged with the responsibility of qualifying them. This should not be a simple financial qualification. Prospects are unique with both property and emotional reasons for their purchases. Agents must take time during the qualification process (the comprehensive interview) to discover their needs.

■ Multiple Choice Questions

1. What is the *MOST* important aspect of personal selling?
   a. One-on-one training
   b. The ability to interact with the prospect
   c. Taking orders
   d. Prospecting

2. Which of the following *BEST* describes an order getter?
   a. Their presentations are considered offensive by many.
   b. They depend on the prospects to tell them the price they will pay.
   c. Their selling style is very effective in tract developments.
   d. They aggressively seek out past customers and search for new ones.

3. Real estate agents who sponsor annual parties for their customers are working the _____ market.
   a. referral
   b. housing
   c. multiple listing
   d. financial

4. Which of the following is *MOST* associated with the expression "stuffing the pipeline"?
   a. Advertising
   b. Farming a geographic area
   c. Prospecting
   d. Public speaking

5. Although rarely shared with the agent, _____ reasons for buying concern how the purchase affects the buyer.
   a. rational
   b. irrational
   c. emotional
   d. motivated

■ Exercises

Exercise 1—Emotions play a role in our purchases. Prospects who say they need a three-bedroom home usually mean to say that a three-bedroom home could solve their need. The underlying need is often an emotional one, such as the need for more privacy. Personal selling must address the emotional reasons people have for buying. Imagine that you are a prospect. Develop some emotional reasons for a purchase decision.

Exercise 2—This exercise links together the need to disclose intent, as was discussed in Chapter 10. When creating customized presentations, agents should remember that the receiver of the information wants to know the intent as quickly as possible. Develop a one-minute customized presentation for a telephone-canvassing project. The presentation should include information on who you are and the intent of the call.

Exercise 3—Public speaking or teaching allows agents to interact with a number of people at once. This creates better efficiency when personal selling is used to deliver the message. Many times, topics for presentations are found in the daily newspaper or real estate textbooks. Make a list of five topics for which you can create one- or two-hour seminars for public presentations. Develop an outline or a full PowerPoint presentation for any one of these topics. If in a classroom setting, make presentations to the class. Remember that agents are trying to sell their expertise and professionalism through the vehicle of public speaking.

13

THE INTERVIEW AND CLOSE

■ Learning Objectives

After the study and review of this chapter, you should be able to

- explain the reason for questions with a purpose;
- identify ways to use the interview when presenting your property or service;
- explain the reason for the interview questions you develop;
- develop interview questions that requires complex answers from prospects;
- describe the difference between negative and positive objections;
- understand and describe the methods used to break down an objection;
- describe the steps used in negotiating and closing the sale;
- describe the use of the trial closing question;
- identify and give practical use to multiple closing techniques; and
- analyze and put into action the final step in negotiating and closing the sale, which includes empathizing with the prospects' situation, questioning the problem, helping the prospects solve the problem, and asking for the order.

■ Key Terms

negative objection	positive objection	trial close
objection	right solution	

The key to a successful interview is finding what motivates prospects to seek a certain solution and then providing the property that will deliver that solution. Misunderstanding the prospects' needs and how they perceive the solution to their problem or providing the wrong answer to a problem results from a poor interview. Throughout the text, we have identified several reasons for a well-organized interview:

- To discover the prospects' needs and the cause of the problem
- To determine what motivates the prospects
- To discover how the prospects describe the property
- To discover how the prospects perceive that the property will solve their problem

Although an interview is regarded as primary data, it is also a personal selling tool that, when successful, puts agents in a better position to counsel their prospects. Agents experience a successful interview when the prospects describe a property that already exists in the agent's inventory. This chapter identifies how questions that are well prepared and asked require profound answers—answers that require more than a yes or no. If questions do not have a strong purpose, a strong reason for asking them, then avoid them. Once on site at the property, prospects may bring up objections. We will discuss how to break down an objection to understand it and overcome it. We conclude this chapter by evaluating some negotiating and closing techniques used in the industry.

■ How to Use the Qualifying Interview

When fully developed, interview questions will not necessarily change with each prospect because the agent seeks to accomplish the same things in each presentation, approach, or interview. What changes are the answers given by unique individuals. You can imagine the differences in answers given by first-time buyers and experienced investors. Each has a different understanding of the subject at hand. However, the agent is still responsible for persuasively communicating to each the benefits of the property or the agent's services.

The time for showing properties after the interview may vary. Most agents show property immediately; others may wait a day. In either case, before leaving the office to view any properties, summarize how the prospects have identified the cause of their problem and what the solution means to them. Agents should have gained some sense of how the prospects perceive the solution.

Agents must be very familiar with the prospects before leaving the office. If there is any miscommunication, it is better to take care of it before viewing any properties. The interview has the greatest effect on prospects when you can remind them of their thinking or the statements they made during the interview.

One example we used earlier was a prospect's need for a four-car garage. Market the features in the home by using the information gathered from the initial meeting.

"As you can see, Richard, the garage is 31 feet long, and the walls are finished and insulated. This should give the boat you and your dad used to fish on the protection it needs, don't you think?"

■ The Qualifying Interview

Agents must be thoughtful when preparing for a qualifying meeting. Qualifying questions will take some time to develop. Each must have a purpose. Over the next several pages are interview questions followed by the purpose for asking each question. After you read the first three or four questions and the purpose for asking them, you are encouraged to read the remaining questions and assign a purpose for them before reading the purpose in the text. The results of a successful interview are prospects who like and trust the agent, who have a complete understanding of what they want and why, who have described the property they will buy from the available inventory, and who want to see the solution now.

Offer the Right Solution

The **right solution** for prospects treats both the property needs and the personal or emotional needs. The initial meeting helps agents learn what the right solution is and how to present it. The reason for preparing so many questions, all of which may or may not be asked during the interview, is so that agents do not damage their credibility by offering prospects the wrong property or emotional solution.

A great deal of thought and time should go into the development of interview questions. Their design should encourage the prospects to disclose as much about their problem and its causes as possible. Through your questions, find out what the solution means to the prospects. Don't provide a thumbtack when a 20-pound picture hook is what's needed.

Questions with a Purpose

Few agents set appointments with prospects without any idea of the kinds of questions they will ask. Many ask about the prospects' hobbies, the number of bedrooms they want, and how much money they make, but the interview can be so much more.

Professional salespeople in all industries take the time to create simple, direct questions that require profound, thoughtful answers. The questions are shaped in such a way that allows the prospects to talk more than the agent does, which develops trust. The questions should help guide the prospects toward discovering their true needs. When agents are familiar with the inventory, they can ask questions that help prospects describe property within that inventory. Avoid designing or crafting interview questions without a purpose in mind. Prospects who call or come to your office already feel they have a problem. The questions you ask will help them share with you what they are trying to accomplish. The following questions are in no particular order and, assuming that the formalities are out of the way, everyone is on a first-name basis, unless otherwise indicated. Let's look at a few.

Suppose a couple comes into your office after reading one of your ads. The secretary shows them into your comfortable conference room. On the walls are certificates showing the educational background and professionalism of the agents in the office.

After the buyers are settled and the secretary has delivered their coffee or iced tea, you enter the room and introduce yourself. Have a seat and make some small talk before going into the qualifying process. How do you begin?

You can begin in many different ways, but remember to develop trust; the prospects must feel you have their best interests in mind. Your initial questions should be conversational in nature. The questions in the opening minutes of the interview should not require a lot of thinking and may consist of simple fact-finding questions.

Questions that require little thought:

"How do you spell your last name?"

"Where are you currently living?"

"How long have you been looking for a home?"

Purpose: These questions give you minimal information, but they help put the prospects at ease in the initial phase of an interview.

The simple questions that require little thought slowly lead to the next part of the interview. In this phase, agents ask questions to find out what and how the prospects think, how they feel about certain topics, and what they like the best and the least about various issues.

Question: "What have you done to resolve this problem?"

Purpose: The answers they give may reveal that they are seeing several agents at the same time. You may discover that they are serious buyers, but they don't want to purchase for at least six more months. They may tell you about the disappointments they had with other agents. All of this information is helpful to you in formulating a plan to help them.

Question: "Have you purchased other properties in the past?" If they have, ask, "What did you like the best about the experience? What did you like the least? What did you like the best about the agent? What did you like the least?"

Purpose: By asking these kinds of questions, the prospects will tell you what they expect. Their reactions are memorable when you paraphrase in your own words how you perceive the meaning of the words they used to describe what they liked the best about their agent, as well as the opposite of what they liked the least.

This last may be a little confusing. Suppose the agent asks the following question.

Question: "What did you like the best about the last agent you worked with?"

Purpose: Many times, you will get a reply that may surprise you, such as, "What I didn't like was how he wasted our time. We told him exactly what we wanted and he continually showed us property that we didn't like."

Keep in mind that the agent asked a question that should have elicited a positive response. However, many marketers who use this question receive a negative response. That's fine. Feed back the negative information in a positive way and paraphrase what you perceive to be the meaning of the prospect's statement.

> "As I understand it, you are looking for an agent who can save you time when looking for a home. You want an agent who will show you property that meets your needs and not the needs of the agent. Is that about right?"

Prospects' reactions to this type of statement are amazing. If you are the first agent they have ever gone to that actively applied positive questioning, empathic listening, and feedback, they may not go anywhere else.

As a side note, don't paraphrase the prospects' responses immediately after each question. If it is a short interview, the feedback can take place at the end. However, when conducting an extensive interview, you don't want the prospects to feel you have lost interest in what they are saying. You might test your understanding of what the prospects are telling you by feeding it back to them after they have responded to five or six questions. The feedback is designed to let the prospects know that you are listening and that you understand, and in so doing you are encouraging them to tell you more. You want to learn as much as you can about the prospects, so encourage them to talk more than you. Let them know that your recommendations depend on how complete they make their answers and how well you understand them. When you feed back their responses, it lets the prospects hear your understanding of their problem. You want to be in the position to offer the right selection of listings the first time.

> *Question:* "The home you are referring to in our ad may work well for you, but it's hard to know at this stage if it is best for your situation. I certainly don't want to waste your time. To make sure we are on the same page, may I ask you a few questions?"

> *Purpose:* Statements like this suggest that you are a professional. They demonstrate to the prospects that you are interested in them and shows that you do not want to waste their time by providing them the wrong solution to their problem.

Agents need to know what the prospects expect of them as soon as possible. The following questions often get some interesting answers.

> *Questions:* "What do you expect from us today?"

> "Would you expect to find this afternoon the home you are going to buy?"

Purpose: Many times agents are uncomfortable when working with a new client. Most prospects feel the same way. Questions like this may appear later in an interview. After summarizing a series of questions, the prospects may respond to a question like this by telling you that they expect to look at only three to five homes, and they expect that one of them will be the home they are going to buy.

The prospects will not say, "Show me three to five homes and I will buy one." They will respond indirectly by telling you things such as:

- They expect you to do your job
- They expect you to discover the cause of their problem
- They expect you to provide three to five solutions from which they can pick
- They expect you to do it today
- They expect to stay in control

Question: "Are there any special people or situations that might affect your real estate purchase?"

Purpose: This question allows the prospects to say that they are not the actual buyers of the property. They can tell you who makes the final decisions for the purchase. They can tell you if a relative or a friend has to have input or has to approve the purchase. They can tell you if they must sell another property or stocks or if they are waiting for a cash deposit from some source before purchasing. It is an open-ended question intended to elicit a more detailed response than asking, "Do you have a home to sell before you purchase?"

Question: "I like to make presentations to all concerned parties. Is that how decisions are made in your family?"

Purpose: This is another way of asking the same question above. Agents can confirm earlier responses by embedding similar, although differently worded questions into the later portions of the interview. This question should not be asked as an immediate follow-up question to the one above, but asked later if the agent has not received an adequate response.

Question: "Many times we find people who come to us with cash from the sale of their home or other property. Is that your situation?"

Purpose: This is a nice way to find out if they have other properties they must sell, or may consider selling, in the future. It also gives you an idea as to the source of their deposit or down payment. Sometimes they may tell you that they have the cash needed for a speedy closing. This is also another way to confirm information received from the "special situations" question.

Question: "What is your impression of what a real estate agent does?"

Purpose: This question often leads to surprising responses. Sometimes the buyers or sellers will tell you what they wished agents would do (if so, take good notes), or they will tell you what their past agents didn't do for them. Many times interview questions need to be asked multiple times, but in different ways. This question could be asked later in the interview if you had earlier asked, "What do you expect from us today?" and you didn't get all the information you needed.

Questions: "If you were to stand across the street from your new home, what would your new front yard *not* have in it?" Follow-up questions could include: "Would you see any weeds? Trees? Cracks in the driveway? A circular driveway?"

"In looking at the home from this angle can you tell me about the roof? Is it tile or asphalt shingle?"

"Where is the garage? Is it on the side or in the front? Is it a two-car, three-car, or an oversized garage?"

Continue with this line of either/or questioning. Help the prospects describe their solution.

Purpose: Notice how the first question is asked. Using the word *not* causes the prospects to pause. It is not the way questions are usually asked. Each question is designed to have the prospects pause and reflect before responding. If you see a quizzical expression on their faces, it just means that you may have to help them. You might ask if weeds in the front yard are okay or if they would want a circular drive or a home without one.

It is very important to understand at this point that agents should employ their knowledge of the inventory by asking give-and-take kinds of questions. Agents might know of listings with garages on the side of the home and others with garages facing the street. The questions that follow the initial question above depend on how the prospects answer the first question. If the prospects said they want a garage with an entrance on the side, the next question should involve features found in listings with side garages. Asking questions this way helps prospects describe properties that are in your inventory. This process continues until there are five or six homes from which to select. Be sure to find out why the features are important to the prospect. As you can see, agents must know the inventory before conducting an interview.

Questions: "If there was a minimum goal we had to meet for you in this area, what would it be?"

"If this goal could not be met but we could come close (we could only get a two-car garage with a side workshop, instead of a three-car garage), what would you think about that?"

Purpose: This question has a lot of application. It is often a follow-up question to almost any topic. For example, you might have addressed multiple areas of the home—bedrooms, family room, the fireplace—and you are trying to find out which was the most important to the prospects. After the prospects identify the most important element (which will help you solve the right problem), you can ask a question like this to find out the prospect's minimum expectations.

Question: "What is more important to you, having my staff and me review your specific needs and locate properties that fit those needs, or pulling some property out of the MLS and driving out to see if they work for you?"

Purpose: A question like this demonstrates competence and develops the prospects' trust in the agent. The prospects' response may also tell you a lot about their motivations. Are they really interested in finding a property best suited to their needs or do they just want to drive around and get a feel for the market?

Question: "Have you ever been with an effective, professional salesperson who found you the right home within a few showings?" Whether the response is positive or negative, follow up by asking, "How did you feel about that?"

Purpose: This question gives you an opportunity to gain some insight into what salespeople have done for them in the past. Whether their response is positive or negative, when you ask the follow-up question you gain a clear idea of what they expect of you.

The questions you design should be well organized; in other words, they should have a sequential order to them. You should start with questions that are easy to answer, then slowly move to questions about what the prospects think, and later to questions about how they feel about their situation, solutions, or the sales process. Take a weekend or two to develop questions that require thought and reflection. The more you let the prospects talk, the more easily they become creative contributors to the solution.

The net result of a well-prepared interview is that you will discover with the prospects the difference between what they have, what they need, and, more important, why they need it. As answers to the interview questions make the solution clear, agents may find it harder to contain the prospects. They are ready for the solution. They have, probably for the first time, a clear understanding of their problem. They have articulated their perception of what the solution looks like.

An important last step in the qualification process is to give them a verbal summary of the nature of their problem, its probable causes, and the prospects' perceived solutions. Some agents may paraphrase what the prospects have told them. Others may use the words the prospects used to answer the questions, with the exception of their transition phrases. Let's try the latter. Request agreement with what you are saying throughout the summary and at the end of the interview. Your summary may go something like this (the prospects' original words are in *italics*):

"As I understand it, you *think that inflation is rising and this will cause interest rates to go up soon.* You *feel that* your *payments will go up if interest rates rise.* You are *looking for a home in the northeast side of town so that you will have enough income left over to enjoy your free weekends out of town.* Is that right?

"You *feel that a four-bedroom home around $560,000 will suit* your *needs.* However, you indicated that *the home must have a detached garage.* We discussed that we did *not need to have a close fit on anything other than the detached garage.* Was I right in thinking that?"

Continue with this detailed summary until completed. You will be amazed at the prospects' response when you finish. Agents have had customers literally get out of their chair, shake the agent's hand, and express their gratitude for being the first agent who really understood their needs! All the agents did was paraphrase what the prospects said to them.

Sample Interview Questions

These interview questions are in no particular order. They are designed to elicit profound answers from the prospects. The agent must give some thought to assigning an order to these questions and possible follow-up questions. The list that follows is in no way complete; nor is it presumed that all of the questions will be asked of the prospect.

- What do you expect from this initial interview?
- What do you expect to do today?
- Why did you come to our firm?
- How did you hear about our firm?
- What are your thoughts on home ownership?
- What are your initial thoughts on taxes?
- How do you feel about real estate as an investment?
- What is your impression of the direction of inflation? Home prices? Interest rates? Population growth in the area? Etc.
- Are there any special people or situations that might affect your real estate purchase?
- When you bought your last house, what attracted you to the real estate office with which you worked?
- What did you like best about the real estate agent?
- What did you like least about the real estate agent?
- What do you like best about where you are currently living?
- What do you like least about where you are currently living?
- Are you working with any other professional real estate agents at this time?
- Do you anticipate doing so?
- How many are in your family?
- You said you had _____ people in your family. How many of them are children?
- Do you plan to stay in the home a long time?
- Many times, we find people who come to us with cash from the sale of their home or other property. Is that your situation?
- What portion of the cash proceeds from the sale do you anticipate using for your down payment?

- What amount are you comfortable taking from your savings for the down payment?
- What do you expect of a real estate agent?
- What is your impression of what a real estate agent does?
- If we were to look at the components of a home—bedrooms, bathrooms, family room, fireplace, and so on—which is the most important to you?
- How important is it that we find the right home for you today? This week?
- What has been your formula for success in finding a home in the past?
- Have you ever been with an effective, professional salesperson that found you the right home within a few showings? How do you feel about that?
- Are you familiar with our school districts? (Don't educate, just ask the question.)
- Would you like to be close to schools?
- What special features or situations would you like us to try to address? How important are those to you?
- When you looked at or bought homes in the past, have you noticed that you ended up looking at a lot of homes that just didn't seem to fit you?
- Can you assign a reason to that?
- How do you envision a real estate salesperson helping you?
- I hate to waste time looking at homes that don't suit the customers' needs. Is that how you feel?
- Often our customers have a preconceived idea of how their new home should look. Are there things about a home that you are totally uncomfortable with?
- Aside from the obvious, are there things in a home you just can't live without?
- Based on all you have said, if we found the house you have described within the first few showings, would you be compelled to look at more?
- I like to make presentations to all concerned parties. Is that how decisions are made in your family?
- What time constraints do you have for finding your next home?
- What would be the driving force that would cause you to want to look at more homes if you were standing in a home that you described in our interview?

Let's summarize this process. The sample questions above are designed to stimulate you to put more thought into the kinds of questions you design. Your list of interview questions should be as complete as possible, but you will not necessarily ask all of them when interviewing each prospect. Attempt to develop follow-up questions that reconfirm what the prospect says. This type of question should be written differently, but should solicit a confirming response to a particular issue. These should not be asked immediately after the initial question. Let some time pass before using follow-up questions to confirm an earlier response. Your interview questions should discover the prospects' perceptions, what they think, and how they feel about certain issues relevant to their real estate purchase.

Let them answer the questions completely. Don't ask another question or follow up on the question just answered unless you are certain they have finished responding. Gain permission to write down their answers before starting the interview. Your questions should be almost Freudian in that they might be interpreted by the prospect in a couple of ways. Do not judge what prospects say. Just write down their responses. Lastly, your interview should have a tactical, well-focused order to it. Design the order of the questions so that the prospect can hardly wait to solve their problem.

■ Negotiating and Closing the Sale

The close may be the most difficult step in the selling process. There is probably no one right way to close a real estate transaction. For new licensees, this is a frustrating thing to hear. Some salespeople say they know when to close because it feels right. That's not much help. Others say that you can tell by watching the prospects. Some agents suggest that if a couple holds hands after viewing a property that they may be ready to purchase. Others suggest that prospects are closer to a purchase when they ask questions about a property or want to spend more time in the property. So how do you help the prospects create that first offer? How do you close them?

Although there is no guarantee, after the comprehensive qualification step, it is very difficult for the buyers not to purchase one of the properties agents present. The reason is that during the qualification step buyers develop a clear picture of the home they will buy. The questions generate an excitement of discovery. Questions help the prospects describe a home in the agent's inventory. When prospects see the home they want to buy, they can hardly believe the agent was able to find almost exactly what they described. Often a high percentage of buyers will ask how they can buy the property. Agents won't have to ask them. Not only will a high percentage of prospects buy, but they will also be very happy that they made the purchase. After all, it is exactly what they said they wanted—and more.

If the prospects don't ask you to buy the property, you will have to look for opportunities to close. Sometimes the prospects will help you. They will ask you a question or bring up an objection. You can either answer the question or you can create a closing opportunity. The prospects might ask how quickly they can take possession. They might ask if the refrigerator is included, if the roof leaks, or any number of other tremendous questions that create an opening for the close.

Let's take the first question as an example.

Prospects: "How quickly can we close the transaction?"

Agent: "120 days." By saying this, the agent just missed an opportunity to close!

Instead, consider this response:

Agent: "Steve, I'm sure you wouldn't ask how long it would take unless you and Pam were interested in the property. Am I right in assuming that?"

Wait for the prospects' positive answer.

Prospects: "That's right."

Agent: "The process can finish up in 130 to 150 days; which works best for you?"

Write their answer down on the purchase agreement and you are on your way. This trial close tests whether the prospects are ready to move forward with you. When you start filling in the offer, it's known as the contract or purchase agreement close. We will discuss this and other closing techniques in just a moment. Let's first understand the trial close and how to break down an objection and solve it.

■ Trial Close

A **trial close** helps the prospects and the agent determine if they are looking at the right property, or if the agent needs more information from the prospects or the prospects need more information from the agent.

Let's say you have an unfurnished home listed. The sellers say they will paint the walls any color the buyers want. Based on what you know about the buyers, you could ask this trial close question:

"In this room, which would go best with your couch and love seat, Cathy, a light blue paint or mauve?"

If the prospects don't respond to this trial close they are lacking the information necessary to make a decision and you are lacking the information necessary to create a close. Additional trial closes of this type help gain that information. This technique works well for agents because prospects may not perceive most trial closes to be closing questions. If prospects respond, then agents can move forward with a formal close. If prospects need more information, they may bring up an objection.

■ Understanding Objections

As powerful as a successful interview can be in generating a smooth transaction, objections will come up and when they do, they have a tendency to unnerve some agents. So, before we break down an objection, let's first understand that there are two ways that prospects might slow you down: negative objections and positive objections.

Negative Objection

An objection has the impact of slowing the forward movement of the negotiations. Professional agents welcome objections because they help overcome misunderstandings. However, **negative objections** block communication. Suppose you are the buyer, and you didn't like a home. As you left the property you probably wouldn't say that much about it. You would get into the agent's car and let the agent drive you to the next property.

If the agent really pressed you and tried to get you to buy it, you would defend your position by coming up with a negative objection. Negative objections don't necessarily slow the process; they stop the forward movement of the close. They also challenge the prospects' sense of trust in the agent. When pressed, prospects may say, "We can't believe you showed us that property!" Subconsciously, they may be thinking, "Great, another agent who isn't listening to what we need." Negative objections are difficult to overcome. The prospects do not want a particular property and cannot believe that you are trying to sell it to them. Agents may be able to recover from this situation by saying, "I was hoping you would feel that way. I wanted to be sure before showing you this next home." However, the damage to your credibility might have already been done. When the qualification step is done well, you will have all of the ammunition needed to keep negative objections to a minimum.

Positive Objection

A **positive objection** is more like a hurdle than a block wall. They should be treated as questions because the prospects need more information in order to make a decision. Suppose the interview indicated a strong interest in homes priced around $463,000. Instead, you show them homes priced around $468,000. This is not uncommon in the industry. When prospects make the positive objection, "That price seems a little high," it is their way of telling you why they are not making the purchase; conversely, a negative objection might be stated as, "We are not interested in something like this." You need to recognize this communication *quickly*.

A positive objection is also an indication that you missed something in the interview. Perhaps if you had asked, "And how close must we come to that price?" the prospects would have responded, "That is our high end. We would prefer homes between $458,000 and $463,000."

■ Breaking Down an Objection

An **objection** is simply a technique used by prospects to slow the sales process. To overcome an objection, agents need to help the prospects break the problem down so that they both have a clear understanding of it.

Suppose your customers want a three-bedroom home. They do not want to spend time doing any yard work. When you try to show them a three-bedroom home on a 1/8-acre lot—a lot size that is considerably smaller than others in your area—the customers object because they don't understand how your selection satisfies their need for spending no time on yard work. Perhaps a condominium might have worked better.

When prospects don't understand how a property gives them the benefit they want, they object. You will discover the benefit they are looking for somewhere in the interview. So familiarize yourself with how prospects define their needs and how they define the solution before showing them any property. When you present the property, demonstrate it from a benefits standpoint.

Interaction between agents and the prospects helps break down objections, which as we said are simply requests for more information. In order to discover the problem, agents should keep their talking to a minimum to get the prospects involved in the solution. When handled successfully, the prospects will disclose what the problem is or they will see how ridiculous their objection is. Both results give them an opportunity to move forward with the agent.

Overcoming Objections

One way of overcoming an objection is by reflecting on the words the prospects said during the interview. To make this simple, suppose the agent asks, "How would you describe the neighborhood you would like to move into?" The prospects may say, "We would like a quiet neighborhood with wide streets, young families, and quality homes." Now suppose after showing several neighborhoods, the prospects object. Several things may be going on in the prospects' minds. The prospects may be wondering what their friends will think after they purchase a home in this neighborhood. They need an answer. Most agents will offer a response. They might explain the advantages of the neighborhood, access to shopping and schools, and a myriad of other things. However, if the prospects can't remember these advantages or they can't relate to them, there may be a problem. It's easier for the prospects to remember their own words.

Therefore, by restating the advantages in the prospects' words, the agent demonstrates how the neighborhood meets or exceeds the objectives laid out during the interview:

> "Based on what you told me in the office, you were looking for a quiet neighborhood with quality homes. Isn't that right?" After a response, the agent continues by saying, "As I recall, Debbie, you also wanted to be located in an area with wide streets and homes that had young families so that your children may have someone to play with. For these reasons, I thought this neighborhood would be well suited to your needs. What do you think?"

By reminding them of what they said, you have given them enough ammunition needed to counter anything they might hear from their friends. Remind the prospects of the interview by pointing out the benefits that make up the total product. Prevent or slow down negative objections by selling quality, service, power, security, satisfaction, respect, pride, and the multitude of other things that may come up in an interview.

Should You Answer Every Objection?

Most agents recognize how fruitless it is to try to have an answer for every objection. Yet some agents try to win that game with prospects. By doing this, every time the prospects object and the agent comes up with a brilliant response, the prospects find another objection. The contest goes on until someone "wins."

Of course, no one wins; not the seller, the buyer, or the agent. If the prospects are the last ones to raise an objection that the agent can't answer, a sale is not made. One of the closing techniques in the next section will help prevent this cycle from continuing. It is called the final objection close.

■ Closing Techniques

Besides the trial close mentioned above, many real estate salespeople still use techniques developed during the sales era of marketing in the 1920s and 1930s. Today, sales trainers in multiple industries have developed closing questions appropriate for their product or service. Zig Ziglar, in his book

Secrets of Closing the Sale, lists over 100 closing questions and responses. Tom Hopkins has conducted multiple seminars over the years that describe similar closing techniques. Several decades ago, J. Douglas Edwards recorded a presentation of 13 closes. These closes set the foundation for many closing techniques. They are common to those discussed by most sales trainers today and are presented here. By combining these closing techniques and the interactive interview, agents have a powerful set of tools to help the prospects get what they want.

Purchase Agreement Close

The purchase agreement close assumes that the prospects are moving forward with you. In other words, agents assume the prospects want to buy the property. To do so, agents must fill in the purchase agreement. During the sales era, this was the first close agents used. It makes sense still today because no matter what technique you use, they all end up with the action of filling in the offer.

The steps are simple. They require that you ask questions and write down the answers on the form. Don't make the initial questions difficult to answer. Remember that you are assuming the prospects are ready to buy, so ask questions such as: "What are your full names?" "What is your correct mailing address?" "What is the correct spelling of your last name?" As they answer, fill in the purchase agreement. You are making this very easy for the prospects and as long as they don't stop you, they have purchased the property.

The Question Close

In the question close, agents ask questions and then remain quiet until the prospects provide an answer. When most people ask a question, they get a response. The question close works for that reason. Some sales trainers suggest that after asking a question, the first person to talk, make a noise, or clear their throat loses this one. As in the first closing technique, agents may ask, "How do you spell your last name?" They write the answer on the purchase agreement and then continue with the purchase agreement close. Questions may help bring up objections that agents overcome with other techniques. The reasons for not buying may remain unknown for lack of a question. Agents use the question close to help the prospects buy or find out why they are not ready to buy.

The Alternative Choice Close

This technique poses a question in such a way that it allows the transaction to continue forward. Agents ask a question that causes the prospects to choose one way or another way. When the prospects answer, they are committing to part of the overall purchase. It is important for the negotiating sequence to continue moving forward. Agents should avoid questions that can be answered with a simple yes or no. The tendency for prospects might be a simple no. An example of an alternative choice question would be, "Would you put your new couch on this wall or the wall closer to the entry?" The prospects may respond, "We'd put it closer to the entry." Now that they are committing to how they would decorate a room, they are closer to making the overall purchase. Other examples of alternative choice questions include:

- "Would you like to take $500 or $1,000 out of your savings for the deposit?"
- "Would you prefer the single-story or the two-story home?"
- "Would you place your pool table this way or that way?"
- "We can close this transaction in 45 days, or would you prefer 60 days?"
- "The window coverings come with the property, or were you thinking of changing them after your purchase?"

Although rare, the prospects may say, "Neither one." In this instance, agents must ask for clarification. The process moves forward when the prospects give a positive answer.

Puppy Dog Close

The puppy dog close tries to get the prospect attached to the product before they purchase it. The owner of a pet store might say, "Just keep the puppy overnight, and give it back tomorrow if you don't like it." Who wouldn't keep the puppy after becoming attached to it overnight? Obviously, this may be difficult to adapt to real estate, but it is possible.

If the prospects seem interested in a vacant home you just finished showing, send them back through to rediscover it on their own. You can wait on the front porch. They can spend more time feeling the ceramic tile, running their toes through the carpet, opening and closing doors, turning the faucets on and off, and many other "kick the tire" activities while you are out of the house or in another room.

After an extensive interview, you may be familiar with the kind of furniture the prospects have. Perhaps you visited their home before showing them property. Some agents use the puppy dog close by helping the prospects mentally place their furniture in various rooms. If they can visualize their furniture in one room, you are that much closer to a purchase. Another approach for prospects that may have an interest is to take digital photographs of the inside (with the seller's permission) and the outside of the homes. If a purchase decision is not made that day, create a montage of pictures for each home and e-mail them to the prospects. Let them visualize how they would use each property and how they would place their furniture.

The Ben Franklin Close

In this technique, you help the prospects list in two columns the advantages and disadvantages of a decision. The column with the longest list should dictate the prospects' action. Most people use the Benjamin Franklin close every day when they make decisions to do or not do something. Many salespeople like this approach because it makes sense to make some decisions this way.

Use this technique when the buyers appear ready to buy but can't quite commit to the purchase. In other words, they aren't signing the document that will get them the property that will solve their problem and satisfy their need. Most agents who use this technique have memorized the story that starts it.

"A story was written about Ben Franklin that described what he did when he found himself evaluating the pros and cons of a difficult decision. Just as you may be thinking now, he didn't want to pass up a good opportunity if one became available and he wanted to avoid those that were not.

"Ben didn't have high technology in those days, just a piece of paper. On the left side of the page, he'd create a column called Advantages. He drew a line down the middle of the page and on the right side, he'd write a column heading called Disadvantages. Then he'd list the advantages and disadvantages of the decision. The process after this was simple: he just totaled each column. The column with the longest list made the decision easy for him. Let's try it; maybe it will help."

As agents swing the paper around and hand the prospects their pen, they remind the prospects of the reasons why they liked the large garage, the maintenance-free yard, or access to the freeway. When the prospects get to the Disadvantages column, agents might say, "Now what Ben would do is put all the reasons against the decision on the Disadvantages side. Go ahead and write those down now."

The agent can help them list the first disadvantage, bringing up one of the main objections that the prospects had about the property. Then the agent shouldn't say anything. Let the prospects write down what is really bothering them. You will probably find that prospects can only list three or four disadvantages. Yet they will have written, in their own handwriting, more reasons why they should buy the property. This was a powerful tool during the sales era and still works today. However, as with all of these closing techniques, agents should remain aware of the obligations they have with regard to fair housing, truth in lending, and deceptive trade practices, as mentioned in Chapter 9. When the prospects are done, count aloud all the advantages and disadvantages of the decision.

"Well, I suppose that helps clear that up, doesn't it? By the way, what was your correct mailing address?"

This last sentence moves you back to the purchase agreement close.

Figure 13.1

The Ben Franklin Close

ADVANTAGES	DISADVANTAGES
View	Only 2.5 baths
Close to schools	Wall color
Big yard	
Square footage	
Cabinets	
Storage	
Entertainment room	
Enclosed storage area	
Freeway access	

The Summary Close

The summary close is designed to help prospects discover why they are not moving forward with the purchase. In a way, this is a verbal form of the Ben Franklin close. It requires that prospects answer simple questions. However, the questions are posed using a technique called a negative yes. Sometimes prospects can't put their finger on why they are not moving ahead with the agent. Something is bothering them that wasn't discovered during the interview. A negative yes closing question allows the prospects to give the answer that is easiest for them—no. However, when the question is shaped properly, the no actually means yes and the prospects are that much closer to finding out what is really bothering them. Let's take a look.

Agent:	"Just to clarify my thinking, what isn't clear—is it the three-car garage?"
Prospect:	"No."
Agent:	"Is it the 42–inch-wide front door for easier access?"
Prospect:	"No."
Agent:	"Is it the deep garage that works well for your boat and trailer?"
Prospect:	"No."
Agent:	"Is it this or is it that?"
Prospect:	"No."

Every no that agents hear means that the prospects are buying that part of the property. Although agents hope that there is only one thing bothering the prospects, often more than one issue may materialize. Nevertheless, this technique is designed to help the prospects move closer toward a decision.

The Similar Situation Close (Storytelling)

The similar situation close uses the technique of telling stories of other prospects that found themselves in a similar situation. Let's face it; purchasing real estate can cause some degree of stress. For many, it is the largest investment they will ever make. Sometimes prospects want reassurance that your solution will work for them. You may need to show that you helped other prospects make a decision that made them look really good; now they have the security of a home with a block wall, they enjoy their new neighborhood and new friends, or they saved money on the purchase price before inflation raised it even higher.

Because these should always be true stories, a licensee new to the industry may not have much to tell. This is why it is a good idea to talk with your fellow agents. Learn about their most unusual sales and tell your prospects about them when appropriate.

The Lost Sale Close

You should consider using this close only when everything else has failed and the sale is going nowhere. Consider the following example. After a frustrating three-hour attempt to get the prospects to okay an offer, you decide all is lost. At this point, you have nothing to lose. Just before you leave, ask if the prospects might help you. You can remind them that you make a living selling real estate and you want to see if they could tell you where you went wrong. Apologize for not being helpful in getting them the home they wanted (for buyers) or in selling the home (for sellers). If the prospects see that you are sincere, you can now switch to the summary closing technique we discussed earlier.

> "I always want to learn from my mistakes and I must have missed something in the interview. Could you tell me what was wrong with the property?"

This close requires that you help the conversation along and apply the summary closing techniques, or the prospects may say that everything was wrong with the property. Don't take a breath after the first question until you add another question:

> "Could you tell me what was wrong with the property? Was it the four-foot-wide hallways?"

When the prospects tell you no, continue asking questions until you find the real problem.

The Call Back Close

The purpose of this technique is to discover what is bothering the prospects so that you have a problem to solve. Sometimes agents make full presentations on a property only to hear the prospects say, "I'll get back to you." This is a difficult situation for agents because they don't know what to do with this comment. The prospects are telling the agent the conversation on this property is over.

Agents should consider taking three steps. First, the agent should attempt to confirm a follow-up date and time. Keep in mind that the prospects may go along with you and set up a date and time only to refuse your call when you try to confirm the appointment, or fail to call you back if you leave a message. Second, assuming that you can get in to see the prospects one more time, do *not* ask if they thought about it. It's too easy for them to respond by saying, "Yes we have, and we are not interested." Third, present something that is new about the property. This should *not* be a material fact, as they should have all been presented in the first meeting. In other words, when you meet again, tell the prospects, "I am glad we were able to get back together again. In our last meeting I forgot to tell you about…" Tell them something new, and then switch to the summary close. Your summary presentation should seek agreement on the solutions offered by the property, as well as the advantages of those solutions and how they benefit the prospects.

The Secondary Question Close

This is similar to the alternative choice close, and consequently is sometimes called the complex alternative choice close. However, the difference between the two is that agents present a major point in the secondary question close and assume there is agreement before presenting a minor question for the prospects to answer.

> "It looks like all we have to figure out is when you wanted to move into your new home. Do you think this location will take five minutes or ten minutes off your commute time?"

The major point "all we have to figure out is when you wanted to move into your new home" was masked by the minor question, "Do you think this location will take five minutes or ten minutes off your commute time?" If the prospects make a decision on the minor question, you have permission to presume that they agree with the major point.

The Sharp Angle Close

This close answers a question with a question, but adds a little more. The buyer might say, "We'd buy this home if the refrigerator was included." Using the sharp angle close, an agent's response would be, "If I can get you this refrigerator are you ready to fill in the paperwork?"

Generally, prospects ask these kinds of questions if they are interested in the property. While it may be tempting to look at the listing to find the answer to their question—you may discover that the refrigerator does stay with the property—little is gained by telling them it stays. Rather than taking the prospects' questions and feeding them back as in the question close, the agent adds a little more to it.

Here's another example of a sharp angle close. Once again, the buyer asks, "Does the refrigerator stay with the home?" Let's suppose the refrigerator is especially unique or color-coordinated to the room's décor. The agent needs to make this point in a way that leads to a close.

Agent:	"Am I right in assuming that you wouldn't ask that question unless you were interested in this home?" This requires a yes.
Prospect:	"Yes."
Agent:	"The refrigerator's features go nicely with the kitchen, don't they?" Prospect: "Yes."
Agent:	"Would you like it included in the sale?" (The sharp angle)

Note the prospects' response on the purchase agreement, and follow up by asking them for the correct spelling of their last name. After that, continue with the purchase agreement close, unless they stop you.

The Think It Over Close

The think it over close helps prevent the need for the call back close. You recall in the call back close we depended on the prospects to consider our proposal before the next appointment. When we arrived at the second appointment, we presented something new about the property to keep the process alive.

In various ways, we have all used this technique. The prospects' statement might have been as simple as, "I'll think it over," as curt as, "I am not prepared to make a snap decision today," or as polite as, "Let me think on this; I will get back to you in the morning."

If agents let the buyers go and wait to see if they return in the morning, they may have to depend on the call back close to create the sale. But with the think it over approach, the agent can say, "I know you wouldn't say that unless you were really interested, would you?" This can lead directly to a summary close. Or ask, "Just to clarify my thinking, what exactly did you want to think over? Is it the 35-foot-deep garage? Is it the 42-inch front door for easy access? Is it the extra-wide hallways?"

As the prospects answer these questions, you have shifted to a summary close. If they are still unsure after hearing all the reasons why they should purchase the property, the prospects may find themselves looking for a way out. As you continue listing the potential objections, prospects may grab one and say that's the reason they're not buying. If this happens, move to the final objection close.

The Final Objection

The final objection close helps prospects reach a decision when agents listen and empathize with their situation, asking them to clarify the problem, and helping them overcome it before asking for the order. Often the most difficult objection to find is the last one. Too often, when agents hear an objection they are quick to answer it. By doing so, they sometimes provide the wrong solution and this brings up another objection. Agents and prospects can go back and forth like this for some time before one or both of them get frustrated. Prospects feel their needs are not being met and agents feel that prospects are stalling, which is probably true. The prospects are stalling because they are waiting for the agent to give them the information needed to make a decision. The objections are surfacing because there is something troubling the prospects. A successful close can't take place until the problem is resolved.

Steps to Finding the Final Objection

1. Listen to the prospects
2. Empathize with their situation
3. Question the problem
4. Help them solve the problem
5. Ask for the order

Discovering the final objection requires patience. The following process covers the steps involved in overcoming most objections and enhances our previous discussion of no hurry. Agents can use this five-step process to move the prospects to a final objection, which, when answered, leads to a purchase decision.

Step 1: Listen to the prospects.   In real estate, your prospects want you to listen, even though you may already have the perfect solution. Agents sometimes make the mistake of hearing a few words and assuming they know what the prospects are going to say, and then proceeding to solve the wrong problem. Without a doubt, agents have heard it all before. The concerns of the prospects before them are the same as those of the prospects they met last week. However, the prospects feel their problems are unique. These are the prospects' concerns, so even if agents guess right, the prospects will be upset if agents don't listen to them.

Step 2: Empathize with their situation.   For the final objection close to work, the prospects must agree that what they told the agent is the reason they are not buying. To help the prospects come to this conclusion, agents feed their statement back to them by paraphrasing.

> "As I understand it, you feel that the fourth bedroom is too small. In fact, you feel the room needs to be at least a foot longer on one side. Is that right?"

The prospects may confirm that this is the reason they are not going ahead with the purchase. Nevertheless, agents do not want to jump on this reason too quickly. Agents want to be certain of the issue they are trying to solve. They need to make sure this is the last objection.

Step 3: Question the problem.   When prospects are allowed to talk, they can help you solve their problems. As we said, we want to be certain we are solving the right problem. Now that the agent has confirmed the objection, the agent must make sure it is the final problem the prospects are having. This step and the next allow the prospects to tell the agent more about what they have identified the problem to be.

> "So, the only thing preventing you from owning this home is that fourth bedroom. If it weren't for that room being one foot short on that one side, you'd buy this property today. Is that right?"

Step 4: Help them solve the problem.   Agents now help the prospects solve their problem by asking another question and listening to their response. This question should confirm what you believe to be the final objection, or it should bring one out. If the prospects have suggested, in some manner, that if it weren't for the room being so short, they would buy the property, ask:

> "Just to clarify my thinking, why do you feel the room is too short?"

The answer to this question helps agents uncover the reason for the objection. The prospects may have a legitimate reason why they feel the room is too short. If they do, the agent may have missed something in the interview that caused him or her to provide the wrong solution.

The prospects may tell the agent that the room is for their new baby, and it just doesn't seem large enough to be used as a bedroom. Perhaps the agent could ask: "Have you ever returned to the home where you grew up? Did you get to visit your old bedroom? Did it look smaller than you remember?"

Sometimes prospects will talk until what they are saying doesn't make sense, therefore resolving the objection, or they will open up and tell you what is really going on. This is what you are looking for. Fortunately, by starting with a well-structured interview, problems like these do not occur very often.

Step 5: Ask for the order.   Depending on how the prospects' response plays out, agents can attempt their last close by switching to the purchase agreement close. Ask for the prospects' correct mailing address or the correct spelling of their last name.

■ Follow-Up

Follow-up represents the last step in personal selling. The longevity of most professional real estate agents is due to their ability to receive referrals. One of the best ways of accomplishing this is by keeping the buyers and sellers fully informed throughout the listing, selling, and transfer processes. Additionally, use the other methods mentioned in the text. Send them greeting cards or brochures and make phone calls to them even after your obligation to them has ended.

As was suggested in Chapter 1, people have come to think that the real estate industry is mostly sales oriented. However, today's professionals take the time to research and segment their market in order to develop comprehensive pricing, distribution, and promotional strategies that result in prospect contacts. When agents apply the techniques shared in this text, their personal selling efforts—including the interview, negotiations, and the close—should result in more sales, more referrals, and a sustained career.

■ Summary

This chapter has reminded us of some of the reasons for a comprehensive interview. In addition to developing the prospects' sense of trust in the agent, an interview helps agents discover what prospects need, what motivates them, and how they perceive the solution. The questions presented in this chapter were designed to give a sense of what might be asked of prospects, other than how many bedrooms are needed or what can they afford. Additionally, the purpose of several questions were described. All questions should be asked for a reason, and every question asked should require a profound answer (more than a yes or no).

As discussed in earlier chapters, agents should have a complete knowledge of the inventory. This is a critical component of a successful interview. As agents guide the prospects through the interview process, the result should be a solution that describes a property in the market's current inventory of listings. Whether the prospects like and trust you or not, it is not uncommon to have objections arise while demonstrating property. Negotiating through these objections requires that agents remind the prospects of how they perceive things and how the components of the property fill needs that were discovered during the interview. By breaking down objections into manageable parts, the prospects and agents are able to understand the points of concern and close the transaction.

■ Multiple Choice Questions

1. Which of the following represents a key factor that should be considered when developing interview questions?

   a. The questions should allow agents to talk extensively to show the prospects that they know what they are doing.

   b. The questions should be structured so that the prospects need to do nothing more than agree with the agent.

   c. The questions should be designed to allow the prospects to talk more than the agents.

   d. The questions should be written to help demonstrate that the agent is goal oriented.

2. Which of the following does the *MOST* damage to your credibility?

   a. Talking too much

   b. Letting the prospect talk too much

   c. Offering the wrong solution

   d. Showing overpriced property

3. When negotiating the sale of a property, it is common to hear objections from the prospects. Objections are often another way of asking for information. They tend to slow the closing process to give the prospects time to think. Objections of this type are often referred to as _____ objections.

   a. irrational

   b. negative

   c. rational

   d. positive

4. When agents say, "Some living rooms have a focal point. As we enter this room, where would you place your grand piano—in this corner or near that wall?" it is an example of a

   a. purchase agreement close.

   b. Ben Franklin close.

   c. trial close.

   d. summary close.

5. When agents have their prospects compare the advantages and disadvantages of a property, they are using a

   a. summary close.

   b. Ben Franklin close.

   c. question close.

   d. trial close.

■ Exercises

Exercise 1—It takes quite a bit of planning to develop questions that require profound answers. Agents want to learn more from the prospects than just the fact that they want a fireplace or a three-bedroom home with a three-car attached garage. Agents want to know why. Their questions should help the prospects discover the underlying need that is solved by having a three-car garage. Develop a series of five interview questions and follow-up questions, if necessary, that treat the single issue of what the prospects expect of the property they will buy and what motivates that expectation.

Exercise 2—The answer to a trial close lets the agent know if the prospects need more information before making a purchase decision. Most trial closes work well because the prospects often don't perceive them to be closes at all. Trial closes can take on many forms. Suppose your prospects have indicated an interest in some of the features in the kitchen and dining room. Given this information, prepare a trial close with regard to any of the features. Remember, you only need to write short, concise questions.

MARKETING PLAN

Real estate brokers and their agents want to know how they can best compete in their marketplace. They want to be positioned in a geographically advantageous area and aggressively market the right product/service to the right people the first time. These things are possible with a well-coordinated plan.

Although every marketing plan is different, the following outline shows how agents put to use the data collected during the research phase. Marketing plans should be the result of realities in the marketplace and written only after organizing, evaluating, and analyzing the data. As you read through this material, keep in mind that the company or the agent (salesperson) should be considered as one and the same. Marketing plans can be created by an individual salesperson to meet his or her needs or they can be created by the owner/broker of a real estate company for all agents to consider or follow.

The organization of the following outline includes a general description of the purpose of the subtopic and brief examples of how it is used, or suggestions of what it might look like in a written plan. The brief examples attempt to draw references from things already discussed in the text. Consequently, connectivity between the topics is not intended. Most marketing plans contain subtopics; however, you should always keep in mind that there is no one format for a marketing plan. Its design is based on what the agent wants to accomplish. Marketing plans could be as simple as two or three pages or as lengthy as the example shown here.

■ Executive Summary

Company Overview

Purpose: The company overview states the purpose of the firm and gives a summary of its background and how its product meets the needs of its consumer. The company summarizes where it has been during the last year or longer through its historic returns, and establishes its long-term objectives with regard to market share and financial returns. This overview can be organized into these subtopics: mission statement, background, objectives, and financial goals.

Mission statement. *Purpose:* The mission statement establishes the purpose of the firm, why it is in business, and the market for its services.

Brief Example:

> ABC Realty will set the standard for professionalism in our area of operation. Our service quality will exceed the expectations of our prospects.
>
> ABC Realty is a member of the National Association of REALTORS® and abides by a strict code of ethics. Our commitment to excellence and our desire to accrue more knowledge, education, and…
>
> This firm will specialize in residential and multifamily residential properties, attempting to limit its inventory to…

Background. *Purpose:* The background provides a summary of where the company has been. It isn't needed in every marketing plan; however, if changes were made to the operation since the last plan was implemented, then mention of those changes and their purpose. If the results of the changes were positive or negative, then agents should decide whether to continue or adjust its implementation.

Long-term goals. *Purpose:* Typically the company lists its long-term objectives for the next year, three years, or five years. These objectives may center on a variety of things including increasing the size of the agency, maintaining brand recognition, or increasing its position in the market.

Brief Example:

- Develop a presence in the three malls by negotiating for kiosk spaces in each.
- Increase market share by 20 percent in the Mesa Verde housing tract by…
- Reduce cost of repetitive operations

Financial goals. Purpose: The agent states his or her expectations for financial returns, given the objectives for the year.

Brief Example:

- Cost savings $150,000
- Increased sales volume from Mesa Verde tract—ten homes or $6,250,000
- Increased commissions from Mesa Verde tract—$250,000 (average based on listing or listing and sales commission)

Real Estate Market Analysis

Purpose: Any marketing mix that is developed must take the market environment into consideration. Agents should take a moment to define the market environment, as it currently exists. When agents define the nature of the market, they take into account many elements that were discovered during their research, such as the direction of interest rates, access to credit, costs of materials (residential, commercial, industrial, acreage), types of properties selling, and the current geographic areas under development. For new opportunities, agents should examine the direction of growth, the population growth rate, and the expansion or contraction of the job market.

Brief Example:

> Although the national markets tend to be slowing, over the past year, the local residential housing market has seen an 11 percent increase in supply and a 23 percent increase in prices. During the period, the Federal Reserve has increased the short-term discount rate three times to its current rate of…

> Residential housing continues selling at a rapid pace, as rents in multifamily housing units continue increasing. The population migration into our community has exceeded those leaving the area. Over three million square feet of commercial space has broken ground and is currently under construction, with most of the construction in the…

Evaluate the Company's (Agent's) Strengths and Weaknesses

Purpose: An evaluation of what the company or the agent can do is needed in light of the established goals. The strengths and weaknesses are discovered by an introspective view of the agent or the company. Agents want to discover any competitive advantage they can exploit, and modify, if possible, any weaknesses. The following list is representative of the topics that can be included. Your topic areas will depend on the purpose of the review.

Brief Example:

Company strengths:

- National franchise with strong local and national branding
- All agents have laptop computers with satellite access to the Internet as well as T1 data line intranet and local area network connections for faster access to the multiple listing service.
- Five strategically located offices in high-traffic areas with easy access for customers
- Sixty-three percent of the sales force with bachelor's degrees in business administration or finance

Company weaknesses:

- Although a nationally recognized franchise, the actual real estate operation has had only an 18-month presence in the area.
- Poor execution when selecting media for promotional messages
- Twelve percent decline in market share in Vista Knolls Estates over the past six months

Agent strengths:

- Recently purchased first home and can relate with first-time home buyers
- Five years experience as a land investor
- Own a motorcycle with an enclosed sidecar. It will safely seat two adults and two small children.

Agent weaknesses:

- Need an improved wardrobe
- Need to develop both written and verbal communication skills
- Currently have no Web site developed

Property (including services) strengths:

- Forty-seven percent of all single-family residential sales within our firm are four-bedroom, 3,100- to 3,400-square-foot homes, in high demand by our target market.
- When compared to the multiple listing service, the company sells the greatest number of homes overall within this price range.
- The target market: (Describe the target market that has provided the company the greatest degree of sales. Also, describe how that market is accessed and any changes in that market.) Our primary market segment for residential housing, without reference to gender, is the 30–34 age group and the 40–44 age group. When segmenting this market by marital status, those who live alone comprise a little over 24 percent of the market when compared to married couples that hold about 56 percent of the market. Married couples, within these age ranges, comprise the bulk of our target market. Further description and conclusions drawn about these age groups include…

Property weaknesses:

- Although our franchise name is nationally recognized, our real estate operation is relatively new to the community.

Pricing strengths:

- For the past year, the majority of our home sales were between $775,000 and $850,000.
- The company's market share results were directly related to the efficient pricing of its inventory and services.

Pricing weaknesses:

- The percentage of buyers who can afford $775,000 to $850,000 homes is dropping, as the affordability index drops.

Evaluate the Company's (Agent's) Opportunities and Threats

Purpose: Agents must also be concerned with the environment that is outside of their control, such as how interest rate increases affect their target market. Nevertheless, the outside environment can create opportunities for the agency, depending on the agency's ability to capture them. The external opportunities and threats involve issues that are similar to those in strengths and weaknesses; however, each is measured by how the outside environment affects those issues.

Brief Example:

Opportunities:

Increasing population at the east end of town has a negative effect on density and traffic. Increased congestion, traffic, stoplights, and smog all contribute to increased stress for the homeowner that is trying to commute to work. Just getting to the cross-town highway takes over 30 minutes. What can the company or agent do?

- Promotional campaigns that stress solutions to the cost of gasoline consumption, reduced stress, easier access to major highways
- List properties with easy access to shopping, highways, and jobs that are not at the east end of town
- Increase market share at north end of town

There is growing awareness about radon, asbestos, flooding, earthquakes, and other environmental concerns. How can the company or agent take advantage of this?

- Develop press releases about these issues
- List properties that provide solutions
- Have open houses that demonstrate features that overcome these concerns

Although the market is still extremely active, sales have slowed because the affordability index has fallen as interest rates continue to climb. The sales of competitors seem to be as affected as our own. How does the company or agent take advantage of this opportunity?

- Conduct a market research study to determine how these changes have affected the current target market (At this point, display the breakdown of the new target market, if one is discovered, and the price range of highest affordability.)

Threats:

- Company A (a competing company) now has a greater market share in Chesapeake Estates.
- With the exception of billboards and political signs, the city has created a regulation making it illegal to post business signs on real property. This includes real estate signs.
- Two competing real estate offices advertise more and with better results (as measured in sales).

Market Segment

If this topic has not been approached already, now is the time to see if the market has shifted. Update the appropriate information (or all of it) and describe the size and demographic and psychographic makeup of the market. What percentage of people in the market are married couples, singles, kids, etc.? What are their incomes, occupations, and interests? What are their recreational activities? What do they read? What are they looking for in a home/service? In other words, summarize and put into words the things discovered from your research, as well as your conclusions about this segment.

Brief Example:

> Single men make up 35 percent of persons living alone, and 65 percent of singles are women who live alone. The singles market is the largest segment of the total market, and single women make up the largest segment of the singles market. Within that segment, the largest group of single women is between the ages of 25 and 44. A little over 65 percent of single women in the 25–44 age group earn between $50,000 and $65,000 per year.

(The analysis continues along these lines until the agent has defined the market segment with the greatest potential.)

Marketing Objectives

Purpose: After the goals for the company or the agent are set, then objectives must be put into place to accomplish them. Agents generally want to maintain what they have or increase their position in some way. The three main areas to consider are sales objectives, profits, and the target market. Other considerations may include maintenance of the service pricing strategy, the brand, the company's position, or the agent's position in the local industry.

Brief Example:

Profits

Agents must determine the costs of operation and how much they may increase given their current objectives. What is the anticipated level of profits desired? When these are added together, agents get a sense of the revenue production needed.

Revenue (sales) and market share

Identify in some detail the number of listings, market share, sales, dollar value of the listings, and the revenues generated by the agency or the agent over the next year (these numbers can also be broken down to a weekly, monthly, or quarterly goal).

- 150 listings generated for the calendar year:
    - Generate 50 listings from the Mesa Verde Estates
    - Dollar value of the listings—$94,000,000
- Revenues created $4,218,750:
    - $1,462,500 commissions from the Mesa Verde Estates
    - $900,500 commissions from multifamily residential sales
    - $1,325,000 commissions generated from…
- Turnover ratio:
    - 4 for homes in the Mesa Verde Estates
    - 2 for multifamily residential units
    - 2 for acreage in outlying areas
    - 4 for vacant residential lots with all infrastructure
- Targeted consumer:

    Based on the results of your research and the conclusions you have drawn, describe the specific target market you will approach with your marketing mix.
    - Married couples with children
    - Income between $58,000 and $64,000
    - Children between the ages of 2 and 14
    - Sports enthusiasts

Strategies

Purpose: Agents give guidance to the development of a marketing mix by listing the strategies they want to use to accomplish the marketing objectives.

Brief Example:

Increase turnover by listing properties that meet the parameters set by the target market. (This has a direct effect on the product and pricing strategies to come.)

Contact target market through weekend sports activities, such as events that are sponsored by schools or community centers.

Marketing Mix

The marketing mix combines the four elements of product, place (distribution), price, and promotion. Each should relate back to the goals and objectives set by the company or agent.

Product strategy (both property and services). *Purpose:* The properties listed or the services provided should meet the needs of the market. When trying to attract the largest segment of a market, the features within the property or service must have value to the targeted markets. Therefore, agents should be selective when adding property to their listing inventory. Properties should be selected that will satisfy the objectives set by the agent. Those objectives are unlimited, but may include satisfying customer needs, increasing profits, increasing market share, and increasing turnover.

Brief Example:

- List two-story homes at market value in Mesa Verde Estates
- Increase market share of listings by listing homes in the Chesa-peake tract that are suitable for the target market
- List properties with walled backyards and home security systems

Pricing strategy. *Purpose:* The pricing strategy is designed to get the seller the highest price possible but at the greatest value for the buyer, while making a profit for the agent. By enhancing the value of the property, buyers feel they got more than the price suggests. Agents should make every effort to market the property (culminating in a sale) as aggressively as possible. In addition to pricing the property correctly for the niche market, an aggressive services pricing strategy may also help.

Brief Example:

- Offer a substantial bonus to all agents through the co-operating agent's broker of 20 to 30 percent of the listing agent's commission, if any co-operating agent sells any of the listing agent's inventory within two weeks of the listing date.
- Consider short-term weekend price adjustments, with price increases after the "sale" day.
- Watch the condition of the economy. In six months, consider increasing commissions on hard-to-sell properties, rather than lowering the selling price.
- Continue promoting properties in the price range that is most attractive to the target market.

Place (distribution) strategy. *Purpose:* The place strategy calls for an inventory that is available in the right locations at the right time that quickly can be delivered to the customer. Additionally, it concerns how the public learns that properties are available for sale. Target markets have specific interests. Those interests can be used to find members of that market and attract them with promotional messages. What can be included in your marketing plan?

Brief Example:

- The volume of sales to commuters (people who live outside our area) has increased. Develop media exposure in newspapers that are read by our commuter market.
- Sponsor a billboard or game clock for a basketball court or baseball or soccer field.

- Develop closer relationships with qualified, professional attorneys, escrow and title officers, lenders, and inspectors to help speed the transfer process.

- Increase customer awareness with additional radio and newspaper advertising.

Promotional strategy. *Purpose:* The promotional strategy creates a direct or indirect connection to prospects by addressing their needs in the messages they receive. Agents develop coordinated messages through their advertising, sales promotion, and publicity to help attract prospects to them. Personal selling is the last step in the promotional strategy because it is the direct face-to-face meeting that often completes the sale.

Brief Example:

- Provide a pick-up service in a motorcycle sidecar for families with children under 7

- Offer coupons or free tickets to professional sports events

- Coordinate promotional messages so that value is added to the properties and services advertised

- Develop promotional messages for billboards and game clocks that are attractive to families with children

The marketing plan cannot be developed in a vacuum. Every firm or agent is restricted by the resources available. Determine in advance what resources you have—time, money, location, education, and experience—and budget them accordingly.

Implementation and Follow-Up

Set a time in the future to evaluate this process and see if it is being implemented. The marketing plan is of no value if it is not used.

GLOSSARY

action Encouraging action starts as early as the first extensive qualifying discussion held with the prospects. Taking action in a sales presentation means that the prospects "buy" your solution. (Chapter 12)

advantage Something that helps the prospects understand how the product is useful or how it works. (Chapter 11)

attention The first step in making a presentation is much like that in writing advertisements; the prospect's attention must be gained quickly. (Chapter 12)

benefit Something that describes how the feature or property satisfies an emotional or product need. Without this element the prospects understand they have a need, but do not understand how the property helps satisfy the need. This element reminds the prospects what motivated them to search for a solution. (Chapter 11)

blockbusting Inciting panic selling in a neighborhood because of a change in the mix of occupants with respect to race, religion, national origin, sex, handicap, and family status. (Chapter 9)

branding Something that creates the reasons people identify with the product. (Chapter 8)

buyer The person with the credit or cash needed to make the purchase. (Chapter 2)

Civil Rights Act of 1866 Defined citizenship as belonging to anyone born in this country. (Chapter 9)

competence Demonstrating capability, knowledge, and experience through your actions. Agents demonstrate competence by being prepared, developing questions for prospects and answers to questions prospects may ask, and sharing with prospects the ways they have solved problems in the past. (Chapter 10)

customer orientation A focus on customer needs. Agents who are customer oriented identify the needs of groups of buyers, sellers, or other agents. This is the essence of the marketing concept. Customer needs consist of both property needs that are known to the prospects and emotional needs that may or may not be immediately known to the prospects. Agents familiar with a customer orientation determine needs before listing property, and establish needs before showing existing listings. (Chapter 2)

data analysis Taking raw, seemingly unrelated data from the market research phase, and reorganizing it into meaningful groups of data from which conclusions may be drawn. (Chapter 4)

decider The person who makes the purchase decision. (Chapter 2)

defining the problem The first step in market research. By asking probing and relevant questions of themselves or their prospects, agents move closer to defining the problem, which gives them a better opportunity to solve it. (Chapter 3)

demographic segmentation Organizes the entire market by multiple factors including age, income, gender, occupation, family life cycle, education, and household size. (Chapter 5)

desire Desire follows interest in a presentation. It is the motivation or need to solve a problem with a specific product or service. (Chapter 12)

differentiated market One that is made up of different recognizable segments that can be attracted by creating multiple marketing mixes. (Chapter 5)

discount rate The interest rate charged to member banks when they borrow money directly from the Federal Reserve. (Chapter 3)

effective marketing An effective marketing plan brings a property to market with the right mix of promotion, pricing, and distribution strategies. (Chapter 1)

enhanced value Something done to help prospects perceive and understand that they are receiving more than what they are paying for. (Chapter 7)

enhancing the property's value A part of the total product concept in which agents deliver more than what is expected. This is done by addressing both the property and emotional needs of the prospects. (Chapter 6)

externalists People that try to conform to or impress the outside environment. (Chapter 5)

family life cycles The stages that people go through in their lifetime. These stages generally include singles, couples, and parents. (Chapter 5)

the Federal Reserve (the Fed) The institution that regulates the banking system within the United States. (Chapter 3)

form utility Measures the usefulness of the property or feature. (Chapter 1)

fraud A form of misrepresentation that relies on deceit. (Chapter 9)

functions of promotion To inform, persuade, and remind prospects about a product or service. (Chapter 8)

gatekeeper The person who controls the information that helps the decider make a purchase decision. (Chapter 2)

gathering and organizing data The second step of market research. Agents must find and collect data that is relevant to solving the research problem. (Chapter 3)

geographic segmentation Organizes the total market by the political makeup, population density and migration, and actual location of property within a geographic area. (Chapter 5)

goal Something you desire or want to achieve. (Chapter 10)

goal orientation Having a goal orientation means applying time management skills that help attain both personal and professional goals. This helps save time and potentially generate more sales. Goal orientation helps agents reach their production goals and the goals of their customers.

group boycott Prohibited actions in which agents conspire to put other agencies out of business, speak badly of those agencies, or refuse to assist co-operating agencies that are asking about their listings. (Chapter 9)

incentives Something used to encourage prospects to make one decision over another. (Chapter 4)

inflation The result of rising or stable demand without offsetting increases in supply. (Chapter 6)

influencer The person who helps persuade the decision maker to make the purchase. (Chapter 2)

interest Interest is gained when agents can demonstrate what the product or services means to the prospects. (Chapter 12)

internalists People that do things based on experience and who are not necessarily influenced by the opinions of others. (Chapter 5)

market research A data-gathering process that helps agents make marketing decisions that reduce risk, save time, and save money. This research helps identify opportunities, customer needs, channels of distribution, the strengths and weaknesses of the company and its competitors, pricing strategies and their impact on the market, and other information agents need to make decisions. (Chapter 3)

marketing concept Identifying customer needs and developing a product to meet those needs. The marketing concept takes into account the needs of consumers when agents develop their personal and professional goals, list property, or develop the services they offer. (Chapter 2)

marketing mix The combination of the right product or service at the right time given the right promotion through the best channels of distribution that produces a buyer that is ready, willing, and able to buy your product or service. (Chapter 5)

misrepresentation Making false statements or concealing information from buyers that may be useful in making a purchase decision. (Chapter 9)

motivation The reason to act. In real estate, motivation is that hot button in a prospect that, once discovered, provides agents with the information needed to help prospects take action. (Chapter 4)

need A motivating force. When activated, a need provides the motivational trigger to act. In real estate, physical needs focus on tangible features or the property. Emotional needs focus more on things such as the need to control, to be a part of a group, to be the center of attention, or to gain respect. (Chapter 10)

negative objections A way prospects block communications that results from the prospects' perception that agents are trying to sell them something they don't want. (Chapter 13)

negligence A situation in which reasonable care is not used when evaluating a property for resale. For example, agents may be negligent for not finding out if a permit was pulled on a patio cover for a listing they have secured. (Chapter 9)

no help A property is of no help when prospects do not understand how it satisfies their needs. If the prospects perceive that the listings shown come up short of expectations then the solutions are of no help to them. (Chapter 11)

no help presentation The three steps used to overcome the no help objection for a product. These steps identify what the product does, demonstrate the advantages of the product, and explain the benefits so prospects can understand how it helps achieve their perceived needs. (Chapter 11)

no hurry No hurry comes from the prospect's perception of potential negative consequences caused by the purchase decision. (Chapter 11)

noise Anything that distracts prospects from the agent's message. (Chapter 8)

no need To overcome no need, agents must discover the problem, discover the cause of the problem, question the prospect, listen intently and clarify the need before providing a solution. (Chapter 10)

no trust It takes time to overcome no trust. If prospects don't feel they can do business with a real estate agent, then business is not likely to happen. Agents develop trust by creating good first impressions, developing goals that meet personal and professional needs as well as the needs of the prospects. Agents develop trust by listening to and relating to the prospects and demonstrating competence and dependability. (Chapter 10)

objections A technique used by prospects to slow the sales process. (Chapter 13)

objective The means by which you intend to accomplish a goal. In other words, what steps are taken to accomplish the goal? (Chapter 10)

open market operations Actions that provide a generally successful way of controlling the money supply through the purchase or sale of government securities. (Chapter 3)

order getters Salespeople who aggressively seek out past customers and search for new ones. (Chapter 12)

order takers Salespeople employed to maintain customers and their repetitive orders. Agents who specialize in this style are often quite effective in selling homes in housing tracts for developers. (Chapter 12)

overheated economy A condition that occurs when the supply of goods (e.g., houses, commercial buildings, usable land, components of construction) and services cannot keep up with the demand for them. (Chapter 3)

packaging Marketing efforts that make the prospects want to experience more. Packaging draws attention to the product; it creates curiosity and encourages comparisons. (Chapter 6)

performance Doing what you say you will do and doing it in a timely manner. (Chapter 2)

personal selling The face-to-face interaction salespeople have with their prospects. Personal selling applies and makes use of the primary and secondary data collected during the marketing phase. (Chapter 12)

physiological needs The basic human needs for good health, food, medicine, exercise, fresh air, safe drinking water, shelter, and clothing. (Chapter 4)

pioneer Salespeople that sell franchises or are responsible for establishing a client base or a method of selling before moving to another project. (Chapter 12)

place Involves the easy transfer of the property from the seller to the buyer. Describes the vendors involved in taking the property from the listing stage and delivering it to the transfer stage. Also describes how, through channels of distribution, the potential customer receives the promotional message. (Chapter 1)

place utility Making product available when and where the customer wants it. Agents address the place utility when evaluating the properties they list. (Chapter 1)

positioning Efforts that lead a market segment to think of one agent or one agency over all others. (Chapter 8)

positive objection A technique used by prospects to gather more information in order to make a decision. Positive objections are more like a hurdle than a block wall. (Chapter 13)

possession utility Requires that the property be deliverable, the buyer be able to buy, and the money be available and at reasonable rates. (Chapter 1)

price The value placed on the property or services rendered. (Chapter 1)

price niche Specializing in properties within a certain price range. (Chapter 6)

primary data Data that is collected and used for specific research projects. It is time consuming and often expensive to collect. However, agents conduct an inexpensive form of primary data collection when they meet with prospects to conduct their qualifying interviews. (Chapter 3)

problem solver Someone that offers facts, choices, information, and counseling to their prospects to help them make decisions. (Chapter 12)

product The property or services offered by real estate agents. (Chapter 1)

profit The amount remaining after all expenses are paid. For purposes of personal service pricing strategies, it is the commission earned. (Chapter 7)

promotion Consists of four main activities: advertising, publicity, sales promotion, and personal selling. (Chapter 1)

promotional campaigns Efforts that seek to position the company or the licensee ahead of all competitors, differentiate its services and products, and characterize (brand) the reasons people identify with its listings and services. (Chapter 8)

promotional mix A combination of activities in advertising, sales promotion, publicity, and personal selling. (Chapter 8)

prospecting The method—based on data gathered during the market research phase—used to find potential customers who can benefit from your product and who are ready, willing, and able to make a buying decision. (Chapter 9)

psychographic segmentation Offers agents a powerful tool in both marketing and sales because it discovers how values and needs motivate people. (Chapter 5)

publicity A free form of advertising. It is not paid for by agents, but the stories should be controlled by agents. (Chapter 8)

qualifying A process of discovering the property and emotional needs of prospects, as well as determining creditworthiness. (Chapter 9)

quality service Measured in several ways, it can be summarized by letting prospects know what to expect, telling them what you will do, and then doing it. (Chapter 7)

real estate marketing A balanced mix of activities that serves two functions. The first, and more common definition, results in both attracting prospects to agents and creating a sale that meets the personal needs of prospects. The second may not necessarily result in a sale, but enhances the reputation of the agent or agency. (Chapter 1)

redlining An illegal practice in which lenders refuse to loan or limit the loans in specific neighborhoods based on the racial makeup of that neighborhood. (Chapter 9)

referral The direct result of a satisfied customer telling others about an agent's services and encouraging them to contact the agent. (Chapter 12)

relating Getting to know another person by discovering what things you have in common. (Chapter 10)

reserve requirements The percentage of funds held in bank reserves that is unavailable for transactions (e.g., loans or withdrawals). The Fed sets this percentage. (Chapter 3)

right solution The solution to the prospect's concerns that treats both the property needs and the personal or emotional needs. The initial meeting helps agents learn what the right solution is and how to present it. (Chapter 13)

sales promotion Generally defined as promotional activities other than personal selling, advertising, or publicity. Sales promotions are often used as incentives to take action. (Chapter 8)

secondary data The result of research studies done by the government or private enterprise. In other words, the data was originally collected for a different research project; however, much of the data can be applied to other projects. (Chapter 3)

services utility Delivering the information necessary for customers to make a decision. (Chapter 1)

standardized output A perception that no matter where a product is purchased, its quality and other attributes do not change. This is a difficult concept in real estate and other services, where the output of one agency is different from another. (Chapter 7)

steering A form of discrimination in which agents show properties in specific areas because they feel the buyer is best suited for that area due to a stereotype or bias based on race, color, religion, national origin, or gender. (Chapter 9)

summary of findings Conclusions drawn from the data analysis phase that break down into a few sentences or paragraphs the limits of an agent's resources, time, and money, and how best to take advantage of the opportunities available. (Chapter 4)

systems orientation Successfully operating multiple tasks without conflict. (Chapter 2)

target market A large segment of the market with similar commonalities that may react in a similar way to promotional stimuli. (Chapter 3)

time management Effectively prioritizing tasks and employing skills, experience, and education to complete those tasks. Prioritizing the most important issues involves the establishment of personal and professional goals. Market research and analysis is another example of employing time management skills. (Chapter 3)

time utility Calls for an adequate number of listings in inventory that are attractive to the largest market segments. (Chapter 1)

total product A quality product or service that exceeds the customer's perceived expectations. (Chapter 6)

trial close A closing technique that helps the prospects and the agent determine if they are looking at the right property, or if the agent needs more information from the prospects or the prospects need more information from the agent. (Chapter 13)

turnover How long it takes to sell homes in a particular price range in a given year. For example, if it takes six months to sell a $500,000 home, then the turnover ratio is 2. (Chapter 7)

user The person who uses the property. (Chapter 2)

value A perception held by buyers and sellers about products and services that is indicated by price. Price is used to compare and exchange things of value. (Chapter 6)

ANSWER KEY

Chapter 1

1. **c** When the strategies that involve product, price, promotion, and place are put into action, it is called the marketing mix.

2. **c** The four parts of a promotional strategy include personal selling, advertising, sales promotion, and publicity.

3. **b** When the real estate agent no longer delivers what the customer wants, that agent will cease to be in business.

4. **a** People who buy a fenced back yard or a productive garden are buying something that is useful to them. This is known as form utility.

5. **c** Possession utility requires that a property is deliverable, that the buyer has the ability to buy, and that money is available at reasonable rates.

Chapter 2

1. **b** When agents exercise customer orientation, they identify the needs of groups of buyers, sellers, and agents within the total marketplace before listing property.

2. **b** This is a breakdown in the system. The listing had sold and the transfer paperwork was underway, but someone didn't remove the listing from the active sheets. System breakdowns can affect the reputation of the office and the agent.

3. **d** Because agents often expend a lot of time and energy gathering information, it's difficult for agents to share this information with the group. Often they feel that this might jeopardize their income in some way. For this reason, broker/owners have difficulty implementing systems orientation.

4. **c** Sellers assume that all agents have product knowledge and they expect agents to show up on time for an appointment, so these traits are common among many agents and won't assure that an agent gets a listing. Sellers also may agree to a discounted commission because that is what they feel the agent is worth, which may not say too much for the agent's marketing plan. When agents demonstrate their uniqueness (through a comprehensive marketing plan, empathic listening skills, product and people knowledge, etc.), listings are more easily attained.

5. **d** A helpful tool in evaluating competitors is called SWOT. The letters stand for Strengths, Weaknesses, Opportunities, and Threats.

Chapter 3

1. **b** Market research provides information to agents that helps them make decisions in the marketplace.

2. **a** The best time to discover the nature of the larger segments in the overall market is before an agent takes a listing. This saves time because the agents can then list properties that meet the needs of larger segments of the mar-

ket, thereby making it easier to find individuals within those segments.

3. **b** Prospecting is often the result of market research. In other words, the evaluation of the market research data may suggest that certain market segments would be profitable to prospect.

4. **b** Sometimes agents fail to establish the right problem because they fail to ask the right questions. Interview questions should require complex, comprehensive feedback. When prospects are given the opportunity to respond completely, it will be difficult for the agent to be unaware of the right problem.

5. **c** Primary data collection is the most expensive form of research. However, there are things agents can do that require little, if any, expense. Primary data collection is defined as an original data collection effort (as opposed to secondary data collection done by someone other than the agent) created for a specific purpose.

6. **b and c** The Federal Reserve (the Fed) is responsible for managing the growth of the nation's money supply and the course and direction of interest rates through the manipulation of the money supply. Congress is responsible for increasing or decreasing taxes and control over government spending.

7. **d** The easiest way to calculate the expansion of money supply for every dollar deposited is to divide the amount deposited by the reserve requirement. The result is the total amount to which the money supply should expand, including the original deposit. In this case, the $1,000 deposit divided by 10 percent equals $10,000.

Chapter 4

1. **b** With an adequate amount of financial resources, agents can hire a professional firm to acquire data, identify trends, and analyze or tie together information that helps answer the question in the research project.

2. **c** Collected data may include the number of people in the total marketplace, the demographics of a local radio station's audience, or the total volume of sales; however, all of these data must have relevance to the solution required for the research project.

3. **c** Exercise, food water, air, clothing and shelter are all physiological needs.

4. **c** Safety and a sense of order are strong motivators. Some buyers see a cluttered, poorly organized home and jump to the conclusion that it is not safe.

5. **b** Some people have a higher need than others to belong and to be socially accepted. People who are concerned about fitting in are also concerned about making decisions that please others.

Chapter 5

1. **a** Wanting to buy a home is one thing. However, the target market must have the ability and authority to buy the home. Agents must also have access to the people in this market.

2. **c** The shotgun approach attempts to make the promotional items appealing to all individuals within the total market. Agents on a limited budget often find this to be counterproductive.

3. **b** Demographic segmentation considers the issues of age, income, gender, family life cycle, marital status, and career fields.

4. **d** Demographic activities center on family life cycle, marital status, gender, income, and age. Psychographics center on how people live their lives—interests in sports, restaurants, or social activities—as well as what motivates them and generally how they perceive the world.

5. **c** Psychographic segmentation looks at the behavior of groups, what motivates them, and how they perceive their environment.

Chapter 6

1. **c** The result of marketing the total product—a property that meets the physical and emotional needs of the prospect—is a sale where the property appears to offer more value than the price suggests.

2. **c** Rising interest rates are the result of inflation and typically cause real estate prices to decline in order to keep properties affordable. Conversely, rising demand for a product that is declining in supply causes prices to increase for that product.

3. **b** Buyers negotiate things of value, which easily could include things such as price, improvements, and the transfer date.

4. **c** The demand for any product in excess of its supply will cause the product price to increase. In this case, it is not necessarily the demand but the lack of supply that creates the problem.

5. **d** The Fed has no control over the taxing or spending policies of the United States government. Decreasing interest rates would run through the diminished supplies quicker. This would cause inflation, exactly what the Fed doesn't want. The Fed has the power to influence interest rates up or down. To slow spending, it would cause interest rates to increase.

Chapter 7

1. **b** One of the best reasons to provide enhanced services is to help agents stand out from their competitors. If everyone is offering the same services then a seller's selection of an agent is only one of chance.

2. **c** When sellers negotiate for a lower commission, agents should explain how the channels of distribution might close down. Other agents may consider showing other properties before showing one with a lower commission. The broker may be reluctant to start a major promotional campaign on a property with a low commission. The overall company profits may or may not decline; it depends on how many properties are sold in a year.

3. **b** Company pricing objectives include a consideration for time and expenses, turnover, and market share. Performance is a consideration when individual agents negotiate fees with sellers.

4. **d** A turnover ratio of 3 means that properties in a particular price range take an average of four months to sell (12 months divided by a turnover ratio of 3 equals 4 months).

5. **c** Increasing sales in an area shows growth in market share. In this example, the company realized a 75 percent market share of the 100 homes sold last year. This year they realized a 92 percent market share of the 130 homes sold in the area.

Chapter 8

1. **c** Place addresses the speed, convenience, and condition of real property. It answers questions such as how long the transfer may take, what to expect during loan processing, and how to save time when the prospects are looking for a home.

2. **d** The four elements that define promotion are personal selling, advertising, sales promotion, and publicity.

3. **c** Real estate promotion communicates, persuades, and reminds prospects of an agent's products or services. The process of persuasion can take a considerable amount of time due to the "noise" of a competitor's message.

4. **c** Place strategies involve the delivery of advertising messages to the consumer. One method of delivery is through newspapers; others include magazines, television, radio, and billboards.

5. **c** Sales promotions are sometimes used as incentives for buyers, sellers, and agents to act.

Chapter 9

1. **c** The three steps in the initial sales effort include preparation, prospecting, and qualifying. Qualifying is one of the steps taken after the prospect is in front of the agent.

2. **a** Preparation includes activities that anticipate questions that might be asked by a prospect.

3. **b** Prospecting is one of the most important elements for a new licensee. Without prospects there would be no opportunities to qualify, prepare offers, etc.

4. **b** Under the Civil Rights Act of 1968, redlining is illegal. It is illegal for lenders to practice redlining in which they refuse to loan or limit the loans in specific neighborhoods based on the racial makeup of that neighborhood.

5. **d** The Civil Rights Act of 1866 defined anyone born in the United States to be a citizen of the country.

Chapter 10

1. **a** One criterion for overcoming no trust is a strong self-image. Agents must believe in themselves, believe in their services, and have a strong conviction for the solutions they provide.

2. **c** When agents prepare for an interview, they create questions that solicit answers that help them locate properties that solve the right problem. This demonstrates their competence.

3. **c** Active listening or listening that is intent on understanding what the prospect is saying is a critical research activity.

4. **b** Questioning and listening provides a tool for agents to discover the cause of the prospects' problem, allowing them to find a solution to satisfy the need.

5. **c** The agent's primary job is to solve problems. To do that an agent compares what prospects have to what they need and take steps to understand why they do not have what they need—the cause of the problem. In this case, the yard may have been beautifully landscaped, but perhaps the 75-year-old buyer did not have the physical stamina to maintain it or the monetary means to hire someone to do it for him.

Chapter 11

1. **c** Agents demonstrate competence to overcome no trust. However, when prospects question the competence of their agent it is a signal that they are in no hurry to make a purchase.

2. **b** Reassuring or supporting a prospect is the method used to overcome no hurry. Identifying features, demonstrating advantages, and explaining benefits are all steps to overcoming no help.

3. **d** Prospects want to make sure the agent's solution is the best for them. To overcome no hurry agents must overcome their doubts by supporting and reassuring them.

4. **b** A legitimate objection from a prospect with a need indicates that they do not have enough information to make a decision.

5. **a** Prospects going through a real estate purchase, especially their first one, may suffer from a great deal of tension. Many emotional triggers may cause them to rethink their position about buying. Prospects may avoid the purchase decision if they think it's more trouble than it's worth.

Chapter 12

1. **b** The ability to interact with buyers and sellers is the most important aspect of personal selling and makes personal selling an essential part of a promotional strategy.

2. **d** Rather than depend on the customer to find the agent, order getters aggressively seek out past customers and search for new ones.

3. **a** Offices that invite past sellers and buyers to an annual party are aggressively working the referral market.

4. **c** Prospecting is a frustrating part of sales. Agents can't always tell if it's working. Often, the best they can do is "stuff the pipeline" with names, appointments, and work until something comes out the other end.

5. **c** Rational reasons for a purchase focus on the product, whereas emotional reasons focus on how a purchase decision affects the buyers (e.g., gets them noticed, provides security, improves relationships).

Chapter 13

1. **c** Questions should be written in a way that helps the prospects discover their true needs and describe in some detail the desired solution. This means that the questions should be short and direct, but require complex, profound answers from the prospects. Therefore, the prospects should always talk more than the agent.

2. **c** Agents that offer the wrong solution damage their credibility.

3. **d** Positive objections allow the closing process to continue. The prospects may bring up an objection to slow the process in the hope of gaining more information.

4. **c** A trial close helps agents find out if they and the prospects are looking at the right house, or if the prospects need more information before making a decision.

5. **b** The Ben Franklin close is a process we use every day to make decisions. It weighs the advantages and disadvantages of a decision before it is made.

INDEX